"Of course," R—
be no discussio—
child support c—
of the child bei—
you will both be—

"I thought I wasn't fr— ~~be brought~~ back to your country."

She wasn't. Even now, looking at Bailey, he felt that intense possessiveness that had him in a stranglehold. Taking her, claiming her, seemed to be the most obvious choice.

Which was what gave him pause. A ruler was meant to be cool. A ruler was meant to direct his actions with his mind, his sense of honor, not with anything half so fickle as desire or heat.

He was forced, then, to weigh his options. To bring back a woman such as this…one he had already decided was unsuitable for his kingdom…was unfathomable.

But honor. Honor and duty were at the center of all of it, regardless of what she made him feel. His duty was to his child.

"That was before I knew you were carrying my heir." He took a step toward her, the word *mine* pounding itself through his head in time with the thundering of his heart. "Of course you are coming back to my country with me now. But not as my mistress. Bailey Harper, you are going to be my wife."

One stolen moment of extraordinary passion leads to dramatic consequences in this stunning new trilogy by *New York Times* bestselling author Maisey Yates in...

Heirs before Vows

Claiming their legacy with a diamond ring!

Three of the world's most impressive and powerful bachelors, connected by fate and friendship, are about to find their lives changed irrevocably!

No one could have expected the shocking consequences that now lead these determined alpha males down the aisle...

...as expectant fathers!

Find out what happens in...

The Spaniard's Pregnant Bride
October 2016

The Prince's Pregnant Mistress
December 2016

This stunning trilogy concludes with...

The Italian's Pregnant Virgin
January 2017

THE PRINCE'S PREGNANT MISTRESS

BY
MAISEY YATES

First Published in Great Britain 2016
By Mills & Boon, an imprint of HarperCollins*Publishers*
1 London Bridge Street, London, SE1 9GF

© 2016 Maisey Yates

ISBN: 978-0-263-92142-7

Our policy is to use papers that are natural, renewable and recyclable
products and made from wood grown in sustainable forests. The logging
and manufacturing processes conform to the legal environmental
regulations of the country of origin.

Printed and bound in Spain
by CPI, Barcelona

Maisey Yates is a *New York Times* bestselling author of more than thirty romance novels. She has a coffee habit she has no interest in kicking, and a slight Pinterest addiction. She lives with her husband and children in the Pacific Northwest. When Maisey isn't writing she can be found singing in the grocery store, shopping for shoes online and probably not doing dishes. Check out her website: maiseyyates.com.

Books by Maisey Yates

Mills & Boon Modern Romance

Carides's Forgotten Wife
Bound to the Warrior King
Married for Amari's Heir
His Diamond of Convenience
To Defy a Sheikh
One Night to Risk it All
Forged in the Desert Heat

Heirs Before Vows

The Spaniard's Pregnant Bride

The Chatsfield

Sheikh's Desert Duty

One Night With Consequences

The Greek's Nine-Month Redemption
Married for Amari's Heir

Princes of Petras

A Christmas Vow of Seduction
The Queen's New Year Secret

Secret Heirs of Powerful Men

Heir to a Desert Legacy
Heir to a Dark Inheritance

Visit the Author Profile page at millsandboon.co.uk for more titles.

This book is dedicated to the librarians.
I spent countless hours at libraries,
reading countless books.
Thank you for giving the joy of reading to everyone.

CHAPTER ONE

IT HAD BEEN a perfect night. So beautiful, the white Christmas lights strung across the facades of the buildings in Vail glittering on the snow all around them. Like the stars had dropped down from the sky to light their way.

Yes, the night had been perfect and Raphael even more so. But then, he always was.

Bailey couldn't quite believe it was real. Even after eight months with him, she couldn't believe it. He was like something out of a fairy tale, and she was a girl who never thought she'd have a happy ending.

But then she'd met him.

Of course, she only saw him every few months, when he flew into Colorado on business, and never for long enough.

She'd been guarded all of her adult life. So cautious when it came to men and dating. But with Raphael…that caution had never been there. She'd just given herself to him with no thought of self-protection, no thought of anything but how much she wanted him.

She was like a different woman with him. A woman in love.

It was always so frantic when he was there. Tonight

was no exception. They'd finished dinner, a walk through the town, then back to the hotel, where he'd consumed her.

There had been an edge to him tonight, an intensity. Not that she was complaining.

She stretched out on the sheets, curling her toes. She was still recovering. She giggled and rolled onto her side, looking toward the bathroom.

The door was closed, a sliver of light visible beneath it. She sighed heavily, waiting for him to come back to bed.

Waiting *impatiently*.

Tonight felt different. Significant and special.

She loved him so much. She ached with it. She'd never thought she could feel this way about someone. Never thought someone could feel this way about her.

She was ready for more. She was ready for everything.

The bathroom door opened, and her heart skipped a little. That made her smile. It was ridiculous how giddy she was over him. But then, she'd never let a man close enough to her to have this kind of intimacy.

In her waitressing job she got hit on by men all the time. She just wasn't…swayed by it. At all. She had been thoroughly disenchanted with men by the time she'd moved out of her mother's home at sixteen. She'd seen too much. Too much heartbreak. Too much screaming.

Bailey had decided to make her own life, her own future. She'd made it to twenty-one a virgin because she'd been so determined to wait until it was right, until she was ready.

And then she'd met Raphael. Her friends barely believed he existed. She'd stopped talking much about him when all she'd gotten were skeptical eye rolls and *Raphael? Bailey, are you dating a Ninja Turtle?*

He'd never met them because he was so busy whenever he flew in. And then she wanted him all to herself. So yeah, she was giddy. She had a feeling she always would be.

"Bailey, shouldn't you be getting dressed?"

She frowned. She hadn't expected him to say that. She spent the night with him all the time when he came through town. "I thought...well." She swept a hand over her bare curves. "I'm ready for more if you are."

"I have an early flight out—I thought I told you."

He looked grim suddenly. She hated that grimness. It grabbed her by the throat and held her tight, filled her lungs with dread, and she couldn't quite pinpoint why. "No. You didn't." She forced a smile because there was no point fighting with him if these were their last few minutes together before he had to leave again. "You have to go back to Italy?"

"Yes," he said, reaching for his pants and tugging them on, covering up his gorgeous body.

She watched him dress the rest of the way, the reverse strip show still arousing even if it had a more depressing ending than the alternative.

His muscles rippled with each movement, his fingers blunt and efficient as he buttoned his shirt. Reminding her of just how *efficient* they were with her.

"Bailey," he said again, his tone vaguely...irritated. She couldn't recall Raphael ever being irritated with her before.

"I'm comfortable," she said, sighing heavily and rolling out of bed. "There. Now I'm not. I hope you're happy." She purposefully wiggled her hips a little bit as she made her way to where he'd torn her dress off earlier. "I hope this survived," she said, picking it up gingerly.

"I'll replace it if it didn't."

"I'm more worried about what I'll wear home." Another sigh escaped her lips. "When are you coming back?"

"I'm not."

She felt like all the air had been pulled from her body. She just stood there, blinking in the dim light, totally frozen while her fingers went numb and her insides went cold. "What do you mean, you aren't coming back?"

"I don't have any more work here in Vail. We're finished up with our meetings."

"Right. So. But… I'm here."

He laughed, a hard, low sound that wasn't like Raphael at all. "Sorry, *cara*, that is not enticement enough."

She was dumbstruck. Completely. And she hated herself for it. "I don't understand. We just had the nicest date and the best… I don't… I don't understand."

"It was goodbye. You have been an especially lovely diversion, but that's all it could ever be. I have a life back in Italy, and it's time I got back to it in earnest."

Dumbstruck turned into sucker punched. "A life? Are you… Raphael, are you married?"

"About to be," he said, his tone hard. "I can't afford distractions any longer."

"You're engaged. Of course you are," she said, words tumbling out of her mouth without her permission. "I bet you…live with her. Of course you only come and visit me every couple of months. I'm such an idiot."

She covered her mouth and stifled a scream. She was too angry to be humiliated. Too wounded to care if she bled all over him. "I was… I was a virgin, and you knew that," she threw at him. "I told you it was a big step for me!" Angry tears welled in her eyes, rolling down her cheeks.

"And I appreciated the gift, *tesorina*," he said, his tone now like iron. "We were together for eight months. It was hardly a fling."

"It's a fling if one of you isn't taking it seriously at all!" A sob rose in her throat, shaking her whole body. "If one of you knew it would end and was sleeping with someone else." She bent down then, picked up her shoe and threw it at his head.

He dodged it neatly, an Italian swear word on his lips.

She bent again, picking up her other shoe and flinging that at him too. This one hit him square in the chest. He closed the distance between them, grabbing hold of her wrist. "Enough." He released her as quickly as he'd taken hold of her. "Don't embarrass yourself, Bailey. Not more than you already have."

"You should be embarrassed," she said, her voice shaking. She pulled the dress on, then moved to pick her shoes up. She hadn't put her nylons back on, but who had the time for that ridiculousness when your heart had just been ripped out through your chest? "You are the one who *lied* to me." She sniffed much louder than she meant to, pulling her coat on over the dress, trying to ignore the fact that she was shaking so hard now her teeth were chattering.

"I never lied to you," he said, his dark eyes burning. "You created the story you wanted to believe."

She let out a feral growl and rushed past him, heading out the door as quickly as she could, feeling like a disgraced hooker walking out of his hotel room in the middle of the night, wearing high heels and a beautiful dress that she was going to have to burn now.

It wasn't until she was outside, until the cold wrapped itself around her, overtaking her, that she fell apart. Completely, utterly. She sank to her knees in the snow, sobbing until her throat hurt.

It felt like her life was over. And right now, she did not have it in her to put herself back together.

Three months later

I'm sorry, Bailey. But I can't have a waitress falling asleep in the kitchen in the middle of her shift. Especially not a fat waitress.

Her boss's voice played over and over in her head as she trudged back to her apartment. She had been right, that night three months ago when Raphael had broken things off with her. Her life pretty much felt like it was over.

She was so far behind in her classes it didn't look like she had the credits she needed to graduate, she didn't have a job anymore and she was so sick and tired she barely cared about either.

Now she was going to have to tell Samantha that she couldn't make rent. Well, this was the crowning achievement on the past months' humiliations, really. She had become everything she had felt so far above for most of her life.

When she had left home, left town, she had blistered her mother's ears with her rant about how she was off to make a better life for herself. One that wouldn't be all about men and an intense dedication to being a victim.

She'd gotten the hell out of metaphorical Dodge. Leaving behind that life of destitution. Where she'd been nothing but unwanted. Nothing but resented, and she'd vowed to do better.

She'd been wise to men, and what they might say to get into your pants, from the time she was way too young to know any such thing. Because she'd heard her mother rant at length on the subject after whatever boyfriend had broken up with her. As a result she had imagined herself as inoculated against such things. Had imagined that she was immune to that kind of behavior.

The truth of it was, she simply hadn't met a man who made her crazy enough. Then she met Raphael. And now, here she was, single, out of a job and pregnant. And all at the age of twenty-two.

She was the cycle. The cycle that she had so proudly and grandly told herself she wouldn't perpetuate. Now here she was. Perpetuating. She was a statistic. A sad statistic wandering around in the chilly, early spring air with nowhere in particular to go.

She stopped, turning to face the small general store across the street. Candy. She needed candy. Since she couldn't have wine. *Damn pregnancy.*

She ducked into the store and made her way to the nearest candy aisle, stopping abruptly when her eye caught the tabloid just above the chocolate bar her hand hovered over.

The man on the cover looked...far too familiar.

Prince Raphael DeSantis jilted by Italian heiress Allegra Valenti just weeks before royal wedding!

"What the actual *hell*?" The shoppers around her

startled when she all but shouted the words, but she didn't care. She reached out and grabbed the magazine, flipping through it with shaking fingers.

Raphael. *Prince* Raphael.

She flipped the pages until she saw it. The article about the scandal that was apparently rocking the principality of Santa Firenze, a tiny dot on the map of Europe. One she'd never even heard of.

It was him. There was no mistaking it. With his arresting good looks, more like a god than a man, and his incredible body...a body they had on show in the article, thanks to a few creeper beach pics. Those broad shoulders, washboard abs and lean hips...

She knew that body better than she knew her own.

"Oh, my..." She reached into her purse and pulled out a stack of tip money, throwing a ten down onto the counter. "Keep the change." She ran out with the candy bar and the magazine, her entire body starting to shake.

What *Twilight Zone* episode had she stumbled into? What kind of a joke was this?

By the time she got back to her apartment she felt like she was going to be sick all over the floor. And, given the theme of the last couple of months, she wouldn't be surprised if she did. Attempting to keep food down was sometimes a superhuman feat. Not that you could tell by her expanding waistline. Which her ex-boss had made clear to point out along with the firing.

She was tragic. So tragic that all she wanted to do was throw herself down on the bed and sleep for the rest of the day.

She made her way into the living room, where Samantha was sitting, looking wide-eyed.

"Are you okay?" Bailey asked, mostly to stave off the question of whether or not she was.

"You have a visitor," her roommate responded.

"Who?" she asked, feeling like the only possible option was that it was someone from the IRS telling her she owed back taxes, or maybe a police officer letting her know she had a warrant for a parking ticket she didn't know she had...something awful. Because that was the theme of the day. The theme of the past few months, really.

"*He's* here," Samantha said, sounding dazed.

There could only be one he. There was only one *he* that would make a woman's voice sound like that. Only one man Bailey had ever met who could render a woman completely stunned by his very presence.

And, as Bailey was processing that bit of information, she heard shoes on the hardwood floor and looked up, up into the dark eyes of Prince Raphael DeSantis just as he exited her bedroom.

He was here. In her crappy little apartment. Looking as out of place as a lion among house cats.

She wrapped her coat more tightly around herself, doing her best to conceal her figure. To hide the bump that she knew was pretty plainly visible without her woolen shield.

"What are you doing here?" she asked. She realized she was also still holding the tabloid with his face on it. She looked down at the magazine. Then back up at him. "What are you doing here?" she repeated.

"I came to tell you that I wanted to start seeing you again," he said.

"Oh, *please*." This exclamation came from her roommate, who had watched Bailey weep into her pillow for weeks now.

"What she said," Bailey affirmed, crossing her arms even more tightly beneath her chest.

"Could we have a moment?" He directed the question at Samantha, then, without waiting for a response, grabbed hold of Bailey's arm and guided her back into her bedroom. He closed the door, enclosing them both in the space.

And for a moment, she was completely lost in him. In his strength, in his very presence, which reached to every corner of the room, and around her. She wanted to lean into him. To rest her head against the solid wall of his chest and release hold of all of the heartbreak, fear and stress she had been enduring for the past few months.

She just wanted to fall into his arms and lose it all. Lose herself.

But that was impossible. He was…he was a liar. On so many more levels than she had realized.

"My engagement is off," he said, as though she were not holding a magazine in her hand proclaiming exactly that. "And, given that, I see no reason why the two of us can't resume our liaison."

"Our…*liaison*. The one where you come and visit me every couple of months for sex?"

"Bailey," he said, his tone exceedingly hard done by. It made her want to punch him. "I have a certain life, certain expectations, and…"

"These expectations?" She turned the tabloid around, thrusting it toward him. "You're a prince? What strange fairy tale did I fall into, Raphael? You said you were a pharmaceutical rep."

"You said I was a pharmaceutical rep, Bailey," he said. "Don't you remember?"

"I…" She remembered everything about the night she met him. The way that her world had stopped completely when their eyes had met. How out of place he looked in the sleazy diner that she worked at, Sweater Bunnies, where the waitresses all wore sweaters with plunging necklines and short shorts, with glittering tights and high heels.

His plane was delayed because of the weather. He had come into town on business. They had ended up talking. And then she had done something she had never done before in her life. She went home with him.

They didn't have sex. Not that first night. But he had kissed her, and she had…well, she'd learned an entirely new definition for the word *want*. Her entire body had caught fire with the touch of his lips, the touch of his hands. They had been talking one moment, and then the next, he had her down on the bed.

"I'm a virgin," she said.

"I don't need you to be," he responded, his voice rough, his hands tangled in her hair. "We don't have to play that game. Unless you want to."

"No," she said, "I really am. Like, a really, real virgin. Who has never done anything like this before, ever."

He sat up. "Never?"

"Never. But, I like you. And…maybe if the weather is bad tomorrow…"

"You want to wait, but you might be ready tomorrow?"

"I don't know."

"We'll wait," he said, kissing her cheek.

And he hadn't thrown her out. Instead, he had poured her a glass of soda and then continued to talk to her.

She hadn't made him wait long after that. The next night she'd made him her first, and she'd already been spinning fantasies about him being the only.

Then…well, then he'd turned out to be a frog. Except he was actually a prince. Which was just insane.

"Of course I remember," she snapped.

"Then you remember that you were the one who laughed at me, and said, 'You aren't a pharmaceutical rep or something, are you?' And I did not correct you. In fact, you will find, Bailey, that a great many of the things you think about me you created."

"So now you're gaslighting me? You're making this whole thing about what I chose to believe? And somehow, you think that will make me want you back. Not as a girlfriend, or anything like that, just as your little Colorado-based… Tell me, Raphael, where do your other women live?"

"I never thought of you that way," he said, his tone fierce. "Never."

"Actions speak louder than words and all of that. You treated me like one. You're still treating me like one. Get out of my apartment, Your Majesty," she spat.

"I am not in the habit of taking orders, you will find. I was all right playing your game before, but now you know. I am a prince, *cara mia*. And what I want, I have."

"Well," she said, flinging her arms out wide, "you don't get this."

He reached out, cupping the back of her head and drawing her forward. "You don't mean that."

"Oh, but I do." She pressed her hands flat against his chest—the better to shove him backward—only then he felt…so much like home. Like everything brilliant and perfect that she'd been missing while her life had been upended.

It was easy to forget he was the one who'd upended it.

He curved one arm around her waist, drawing her body flush against his. And then he frowned.

And she came back to reality, hard.

"Don't touch me," she hissed, pulling away and straightening her coat a little bit frantically.

She didn't want him to see that she was pregnant because…

Because she didn't know why. She'd resigned herself to her fate as a single mother because he was supposed to be married to someone else. Because the text she'd sent out to him after the fact saying she needed to talk to him had gone unreturned.

But he was here now. And he was a prince, damn it all.

Her own father had never been around, and she and her mother had suffered financially for it. Raphael could support their child. Could make sure they didn't struggle.

She flicked the top button of her coat open, her heart pounding. "I'm not going to be your lover, Raphael," she said, her voice trembling as she continued undoing buttons. She let her coat fall free and revealed the bump that was only just now visible beneath her tight-fitting sweater. "But whether you want to be or not, you are the father of my baby."

CHAPTER TWO

IT WAS RARE that Prince Raphael DeSantis was rendered speechless. But then, it was rare for him to be rejected.

And that had happened twice in the past week.

Were he a man with any insecurity, he might be wounded. However, he was the Crown Prince of Santa Firenze, a man who had been born with the world in hand and every advantage available to him. A man who—upon his birth—had been worshipped by the palace's many servants, simply because he existed. Reverence was a gift bestowed upon him from his first breath. And he had spent his life ensuring that he maintained the admiration of his people.

And this little waitress had refused him. Then gone on to reveal a surprise he certainly hadn't seen coming.

"You are certain it's mine?" He knew the question would earn him more of Bailey's ire, but he suddenly felt as though everything was hanging in the balance. This woman, who looked at him as though she wanted to do him bodily harm, was carrying the heir to the throne of his country.

She recoiled from him. "How dare you ask me that?"

"I would be remiss if I did not."

He tried to ignore the hurt in her blue eyes. This

changed things. It changed everything. Bailey had been a diversion he wasn't looking for. And he had allowed himself to get caught up in it. To enjoy the fiction that she had built up around them. That he was a businessman, coming to Vail once every couple of months for meetings and to spend time with her.

Somehow she hadn't seemed to know who he was. But then, part of maintaining the admiration of his people had been keeping himself out of baser things like tabloid news. Which he had clearly failed at recently. He attributed that to his former fiancée, Allegra.

But it had all come to an end three months ago. He had known that he couldn't continue his assignation with Bailey right up until his marriage. He had never touched Allegra, and he didn't love her, but he had intended to be a good husband to her. A faithful husband. Or at least—depending on the agreement they ultimately reached—a discreet one.

When the engagement had ended, however, he had immediately thought to come back to his mistress.

The world was crumbling as he knew it—a slight exaggeration perhaps, but the cancellation of a royal wedding could hardly be deemed insignificant. It had made him tabloid fodder.

His father, the late ruler of Santa Firenze, had despised all forms of media and had felt it wholly beneath a leader to become a headline when he should be aiming to be part of history.

He had instilled this in Raphael, along with strength and steel. There had been no softness allowed in his childhood, and Raphael could see it for the benefit it was now that he was a man, both of his parents long dead and an entire nation left to him to oversee.

In fact, his marriage to Allegra was a testament to that strength. That he had been more than willing to set aside the desires of his flesh for the betterment of his kingdom.

Bailey, no matter that he desired her, could offer no political advantage to his country. Allegra, on the other hand, would bring an alliance with one of Italy's oldest families and a great deal of influence within the business community thanks to both her father and brother.

Bailey heated his blood. But his time with her was outside the norm…something separate from Santa Firenze. Something he could not afford to bring back there, he had known with certainty. Not only was she beneath him in status, she was a distraction. The sort his father had always warned against.

The only thing Bailey had…was his heir. And that was something that could not be ignored.

He had not foreseen this complication.

"Yes, Your Royal Jackass, it's your baby. Since you were the one to take my virginity, I would think you would know that."

"Nearly a year ago, Bailey. Many things could have happened since that first time we were together. I was not always here. And it has been three months since I left you. For all I know, in your grief, you sought solace with another man."

"Yeah, it's been a nonstop orgy since you dumped me. I figured, why not just go for it? After all, your royal scepter paved the way. Might as well allow the common folk a chance."

"Enough. You are being crude, and it doesn't suit you."

"Yes it does. It suits me perfectly. As you well know.

I am not the kind of woman that you could ever take back to your country, so you *must* think that. I'm a waitress. A lowly server that you met in a sleazy restaurant better known for the waitresses breasts than the chicken breasts. I would say this behavior suits me perfectly."

She was vibrating with rage, angry like she'd been the night he had ended things with her. When she had screamed at him, thrown a shoe at him. *Hit* him with a shoe. It had been the exact response he'd been looking for. He could not have her coming after him. Could not have her being tempted in any regard to find him, not when he was ready to get married and begin producing children. He had made their separation as devastating as possible so she would not seek him out.

Better to spoil her memory of him than leave her longing. Of course, he had changed his mind about that. Which he reserved his right to do. He was a prince, after all.

"You are carrying my child," he said, looking down at her stomach. She wasn't showing dramatically, just a vague bump beneath her sweater. Her curves looked a bit more abundant. He considered himself an expert on Bailey's curves, so he was certain his assessment was correct. "How far along are you?"

"Close to four months," she said. "It happened before we broke up. But I didn't know until after."

"Did you try and get in touch with me?"

That question seemed to make her angry, too. "Yes. I did. Though, since I didn't know your actual identity, it was a little bit tricky. I texted you."

The only number that Bailey had was to the phone that only she used. He had been careful to keep everything with her separate. Particularly when he had dis-

covered that she truly didn't know who he was. There
had been something so enticing about it. The chance
to come here and be with a woman who had no expectations. To be more himself than any other venue
allowed.

And when he had ended things with her, he had gotten rid of the phone. Cutting off his temptation. He
didn't need to save messages from her. Or the occa-
sionally suggestive photographs that she had provided.

"I no longer have that phone," he said.

"Wow. When you break up with a girl, you really
go hard-core."

He frowned. "You keep using that word, Bailey. As
though you were my girlfriend. From my point of view,
we never had that kind of relationship." He realized,
even as he spoke the words, that he was being extraor-
dinarily unfair to her.

With most women, he laid out the ground rules from
moment one. He had not been seeking Bailey out. Not
at all. He had come to Vail to visit a friend's resort and
see about investing in the property and its expansion.
And then a blizzard had waylaid his travel.

Not even a man such as himself could control a
storm.

He had wandered into a restaurant not far from his
hotel, and had nearly walked right back out when he'd
seen what sort of establishment it was. But then he had
seen her. Somehow, in spite of the tacky surroundings,
the horrendous uniform and the dim lighting, she had
shone.

He had been able to think of only one thing. One
word. *Mine.*

And there had never been a single thing in his life

that he had wanted and had not gotten. He had purposed in that moment that the waitress would be one of them.

When she had made assumptions about who he was, he had allowed her to do so. He had encouraged it. And he had not done as impeccable a job as he usually did of ensuring that the relationship stayed in the bedroom. But he had reasoned that he only ever saw her for a long weekend every couple of months. And it would be wrong to keep her in a hotel room the entire time.

So he had taken her out. He had no connections to Vail other than that one visit to see about investing. The press never had any reason to take an interest in him being there. Or even think that he would be there.

There were a great many advantages to having a relatively low profile.

"What I mean," he said, attempting to soften his tone, "is that I have lovers, not girlfriends. Women that I carry out affairs with. I don't date. That's the issue with being a prince. You cannot simply go public with women, not without expectation being attached. However, I was hardly going to live my life celibate."

"You had a fiancée." The words were low, carrying with them an edge of violence.

"Allegra was nothing more than a convenience. She is from one of Italy's most revered families. She was a reasonable choice for a man in my position. She was not my lover."

"Well, I guess that's something," she said. "So. I figure we need to come to some kind of child support arrangement? I'm having your baby. If you need me to get a paternity test, fine, whatever. I'll hate you, but I already do. Whatever you need. A cheek swab, my

blood. Though I'd prefer not to give blood. I've already
bled for you. I'm not doing it again."

"What are you talking about? A child support?"

"Presumably you have a castle. I would like to not
live in a heap."

"And so you want money?"

He found her fascinating. This woman who had not
known who he was. This woman who was standing
there with a tabloid featuring him at her feet, who had
been a virgin when he'd first taken her. Who was asking for child support, and not threatening to go to the
press. Not demanding a pied-à-terre in various cities or
pieces of the crown jewels.

Clearly, she had no understanding of the situation she
found herself in, in spite of what she thought.

"I don't think it's unreasonable," she said. "My own
mother was single. And my father didn't give us anything. I'm not going to consign my son or daughter to
that life if I can make it better. I have a responsibility.
And so do you."

"Undeniably I have a responsibility to this child,
but I do not think you understand exactly what you're
dealing with here," he said, staring at her, mystified.

"I'm dealing with an unexpected pregnancy and the
best way that I can think to handle it. I want to make
sure that you are not living in the lap of luxury while
your son or daughter has nothing."

"Oh, I have no intention of my son or daughter
lacking for anything. But if you think that I'm leaving them here in Colorado to be raised alone by you,
you have failed to understand the man that you are involved with."

Her entire face turned pink, her rage seemingly

silent for the first time since he had aroused it three months ago.

"I am not sending child support checks, *cara*. There will be no more discussion of it."

"What do you mean you aren't allowing me to raise my child in Colorado? Under what authority? This is America! And last I checked, you probably aren't a citizen."

"Diplomatic immunity," he said, waving his hand, "and a desire to preserve relations with my country, will no doubt see any kind of court battle you should wish to wage fall in my favor. Who would give custody to a waitress from Sweater Bunnies when a prince is on hand to raise the child to rule?"

"You're going to take my baby from me?" Her voice had turned shrill, and he could see that she was looking around the room, her eyes darting back and forth. Probably looking for a weapon.

"It should not come to that."

"Start speaking slowly, and spelling out what exactly you're implying. Obviously I'm not picking up on it."

"Of course," he said, "there will be no discussion of my sending you child support checks, and no discussion of the child being raised here, because you will both be in Santa Firenze."

"I thought I wasn't fit to be brought back to your country."

She wasn't. Even now, looking at her, that intense possessiveness had him in a stranglehold. Taking her, claiming her seemed to be the most obvious choice.

Which was what gave him pause. A ruler was meant to be cool. A ruler was meant to direct his actions with his mind, his sense of honor, not with anything half as fickle as desire or heat.

He wondered what his father might have done in this instance. And then had to concede that his father would never have been so foolish as to get himself in this situation.

He was forced then to weigh his options. To bring back a woman such as this, one he had already decided was unsuitable for his kingdom…it was unfathomable.

But honor. Honor and duty were at the center of all of it, regardless of what she made him feel. His duty was to his child.

"That was before I knew you were carrying my heir." He took a step toward her, the word *mine* pounding itself through his head in time with the thundering of his heart. "Of course you are coming back to my country with me now. But not as my mistress. Bailey Harper, you are going to be my wife."

CHAPTER THREE

"YOU HAVE A private jet."

"Of course I do," Raphael said, brushing past her and walking up the stairs into the sleek-looking aircraft.

"Were you in your private jet the night that we met?"

He treated her to a withering look. "I wasn't flying economy."

"I just…" She let the words trail off. There wasn't much to say. Not really. He was not the man she had thought he was. That had become apparent when he'd broken her heart the way that he had, when it had been revealed that there was another woman in his life. This was just another layer to it. She supposed that some people would view this as good luck. The fact that the man who had gotten her pregnant was wealthy, titled and powerful should be some kind of boon.

She looked up at the plane. She didn't really feel like it was a good thing. Not now.

She just felt small. Small and so desperately out of her depth.

She had argued with him about the marriage thing, and she intended to argue with him even more. But… what could be done? He presented a pretty ironclad case when it came to how he would go about getting custody. And she didn't want to lose her baby.

Are you sure part of you just doesn't want to go off with him because it sounds easy?

She banished that traitorous voice, began to walk up the steps and into the jet. And that feeling of being tiny only increased. She was nothing. No one. Just a girl from Nebraska who had gone to Colorado seeking mountains and a fresh start. A girl raised by a single mother in a drafty house built in the 1920s with a sagging foundation and a crack in the ceiling.

She looked around the cabin, her jaw a little bit slack. It was…she had never seen anything like this on the internet. She had idly scrolled through the odd slideshow on various lifestyle websites showing the ridiculously luxurious way that the rich and famous traveled, but she had never imagined she would be standing in the middle of it. Much less ready to fly on board.

"There are bedrooms back that way," he said, gesturing past the plush living area and bar to the back of the plane. "There is also a bathroom and a shower."

"There's a shower?"

"Of course there is." And that was it. No further explanation. As if it really were the most typical thing on the planet for a man to have a shower on his plane, and she was the absurd one for thinking otherwise.

"Okay then. I will keep that in mind in case I feel a little bit travel stale."

Her heart began to hammer loudly, her hands shaking as the door to the plane closed.

"You know," she said, "we don't have to go now. I have… I have school to finish."

"You mentioned. In your rant as you packed your things."

She was failing right now, but still. "Well, it was a valid rant. I worked hard to pay my way this far through school, and if I don't finish this term, I'll be out the money for the classes."

He sat down on one of the tan leather couches, spreading his arms wide over the back, his posture laconic. She had to wonder how on earth she hadn't realized he was royalty. Sure, she had never been in the presence of anyone who could be considered royal, but he exuded it. How had she ever thought he was a normal man?

You never did. You saw him and the world stopped.

"Come now," he said, "*cara mia*, the cost of your college tuition will be the least of your concerns. I can arrange to have you complete your courses remotely. Or you may transfer to one of the universities in Santa Firenze. Of course, you will have to take classes at the palace and not on campus should you choose to do that."

"Why can't I go to the campus?"

"You would create a circus." He tapped the back of the couch with his fingertips. "I am not a man accustomed to getting tabloid attention. My family name has always been upheld, whispered reverently, spoken of with great respect. We are not part of the nouveau riche royal set who takes great pride in posting our social engagements on various online accounts. We take pride in the title. My father did before me, and I do it now. That headline you saw today was an aberration. There is a reason that you were not aware of my identity. I simply don't court publicity. That is the vocation of celebrity, and I am not a celebrity. I am the ruler of my country." He sighed heavily. "I dislike the position I find myself in. Because you...you will be a problem."

"Oh, will I? Excellent. One hopes that I will be too much of a problem for you to want to take on."

He waved a hand. "Not at all. You see, *cara*, you are carrying my baby. The most important thing on this earth is the birthright of that child. You must be married to me in order to secure that birthright."

She blinked. "Is this the Middle Ages?"

"No, this is Santa Firenze. And this is the cost of being royal."

"Good thing you're rich. It seems damned expensive."

"You have no idea. But, suffice it to say, your tuition is not my concern. In fact, it isn't your concern, either. You have no more financial concerns."

His words were strange. Made her ears feel fuzzy. She could hardly comprehend them. All she had worried about—from the time she had known what it was like to be hungry, from the moment she had experienced her first night in winter with the heat off because the electricity had been interrupted by the power company—was money. To have this man look at her, snap his fingers and say it was no longer a concern was...it was beyond surreal.

"I don't... I don't understand...any of this."

"It is simple," he said as the engines to the plane fired up and the aircraft began to glide down the runway. "I am a prince, I cannot have a bastard. I would have preferred a more suitable wife, a wife with a title or a pedigree of some kind. However, you are the one carrying my baby. That means I will have to make do with what I have."

"More flattering words have never been spoken, I'm sure."

"This is not about flattery. This is about reality."

The aircraft lifted off, and as it rose higher, Bailey's stomach sank into her feet. The longest plane ride she had ever been on was the short trip between Nebraska and Colorado. And nothing more. Which brought to mind other concerns. "Wait," she said, her heart kicking desperately against her chest, thinking that perhaps she had found a reprieve. "I don't have a passport."

He laughed. "That is of no concern to me. I can arrange to have one secured for you."

"Not by the time we reach your country."

"That is the thing. It is *my* country. No one is going to deny you admittance if I say you may have it. And as for coming back to the States, you certainly will eventually. So, we will secure you documentation for that eventuality. However, either way you'll be fine. You will be traveling with me."

He was maddening. Nothing fazed him. Nothing even made him pause. He was going about this with all the ruthless efficiency of a commander going into battle. And each and every protest issued from her lips, he struck down like an enemy of war.

"Does none of this bother you?" she asked. "I mean, you say you don't like being in the tabloids, but you say it with all the fire and passion of an iceberg. Meanwhile, I feel like my life is falling apart. I feel like I've been dropped into some third-rate reality show."

"That's insulting. This is first-class," he said, his tone dry, "all the way."

"Is this a joke to you? Your life has been easy, I get that. It radiates off you in waves. Your privilege. Your wealth. Everything I've had I've worked for. Every day of my life has been infused with some kind of struggle. Every single thing I own was purchased at great cost. You spend more on bottled water in a week than I spend on groceries in a month."

"That is probably true. But now this is your life. Do not worry about your roommate, by the way. I made sure to give her several months of rent so that she would not feel your absence too keenly."

"Nice of you to consider her feelings," she said, though she was grateful that Samantha wouldn't be left high and dry. Suddenly a wave washed over her, leaving her feeling adrift. Weightless. "I think I'm in shock," she said, sinking further back into the chair across from him, her limbs suddenly feeling very shaky.

"Bailey," he said, his expression concerned. "Are you able to breathe?"

She laid her head back, feeling dizzy.

"No," she said.

Suddenly he was next to her, his large hands cupping her face. He was warm, and he was so very Raphael. "Bailey," he said, his tone stern. "Keep breathing."

Her vision went fuzzy around the edges for a second, then dark...

It came back, with too much clarity, too much brightness. She felt sick to her stomach, a cold sweat on her forehead, her fingers icy. "What happened?" she asked.

"You passed out," he responded. He looked...he looked genuinely concerned. Though she wondered if it was for her or for the baby.

"Don't touch me," she said, pulling away from him. He complied, removing his hands from her face. She hated it. Hated that when he touched her she still felt something. Hated that he wasn't touching her anymore. Hated herself for caring.

"Have you been passing out regularly?"

"No," she said, trying not to watch him as he stood up and crossed to the bar. Trying very, very hard not to pay total and complete attention to his every movement. "I've had a little bit of a shocking day. I walked into a grocery store and saw that my ex-lover was a prince. Seeing as I knew I was having his baby, it suddenly occurred to me that I was having a prince's baby. Then I went home, and said prince was in my bedroom. Then he dragged me onto a private plane, all the while demanding that I marry him or he'll take my baby away. I think I'm just suffering the aftereffects."

He opened up a bottle of sparkling water and poured it into a glass, his movements deft and swift. Then he crossed the space to her, handing her the drink. "I found out I was going to be a father today, and I seem to be handling it well."

"Because you're a robot," she replied, taking a sip of the bland, fizzy liquid.

"I think that you can attest to the fact that I'm all man, Bailey. Not a robot."

"Not all. Parts of you," she said. "You seem to have Tin Man syndrome. No heart."

"I love my country," he responded, his tone cool. "I am eternally loyal to it. And I will do whatever is necessary to preserve the legacy. There is no reason for me to panic about the situation we find ourselves in. There is no question that I must marry the mother of my child. And while who you are will require a little bit of damage control, I was already set to be married in the next month. And, presumably, sometime after my wife would have given birth to a child. That has always been the course plotted out before me. All in all, only the bride has changed."

"So…women and the children they bear are interchangeable to you?" she asked.

"A wife and child are necessary components to my life," he said, his tone hard. "Essential to the continued health of the kingdom and bloodline. The importance cannot be overstated."

"But who the woman…"

"Matters in terms of bloodline, political affiliation and the ability to have children. You have one out of three—I think you're smart enough to guess which."

He said it with such calm. As though the bride were the most incidental part of the marriage. As though he didn't care at all whether he was married to her or to the shiny brunette she'd seen in the tabloids. "You're horrible. Just horrible. How did I manage to convince myself for eight months that you were Prince Charming? No reference to your *actual* royalty intended."

"We see what we want to see, Bailey. You wanted to see me as something that I wasn't. It was convenient for you at the time. I was an easy lover for you to have. Don't pretend that it didn't suit you on some level to be with a man who was only around part of the time."

"Or I was an idiot virgin who had finally found a man that she wanted to sleep with, and had her judgment completely clouded by her orgasms."

Her words hung between them, tense and heavy. She despised herself for bringing that up. For bringing up the pleasure they had found together. She would rather forget it. It kept her up at night. All day, she would drag herself around, feeling exhausted and heartbroken. But night was worse. Because then she would dream. And when she dreamed, it was that Raphael was in bed with her. Touching her, kissing her. And when she woke up, she was alone. Hideously, depressingly alone, and she ached. For a touch she would never have again.

"I am sorry you were hurt," he said, his tone clipped. "That was never my intention. But I have known who I was to be, what sort of woman I was to marry, from the time I was a boy."

"And that woman isn't me."

"No." He pushed his hand through his dark hair. "It is important to make the best choices I can for my country. And someday my child will do the same. It is what was instilled in me from the beginning. My mother reinforced my father. She had been raised to be the wife of a prince, and she knew her place. That is what it takes to raise the heir to a throne, Bailey. You must understand it is not snobbery on my part—at least not entirely—when I say you are not suited."

"I…" She swayed slightly in her seat. "I really don't even know how to have this conversation."

"You should get some rest," he said, stunning her with that declaration. "When we land we will be very close to the palace, and you can get settled in. In the meantime, I am afraid that you are overtaxed."

"I don't feel like you've earned the right to comment on my level of taxation."

"As ruling government of an entire nation, taxation falls under my purview."

"Oh, well, that's fabulous. I guess we know which things are certain. Death, taxes and Raphael."

"I'm hardly going to kill you, *cara*. I'm going to make you a princess."

Suddenly, she felt so tired she could barely hold her head up. She could not be a princess. She was a waitress. And waitresses didn't become princesses. "I'm going to have that nap now."

Bailey wandered to the back of the plane, opening the door to the bedroom, then closing it tightly behind her. It was bigger than her bedroom in her apartment. With a large, ornate bed that looked like it was designed for much more than sleeping. It was ridiculous. *He* was ridiculous. This whole thing was ridiculous.

She kicked her shoes off, crossing to the bed before throwing herself down on her face like some tragic cartoon princess. She shut her eyes tight, trying not to give in to the tears that were building behind them.

This had to be a dream. All of it. When she woke up in the morning, her head would be clearer. She would be single, alone and pregnant. Her ex-boyfriend would be nothing more than that jerk pharmaceutical rep from Italy who had left her in the lurch. He would absolutely not be the prince of some obscure country, and she would not be a future princess.

The alternative was unthinkable.

When they disembarked in Santa Firenze, Raphael had them pull the car right up to the plane. He was feeling more than slightly concerned for Bailey's health. Or, at the very least, the health of their unborn baby.

She had been especially pale ever since he had first seen her in her apartment, and she had gotten only more waxen as the trip had worn on. Though he had only seen her once after she had gone to the bedroom to sleep, and that was only to use the restroom about a half hour before they landed.

He was confused by her. By their every interaction. She was not grateful for the offer of marriage. Not especially pleased that he was giving her the chance to be a princess. His wife. A position of great honor. One that most women would fight over.

And yet the two who'd had it offered to them both seemed to have rejected it.

Allegra was a separate issue.

"The car is waiting," he said through the closed bathroom door.

Bailey emerged a moment later, wet-haired, gritty-eyed and cranky, wearing a university sweatshirt and a pair of stretch pants.

"I see you availed yourself of the shower," he said.

"How often do you get a shower at thirty thousand feet? I thought that if I didn't at least give it a try, I would be seriously failing in the luxury stakes."

"Well, you will have ample opportunity to use the facilities again. Even if I upgrade jets, it will still have a shower."

"You're assuming that I will be making use of your jet in the future."

"Of course, you're marrying me. Pretending otherwise is ridiculous." He grabbed hold of her elbow, leading her from the plane, carefully helping her down the steps. "Now, come get in the car."

She sputtered, "Just because you say nothing else makes sense does not mean that nothing else makes sense."

He opened the door to the car, gesturing for her to get in. She shot him a deadly glare, then complied. He got in beside her, slamming the door shut. "You seem to be misunderstanding," he said, feeling very much like he was speaking a different language. Because Bailey seemed to persist in misunderstanding him. "I am the ruler of Santa Firenze. No one in my family has produced an illegitimate child. Not one. No one in my family has ever been divorced. We are a hallowed and storied lineage. I am offering you a chance to become part of it. The fact that you have rejected me is outrageous on so many levels I cannot even begin to list them all."

"By all means," she said, leaning back in her seat. "List them. If you have time."

"It isn't that long of a drive to the castle."

She blinked. "Castle?"

"What part of *prince* are you having trouble comprehending? I speak very good English, though Italian is my first language. You, however, are making me question my linguistic skills."

"I would hate to be the cause of you questioning your linguistics. I'm sure that they're fantastic."

"They can't be overly fantastic, because you do not seem to understand anything of what I am telling you." There was no point arguing.

She would understand the moment his family home came into view. It was the jewel of Santa Firenze. Settled in the middle of the Alps, overlooking one of the deepest and bluest lakes in Europe, craggy peaks rising up around it. She would understand then. What he was offering. Understand what a gift he was presenting her with.

As the car made its way down the narrow, winding two-lane road, Bailey insisted on shifting constantly in her seat and letting out long, huffy sighs.

"Your distress is noted," he said.

"Not overly. You keep accusing me of not understanding, and yet I think you're the one who has not
fully taken on board that I am not happy about this."

"I am offering you marriage. Legitimacy for your
child, an end to your financial concerns."

"About that," she snapped. "Where was your offer to
end my financial concerns when I was working double
shifts at that horrible restaurant? As I was killing myself
to get through college, and you were presenting yourself as a businessman there on your company's dime?"

"Would you have accepted my offer of financial assistance?"

Her face went blank then, her mouth settling into a
stubborn line. "Yes," she said.

"You're a terrible liar. You would not have accepted.
Not from Raphael the businessman. And you seem to
like Raphael the prince a lot less."

"That's because the first time I met Raphael the
prince was when he was breaking up with me at midnight after what I had thought was a very romantic date.
Only then you threw me out into the snow."

"I wanted a clean break. I felt it was better for both
of us."

"Don't try to convince me that you lost any sleep
over any of that."

He *had*. She had no idea. He had lost countless hours
of sleep, lying there hard and aching, wanting something that only she could give to him. She had cast a
spell over him from the moment he had first seen her,
and he had never been able to explain it. He only knew
that she affected him in a way no other woman ever
had. And it had nothing to do with skill.

He could remember the first time she had knelt

down before him and taken him into her mouth. The way that she had tasted him, with shy, timid strokes of her tongue, how she had taken him in as deep as she could, her every movement uncertain. It was not her skill that enticed, but her sincerity. Her intense dedication to him. He was a man who had always felt a certain level of worship was his due, but it meant so much more coming from such a willing supplicant, rather than a trained one.

So yes, he had lost sleep. He'd had no desire to touch another woman, and, in fact, that had worked to his advantage, since he had purposed that he would not until his wedding night with Allegra. In that time he had attempted to drum up some kind of enthusiasm for the woman he was engaged to. But he had found none. Allegra was beautiful, with golden skin and dark, shimmering curls.

But he had craved the pale, flaxen-haired beauty of Bailey.

It was all vaguely ridiculous. He was fantasizing about a university student named *Bailey*. Princess Bailey.

But that was the thing with honor. It was supposed to matter even if it was hard. A truly strong oak didn't bend in the wind, and neither could the ruler of Santa Firenze.

As a boy, when he'd hurt himself, his father had not allowed his mother or the servants to comfort him. It had been up to him to breathe through the pain and carry on. That, his father had told him once, was how a man learned to soldier on in all things. If you could do it with a cut, you would do it with an emotional wound, too.

When he was older, his father had told him it applied to other physical aches, as well. A man might want a certain woman, might burn for her, but if there was potential a dalliance would harm the country, that craving—like all other harmful desires—had to be cast aside.

The prince of Santa Firenze could have whatever his heart desired. And that was why his heart, soul and sense of honor had to be made strong.

Raphael knew that he was strong. Had been, utterly and completely all his life.

Until her.

It was *truly* ridiculous. But here they were. And she, somehow, felt like she was in a position to play hardball.

The limo wound itself around the last curve, and, finally, the stately palace gates came into view. Wrought iron and scrolling, the family crest emblazoned upon them. They parted for the car as if by magic, and the limo rolled through a lane lined with hedges until they reached the magnificent courtyard in front of the palace.

The ground was overlaid with brick. A giant fountain dominated the center. At its top was a golden statue and there were many others fashioned from marble all around, representing the great leaders of his country. His very bloodline carved into stone in front of this hallowed castle that had housed generations.

He looked over at her and was satisfied to see that, finally, she had the decency to look impressed. She was staring up at the castle, at its turrets, with ivy climbing up the side and the blue-and-white flags of his country waving in the breeze from the very top of the shining palace.

"This is my home," he said, stating the obvious for

dramatic effect. "And when you are my wife, it will be your home. When our child is born, it will be his home. Do you still think you should raise him in an apartment in Colorado with your roommate?"

"I... I had no idea."

"It is not my fault you don't pay attention to current affairs. Or perhaps it is my fault, for keeping my country financially sound and free of most of the conflicts that happen in the world. We have very few reasons to be in the news because the citizens are happy, the coffers are full and we have no national security crises or natural disasters to speak of."

"Is this Narnia?"

"If it were, then a breath would turn all of the statues back to flesh. However, it is the real world. And they are only stone."

"That's a shame," she said. "Then all I would have to do is walk back to the wardrobe and I could be free of you."

She was mutinous. And he had never dealt with mutiny before. Like his father before him, he'd made Santa Firenze his life. Nothing had ever come before it. And as such, no one in his country had ever had cause for complaint.

"You don't actually want to be free of me," he said. How could she? "You're putting up a fight because you have an idea of what your life should be. I would argue that you are putting up a fight additionally because you have an idea of what consequences you should suffer for your sins."

"My sins?" she asked.

"Yes," he said, "your sins. You think you should be punished for this. Because you allowed yourself to get pregnant. And now you must pay penance. The sad, single mother, waiting tables, having been abandoned by her lover. It's a very nice narrative, but it is not a situation you find yourself in. You have a man willing to step up and take responsibility. More than a man, you have a prince. Saying anything but an emphatic yes is a waste of your resources."

She looked up at the palace, her eyes wide, her lips parted slightly. He was struck in that moment by the fullness of her beauty. Just as he had been the first time he'd seen her. And now she was carrying his child. She would be his wife.

Mine.

He pushed that word to the back of his mind. This wasn't about that. It was a necessity. What he must do. It had nothing to do with want. With that thing Bailey made him feel that was so perilously close to weakness.

"Come," he said, opening the door and extending his hand to her. "We must get you to your room."

CHAPTER FOUR

BAILEY TRIED NOT to stare too gauchely as she entered the palace, her heart thundering loudly. Loudly enough that she was pretty sure it was echoing off the marble walls of the massive antechamber they were standing in now. She had never seen anything like this in her life. It was like something out of a movie, except in a movie she had a feeling she would be heading toward some sort of fun montage where she would try on lots of dresses and upbeat pop music would play in the background while a sassy stylist told her how amazing she looked.

Instead, she was standing there wearing nothing more than a sweatshirt and pants that had seen better days, feeling like something a very large, overly self-satisfied cat had dragged in.

There were servants wandering around the palace, not making eye contact with Raphael, as though any unsolicited contact would be far too presumptuous on their part.

They did not look at her, either. Not with any kind of curiosity. In fact, she seemed beneath their notice. As though she were merely a package he had brought in after a day of shopping.

"It's so quiet in here," she said, her voice reverberating around them even though she was speaking softly.

"There are so many people in the palace at all times, it would be difficult to think if everyone were carrying on a conversation, don't you agree?"

"So you have a...silence policy?"

"There is no policy. But my father was one to train the servants to ensure they were rarely seen and rarely heard. I have done nothing to revise that code of conduct, as it suits me." He, on the other hand, didn't seem to feel like he was speaking too loudly. His voice echoed across the room, and he was not bothered by it in the least.

"You are definitely an *elevated* personage," she said, following him just slightly behind. "Aren't you?"

"This is my palace," he said, making a broad, sweeping gesture. "Of course I am elevated."

"It's just... I had the feeling royalty was a bit more modern nowadays. Prince Harry is out greeting soldiers and things."

"And getting caught with his trousers down at hotels in Las Vegas."

"We both know your trousers have been down, Raphael—it's just that nobody was there to take pictures. Actually, I could have taken pictures. I should have. I sent you some scandalous shots and sadly, never got a nude pic from you. Think of the leverage that would provide me."

His eyes sharpened. "I see you're finally considering the angle of using the press against me."

"I don't want to. Not particularly. To what end? So that we're both embarrassed? So that our child can look at the headlines in the future and see all the ugly things we said about each other? That isn't what I want. We both know that even if I were able to disgrace you by giving sordid details of your secret affair with a waitress, I would be the one who was called a whore."

"You speak the truth," he said, resting his hand on the solid marble banister, one foot on the first stair. "That is how it has always been."

"Yes, indeed," she snapped.

He arched a dark brow. "Don't look so angry with me," he said. "I don't rule over the whole world."

She sniffed. "You act like it." He continued up the stairs. She followed. "What about my things?"

"They are being handled. Though I sincerely doubt that any of your things will be deemed suitable for your new position."

She thought of her collection of clothing, all relatively dear to her, since she was a pretty intense bargain shopper who saw the experience as something of a covert ops situation. "I like my clothes."

"You will have new clothes. Better clothes. More than you could possibly wear."

"I don't understand the point of all of this."

"The point is that you are to be my queen. And you will look like my queen. When we break the news of our impending marriage, it will be with the view of presenting you in the best way possible. It does not benefit me to embarrass you, either."

"Well, at least there's that." Her stomach sank, tightening a little bit. "I don't...what is all of this going to entail?"

"You have seen movies where the people stand out on the balcony and wave at their subjects below?"

"Of course. It's a cliché."

He didn't miss a beat. "Prepare to become a cliché."

She took the steps quickly, trying to keep up with him. "You can't be serious. We're not really going to… that isn't…you don't expect to present me to the entire nation."

"Don't be silly," he said, and she felt herself start to breathe again. "I will be presenting you to the entire *world*."

Her heart slammed against her sternum. "The *entire world*? The entire world isn't going to care about me. I'm just… Bailey Harper from Nebraska. And two days ago I was a waitress."

"That is exactly why the world will be interested in you," he said, his tone fierce. "They will hold you beneath greater scrutiny than they ever would have held Allegra. They will turn over your every potential scandal. They will bring up the fact that you were waiting tables in a restaurant designed to flaunt the female figure. They will bring up the fact that you were pregnant prior to our marriage. The fact that I very likely had to marry you. They will find out the details of your childhood, of your parentage, and they will use it against you. Because that is what the media does."

"You make it all sound so exciting," she said, deadpan, trying to keep the abject horror out of her voice.

"It is simply the truth," he said. "It is why I have done my very best to stay on the right side of things. But I cannot do anything about the fact that this is going to create a scandal."

"What if I just went back to Colorado? What if we just…forget this happened."

He stopped again, turning to look at her, his eyes

fierce. "I cannot forget this happened," he growled. *"Ever."*

"But you could marry a more suitable woman. And you could kind of do it like they did back in the days of yore. You know, pay off your mistress, pretend that your bastard doesn't exist. That's kind of the way they did it, right?"

"It is not the way *I* do it. I am a man who is more than able to own his mistakes."

"Oh," she said, "excellent. I get to be something you own. A mistake you own, even. I'm the luckiest girl in the world."

"Whether or not you realize that, you are," he returned. "You are to be my princess—is there something degrading about that in your eyes?"

"No, there is something degrading about being seen as so far beneath someone that they lie to you about who they are, keep you as their dirty little secret, then abandon you so that they can marry someone who's more suitable, only bringing you back to their country when they realize that you are pregnant with their baby. None of this has anything to do with me. So why would you expect me to be flattered?" The words came hard, fast.

She didn't even know why she was so angry, because she shouldn't care. She should be happy, come to think of it. She should be happy that she didn't have to worry about the future of her child. That she wouldn't be destitute, waiting tables for the rest of her life. That she could give her baby something more than the kind of unstable situation she'd had growing up.

Except she didn't feel triumphant. Because at the end of the day, she hadn't really broken the cycle. She had still fallen into it. It was just that she had gotten pregnant with Raphael's baby, and not some random auto mechanic she'd met while passing through a dusty town in the Midwest, as her mother had done.

Bailey had just been more fortunate in her mistake, that was all. She couldn't feel triumphant about it. She couldn't feel anything but stupid.

"We will argue no more," he said, his voice hard. Then he turned and continued on up the stairs.

She let out a hard breath and followed after him. "Does the staircase ever end?" she asked.

He said nothing. Rather he let the answer become self-evident when they reached the top and a grand corridor opened up in front of them. Art that looked to be painted by the masters hung on the walls, various suits of armor positioned between each grand painting. The place was a museum, from the intricate scrollwork carved into the stone to every painting, every artifact displayed throughout.

"Your room is just here," he said, opening up a set of broad blue double doors that revealed a lavish sitting area that graduated up to a bedroom set. The bed itself had a velvet canopy that hung down and enough pillows stacked on top of the plush bedspread that it looked like it was prepared to accommodate an entire harem.

"Just how many people are supposed to sleep in that bed?"

He said nothing. Instead, he simply looked at her. And it burned all the way down to her toes.

"I didn't—"

"You have your own bathroom, shower and bath, as well," he said, cutting her off. "And this door here connects to my room, which shall make things convenient for us."

Her heart stopped cold. "How will it be more *con-venient* for us, Raphael?"

"We are to be man and wife, *cara*. There are certain expectations that go along with that."

She seriously thought her head might explode. His outright arrogance knew no bounds. She was astounded. *Enraged.*

"You honestly think I'm going to sleep with you?"

"You have done so before," he said, gesturing toward her midsection.

"Yes," she said, "I did. When I thought you were a normal man. A man with a heart. A man that I might have a future with."

"Clearly you have a future with me. We are to be married."

"We are to be married only because your fiancée dumped you at the last minute." She took a step toward him, seething. "Only because I'm carrying your child. And had your fiancée not broken things off, you wouldn't even know that I was having a baby, because you never bothered to respond to my text."

"As I told you before, I had gotten rid of the phone you used to contact me."

She blinked. "And a prince wasn't concerned about missing calls or texts going to an old number?"

"It was a phone that was only for you," he responded.

"A burner phone." She shrieked the words. "You had a burner phone for me. I really was your filthy secret, wasn't I? What would have happened if people had discovered your assignation with me? How *humiliated* you would have been." She laughed, and once she started she had a hard time stopping. It wasn't funny. It cut her down deep. But it was either laugh or curl into a ball and weep. "Well, now the entire world is going to know. Funny how things work out, isn't it?"

"I am going to do my best to make it as painless for both of us as possible."

"You're a saint, Raphael," she spat. "You really are. But if you think you're a saint that's getting anywhere near my body again, you are fooling yourself."

"I don't understand what the issue is. We share a mutual attraction…"

"I trusted you," she said, her voice low, vibrating. "I trusted you with my body, and you knew that cost me. I didn't even know who my father was," she said, "and I was determined that I would never be like my mother. That I would make better decisions. Instead, I met you. And you set out to make sure that I became exactly like her. I don't trust you anymore." Her voice was trembling now. "I don't think I will ever trust you again. I will marry you, Raphael. I will marry you because it is truly the best thing for our child. I will marry you because I don't know what else to do. Because I want this baby, because I want to not be a waitress forever. Because I don't want my child to go to bed hungry, to go to bed cold. For those reasons, I will marry you. But I will not be your wife. Not really."

His face hardened, his eyes growing cold. "Do you expect me to be celibate for the rest of my life?"

"I don't care what you do. As long as you don't come anywhere near me."

"We shall see," he said, his tone made of pure ice now.

"There is nothing to see," she said. "My decision is made. And unless your particular brand of bastardry extends to forcing women into bed with you, I can safely say that you will not be having me in yours ever again."

"I have never had to force a woman into my bed," he gritted out, "you least of all. The reason I said *we shall see* is that I hold out very little hope for your self-control, *cara*. I believe that I can have you begging for me with the proper flick of my wrist between those pretty thighs."

She ignored the desperate well of longing that opened up inside her, making her conscious of how empty she was, of how lonely. Of just how much she desired him. "Never," she said, tilting her chin up.

He said nothing. Instead, dark eyes burning into hers, he closed the space between them, wrapping his arm around her waist, his grip like an iron bar. He looked… she could see almost nothing of the man she had known in Vail. This was the prince. Commanding, ruthless and so beautiful she could scarcely breathe for it.

Perhaps this was more evidence of just how weak she was. Or perhaps it was simply a testament to Raphael. Either way, she found herself looking back at those black, fathomless eyes, desire yawning through her, stretching all the way down to her toes, hitting everyplace in between.

It didn't matter that only a few hours ago she felt like she was near death. It didn't matter that she was wearing nothing but stretch pants and a ratty sweatshirt. It didn't matter that her hair was unkempt, unstyled, and that any makeup left behind was a mere ghost of what had been applied the night before. Nothing mattered but this. But him holding her, and her wanting him.

Before she had a chance to protest, before she had a

chance to even consider if she might want to, his lips crashed down on hers.

It was as fast as it was ruthless, a claiming of her mouth that mirrored the way he had stormed back into her life today. Taking ownership, making her his.

She left her arms at her sides at first, and then she could no longer resist. She clung to him, curling her fingers around the soft fabric of his shirt, holding tightly to him, because if she didn't, she would fall to the ground.

Three months.

Three months she had been without this. Without him. It was so much better than she remembered. So much more.

And then he released her, his top lip curling. "As I said. We shall see."

Then he turned and walked out of the room, leaving her there with her shame and with a burning desire that refused to be quenched no matter how much her brain and her heart tried to put it out.

CHAPTER FIVE

THE NEXT MORNING when Bailey did not appear for breakfast, Raphael went in search of her. She was not in her bedroom. Which was a surprise. He had expected to find her there, sleeping late, as Bailey had often done when she had spent nights in the hotel with him. But she was nowhere to be found. He wandered the halls, wondering if there was any way she had possibly made an escape. And to what end. She must know that he would find her. There was nowhere on earth she could go to hide from him. As evidenced by this morning's headline, the paparazzi had already identified her as his potential lover. And were speculating about whether or not she figured into his breakup with Allegra. She was not anonymous. Already she was conspicuous.

And he had almost infinite resources. There was no way she could avoid him for too long.

He remembered then that she had no passport. And his lips curved into a smile. She could go no farther than the borders of his country. And that meant he wouldn't have to cast a very wide net at all to find her.

One of his servants rushed by, her eyes downcast.

"Where is Bailey?" he asked.

The woman stopped and looked up, her expression

serene. "Ms. Harper is taking her breakfast in the library."

Well, he had to give her full marks for knowing exactly who he was talking about and where she was.

"Thank you," he returned. He made his way down the corridor, flinging the doors wide when he reached the library. Bailey, who was settled into an armchair with a book in her hand, startled.

"How did you know I was here?"

"I have staff."

"Yes, I am aware of that. They're the ones who brought me breakfast," she said, lifting up a cup. "And tea. They're all very nice. Maybe you should talk to them instead of ignoring their very existence unless you have a pronouncement."

"I do not ignore them. They maintain distance out of respect. If I were to stop and speak to each and every one of them, no one would get any work done, myself included. I am a fair ruler and a very good employer. They do not need me to co-opt their time in order for them to feel that. Just as I do not need fawning to know that they revere me."

"Wow," she said. "You're…a whole thing."

"So very nice of them to aid you in hiding away in my home," he continued as though she hadn't spoken.

"I'm not hiding. It's just that this place is the size of a small city. I practically need a cab to get across it."

"Dramatic as ever. I have taken the liberty of procuring you a new wardrobe."

She set her teacup down. "Like…you personally?"

"Don't be ridiculous."

"Right. Well, you procuring me a wardrobe is somehow not ridiculous?"

"There is nothing ridiculous about me."

She laughed. "Are you kidding me?" Bailey stood, stretching, the soft fabric of her T-shirt conforming to her breasts and to the soft swell of her stomach as she did. "You, who were carrying on a secret affair with a university student in Colorado but is secretly a prince with a castle and a superiority complex that would suggest you have little going on in your...trouser region."

"Well, we both know that isn't true."

She waved a hand. "I have nothing to compare it to."

"Regardless, you know every inch of me. And know I am not ridiculous." Her cheeks turned a deep shade of pink, and he felt an answering fire in his gut.

"That's one man's opinion," she said, her tone arch.

"The only opinion that matters in this country."

"Ridiculous," she muttered.

"The press conference will be today."

"What?" she asked. "I'm...jet-lagged still."

"It cannot be helped. The wedding must take place as quickly as possible. I'm sure you understand that."

"But weddings take time to plan?" It was phrased as a question, her voice slightly tremulous.

"Not when you have infinite wealth and power."

"Well, I really wouldn't know anything about that."

He frowned. "No. Nor will you. But we should discuss your monthly stipend. It will be quite generous, of course."

"I..." She blinked. "I don't know what to say to that."

"You'll need your own card, naturally. You will want to shop. Dine out with friends."

"Are you offering me an allowance like a child?"

"No," he said. "I am offering some independence."

"To spend your money. At least, an amount you determine is acceptable."

"I can give you a credit card without a limit, conversely. I'm not worried about your spending habits. You're a *terrible* gold digger, Bailey. You failed to recognize you had hooked yourself a prince. Then you didn't go to the tabloids, and when I mentioned you were getting a new wardrobe your eyes did not glitter with anything like triumph. In fact, you look slightly like you want to kill me."

She pursed her lips in thought. "*Kill* is a strong word. I don't want to kill you. *Maim*, possibly."

"Well, that is reassuring. I would try to keep jokes about harming my royal personage at a minimum around my Secret Service. They take a dim view on that."

She cocked her head to the side. "Where were they when you were with me?"

"As I told you already, I have a fairly low profile. If I don't want to be recognized, casual dress and a pair of sunglasses generally does it."

"The Clark Kent of royalty."

He frowned. "Excuse me?"

"Because nobody recognizes that you're Superman when you have your glasses on."

He found himself laughing, which caught him by surprise. That was more like the relationship he'd had with her before. She always had a way of amusing him, often when he least expected it. They should have nothing to talk about. He had often thought that when the two of them had been together. And it wasn't because he wanted to get to know her that he had initially pursued that connection with her.

Attraction. That was what had hit him upon first seeing her. Need. Want.

He had expected to sleep with her. What he hadn't expected was to spend hours talking to her. And enjoying those conversations.

A man in his thirties, raised to be royalty of a small country in Europe, should have little in common with a university student in her twenties from the United States. And perhaps they didn't have much in common. But she intrigued him. She surprised him. And he found he quite enjoyed it.

Surely, since she was going to be his wife, that was okay.

"I suppose that's true," he said. "I didn't make any announcements about coming into the States. I was there to visit a ski resort owned by a friend. And see about investing. That night, as you know, there was a blizzard, and I was unable to fly out."

"Then, to paraphrase, of all the diners by the airport, why did you walk into mine?"

"I nearly walked back out. I didn't realize what sort of establishment it was. And while I was reasonably confident no one from the press was nearby, I cannot take the chance that I might be seen somewhere of that nature. But then I saw you."

Color rose in her cheeks. "I made you stay?"

"I wanted you," he said, his voice rough. "From the moment I saw you."

He didn't know what he had expected. Really, he needed to stop expecting anything when it came to Bailey. She did not behave in any way that made logical sense to him. But he did not expect for her to frown.

"You make it sound like I was a watch."

"You're going to have to clarify," he said, his tone dry.

"Like, you saw me, and you wanted to buy me. Like I was something you might see in a store."

She wasn't wrong. It was the exact same thing to him. He wanted something, he got it. Women were no exception. Much like watches or cars. All of them were expensive, and often a lot of trouble. And yet he went to great lengths to acquire them. He didn't see how that was offensive.

"People are not things," she said, her tone hard, her expression matching it. As though she had been able to read his thoughts.

"Perhaps not. But things have value. It is not the insult you make it sound like."

"You're not supporting your case."

"I do know that people are not things," he said. Still, the acquisition of things, favors or the affections of women all often went much the same for him. What he saw, he soon had.

"I'm skeptical."

"You are welcome to remain skeptical. However, we must get you ready for today's conference. We have three hours. I have someone coming in to do your hair and your makeup. Then your dress will have to be fitted quickly. I imagine it will be close enough. Still, your figure has changed a bit since the last time I saw it completely uncovered. I did my best to guess."

"I...that all sounds a little excessive."

"Not at all. Your face is going to be on magazines around the world. On the front page of newspapers everywhere."

Her lips twitched. "Okay. I suppose I can submit to having a little bit of assistance."

"What's that?" he asked in mock surprise. "Is Bailey Harper actually submitting?"

"To my vanity. Not to you. Don't get used to it."

"I will see you in two hours. And I expect for you to look like a princess."

Bailey had spent the past few hours being waxed, styled, plucked and polished until she glowed. And when she looked in the mirror, she couldn't help but marvel at the incredible work a professional could do.

She had only ever had her makeup done for her once. And that was when she was in high school, and she'd decided to check out one of those makeup counters in a department store. She had come out of that experience looking like a 1980s reject, with far too much blue eye shadow and a generous helping of glitter.

This was an entirely different experience. She could hardly recognize the woman staring back at her. Her eyes were large, smoky, the charcoal gray of the shadow emphasizing her blue eyes. Her lips were painted a lovely pink color, dark and matte, very subtle.

Somehow, they had managed to style her hair into a smooth, sleek bun, the likes of which she never would have been able to manage on her own.

And the gown...it was beyond anything she had ever imagined wearing. A light shade of pink entirely covered with some sort of netting. And sewn into it were thousands of little glass beads, concentrated around the middle and dispersing over the bodice and the skirt.

With her every movement, she sparkled.

Even she could almost believe this. Even she could almost believe that she was a princess.

The dream, the fantasy hovered at the edges of her consciousness, made her soul feel like it might grow wings and fly. Or might be crushed once and for all if it went wrong.

You're nothing but a weight. You've held me down for sixteen years, Bailey. Don't think I'll spend one day missing you.

Her mother's words rang in her ears, quick to dull some of the brightness of the moment.

Whatever. She was a princess. How much of a weight could she be?

"Look at me now," she said.

She wasn't sure what she thought about all of it, not in the grand scheme of things, but in this moment, she felt pretty good.

There was a heavy knock on her bedroom door, and she assumed it was another servant, come to add another layer of makeup or perhaps to take her to meet Raphael.

"Come in," she said, not looking away from her reflection in the mirror.

The door opened, and she looked up, meeting Raphael's dark gaze as he entered the room. Her heart was thrown forward, slamming hard into the front of her chest.

"You are ready," he said.

She kept her eyes on his in the mirror, the fact it was a reflection acting as a slight buffer. "Yes. Your team of experts is in fact quite expert."

She saw a lick of fire in his eyes. "They are indeed."

"I thought we were going to meet somewhere."

"We are. Here."

She didn't want him in here. She didn't want him

looking at her like that, not with the bed so close by. She didn't want to acknowledge her own weakness.

"Well, here we are," she said, looking everywhere but at him.

"You're missing the most important part of what you'll need today," he said, stepping toward her.

She whirled around, gripping the edge of the vanity. "What's that?" she asked. "Your royal visage?"

"Not quite." He reached into the interior pocket of his jacket and pulled out a little black box.

She was pretty sure her heart stopped completely. "What are you doing?"

He opened the box, revealing a square-cut diamond on a thin band that was also encrusted with stones. Beneath it was another band, glittering yet brighter. She didn't think she had ever seen something so valuable this close. All she could think of was how much money it represented. How many months of rent it could've paid. How many months of groceries and electricity it could have provided.

It was impossible to think differently. When she had gone through life as she had.

"These are for you. Of course, just the engagement ring for now." He took hold of it, grasping it between his thumb and forefinger and holding it out to her.

And suddenly, it wasn't the value that concerned her. Her heart felt like it was shriveling, like everything was being squeezed from it. She had imagined this. Raphael proposing. Before she knew.

The ring she'd pictured had been nothing like this, and the setting had been something entirely different. She had thought he might do it that night in Vail. Out on the snowy streets, or even in his hotel room. When they were both still naked, flushed with passion.

She had fantasized about him getting down on one knee. Looking up at her, telling her she was beautiful. That he loved her. That he couldn't live without her.

Here she was, in a castle, wearing the most beautiful dress imaginable, being offered the most incredible ring. And it paled in comparison to that small, dark fantasy she'd had of him kneeling before her wearing nothing but the naked longing he felt for her on his face.

He was a different man here. There was nothing human or vulnerable about him. Nothing real. His face was stone. As though he were already preparing to become a statue on the grounds.

He wasn't asking. And she was in no position to do anything beyond taking the ring and putting it on her finger. So that was what she did. As she slipped it onto her finger, it killed her by inches.

She looked down, not quite able to believe that she was looking at her own hand. That she was wearing something quite so ostentatious.

"You do not seem pleased, Bailey. Is the ring not large enough for your taste?"

She tried to formulate a response, but the words stuck in her throat. How did she tell him that she had never imagined getting engaged, until she had met him? And then she had imagined it endlessly. And that this, though it was so much more spectacular than that initial fantasy, was nothing more than a pale imitation?

She hadn't imagined the ring.

She had imagined how full her chest would feel. How happy she would be to move forward in her life with someone by her side. To have the kind of relationship she had never dreamed she would.

Well, this was something she hadn't imagined, but she didn't feel full. She felt drained. Missing someone who had never really existed. Suddenly, she resented the man in front of her. It was easy to think he had stolen her lover from her. That they were two different people.

"You think the size of the ring is the problem?" she finally asked.

"You look upset."

"Because. Because this should have been the most romantic moment of my life. But this is all for show. There's no romance in it. There's no feeling. Just a diamond."

"A diamond would be enough for most women. And if it were not, the title of princess would supplement."

"I never dreamed of any of these things." She had never dreamed of love, either. Not before him. Dreaming was dangerous. Devastating in ways she hadn't fully realized until she'd seen those same dreams ground into ash.

"Does not every woman dream she perhaps might be a secret princess?"

"No. Sometimes a woman just dreams that she will be able to escape instability. Get an education, work for a better life. I was never afraid of that. But I was afraid of destroying my hard work. I was afraid of losing my head with a man and ending up in the exact same position as my mother. And so I did." Her voice broke on that last word, and she despised herself. For being so vulnerable with him. For giving him any more information about herself. She had been in a whole relationship all by herself back in Vail. She could see that now.

She had told him so much about who she was, what she wanted. And he had given her nothing in return. He was so skilled at keeping things focused on her, of making small talk that filled the hours but never became personal.

In combination with the physical intimacy, it had been so easy to believe that they were close. But she had never known him. And he had never intended to allow her to.

"You keep saying that. You keep comparing yourself to her. But you are here." He swept his hand across his body, indicating the space they were standing in. "As am I. I fail to see how your situation equates with hers."

"Because," she said, feeling like she was on the verge of screaming herself raw. "If you weren't a prince, if your fiancée hadn't broken up with you, I would be her. It's only your obligation and your money that separates us."

"But you have it. And you have me."

"As though that solves all of my problems without creating more."

"Yes. Terrible problems. Such as which car will you take out shopping today, which of the many forks on the table will you use to eat the delicacy laid out before you, and how on earth will you become accustomed to referring to yourself as princess?"

"Those are things," she said. "That's all."

"It is everything. As you said, you dreamed of a better life. This is a better life."

"I would have been happy with a house in the suburbs and a husband who wasn't too arrogant to function."

"I function just fine, Bailey. As you know. Though perhaps I need to refresh your memory?"

She pressed herself flat against the vanity, trying to put some distance between them while he advanced on her. Her heart was hammering a steady rhythm, so loud she was sure he could hear it. She didn't know what she wanted.

She hated that most of all.

The certainty that she shouldn't. The certainty she wished she could. Jumbling together to create a complex tangle of need inside her.

She needed him to touch her.

She needed him to stay away.

He moved to her, extending his hand and tracing her features with the tips of his fingers. She couldn't breathe. She couldn't think.

She just wanted.

"Regrettably," he said, dropping his hand back to his side, "I will have to remind you later. It is time to introduce my people to their new princess."

CHAPTER SIX

BAILEY FOUND HERSELF being ushered down a corridor of the palace at high speed. Raphael was holding tightly on to her arm as they made their way to what she presumed was the clichéd balcony they had discussed earlier.

Heels clicking loudly on the marble, an aide of some kind ran up to Raphael, her cheeks flushed, her expression tense. She handed him a piece of paper, offering no explanation. Raphael didn't pause, instead, he looked at the scrap, frowning deeply. Then he shoved the paper into his pocket, speaking past her in Italian.

He didn't bother to try to clarify what had just happened. And the only words she knew in Italian were dirty, because he'd taught them to her in bed.

She did her best to keep those thoughts at bay as they kept on rushing. Then they stopped suddenly, in front of double doors with heavy brocade curtains over them.

"You will not have to speak," he whispered into her ear, his breath hot, fanning over her neck. "Just stand next to me. Smile and wave when I do. And for God's sake, Bailey, try and look poised."

And then the doors parted. She found herself being whisked out into the fresh air as quickly as she had been dragged down the corridor. The sun was stunningly bright, washing over the mountain view. It was a shocking blue, with sharp peaks and slashes of bright white snow, fading down to the crystalline lake below. It was so intense, so beautiful that it seemed more like a painting than real life.

More surreal still was the immense crowd of people who had gathered below in the courtyard. They were hushed, standing there, still, waiting to hear from their monarch. She had never seen anything like it. And she had certainly never been in front of this many people. It was like some bad dream from junior high. Except she wasn't naked. She was wearing a designer gown.

"I am aware," Raphael said, speaking in front of a microphone that amplified his deep, rich voice, "that there has been some confusion regarding my future, and the future of this country as a result. Regrettably, my engagement to Allegra Valenti came to a rather abrupt end. And, as you have already seen in a great many of the tabloids, there has been speculation on the reasons for such a thing. I cannot deny that there is some truth to those rumors."

She had no idea what rumors he was talking about. The only headline she had seen was about the dissolution of his engagement, nothing more. She thought back to the scrap of paper he'd been passed in the hall. Had he been given all of this information only a few minutes ago? She knew Raphael was smooth. But that was impressive, even for him.

"Allegra and I wanted to do the right thing, both for my country and for her future," he continued. "But it has become abundantly clear that we were wrong in our methods. Otherwise, we would not have found ourselves in the situation. It is true—Allegra is now with someone else. And I will not deny that I am, as well. It took Allegra's courage for me to see the light, but now that I have, I hope that you will trust what I am giving to you now." His voice was solemn, sincere, and Bailey found herself being drawn in. Hanging on his every word, wondering what he might say next.

"What I am sharing with you now," he continued, "is my heart. I had thought there was perhaps no place for such a thing in politics. But I have faith in my people. Bailey Harper is the choice my heart has made. She is not from a wealthy family. Not from a blue-blooded lineage. But she is going to be my princess, and I believe in time you will all grow to love her as I do."

Bailey was sure that she was dreaming. Any minute now, she was going to wake up in her bedroom back at her apartment in Colorado. Any minute.

Rather than gaining any lucidity, things only got stranger. The crowd erupted below in a roar. Cheering. Cheering him and her and...well, both of them.

She'd never had so much positive affirmation in her life.

And then Raphael wrapped his arm around her waist, drawing her close.

He gripped her chin with his thumb and forefinger, pressing his nose against hers, his dark eyes blazing a trail of heat all the way down to her core.

She couldn't pull away. Not now. Not when they were putting on a show for the country. So, she simply had to stand there, held captive as the crowd was below. Knowing with every fiber of her being that all of the things he just said—all those words that had been so carefully crafted to sound sincere—were exactly that. A meticulously woven fiction designed to spin a tale that would sit well with a nation. Designed to create an impenetrable argument.

Anyone who rejected her now would seem spiteful. Shallow and petty. He had acknowledged that she was beneath him, and even though the words had been beautifully chosen, that was the thrust of all his argument.

Yes, she was lowborn. Yes, she was beneath him. Yes, he had tried to want someone more suitable.

But he had also lied. He had said she was the choice of his heart, when in reality, he had only chosen her because she carried his child in her womb.

She wasn't the choice of his heart. She had been the temporary choice of his libido, and that was not at all the same thing.

But he was looking down at her with such ferocity, such possessiveness, that it was difficult to reason all of that out. And anyway, there was nothing she could do now. She couldn't protest. Not even for an infinitesimal moment, because there were cameras everywhere, the entire world poised at the ready to find fault with her. And so she simply let her eyes flutter closed. Allowed him to lean in and press the softest of kisses to her lips. Almost like a brush of a feather.

Except there was such weight in it. Enough that she thought it might destroy her. That it might crack her irreparably. Reduce her to nothing where she stood.

They parted quickly, and then he raised his hand in a stiff, formal-looking wave. And she knew this was the part where she was supposed to imitate. So she did, feeling like she was playing a part in the theater. Trying to imitate her best approximation of the royal wave as she knew it from movies and parades.

Then, just as quickly as they had appeared, she was being whisked back behind the doors, carried away.

"That was it?" she asked.

"I don't answer questions. I give speeches. I do not give explanations for my decisions. What I decree is law."

"Wow. You really should see someone about that ego."

"It is not an affliction for me."

"It is for those around you," she countered.

"My ego prevents me from feeling overly concerned about that. As I am quite comfortable."

He was so handsome. Even when he was being ridiculous, so arrogant it was amazing she hadn't hauled off and slapped him. He was utter perfection. Those dark eyes and blade-straight nose. The sharp jaw. And his lips…the only soft thing about him where everything else was unyielding as granite.

"What was on that paper they gave you?" She asked the question mostly because she needed something to distract her from how very *Raphael* he was.

"Headlines are already set tomorrow to announce the engagement of Allegra Valenti to Cristian Acosta."

"Your ex is marrying someone else?"

"More importantly, she's pregnant with his baby. Which will also appear in tomorrow's headline. We will be lucky if your pregnancy doesn't appear either. Rumors are apparently already circulating. I didn't want to bring it into today's announcement, as I didn't want to undermine my points. But I saw no reason to sidestep the issue of Allegra being engaged."

"Oh. Well, that was quite the good off-the-cuff speech then."

"I have my moments. I know what my people want to hear."

"Well, that's...romantic."

"As you well know," he said, reaching up and loosening the knot on his tie. Her fingers itched to wrench it free completely. As she'd done so many times before. "There is little that is romantic about this. It isn't about romance. It's about doing what's right."

And just like that, desire turned to anger. "Oh, I do hope we can have that engraved on my wedding band."

"We *could*."

Such a strange, arrogant creature he was in his natural habitat. He could scarcely recognize her sarcasm. "No, thank you," she said, speaking slowly. "I have no desire to have that inscribed on my wedding band. I was messing with you."

"Messing with me?"

"Yes. Which I did often when we were together in Vail. It just seems sometimes like you don't remember."

"I think maybe I wasn't listening to you very closely back in Vail," he said. "Typically, I was blinded by the desire to have you."

Those words were like a clean, vicious stab through her chest. "I see. So the contents of my bra were a lot more interesting than the contents of my brain?"

"Talking to you never served a purpose," he responded, neatly sidestepping the question. "I always knew that our association would be temporary."

"But sex somehow made sense?"

"Most people assume that a sexual liaison will be temporary in some way. Unless you're looking at marriage, and often those end, too."

It was so simply put. So pragmatic. And really, not

wrong. It enraged her. Because she wanted to feel mortally wounded. Wanted to feel justified. Wanted how blindsided she had been to be about him, and not about her.

She sniffed. "Well, you lied to me."

"By omission."

Anger burned through the last shred of her pride. "You're so full of crap." She stamped, her gorgeous dress swirling around her legs. "You *absolutely* let me believe, and build off those assumptions I made early on. You did it so easily. Effortlessly. And I saw that reflected in the way that you made the announcement today. You're very good at saying what people need to hear."

"I would say that's a good quality in a leader."

"It matters much less than *doing* something. Than being sincere. What does it matter if your words make somebody feel warm all over when they listen to you talk, and then your actions leave them cold? In my case, *literally* out in the snow."

"Any dramatic tossing into the cold was your own doing. I didn't chuck you into a snowbank."

"Well, I collapsed in the snow." She watched his expression, neutral and shuttered. Maddeningly still. "In *distress*," she added. "I hope you're happy."

"It does not make me happy to have hurt you. But I fail to see how your unrealistic expectations were my fault."

"I think you fail to see how anything could be your fault ever," she spat.

"I am held to a different standard. As a result, I live my life by a different set of rules. Again, that is hardly my fault. I am under greater scrutiny. I carry heavier weight—there must be some perk to that."

"What perk? The feeling that the entire world is a trinket box you can reach into and rummage around, pulling out whatever you want and then casting it aside when you're finished? The idea that people are as disposable as *things*? That everything is here for you to use to your satisfaction? I think that goes a little bit beyond the benefits you could expect for being royalty."

"I see. And what benefits do *you* suppose I deserve? For bearing the weight of an entire nation and all of the people in it?"

"Dental? I don't know. But definitely not the right to lie about your identity."

"I wanted you," he said, grabbing hold of her arms and pressing her back against the wall, his movements sudden, swift, shocking.

He held her tight, his voice suddenly low, rough. Gone was the prince. Somehow she had managed, with a few words, to strip him back down to the man.

"I thought of nothing else but having you," he continued. "I was engaged to someone else. I knew that there was no future, and I took you anyway, because I could not imagine living in a world where I had seen you, and desired you, but not satisfied that desire. I am not a man who understands failure. I'm not a man who understands *no*."

"So you approached me as a child throwing a tantrum over a toy might?"

He growled, rolling his hips forward, the evidence of his arousal plainly felt, even through the layers of her gown. "I am not a child. And what I had was nothing like a tantrum."

He leaned closer to her, and she nearly melted. His smell, his touch, his heat...it was all too much. Too good. "Have you ever felt like your blood was on fire?" he rasped. "Have you ever felt like you would die if you didn't have something? When I saw you, that's what it was. Nothing but fire and need. I cannot explain it. Perhaps I acted uncivilized. Perhaps I played the role of villain in this. But I would do it again."

"Even knowing it ends here?"

He looked stricken by that. His dark eyes haunted. "I... I can still see no other option. Because the alternative is walking through life ablaze, and never having a chance to try and put it out."

He didn't know what was happening to him. He was... shaking.

And he knew with certainty it had nothing to do with facing a crowd of thousands, nothing to do with the eyes of the world being trained on him. Not in the least. That attention, that deference, was his birthright and he wore it with the ease he wore his own skin.

Only one thing had ever made him do this. Tremble like a child.

Bailey.

Always Bailey.

From the first.

It enraged and invigorated him in equal measure.

Because she was out of his reach. She had been. Always. He had carved out a moment of time when he could have her, just a moment. Swaths of time removed from Santa Firenze, spent in a town in the States, mostly in a hotel room with a woman he'd known he could only possess for a short while. And then a change in the tide had brought him back to her. Only now she had made it clear she wouldn't touch him. That he could never have her again, and had happily given rights to his body to other women. But there were no other women.

There hadn't been. Not from the moment he'd first met her.

Never in all his life had Prince Raphael DeSantis wanted anything that compromised the future of Santa Firenze. Never had he taken such an inconvenient mistress. Never before had he chosen a woman on the other side of the globe. A woman he could see for only snatches of time. Going more than a month without sex, often, because he couldn't slip away to Colorado. And because he could find no excitement in himself for anyone else.

The entire point of a mistress was to bring pleasure. It was the meaning of their existence.

He had certainly found pleasure in Bailey's arms, but there had been a cost. She didn't conform to his schedule, his map or his station in life. He'd had to bend to accommodate her.

He'd had her…countless times over days that were easily counted. And still, she made him shake.

Still, she treated him as if she was above this. As if she could turn away from their attraction so easily while he could not.

"I am on fire," he said, the words strong, hard. "And there you stand like ice."

"You doused the fire, Raphael. It's a bit late to regret it."

"More insipid jokes about me throwing you into the snow?"

"That's not a joke," she said. "A part of me *died* that

night. A part of me that believed in something other than my own grit for the first time in…ever. I believed in you. I believed in us. And you took it from me. You're a liar. You're a liar who would have abandoned me to raise a baby alone if not for a twist of fate."

"We met by a twist of fate," he said, releasing his hold on her arms and pressing his palms against the wall, trapping her between them. "How could our reunion have ever been anything else?"

"It could have been anything. You're a man who acts like he controls the entire world, but you're going to pretend you couldn't control what happened between us?"

"If I could have controlled what happened between us, I never would have touched you."

"Rail at fate, Raphael. Not at me. Or maybe for once rail at yourself."

She moved, as though she were going to try to dodge his hold, and he pressed himself closer. Her blue eyes glittered, anger visible there. She was ready to lash out at him if he did something she didn't want. But that was fine. He was more than ready to lash out in his own way.

Quickly, he removed one hand from the wall, sliding it around to cup the back of her head. Then he pulled her forward, claiming her mouth with all the arrogance he possessed that she claimed to be so disdainful of. She was not disdainful of it. She was weak for it. Needy. And he knew it. No matter what she said. No matter how she pretended she didn't want him anymore.

She could play it like she was disgusted with him. With all of his perceived flaws, which she was more than willing to list at the drop of a hat. And yet, without them, she would not go up in flame like this.

She pressed her hands against his chest, attempting

to push him back. But he would not be moved. Instead, he closed the distance between them, pressing her head up against the wall. His hand was trapped between her head and the hard surface, crushing his bones. But he didn't care.

She wiggled, as though she were attempting to get away. Then he angled his head, sliding his tongue across hers, the movement slow, sensual. And he felt the exact moment she went limp. The exact moment she gave in to this thing that raged between them like a starving beast.

He heard footsteps behind them, sensed that household staff members were wandering this very corridor looking the other way. He didn't care. They could stare all they wanted. She was his. She was his princess. She would be his wife. She carried his child in her womb.

Mine.

That was the word. The one that he had been a slave to, driven by, that first night he'd seen her. And he saw it now for what it was. A prophecy. He possessed her now, in every way that mattered.

And this moment, this capitulation, made it clear that he would possess her body again. She would not resist. Could not. Because regardless of how she tried to act, she was as helpless as he was. She was. He was not the only one who shook.

This little creature who seemed to imagine that she was too good for this, too good for him, was shivering in his arms like a leaf in the breeze. He was not beneath her. But, soon enough, she would be beneath him.

He rocked his hips forward, pressing his hardness into her softness, glorying in the soft gasp that he sipped from her lips.

He abandoned her mouth for a moment, kissing her

neck, down to her collarbone. He could bare her breasts here in the hall. Suck her glorious pink nipples into his mouth, so sweet, like candy. He could lift her skirts, free himself from his pants and thrust himself deep inside her.

Not a single servant in his employ would report what they had seen. They were all far too discreet, and far too well taken care of to take a chance at compromising their position in the palace.

And he did not care for his own modesty. This was his palace, after all. If he wanted to have a woman against the wall, that was his prerogative. Of course, he never had. But Bailey...he needed her. He needed her like water. Like air.

And he could feel the deprivation keenly, just as he could those other things.

He raised his hand, curling his fingers around the top of her gown, tugging the bodice down, exposing one rosy peak.

She gasped, wiggling away from him. And he was so shocked that he didn't stop her. He had lost himself. Had lost his sense of time and place.

"What are you doing?" she hissed, pulling her dress back in place. "There are...people." As if to underscore her point, a staff member, dressed all in black, rushed by quickly, her head down.

"All that you see here is mine. Mine to do with as I will. The people that work here have no other purpose but to see that my will is done. If my will is to have you out in the open, I will hardly curb my behavior for the sensibilities of those who live to serve me."

"You arrogant son of a—if you aren't concerned for your servants, if you aren't concerned for your own modesty, what about mine? And even more than that, what about the fact that I said you were not to touch me?"

"You are welcome to make edicts, Bailey. That does not mean I will comply with them. I am a law unto myself. What I want, I will have."

"So you have said. But, Raphael, do you have me?" She tilted her chin up, arching one pale brow, her expression defiant. He had never had anyone look at him like that before. As though he were something beneath contempt. "No." She supplied the answer herself. "You don't."

And then she turned on her heel and stormed down the hall, leaving him standing there, aching, desperate and in a position he did not understand.

He had shown her power. He had presented her to his people. He was giving her a title. Had installed the ungrateful creature in his palace. He had aroused her body, had proven that the fire between them was not gone.

Still, she had turned him down. Still, he had failed at an objective.

He had offered her everything in his possession, and it had not brought her to heel.

Bailey Harper was an enigma. Raphael deeply disliked enigmas.

But he would have to put the mystery of Bailey on hold. A royal wedding had been planned to take place in a few weeks' time. And by God, it would.

If not by God, then by his own hand. That, at least, would not fail.

CHAPTER SEVEN

IT WAS SURPRISINGLY simple to be the bride in a royal wedding. Given that such a thing was a worldwide spectacle, Bailey supposed it would be a great deal of work. It appeared it was not a great deal of work for the stars of the show.

It was probably helpful that most of the details had been in place already. Invitations already sent out. When she had found out that an amendment had been sent, letting people know that the name of the bride had in fact changed, she had wanted to melt into the floor and die a thousand deaths, and any number of other overdramatic and fatal things.

Focusing on her humiliation at being Raphael's pregnant replacement bride was a lot easier to handle than thinking about her disgrace in the hallway a couple of weeks back.

He had…well, he had been perilously close to having her in a public space. Had been perilously close to breaking her resolve absolutely and completely.

But then, after her foot-stomping tantrum, he'd been distant. Nothing if not circumspect. Which was just weird. Because Raphael was never circumspect. He had all the subtlety of a wrecking ball.

She startled as Raphael entered the dining room, his manner purposeful, his gaze direct. "Good evening, Bailey."

"What are you doing here?"

"Is that the customary greeting we give each other nowadays? Manners really are a dying art form."

"I haven't seen you at dinner for two weeks. And here you are. To what to do I owe the pleasure?"

"We have a menu to plan."

"Isn't the menu already planned?"

"Yes. But to Allegra's specifications. She had chosen the design for the cake and the flavors. In addition to the meal that will be served to the guests. I thought you might want your own preferences considered."

"I...well..." She didn't actually. She sort of wished that none of it was up to her. That none of it had anything to do with her. She wished that he could feel impersonal. That she could feel a victim, like she was being dragged along on this crazy, luxurious journey against her will. But when he did things like this, like acting as though there would be consideration for her as a person, and not just a trinket...

Not just another weight.

It tugged at tender, recently wounded spaces inside her. Made her hope where she desperately needed hope to be dead.

"It's cake, Bailey. Do you want to help choose it, or not?"

"Sure," she said, crossing her arms and sitting back in her chair. He had a way of taking all of his nice gestures and twisting them. Making them feel like a grievance.

"Come in," he commanded.

Bailey was confused for a moment until two members of staff came in pushing two different carts carrying covered platters. It was all set in front of her and the lids were removed quickly, revealing an array of entrées, and behind them, plates filled with miniature cakes.

"I..." She could feel her eyes go wide, could feel her entire face lighting up. She couldn't disguise it. Couldn't disguise that she thought this was pretty cool.

"A tasting menu. For your enjoyment."

"And for you?"

In answer, a new staff member came in, carrying a single platter.

"Steak for me," he said.

Then, as quickly as they had come in, the staff melted back out, leaving her alone with Raphael and several beautifully colored cakes.

Honestly, she preferred the company of the cakes.

She looked at the entrées, unsure of where to begin. There was salmon, steak, chicken and some kind of vegetable mixture.

"Vegetarian option," she said, lifting her fork and poking at the eggplant. "How very inclusive of you."

"I am nothing if not generous and exceedingly modern."

She snorted. "If you say so."

"I have to. No one else will."

"That does not surprise me." She took a bite of the vegetables, shocked when rich, buttery flavor exploded over her tongue. "Okay, that's better than I thought it would be."

"I have one of the most accomplished chefs in the world at my disposal."

"Honestly, food has been slightly difficult for me. Just hasn't tasted right for the last few weeks. I'm surprised that I'm enjoying anything." She took a bite of the chicken this time, then went down the line sampling. "I don't know how I'm supposed to choose!"

"You could choose everything."

She laughed. Because it was absurd. "Okay," she said, "I choose everything."

"Done." A member of the waitstaff came back, this time with a carafe and two cups. "Decaf for you," Raphael said, pouring a mug of coffee and passing it across the table to her.

The cakes, she saw, had little labels. Lemon chiffon with raspberry filling. Chocolate with a ganache icing. Hazelnut with mascarpone.

"I can guarantee you I'm going to need to be rolled out of here when I'm finished," she said, picking up a fork and holding it poised, unsure of which delicacy to take a bite of first.

"Go ahead," he said.

She bit her lip, trying to decide where to start. Then Raphael stood, rounding the long table and striding purposefully down the other side toward her. She stopped, watching his movements. He shoved the chair out of the way, sitting on the edge of the high-gloss surface. She blinked, a wave of shock and heat coursing through her. It had been…well, it had been two weeks since she'd been this close to him.

She had begun measuring her days in terms of how long it had been since she and Raphael had first started their relationship. She always knew exactly how long it had been.

Two weeks since they had kissed. Since he had touched her.

Three and a half months since she had said good-bye to him at the hotel. Since he had been inside her.

Suddenly all of that time felt weighted. Like it was pressing down on her, making it difficult for her to breathe. She looked up, her eyes clashing with his. His lips curved upward into a slow-burn smile that scorched her through and through.

"You like chocolate," he said, sliding his fork down through the rich, dense cake. Then he held it out to her, poised in front of her lips. "You should try that first."

Her heart was pounding, the blood rushing through her veins, hot and fast. "Haven't you ever heard of saving the best for last?"

"I believe in having the best all the time." He leaned in, the intensity in his gaze touching her deeply. "Open for me."

Those words sent an echo of sensual memory through her. Of times he had spoken those words when she was down on her knees in front of him. His voice rough, demanding. When she had wanted nothing more than to please him. And to please herself.

And, just as she had then, she parted her lips eagerly for him.

Sweet flavor burst on her tongue, dark, bitter notes following. It was like a metaphor for their entire relationship. Decadent. Intense. And something she couldn't resist, even if she should. Something she knew she shouldn't have too much of, but that she craved. All of it. Every bite.

He set the fork down, lifting up her coffee cup and handing it to her. "To cleanse your palate."

"I'm not sure coffee is a palate cleanser," she said, taking a sip anyway, her fingers brushing against his as she took the cup.

Lightning streaked through her. Would she ever be able to touch him and feel nothing? Would his skin ever just be skin? Or would it always be gasoline against her lit match?

He slid the fork through the lemon and raspberry. "Now, I think this is good, too. And it reminds me of you."

"Why is that?"

"Because," he said, bringing the fork to her mouth again. "It's tart."

He slipped the cake between her lips. "Did you just call me a tart?" she asked after she'd swallowed the bite.

"No. You aren't a tart. You are *tart*. You don't let me get away with anything. There is nothing I have done that you won't force me to answer for, is there?"

"Do you think you should be allowed to get away with not answering for your actions?"

"Yes, damn it," he said, humor playing with the edges of his mouth. "No one has ever expected me to be responsible for my actions."

"What kind of childhood must you have had?"

"One filled with everything I could have ever wanted. My needs were anticipated before even I knew them. I had a dedicated staff all to myself from the moment I came home from the hospital. Actually, I had a dedicated staff at the hospital. To hear tell of it, the entire floor was reserved for my mother when she gave birth."

"That's an extravagant beginning."

"I have never been anything but extravagant from the moment I came into this world."

"Did your dad hold you out over the balcony like *The Lion King*? Or maybe like Michael Jackson."

"I was presented to the nation when I was three days old."

"And you were adored by all," she said.

"Of course." His grin took on a decidedly arrogant tilt. "Though it was not all parties and presentations. I had to learn to be strong. For the kingdom. I could not be indulged. However, we are both indulging now. Try the next one." This time, he cut a slice off the cake, then picked it up between his thumb and forefinger. His fingertips brushed her lips. "Open for me," he said, his voice getting deeper, huskier.

She did, and he slipped his fingers and the cake into her mouth, retreating slowly, the salty flavor of his skin lingering. Arousal shot through her, need. Memory.

She couldn't really concentrate on the cake. Everything in her had zeroed in on him. On her desire for him. On this moment they were in. This little bit of connection that made her feel like maybe she did know him. Or, at least, that maybe she could. It was difficult to remember why she was so angry with him. Here, in the silence of the dining room, with the night sky beyond the window clear and bright with stars.

The two of them at this massive banquet table, with a private feast. It felt much more like fantasy than reality. These past weeks had, but this was something more. Something different. Not like some overblown princess fantasy, but something intimate. Something real.

It made her feel like she was cracking apart inside. On the verge of giving in to something she had sworn she wouldn't. But he was right there, and so warm and so very much what she really wanted.

And he was trying to make this work for her. Having her taste the food, having her sample cake. Trying to make this a little bit about her, instead of just an amendment to the wedding invitations. Almost as if he understood how she felt. As if he cared.

"There," he said, his eyes molten. He lifted his hand, dragging his thumb slowly across her cheek. "I think I have proven that I am not the selfish beast you think I am."

Something about those words sliced through the haze she was lost in. "You knew that this would…make you look like you cared."

"Of course."

"This is part of your plan. It's a thing you're doing to try and make me like you. Try and make me think you care."

"I thought of it. I thought you might care what kind of food and cake you had at the wedding."

"That's not the same as caring about me having something that I wanted."

"Yes, it is."

"No, it isn't," she insisted.

"Perhaps we are experiencing something of a language barrier. I knew you would care—therefore, I set out to do this for you. I fail to see how that proves my overwhelming selfishness."

"Did you do it because it would mean something to me, and that mattered to you? Or did you do it because you knew it would manipulate me?"

"If the result is the same, does it matter?"

"Of course it matters!" She pushed down on the table, launching herself into a standing position. "It isn't enough for you to simply know how to pull my strings. In fact, it's abhorrent."

He laughed, a hard, mocking sound. "Yes, how dare I? What a monster I am. I have brought you into my home, given you an entirely new wardrobe and presented you with a feast of cake. Truly, the abuses you suffer are beyond what anyone should be expected to endure."

"I can't be a game to you for the rest of my life. Some little puzzle that you're trying to work out constantly, and if you can make all the pieces fit, maybe you'll get me back in your bed."

He frowned. "I don't understand you," he said, frustration wearing through his aristocratic tone.

"You don't care. That's the problem. You're playing with me as if I'm a toy, and it is completely different than giving something to me because it came from a desire to please me. You only cared about what it would make me do, not what it would make me feel."

"That isn't true," he said. "I cared about what it would make you feel."

"Because if I felt good, you thought it might make me fall in line." He said nothing, his square jaw set as though it were stone. "That's what I thought."

"Why do you insist on being impossible?"

"I don't know. Why do you insist on being a liar? Why do you insist on being a prince? Why do you insist on being nothing like you were supposed to be?" She turned away from him, beginning to storm out of the room. He grabbed hold of her arm and pulled her back.

"I'm sorry there are no snowbanks outside. Nothing to fling yourself into dramatically. Perhaps you could stay here and talk to me like an adult instead of storming off like a little girl."

"I'm not a little girl," she said, consciously echoing words he had spoken to her, "as you well know."

"You do throw a very convincing tantrum."

"It's the only control I have," she launched back.

"You have me parading around the palace, putting together tasting menus and miniature cakes. Is that not control, Bailey? You have me jumping through hoops to try and gain something other than a sour expression from you. And you claim you have no control?"

"What does it cost you?"

He said nothing to that, his dark eyes inscrutable.

"Exactly," she said, turning away again.

"I don't understand the point you're trying to make," he said finally, when she was halfway between him and the door.

She turned. "You act like you're so aggrieved because you had to do something considerate for me. Something that was going to benefit you anyway. But your kitchen staff prepared the food—all you had to do was ask. You didn't give me anything at cost to yourself. It was all in service of yourself."

"If all that will ever matter to you is my reasoning behind my actions, and not my actions themselves, then we will never reach any kind of accord. I don't see what my motives matter."

"My mother kept me alive, but she let me know every day what a hardship it was. Do you think that didn't matter?"

"Of course it did," he said, his tone clipped. "But I have a responsibility. I am who I am."

"A stone?"

"Maybe so," he said, his voice hard. "But that is what withstands. It is what a nation needs. It is what our child needs. If you're going to flail around dictated by your emotions, one of us has to be firm. I am built to withstand storms, anything that might befall my country. I have to be willing to do my duty at all costs. I must be willing to sacrifice. If I am hard, it is only because it is an essential quality in a leader. I am everything I am supposed to be. I will not apologize to you."

"Good. I wouldn't want it anyway. Because you wouldn't mean it." She turned and stalked out of the room, rage making her limbs feel weak.

Dimly, she thought she might be overreacting. But she didn't really care. She had been manipulated by him from moment one. From the first moment they had seen each other. Everything he had done was suspect now. All of the things he had said since she'd come back to the palace were building on top of one another, a boulder that lodged in her chest, blocked her throat and made it impossible to breathe.

She was unsuitable. Beneath him.

You make him feel like he's on fire.

That traitorous thought glowed in her chest like an ember. Refusing to be doused. It would have to be. It just had to be. She had to get some control where he was concerned, so she wasn't continually taken in by his machinations.

She had two weeks. And then she would be his wife. It all felt so permanent. So final. Yes, there was always divorce, but she doubted it would be easy in her current position.

She was already bound to him. He wasn't just going to let her escape. She wandered over to the end of the corridor, looking out the window, over the view below. The scenery here was so beautiful, crisp and vast. It gave her the sense that she might be able to melt into it. But she couldn't. He had an army, and she had nothing. She didn't even have a passport. They wouldn't let her back into her own country.

Her throat closed tight, a sudden feeling of helplessness overwhelming her. She was marching toward this wedding day, whether she wanted to or not.

She was already in shackles. It was just that once this was over, she would be a princess in chains, rather than a commoner.

She supposed that was as good as it was going to get.

CHAPTER EIGHT

THE DAY OF the wedding dawned bright and clear, and Bailey felt it made something of a mockery out of just how stressful all of it was.

Of how much she wanted to escape into the mountains, regardless of the fact that she was pregnant, and starting to show in a completely undeniable way, in spite of the fact that there was no escape from the long arm of Raphael. Logistics were beginning to matter less and less. There was only a sense of gnawing desperation.

The only thing she could really do was try to keep her head together. Try to remember exactly what this was. It was an agreement the two of them were entering into. She would have to find a place, of course. She wasn't going to be his wife, not really. She was determined on that score. She had pride. And she had a heart to protect.

But she also wouldn't be able to sit around being idle. Motherhood would certainly take up a good portion of her time. But she wondered if there were any other things she could busy herself with.

She was in the process of getting a business degree, because she had thought it was a nice all-encompassing goal. That way, she would have the opportunity to work in a lot of different environments, and ideally start a company of her own. She had no idea what a princess might do with a business degree. Sort of moot, since at the moment, she couldn't see herself finishing it.

She had been consumed since the moment she had gotten to the palace, and studying had been low on her list of priorities. As had figuring out how to make up classes. She was in survival mode. Midterms had no place in that.

Someday, maybe. But not now. As much attention as had been paid to her appearance the day she was presented to the country, the preparation for the wedding was even more intense. She had been given some sort of scrub that was supposed to make her glow, and indeed it did.

Then she'd been made up, her hair expertly arranged, a work of architectural brilliance, and her wedding gown given a final fitting, to ensure that it flowed over her stomach so as not to draw too much attention to her expanding figure.

The announcement about the baby would wait until after the wedding, and she definitely understood why. There would be no hiding the fact that she had been pregnant prior to their marriage, but she had a feeling that once everything was settled, it would all be accepted with a bit more equanimity.

The fait accompli was definitely one of Raphael's preferred methods of operation.

In fact, it was his exclusive method of operation. If he had ever given her a choice in anything, she couldn't remember.

Liar.

She thought back to that first night. That night they

had met and he had kissed her. When passion had nearly carried her away and into his bed only a couple of hours after their first meeting. And she had told him the truth. That she was nothing more than a nervous virgin.

He had given her a choice then. He hadn't pressured her at all.

But he had seemed so different then. Yes, he had still had notes of the same arrogance she saw now. And, yes, he had definitely still liked getting his way. But it hadn't been quite so hard, or so heavy-handed.

She looked around her bedroom while the women who had been hired to prepare her for the big day continued to fuss with her hair, adding little bits of flowers to her curls and adding to the bouquet she held in her hands at the same time.

But of course, in Colorado, he hadn't been the prince of anything. Well, of course he had been, but it had been different. All of this was under his domain, which he was always the first person to remind her of. It was only just now that she realized the enormity of that.

It was about more than just a palace. It was about all the generations that had lived in it. His entire line that had ruled this country for...she didn't know for certain how many years, but she was certain that he did. Was sure that it was written on his heart. Because for all that he was insufferable, and in general kind of a beast, she had no doubt that he would bleed for his country.

As one of the women assisting her settled a necklace over her collarbone, clasping it, the weight suddenly felt excruciating. So heavy on her chest it was almost like it was suffocating her.

Bailey Harper, originally of Nebraska, was stepping into this legacy that wasn't meant for someone like her.

And he was well aware of that. He was carrying extra weight because of it.

His family tree went back hundreds of years. Hers stopped at a garage somewhere in the middle of nowhere where her mother had hooked up with a random guy.

It made her feel small. Rootless. Adrift.

Suddenly, she felt completely unequal to the task. And it had nothing to do with being his wife, or sharing his bed, which she was still determined not to do. But everything to do with the fact that she was being set up as a symbol for this country. This country that she didn't even know anything about. She hadn't even known it existed until last month.

She could see why he had chosen someone else. Why he had attempted to leave their relationship back in Colorado, where at least it made some sense.

She took a deep breath, trying to steady herself. And then the door to the bedroom opened.

"Are you ready, Princess?" It was one of Raphael's closest aides. And it was the first time he had called her princess.

She wasn't ready. She didn't think she ever would be. But it was happening all the same.

"Yes." She swallowed hard. "Yes, I'm ready."

The crowd overflowed the massive old church, just as expected. Thousands of people were in attendance, ready to see the Crown Prince of Santa Firenze finally claim his princess.

Raphael stood at the head of the altar, surveying the traditional surroundings. In this church, generations of his family had married. Generations of political alliances had been struck. That was what his marriage to Allegra was supposed to be. A marriage for his political gain. To gain the ally status of one of Italy's oldest families. It was always best to be on friendly terms with a close neighbor, and he had intended to make inroads via his wife.

Now here he stood, poised to become the first person in his family to marry for a reason other than politics. Perhaps Bailey was right. Perhaps there had been other illegitimate children, swept under the rug and cast aside. But every single marriage in the history books of the DeSantis family had been one of political importance.

Except for this. Except for him.

Raphael wondered what his father would say about such a thing if he were still alive. Would he be disappointed?

He shoved that thought off to the side. His father would have understood that this was the most expedient thing to do. This was an age of transparent media, and bastards were not so easily hidden. Not when every person on earth had a platform thanks to the internet. It would have been easy for Bailey to broadcast the fact that she was pregnant with the DeSantis heir. Easy for her to make a spectacle of his family name and his country.

His father would understand this marriage. It was not a decision driven by emotion. But a decision driven by necessity. He had weighed the cost, and he had acted.

Anyway, even without Bailey his marriage to Allegra would not have gone forward.

Yes, this was purely logical.

As the back doors to the church opened, and the music changed, his heartbeat changed, as well.

She was like an angel. An angel with a mouth that was made for sin.

She took her first step into the sanctuary, and everything in him seized tight. Her dress flowed over her curves, but it was plainly obvious to him that she was pregnant. The soft chiffon gown conformed to that small bump, and her breasts were much fuller than they had been only a few months ago. But perhaps not everyone was so in tune with changes in Bailey's figure. Likely, no one else was.

But she was his. So of course he noticed. He noticed everything about her.

He had done his very best over the last couple of weeks not to notice her at all.

They had barely spoken. Had barely made eye contact when passing each other in the hall. She had seemed happy to keep it that way, and he would not be the one to break the silence. He had refused. His pride refused. He would not bend, not for this woman.

A *nation* bowed before him. He would be damned if he bowed before one petite blonde.

And yet, as she continued down the aisle toward him, there was only that one word. That one word that he always heard echoing in his mind when he looked at her.

Mine.

And after today, she truly would be his. She would be bound to him, legally, yes, but also with vows that were as old, if not older, than the church they were standing in. She would make promises to him here, in this place where every royal baby in his family had been christened, where every royal couple had been consecrated.

He was a man of practicality. He did not believe in

mysticism. However, he felt that making vows here had to carry more weight. That there was something truly binding in the stone walls that had witnessed so many other reverent and sovereign occasions.

All of these thoughts tripped around his mind, but none of them were as loud as the word.

Mine.

She held her head high, tilting her chin up, and he could see that her eyes were glittering. That she was fighting back tears. Bailey, his Bailey, had every emotion so close to the surface. She was hotheaded. Temperamental. And so completely genuine it was difficult to feel any annoyance about it.

She had more conviction in her every word than he had in all of his body.

But his country didn't require conviction. It required a cool head and clear leadership. That was all that had ever been required of him. He fulfilled that position without equal. Still, she seemed to find fault. She always could, his Bailey. No one else ever seemed to say anything negative at all.

Everyone else worshipped him.

Her blue eyes locked with his, and he saw no worship, no deference at all. He saw a challenge. He saw a will of iron, anger that refused to be extinguished and desire that still burned bright.

He saw a woman who was most certainly an asset to his country. Strong enough to be his princess. Strong enough to rule. How had he ever thought she was not royalty? She was. Down to her core. A woman of immovable conviction. Of deep feeling and moral standing.

She would care for his country as he did. He knew

that she would. He knew beyond anything that she would give to Santa Firenze all that he did and more. If for no other reason than to try to show him up.

Such was her stubbornness.

In that moment, he treasured it. Valued it. Because he could see that it was her strength.

She had told him about the way she had worked herself through school, how she had scraped, saved and struggled for everything she had ever had.

How had he ever seen that as anything less than equal to his own standing?

When she reached him, he took her hand in his, drawing her close. And as the priest intoned the words of the service, he let it all wash over him like a wave, absorbing it all rather than hanging on every word.

When it came time for the vows, he spoke without hesitation. He was not a soft man, not a man geared toward romance. But he was a man who knew commitment. A man who kept his word. He did not give it easily, and he had not given it to her at all prior to bringing her here, but he was giving it now. And that meant it was cast in stone.

"Upon my life," he said, his every word ringing out true and clear through the sanctuary, "I will bind myself to you. Keep myself only for you. Pledge myself to you. Body and soul. Until death separates us."

Color washed over her face as he said the words, and they resonated deep inside of him, ringing with a truth he could not deny. There was no question then of whether or not she would be his wife in body, in soul. He had spoken the words, and so they were.

For his part, he could never touch another woman, ever again. It had been so from the moment he had seen her. As deeply imprinted in his soul as that sure and knowing possessiveness that had gripped him from the first moment he'd laid eyes on her.

Mine.

And he was hers, and no one else's.

She repeated his same words back to him, her voice muted, her eyes downcast. And he could see that that same certainty that he felt, down to his very soul, was not shared by her.

It could not be so. She was *his*. His and no one else's. He had bound himself to her. And he had meant his every vow. He would keep it. He would keep every one.

And then it was announced that he could kiss his bride.

He wrapped his arm around her waist, pulling her close, gripping her chin as he brought his face down to hers, and kissed her like it was a brand. As though he were trying to burn that same mark onto her soul that he bore on his.

When they parted, her eyes were bright, her breathing swift, rapid.

He looked at her, everything in him on high alert, determined.

Then, as the crowd cheered for them, for their marriage, he leaned over, his lips brushing against her ear. "You are mine," he whispered. "And I have decided that I will have my wedding night."

It was absolutely impossible to concentrate on the wedding feast, on the chocolate cake that she had chosen and the delicious steak that she had been served earlier. Difficult to do anything but smile brutally as well-wishers filtered through, telling them how pleased they were to have her as princess.

Every voice was a dull, murky mumble. Every taste bland. Because all she could think of was that husky whispered promise he had made up at the altar. Not his public proclamation, but that carnal vow made only for her ears.

That he would have his wedding night.

She had been determined that he wouldn't. And she had been certain he had understood. After all, they had barely spoken at all for the last couple of weeks. Why would he think anything had changed?

She was…she didn't know how she felt. She didn't know what to think. Except she wished that this interminable reception would continue to be interminable. Wished that it would go on so that she didn't have to face being alone with her new husband.

Her *husband*.

She had just stood in front of a nation, in front of the world really, and made promises to this man that she would never be able to break.

She was his captive. She could see clearly enough that she had been from the moment she had first stepped onto his private plane. Perhaps from the moment she had taken his hand outside the diner and said she would, in fact, go home with him on that first night they'd met.

The marriage was just a formality.

She had fooled herself into believing that she had some kind of bargaining power. That he had seen her side of things. That perhaps he understood that things would be better if they didn't have an intimate relationship. Clearly, it had all been a ruse. Something to lull her into a false sense of security.

Or maybe to keep her from screaming at him every day for the last two weeks.

She looked over at him, her eyes catching hold of his. Her heart felt like a bird fluttering in a cage, desperate to get out. At least if her heart escaped, it might be able to fly away from this place. Away from this man who had the potential to be so devastating. If she could only keep her heart safe, then maybe the rest would be okay. She enjoyed having sex with Raphael.

She pressed her mouth into a thin line. That was such an insipid description of what being with him was. It was never about the physical. It never had been. Yes, it felt amazing. Yes, he gave her pleasure unlike anything she'd ever known. But it had never ended there. Not for her.

She had felt connected to him from the moment she'd met him. And when his body had joined with hers, she had felt like everything made sense. Like he had uncovered hidden pieces of her that made so many other things fall into place.

She could not separate that from emotion. Couldn't excise it from what she felt for him.

Whether it was anger or love, there was always something. Always something bigger than she was.

She had loved him back then. Truly. Desperately. Had been ready to spend the rest of her life with him. But then she had to face the fact that she didn't know him. Then he had broken her heart. Then he had swept her off to a castle and shown her demonstrations of power the likes of which she had never seen before.

She had loved the man he was. She didn't know how she felt about this man. This man she had just married. This man who was, sadly, the reality of her fantasy lover, who she'd had over long weekends every couple of months.

She felt silly just then. That she had managed to create such intense feelings for someone that she really hadn't spent all that much time with. That she had allowed herself to fall in love with a man who was so clearly a work of fiction. And that she was now bound to his true self, someone who would never love her. Someone who would only take.

They continued to make their way through the reception, managing to speak to just about everyone but each other.

And then came the time for their grand exit. It was very traditional, with rice thrown as they walked out of the elegant reception hall. She tried to smile. Tried to look like a new bride should. But she found she could not. It was far too difficult. Not when she felt like she was made of lead.

They made their way outside. It was cold and crisp, the night air like a baptism, washing away the events of the day.

But only for a moment.

He led her to the palace, up the steps and in through the massive doors.

They stopped in the entryway, and he regarded her closely. "This is your home now," he said. "Truly. It is a part of you."

She looked around, her pulse throbbing a steady rhythm at the base of her throat. "And to think, my biggest aspiration was perhaps to one day own a house in a nice neighborhood."

"Well, look at it this way. You won't have to deal with a homeowner's association here."

"Just legions of staff and a husband who thinks he rules the world."

"Only a country," he responded. The heat in his dark eyes grew more intense, and he lowered his head, his face a breath away from hers. "Let's go to bed."

"I told you. I told you that I was not…that we were not…"

Something changed in his expression then. He was still perfectly pressed. Still dressed in that meticulously tailored tuxedo he had worn to the wedding. His hair was perfectly styled, not a bit of it out of place.

But it was like a switch had been thrown, and every last vestige of civility was gone from his face.

He was wild just then. Feral.

A predator who had most definitely set his sights on her.

"I know what you said," he responded. "But I made vows to you before my country. Before my ancestors. And I, for my part, intend to keep them. You may not wish to have me as your husband, but I am going to make you my wife."

And then he swept her up into his arms, holding her against his hard chest. She was too shocked to protest. He propelled them both toward the stairs, toward his room.

She knew then that the decision had been made. That, as with all things, once Raphael had set his mind to something, he would not be deterred.

She held on to him, because, after all, she didn't want him to drop her. Held on to him until he brought them both to his chamber, a set of rooms that she had not been in before. He carried her over the threshold, as though he were any groom on his wedding night.

He turned and shut the doors, the sound one of absolute finality.

Then he faced her, his expression all lean hunger.

"And now, my wife," he said, taking a step toward her, "you will be mine."

CHAPTER NINE

BAILEY SEARCHED HIS face, looking for a hint of calculation. Searching for an indication that this was part of his plan.

But there was nothing. That cool sophistication was gone. Burned away. He wasn't the man she'd met in the diner back in the States, and he wasn't the prince.

He was something else entirely. Something foreign and familiar all at once.

He advanced on her, his eyes a broad spectrum of flame, burning with every dark emotion. Rage. Need. Fear.

Of himself or her she didn't know.

It didn't really matter, either, because an answer to that wouldn't change his course. Wouldn't change what was about to happen here. She backed against the wall, letting him advance on her.

He reached out, grabbing hold of the delicate neckline of her wedding gown and tugging hard. The whisper-thin layers of fabric tore, the bodice separating at the seams, exposing the strapless, lacy bra she wore underneath.

She gasped, pressing herself more firmly against the wall.

"Is that how you look at me now?" he asked. "As though I am your enemy?" He cupped her cheek, sliding his thumb across her delicate skin. "As though you don't know me? As though I have not known your body in nearly every way possible?"

"That was different," she said, her tone stiff. "It is different. I don't know you. Not anymore. I never did. The man that I met, the man that I thought you were, doesn't exist. And I'm not going to have sex with a stranger."

"A stranger?" He chuckled, a humorless sound. Then he leaned in, pressing a kiss to her neck, his lips hot and enticing against her skin. "Would a stranger know that if he were to touch you here," he said, sliding his hand down to cup her breast, his thumb resting beneath the lower curve, "that you will start trembling?"

Her traitorous body did exactly that. Shaking beneath his touch, a quivering, needy thing. She was every inch his creature, and he knew it. The bastard knew it.

"Would a stranger know," he said, "that if he were to taste you like this—" he slid his tongue down the side of her neck "—that you will go up in flames?"

She did. Just like that, she did.

"Trust isn't the same thing," she said, panting. She was ashamed that she was so transparent, but she didn't know if there was anything for it.

"I don't care about your trust, *amore mia*. I care about this." He kissed the edge of her mouth, and a lightning bolt shot through her.

She turned her head to the side, closing her eyes tight. "No," she said.

He growled, gripping her arms and looking into her eyes. "What will it take? What do I have to do? I have already lowered myself to admit to you that you make me burn. That I have not been the same since the moment that I saw you in that diner. I have confessed these things to you, and it is not enough. What will it take?" he ground out.

"N-nothing," she said, the lie tasting bitter on her lips. "There's nothing you can do."

"Do you want me to beg?" he asked, the words hard, full of disdain. "Is that what you want? My waitress wife, do you suppose that you are worthy of me lowering myself for you?"

"I suppose that I deserve nothing less than absolute contrition from the man who abandoned me when I was pregnant with his child. The man who would never know that he was having a baby were it not for a freak change of circumstances." And that was not a lie.

"Contrition doesn't come for free." His black eyes glittered like obsidian. Hard. Sharp. "Perhaps you should remind me of what I enjoyed about you in the first place. Because at the moment, I am having a difficult time remembering."

"Or, perhaps," she said, "you can go to your room and find comfort with your right hand. I am not a thing that you can use. I am a woman. You cannot treat me like something you can simply retrieve at will, then toss back when you're finished."

He dropped to his knees in front of her, curling his fingers around the material of the gown as he went, dragging it down into a pool of ruined material on the floor. "Begging is what you require then?"

Her breath hitched. "I didn't say that."

"You would have me beg to be with my own wife. Then so be it." He looked up at her, his expression hard, and then he grabbed hold of the waistband of her white lace panties, tugging them to her knees. "Consider this my supplication."

"Raphael—"

Whatever she had been about to say was lost as his strong, firm hands grabbed hold of her hips, steadying her. Then, he leaned in, inhaling deeply, pressing his face against the tender skin of her inner thigh. "I have dreamed of this," he rasped. "I have dreamed of you."

He moved to her center, sliding his tongue over wet, needy flesh, tasting her deeply. She shivered, pleasure cutting into her like a knife. She reached out, grabbing hold of his shoulder, curling her fingers around his jacket, clinging to him.

Was she so weak?

As he moved even more deeply, his tongue created a wicked kind of magic that moved through her body like a dark enchantment.

She wanted to cry. Because of how good it felt. Because of how weak she felt. Because she was failing herself. But she realized she wanted to have him force this seduction on her. She wanted to submit to it. To tell herself that she was unwilling. That all the power was with him, so that she could absolve herself of any sin. Of any guilt.

You want it. You want him.

She squeezed her eyes shut, letting go of him. But she didn't move away from him. She raised her arms up over her head, pressing her knuckles firmly into the wall, as though she were releasing her culpability in this.

Her heart beat a steady rhythm, each and every pulse calling her a liar. As Raphael continued to push her higher, further, faster. He was ruthless in his exploration of her, his tongue and fingers seeking out each delightful point of pleasure.

He dragged his fingers through her slick folds, pressed a finger deep inside her as he continued the wicked assault with his tongue.

She hadn't allowed herself pleasure since he had left her. It had been punishment for her stupidity, and then, when she had come here to the palace, something she refused to allow herself because she would only be imagining Raphael.

She was strung so tight she was certain that it would take very little to snap her in two.

He knew it, too. He could feel how wet she was for him, how needy. She knew that he could feel her now, her internal muscles tightening around him as he continued to pleasure her. He knew how close she was to the edge.

That bit of humiliation should have pulled her back. Instead, it spurred her on. Brought her arousal up to impossible heights.

"Raphael," she gasped. "Raphael... I can't."

"You can," he said, his breath hot on the source of her pleasure. "And you will. Come for me, Bailey."

The command was as arrogant as any he'd ever issued. As though he, and he alone, had dominion over her body. As though she were powerless to resist any command he might issue, even one such as this.

He was right.

The words pushed her over the edge, sending her hurtling down toward the very bottom of an abyss. And when she hit, she shattered. She became a thousand sparkling pieces, shimmering with pleasure, with the glorious release that made her feel weightless, free. For the first time since her life had been broken apart and glued back together, badly, she felt free.

She felt like herself.

As though he had not just given her a physical release but had released a part of her she had ruthlessly squashed, shamed, left for dead.

She inhaled sharply, and then, suddenly, he was in front of her again, claiming her mouth with his, the taste of her desire on his lips. Carnal. Wild.

He swept her back into his arms, carrying her across the room and depositing her on the bed. Her heart tripped over itself as she watched those deft, blunt fingers working the buttons on his shirt, wrenching his tie free, casting the last vestiges of civility down to the floor.

She drank in the sight of him, hunger roaring through her, as though she had not just found release.

The dim light cast his muscles into sharp relief, the dips and hollows of his abs exaggerated in the glow cast over him by the one lamp that was lit. She was breathless. Caught up in her desire. Just as she had been from the beginning.

There was no thought of consequences. No deference paid to self-preservation. What was the point? She might live a life preserved, but she wouldn't be herself. She would be squished and hidden. Safe but unused. Like a book that had never been read.

She watched, transfixed, as he worked his belt through the buckle, slid it slowly through the loops on his pants. She looked up, looked into his eyes. They burned her, straight down to her center, down to her soul. It wasn't enough that he had complete and total reign over her body, he seemed to demand it in every other capacity, as well.

Nothing more could be expected of Raphael, not really.

His arrogance knew no boundaries—why should it find any here?

She let her eyes drop again, and this time she was held transfixed by the outline of his erection, the absolute evidence of his desire for her. That he was just as weak, just as mortal as she was right now.

It had been so easy to remember the control this yawning, needy thing had exerted over her that she had forgotten about the power she held over him. How had that happened? Hadn't he demonstrated it when he'd fallen to his knees in front of her?

He had shown her, at every turn, that she held sway over him, and yet she had focused on the needy sense of powerlessness inside herself.

Something inside her turned, like a key in a lock, and she felt as though she was seeing all of this differently now. As though a revelation had tumbled down upon her, and she couldn't go back to viewing it quite as she had before.

She rose up onto her knees, reaching behind her and undoing the four little hooks that held her bra in place. She threw the insubstantial confection down to the floor, kneeling there before him, completely naked now. She refused to hide, refused to cower.

Refused to feel ashamed.

That had nothing to do with Raphael, or anything he had ever made her feel. But with herself. She had been bound up in this idea of failure. That desiring Raphael, that desiring anyone, had led her to her doom. That it made her lesser.

But all of that was her baggage. Bound up in cracked pride, because she had always been just a little bit disdainful of her mother and her actions. But it was only pride. Pride that kept her bound and lonely, that would never keep her warm at night, that would never bring her any sense of fulfillment. And maybe Raphael wouldn't either. Maybe this was simply the road to fresh heartbreak.

But she wanted him. And he wanted her back.

It was enough for now. For this moment.

"You made me wait too long," he said, his voice rough.

He shoved his pants down his lean hips, uncovering his body. Her breath rushed from her lungs. It had been way too long since she had seen him naked. Of course, images of him were burned into her brain, fantasies that wouldn't leave her alone even when she desperately needed them to.

But it wasn't the same. Wasn't the same as being so close to him she could touch him. Could taste him.

She moved to the edge of the bed, reaching out slowly, curling her fingers around his shoulder. Then she bent down, kissing his chest lightly. His muscle jumped beneath her lips, his entire body jerking backward, as though he had been burned.

Oh, yes, she had power here.

She nibbled her way up to his jaw, traced that square angle down to his chin with the tip of her tongue, then worked her way up to his lips, sliding her tongue between them, tasting him in a way that mimicked what he had done between her thighs only a few moments ago.

He wrapped his arm around her waist, growling, pushing her down onto the bed, onto her back. He kissed her deeply, taking absolutely no quarter, employing no gentleness at all. But that was fine. That wasn't what she needed. She needed him out of control, as he had been from the moment they had first come into this bedroom. That realization made something bloom, hot and hopeful, in her chest.

This wasn't calculated. This was nothing like their cake tasting two weeks ago. He wasn't doing this to manipulate. He was doing it because he had no other choice. Because he was at the end of his control.

Satisfaction pooled hot and low in her stomach, arousal wrenching itself tighter inside her. His hardness was settled between her legs, sliding against where she was already beginning to feel needy for him again. But an orgasm alone wouldn't be enough this time. She needed to be filled by him. Needed him inside her.

The words hovered on the edge of her lips, but she felt like they might cost her something much dearer than she was willing to pay. There wasn't room for that.

"I want you," she said. "I want you inside of me."

He groaned, the sound a prayer and a curse all at once. Then the blunt head of his arousal pressed up against the entrance to her body, and he tested her, slowly, taking all the care he had taken with her the first time.

Tears stung her eyes. She didn't want tenderness. She wanted fierce, hot and fast. She wanted to satisfy this growling beast inside her.

She braced her hands on his back, then slid them down to his rear, grabbing hold of him tightly and urging him deep inside her. She gasped as he filled her, wholly and completely, nearly to the point of pain.

She relished it. All of it.

She looked up at him, at the tension in his face, the cords of his neck standing out, evidence of the intense amount of power it was taking for him to control himself. She loved that. Seeing how profoundly she affected him. Truly realizing that she wasn't alone in this insanity.

He had lied to her. He had broken her trust.

But this was true. It was real, and it was honest. It was everything. She wasn't entirely sure she knew everything of who he was. Wasn't sure where the truth of the man she had first met ended and the reality of this prince who she'd married began.

She didn't know. She wasn't sure she ever would. But this, this meeting of their bodies, this intense, deep connection that occurred when the two of them were together, was honest. It was the same now as it had been then. He didn't feel like a stranger.

She knew him in her soul.

She knew him in this honesty. In his every touch and his every thrust as he began to move inside her. This was real. Pure and true, and the fact that she had ever felt ashamed seemed wrong now.

She exulted in it. In him. In the rightness of it. Nothing had felt right for so many months now, but this did.

She was caught up in it, in him, swept away on a tide of pleasure as release washed through her again and again. And when he shattered, when he found his own, she gloried in that, too. In his big body shuddering as he spent himself deep inside her.

When it was over, there was no sound but their frac-

tured breathing echoing off the walls, nothing but a profound feeling of finality. It was no longer a question,
whether they would end up here. Because they had. No
longer a question of whether he would continue to pur-
sue, and she would continue to resist. It was done. And
now that it was, she knew there would be no going back.

And now she wondered why she had wanted to in
the first place. Raphael was the only man she had ever
wanted. It didn't matter whether she thought he was a
businessman or knew that he was a prince. It didn't matter if it was back in the United States or if it was here.

He was the thing her heart desired, more than anything. And she was justly entitled to her anger and her
heartbreak over how he had treated her. But they had
this chance. This chance to be married. To be together.
And she had been choosing to cling to anger.

Anger was a hot, destructive shield to use. And she
was beginning to realize there was a great cost to protection anyway. For the sake of pride, for the fear of
being hurt, she had been intent on keeping something
she wanted from herself.

All of it tangled up in that self-flagellation she'd been
lost in for so many months.

If she was going to live with him, raise a child with
him, be his wife, there was going to be a certain amount
of letting go involved. Of deciding to put the past behind
them. Of making where they ended up more important
than where they had begun.

She breathed in his scent, wrapped her arms around
his neck, held him close. And she let all the rest go.

CHAPTER TEN

WHEN RAPHAEL WOKE up in the morning there was a woman wrapped around him. It was notable, because it had been so long since that had happened. He opened his eyes, looking out across the broad expanse of his chamber. And he saw a wedding dress, torn into two pieces and left on the floor like a moth that had been stripped of its wings.

He remembered then. Backing Bailey against the wall. Tearing the top of her gown. Holding her tightly against his mouth while he had unleashed all the pent-up anger and need that roared through him like an untamed animal.

Yes, suddenly he remembered all of that.

He sat up, and the swift motion disturbed Bailey, who had been wound up in him in such a way it was impossible for him to take a breath without affecting her.

She opened her eyes, the foggy, sleepy blue sending a wave of longing through him that made his teeth ache. He had no idea what that meant. No idea why. She was here, and she was naked, which meant there was absolutely nothing for him to long for. He had everything.

This woman, who was now his wife, this palace and

his kingdom. There was nothing else. No reason for the hollow, bone-chilling ache that pervaded him now.

And yet it persisted.

"Good morning," she mumbled.

"Is it?" he asked, clipped.

He found himself extricating himself from her hold and getting out of bed, walking across the room, kneeling down to examine the damage he had done to the dress.

"It's a little bit late for regret," she said, sitting up, holding the sheet up over her breasts. Her cheeks were extra pink this morning, her mouth a bit swollen. He could not remember how many times he had reached for her last night, desperate to sate the desire for her that had built itself inside him to a fever pitch.

She bore the marks of that. Of his passion. Of his selfish desperation. As did the dress.

"I should have thought it was never too late for regret. In fact, you have been demonstrating that to me over the course of the past month. Just how very much you regret me. I'm beginning to think that perhaps you're not entirely crazy to feel that way."

She frowned. "Yes, well, nice to know you won't become completely crazy, now that you've married me."

"I wasn't myself last night."

"Yes, you were. You were completely yourself. You felt you were entitled to something that you weren't being given and reacted as you do."

"You said you wanted me," he said. He was thinking of that moment when she had told him, with that desperate, needy sigh on her lips, that she wanted him inside her. She had said that. She had wanted it.

"Yes, I did. I have. From the moment you came back to me, I've wanted you. That isn't the issue."

"What is?" He stood, holding the remaining pieces of the dress in his hands. "Because, for someone who claims to want me, you did an admirable job of resisting me at every turn."

"I don't want to be a salve for your wounded ego. And I don't want to be a challenge to your masculine pride. That's what I was saying. You're a man who is accustomed to having everything he wants. I don't want to be just another one of those things. I want to mean something more than that to you."

"You want to cost me something," he said, understanding filling him slowly. "That is what you said the other day. That my gesture with the cake was empty because there was no cost to me."

"You've cost me an awful lot, Raphael. I don't suppose it's extremely selfish to wish that I cost you a little something, too."

"You think you have not? I have vowed never to touch another woman."

"The bare minimum requirement for marriage, I should think."

"I am the first person in my family to marry for a reason other than political gain." Finally, finally that elicited some reaction from her. Finally that caused a change in her expression. "I broke centuries of tradition to marry you. You have no connection that could possibly benefit Santa Firenze. What I did, I did for our baby. Yes, I could have hidden you away. I could have paid you off, given you some exorbitant sum of money, but that isn't what I wanted. I wanted my child here. With me."

"And me?" she asked, her voice small.

He let the dress fall to the floor, and he crossed the space between them. He looked at her, and she turned her gaze away. He reached out, taking hold of her chin, directing her eyes back to his. "I have not been with another woman since the day I met you. When I broke things off with you, I did my very best to try and turn my focus to Allegra. She and I never had much of a connection. We hardly had anything to do with each other. She and her entire family would accompany me on various holidays, but she and I were never tempted to spend time alone. She was ideal, in other words."

"How is it ideal to not want your wife?"

"It is ideal to not find your wife a…a distraction. I hoped… I sincerely hoped that when I ended things with you I would be able to find some sort of desire in myself for her. She was going to be my wife, after all, and a life wanting someone else was unthinkable."

"And how did that go for you?" she asked, looking comically hopeful.

"The next time I saw her after you and I broke up, I purposed that I would kiss her." He cleared his throat. "A real kiss. Not just a kiss on her head. But then I saw her and… I could not. I kept seeing you. Every time I saw a woman with blond hair, I would hope that she would turn around and it would be you. I want you to distraction, Bailey. It is wholly inconvenient."

"So, I'm not a completely negligible part of this package?"

"I suppose I wasn't being entirely truthful when I said that I didn't marry for any kind of gain. When I saw you walking down the aisle toward me yesterday, I realized that your strength is only going to be an asset to me, and to this country. You may not have political connections, but I admire you. You worked very hard to get where you are in life, and I don't know very many people who can say the same."

"You work hard, Raphael."

"Undoubtedly," he responded. "But I was given all of this. That's different."

As soon as the words left his mouth, he realized how true it was. How his confidence, his power, was built on something handed down. And in order for it to be handed down effectively, his father had handed his arrogance and certainty down, as well.

He had molded him perfectly. Taught him with so many gestures that there was nothing he could not have while demonstrating at the same time there was nothing more important than the country.

"That's more impressive in some regards," Bailey said. "Seeing as when you haven't earned something often it means less. And it would be easy for you to feel less of an obligation to your country because you didn't achieve your position through hard work. So, I can easily make an argument to support the fact that you're actually pretty amazing."

"Suddenly you have kind words for me, Bailey? Please tell me you did not sustain a head injury last night."

She smiled, a rather impish expression that tugged something deep inside him. It was strange, and not entirely unpleasant, to have a moment where she wasn't at odds with him. He had told himself that it didn't matter, that the only thing that was really bothering him was the prolonged celibacy.

He had told himself that he didn't miss her companionship, just her body. That the entire relationship they'd had back in Colorado was something of a farce. A strange experiment on his end. Being with a woman who had no idea who he was, interacting with her as a typical man would.

But her smile sent such a ferocious flood of warmth through his body that it was difficult to believe that now.

He wanted to do something for her. But he couldn't think what. He had married her, after all. Made her a princess. He wasn't exactly sure what you did to top that gesture. Though, perhaps, a honeymoon.

"Have you ever been to Paris?" he asked.

"No," she said. "But I still don't have a passport."

"You are the princess of Santa Firenze. Your travel documents will be sorted by the palace." He watched her cheeks turn pink, her pleasure obvious. "You are excited about the idea of going to Paris?"

"Of course I am. Who wouldn't be? I've dreamed about seeing it, but I never thought I would. My fantasies ran toward cutting myself above the poverty line. Getting a good job. World travel never really featured."

"Well, world travel is essentially in your job description now."

"Lucky me," she said. "And I mean that. That was not sarcasm."

"No sarcasm?" he asked, with mock shock coloring his tone. "It's amazing you didn't injure yourself."

"You're giving me Paris. I felt, at the least, I owed you a little sincerity."

His chest tightened. He wasn't sure why, but he had the strange feeling of impending doom, rolling over his shoulders like a dark, heavy cloak. "I wouldn't give me too much. But I shall alert the staff of our plans, and they will pack your things."

"We're going now?"

"Paris has waited for you long enough."

CHAPTER ELEVEN

THE FIRST SIGHT of the city took Bailey's breath away. Everything was so old. She had noticed the same thing in Santa Firenze. Maybe that was a strange observation, but everything in the United States was relatively new, particularly things in the West. They didn't have this sort of history, embedded into every brick, into each and every fine scroll carved into the stonework.

The art, the history, was like a living thing, making the architecture, the very air around them, seem like so much more.

They drove along a road that bordered the Seine, the gray water reflecting the clouds above, the row of buildings, old churches and museums on the other side of them like an impenetrable sentry wall.

The penthouse that Raphael had secured for them was rich in details, from the crown molding down to the gold fixtures in the kitchen and bathroom. There was a spread of cheese and bread waiting for them upon arrival, along with a bottle of champagne that Bailey would not be availing herself of.

The master suite was brilliantly appointed, and the closet was already full. Full of beautiful garments that,

Raphael informed her, a personal shopper had chosen specifically for Bailey.

Among them was a rich, green gown made of flowing silk. Silk that would undoubtedly show her growing pregnancy.

"When am I supposed to wear this?" she asked, brushing her fingertips down the fine fabric.

"Tonight," he said, his tone nonchalant.

"I didn't know we had plans."

"There is a private dinner and art exhibition at the Musée d'Orsay tonight. I thought it was something you would probably enjoy, and I thought that the man in charge of the event would likely enjoy the attendance of royalty, even if it were last minute. I was correct. At least on that score. I hope I was correct about you, too."

His expression was so sincere, his tone hopeful. It was…it was so unusual to see Raphael looking something less than certain. But he did. Just as he had done this morning after their wedding night. He had been concerned that he had crossed a line. The fact that he was capable of such concern was encouraging.

He wasn't pulling that veil of arrogance back into place at every opportunity. At least, not today.

"Of course I want to go. A beautiful dress, wonderful food, famous art. What's not to like?"

His smile was slow, and he nodded. "Yes. You are correct."

"You were afraid that I wouldn't like a beautiful dress and a private evening at a museum?"

"I am eternally at a loss with you," he said, his frustration clear. "I had imagined that you would fall to your knees in gratitude the moment I told you I would marry you. That you would see what an honor I was bestowing upon you when you caught sight of my palace. So far, you have been distinctly unimpressed with me."

"It's not you I'm unimpressed with," she responded. "Just the things."

"I am the things," he said.

She frowned, taking a step toward him, reaching up, pressing her palm to his cheek. "How can that be? Didn't I meet you before I knew you had any of that?"

"That was different."

Her heart sank a little bit. "Yes," she said, "it was different."

It was different because it had been completely genuine on her part and a ruse on his. Different because she had imagined they would have a future, while he knew for a fact they wouldn't.

"We will leave in a couple of hours for the party."

"I might want to… I mean, I might take a walk. Just for an hour or so."

He frowned. "You can't do that."

"I'm in Paris. I would like to have a look around." And she needed just a little bit of distance to catch her breath. It was difficult to be under the influence of Raphael. He was so very much. She was trying to find that line between protecting herself and sacrificing herself.

She didn't want to wall him off, not completely, but she needed to have some defenses in place, surely.

"You are royalty. You cannot simply walk around the streets by yourself."

"You really think anyone will recognize me?"

"You are the favored headline at the moment, *cara*. I think you would be recognized within seconds."

"Then I guess I'll get ready," she said, monotone.

"What else could I possibly want to do in Paris but apply makeup?"

"How quickly the tide turns." His expression was grim. "I'm not trying to ruin your life. I'm just being realistic."

She frowned. "Okay." She let out a long, slow breath. "I'm sorry. I'm actually being a little unreasonable. I'll just get ready."

By the time she got herself beautified, it was time to go. She looked at herself in the vanity mirror, frowning. Yes, it was very apparent that she was pregnant.

"I hope you're prepared for the fact that we are essentially making an announcement tonight," she said, walking out into the main living area of the penthouse.

Raphael looked up from his newspaper, his jaw going slack. "Oh," was all he said. More of a noise than an actual response.

"What does that mean?"

He stood, closing the distance between them. He stopped just short of her, not touching her at all.

"Come on, Raphael—you have to say something, or I'm going to go back into the bedroom and change into my sweats."

"No, you will not," he said, his expression fierce. "You are perfect. A jewel come to life."

"I didn't even have a professional makeup artist tonight," she said, pressing for yet more compliments, because this one made her feel warm all over. "And," she added, reaching up to play with a strand of loose hair, "I did my hair, too."

"It suits you. Possibly because it is you. Utterly and completely."

He leaned in, kissing her forehead. It was a strange,

affectionate gesture, void of the usual carnal sexuality that was typically laced through their other kisses.

Then he angled his head and kissed her lips. This one had all the usual carnal sexuality and then some.

"We have to go," he said. "Or I will have you out of that dress, and we will never make it to the museum."

"People are going to know I'm pregnant," she prodded. "You didn't say anything about that."

"I'm proud of your pregnancy. Of the fact you are my wife, that you are carrying my child. I'm pleased to show the world."

"That was the right thing to say," she said, stretching up on her toes and kissing him.

"There's a first time for everything," he said, amusement in his voice.

Somehow they managed to make it to the museum with all of Bailey's makeup intact, which was a miracle, seeing as Raphael had done his very best to kiss most of it off in the car. The museum was beautiful, set for a dinner in one room with ornate table settings and large bouquets of lushly colored flowers.

Men in black suits and women in gowns that ran the spectrum of the rainbow milled about the room making conversation, moving through the large building, looking at the various exhibits that were open to the guests.

The hors d'oeuvres that were being served looked lovely, but Bailey found she was more interested in examining the art.

She managed to tear herself away from one of the overly enthusiastic women who had grabbed her upon entry, excited to meet a princess. And had been obviously angling to get Bailey to comment on her condition. Bailey found it all extremely strange. Being the center of any kind of attention.

Only a few short weeks ago, she'd been the wait-staff. Now she was a princess. A guest of honor. It was enough to make her head spin. And definitely enough to make her seek out a quiet moment.

She made her way to the wing of the museum that housed the sculptures. Bailey wandered through the exquisite marble figures, marveling at the expressiveness of the features. They weren't cold, in spite of the smooth, white stone that was used to fashion them. In fact, she could almost believe that any moment they might come to life.

She paused in front of the statue of a kneeling woman, one of the rare female figures that was fully clothed.

"Here you are."

She turned to see Raphael coming toward her. Her heart clenched tight. And so did other things. Really, he looked amazing in a tux. He shouldn't wear anything else. Unless he was naked. He could be naked.

"Over relating to the plight of Joan of Arc?"

She looked down at the statue's small plaque. "I guess I was."

"Great is your martyrdom."

"Sometimes it feels like it is."

"A very brave creature you are, Bailey Harper."

"That's Princess Bailey DeSantis to you," she said, keeping her tone arch.

"My apologies for the grave error." He moved closer to her. "You're enjoying the art?"

"Yes. I've never seen anything like it. I mean, I've been to museums before, but nothing with works like this. This is…it's exquisite."

"You know, only this floor is open to guests tonight."

"I know."

"I made arrangements to get us up to one of the top floors. I thought you might like to see Manet."

She looked over at him, her heart pounding heavily. "I would... I would love that. But it isn't supposed to be open."

"I am Prince Raphael DeSantis," he said. "The rules of mere mortal men do not apply to me. Nor should they."

She laughed. She couldn't help herself. "I'm sorry— sometimes I forget I'm married to a demigod."

"You wound me so. Only a demigod?"

"I'm sorry. Jove reincarnated?"

"Much better." He extended his arm. "Shall we?"

They took an elevator until it was required they take the stairs, then made their way to a silent floor, high above the activity that was happening below. The settings were sparse, nothing but blocks of black walls dividing a large space. But that was because the show belonged to the artwork that was hanging there.

Raphael stayed silent while they wandered through the displays, while she paused at the paintings. Strangely, while standing in front of one that featured a woman at a picnic—the men were dressed, and she was naked—Bailey could suddenly relate to that woman. Uncovered like that for all to see while her companions were covered still. Out of place, where they blended.

Bailey's eyes filled with tears.

One tear tracked down her cheek, and she tried to wipe it away before Raphael saw.

"What's wrong?" he asked.

"Nothing is wrong," she said, her throat tight. "Except...this is beautiful. And it's so much more than I ever thought I would have. It just feels wonderful right now, and I can't believe that something won't go horribly wrong."

It all rolled over her like a thunderstorm, lightning and rain lashing at her soul. She was in this beautiful place, this place that had only ever been a dream to her, a place she had imagined would always only be a dream, with a man who transcended fantasy. A man she hadn't known she was waiting for, a man she had never imagined she could possibly have.

She was...she was a princess. She was going to be a mother.

She was suddenly standing in a life she had never expected, one she could still barely believe she was living.

"What if I wake up and it's all just a dream?" she whispered.

He put his warm hands on her shoulders, sliding them down her bare arms, holding her tight. Then he leaned in from his position behind her, his breath hot against her neck. "Does this feel like a dream?"

"No," she said, her voice trembling now.

"Why would you think this was a dream?"

"Because. I used to have such vivid dreams when I was a child. I would go to bed hungry, and then spend all night dreaming that I was somewhere warm. About to have dinner. And then I would wake up just as hungry as I'd been when I'd gone to sleep and I would cry. Because it wasn't real. And that was when I realized it wasn't enough to dream. Because dreams aren't real, Raphael. They aren't." She swallowed hard. "When I met you...that was the first time I'd dreamed since I was a child. Only then I woke up. And you weren't any more real than all those other dreams. I was still hungry." She forced a smile. "And now I'm here, but it's just so difficult to believe that I won't wake up again and find it all gone."

He wrapped his arm around her waist, his large hand flat on her round stomach. "I am here," he said, his voice fierce. "I am your husband. I made vows to you, and I will keep them."

She nodded, unable to speak around the lump in her throat.

"This is beautiful," she said finally, dashing away another tear. "So beautiful it made me cry. So perfect... I can barely believe it." She turned to face him, his face another piece of art in a room filled with masterpieces. And she realized then that she was all his. Always and forever. That there was no self-protection to be found, and there never had been.

She loved him. With everything she was and everything she would be.

"Are you ready to go back down for dinner?"

"Yes," she said.

They began to walk back toward the stairs, and then she stopped in front of a massive clock built into a window, overlooking the city below.

The buildings were lit, casting a golden glow onto the river. She stepped up, moving nearer to it, leaning against the railing that was designed to keep people a safe distance from the glass, and gazing at the scene.

"Do you still feel like you're dreaming?" he asked, moving closer to her.

"No matter where you come from, I'm not sure this can feel real."

"A private art showing? One of the most beautiful

views in the world? That feels all too real to me. But you…you might very well be a dream."

She turned to face him, her heart thundering fast and hard. "Me? I thought it was a lot closer to a nightmare."

"Bailey," he said, and not for the first time she was struck by the absurdity of her extremely American name spoken in his cultured accent.

But he made it sound sexy. And no one else had ever managed to do that.

He pressed his hand between her shoulder blades, drawing his fingertips down the line of her spine until his hand reached the rounded curve of her butt.

Her breath hitched as his touch became more and more intimate, something about the effect of his hand over the silk making her feel extra sensitive.

He leaned in close, pressing a kiss to her neck. "I promise you—this is very real."

She closed her eyes, then forced them back open. Forced herself to keep her eyes on the incredible view below as he began to gather the fabric of her skirt into his hand. Began to draw it up her legs.

She gasped as the cool air hit her skin, and he moved his palm over the bare curve of her bottom.

Then he moved his hand, dipping it between her legs, his fingers delving beneath the edge of her panties.

"Raphael," she said, her voice a fierce whisper. "Someone might come up."

"No one is allowed to come up here." He shifted his movements, pushing his fingertips forward, grazing that sensitized bundle of nerves at the apex of her thighs. "And even if they did, I would simply order them to turn back around."

"But they'll see."

"Then let them," he said, his voice firm, authoritative. "You are my woman." There was something about that proclamation that affected her on a visceral level. He had called her his wife, he had called himself her husband. But there was something different about this. Something that laid elemental ownership that went beyond legal paperwork.

She let out a slow, shuddering breath as he continued to stroke her. "Do you...do you mean that?"

He wrapped his arm around her, grabbing hold of her chin, his forearm braced against her chest as he held her against him. "My word is law," he growled, rocking his hips forward, his hardness brushing against her.

"Of course it is. But...but I need to know."

"What do you need to know, *cara*?"

"Am I your woman? Or am I a burden? A duty?"

He hesitated for only a moment. "Everything I have was presented to me. That is my duty. What was passed to me. What I inherited. But you... I chose you."

Relief washed through her, tears prickling her eyes. She just couldn't face being a millstone around his neck. Not after her mother.

He *chose* her.

Raphael held her tight for a moment, stroking her until she was gasping for breath. Until she could hardly see straight, the city lights blurring in front of her, turning into a glittering, impressionistic work of art right before her eyes.

She clung to the railing. It was the only thing keeping her upright.

Then his fingers were replaced by his arousal, as he flexed his hips forward, pushing his erection through her slick folds.

"Bend forward," he commanded, pressing his hand against her stomach and drawing the lower half of her body back slightly as she complied with his order. He slipped his hand to her hip, holding her tight as he tested her entrance with the blunt head of him.

"We can't do this here," she said, her whisper swallowed up by the expansive room.

"Do you want to?" he asked, pressing in another inch.

She lowered her head, pleasure chasing need down her spine. "Yes." She shuddered.

"Then we can."

He pushed home then, a harsh groan on his lips as he seated himself fully inside her. He turned her face, kissing her as he established a maddeningly slow rhythm that was designed to torment her—it must have been. He kept her poised, on the brink, sending little ripples of pleasure that promised to become waves but never did, as he kept himself in firm control.

She began to rock back against him, meeting him thrust for thrust, trying to increase the pressure, to entice him to go harder, deeper, faster. And when those subtle enticements failed to fracture his command, she said the words. Over and over again, until she felt him splinter, until he began to break apart, piece by royal piece.

His hold became punishing, his blunt fingertips digging into her flesh as he pounded himself into her, over and over again. He was saying things, harsh, broken things, in a language she didn't know, his breath hot on her neck as he whispered promises her body understood even if her brain did not.

His arm was an iron bar across her chest, his grip tight at the base of her throat, while he slipped his other hand between her thighs, working wicked magic at the center of her pleasure.

"Please," he said, his voice as fractured as the rest of him. "Please. I can't hold on much longer."

His desperation, his plea, was the thing that turned the key, unleashed the flood of pleasure inside her. She came hard, a hoarse cry on her lips as her internal muscles clenched tightly around him.

He held her up as he thrust into her two more times, shaking as he cried out his own pleasure, the sound echoing off the walls around them, a new addition to the gallery that already contained so much beauty. Now it held this. Them.

Surrounded by so much history, it made everything feel more weighty. Made this feel more real. Made it feel like perhaps it wasn't just a dream.

As he held her tight, clung to her while they waited for the aftershocks to stop, she realized there was no way on earth this could be a dream. She never could have spun this out of thin air. She didn't possess the raw material to do it. Her life, that life of hunger and vague neglect, hadn't allowed her to dream of anything half so big.

And it had nothing so much to do with Paris, or the beautiful gown she was wearing, or the fact that Raphael was the most incredibly handsome man she'd ever seen. It was just him. The warm press of his chest against her back, that tight grip he kept on her. Making her so very aware of his strength, and yet so very safe at the same time.

"Would you still like to go down to dinner?" he asked, moving away from her, smoothing her dress back down and turning her to face him. He began to tuck her hair back into place, smoothing her, wiping away a smear of lipstick from below her lip.

"Is there another option?" she asked, sounding as shaky as she felt.

"Perhaps we could take that walk around the city?"

He whisked her quickly back through the museum, with such an air of command about him that no one dared to try to stop them. His hold on her was so possessive, so protective, and she gloried in it. In belonging to him. In feeling like she mattered.

"Are you going to call your driver?"

"No," he said, "we should walk."

He released his hold on her, shifting so that he could clasp her hand, just as he had done that last night in Vail, just before he had broken her heart. That simple, sweet gesture that had meant so much to her then and felt amplified now.

He led her down the sidewalk, the streets still alive even at this late hour. She had a feeling they looked out of place, she in her long black coat, her green dress shimmering around her feet, and Raphael in his tuxedo strolling along the river.

She looked up, her breath catching as she saw the Eiffel Tower in the distance, lit up for the evening.

"I never thought I would see that in person," she said.

"The Eiffel Tower?"

"It's surreal. I've seen it in so many movies…and there it is. Right in front of me."

"Then I think you will enjoy what I have in mind next."

She did. A small café just across the street from the tower. The base was visible from the little alcove they were seated in. They had coffee and simple sandwiches with bread, cheese and ham that tasted anything but simple. It wasn't the lavish, elegant dinner that they would have had if they'd stayed at the museum, but it meant more to her. It meant everything.

Hours passed that felt like minutes, and it was time to start walking back. It was late now, and her feet hurt, but she didn't want to get a car. She wanted to keep walking. She wanted to extend this night, forever. To keep existing in this moment, with the man as he was now. His guard had dropped somewhere along the way, and she wanted to keep him here.

Far too soon, they were back at the penthouse, but it was quickly clear to her that the night wasn't over. He took nearly as long getting her undressed as she had taken to get dressed before they went out.

When he pressed her into the soft mattress, he spent time thoroughly tasting each and every inch of her. Then he went over all those tender places with his hands, taking her to the brink over and over again.

When they both went over, it was together, and with all the pleasure pounding through her, images from earlier in the evening, from their time together in Colorado, mixing together inside her, painting a picture of a reality more beautiful than dreams, there was only one thing she could think to say.

"I love you."

Much later, when Bailey was asleep, Raphael stood on the balcony of the penthouse, gazing out at the city lighting up the night sky below. He wrapped his fingers tightly around the balustrade, Bailey's admission ringing inside him.

He had said nothing in return. And she had fallen asleep soon enough. But a response would be needed. Still, he could not give her the response she wanted.

If he had learned one thing about ruling from his parents, it was that there could be no greater attachment in the entire world than the attachment to the country. To the cause.

Certainly, a man could care for and treat his wife and children well, but love was an entirely separate issue. Love was something reserved for citizens, for the land and old stone buildings, the family history. Love was something much more like patriotism than what Bailey was talking about. At least, in his world.

Love kept its distance. It served others, not always those closest. His father had always made that so very clear. In the rules he established, the limited time he allowed his mother to spend with him.

When you were royalty, love wasn't personal. It was broad, spread out over everything that fell beneath your rule.

It could be expressed least of all beneath your own roof. Not in the ways that were shown on movies and in TV shows. A ruler cared for his subjects by seeing to their needs, and his father had always done much the same with Raphael and his mother.

The things he presented them with were there in his stead.

But still, he would have to say something to her.

He could say the words. They would cost him nothing.

His chest seized up tight at the thought. He had never told a single person that he loved him or her, ever. He didn't like the idea of starting now, particularly not when it was simply to soothe her feelings.

No, there had to be something else.

He took his phone out of his pocket, tapping the screen as he continued to formulate a plan in his mind. Then he dialed the palace in Santa Firenze.

"I'm going to need gifts sent up to the penthouse in Paris by tomorrow morning. A diamond necklace, flowers—enough to fill every surface in the place—and a lavish spread for breakfast. The best croissants you can find, meat, cheese. Something for the princess to drink that doesn't contain alcohol."

He cut the call off, turning and facing the doors to the penthouse. This would suffice. He would make her happy. He knew that he could. He was a man with near limitless power and deep pockets. Whatever she desired, he would give her.

He thought of her face tonight as she had looked at the art, of the way she had begun to weep with happiness. Yes, he could continue to give her things like this. Continue to make her happy. Keep her in this dream she was afraid of losing. She never had to lose it. He would make sure she didn't.

She would not be hungry with him. She would never be cold. She would never want for a damn thing.

As long as she didn't continue to ask for his love.

CHAPTER TWELVE

WHEN BAILEY WOKE up the next morning, Raphael wasn't in bed. There was something niggling at the back of her mind, but she couldn't quite think of what it was. She got up, putting on one of the silk nightgowns that were hanging in the closet. She had slept naked. Honestly, there was no point wearing clothes when Raphael was around.

Still, she was not going to walk into the living room naked.

She stopped the minute she walked out of the bedroom, shocked. There were red roses everywhere. Like grand-gesture-at-the-end-of-a-romantic-comedy level of everywhere.

She walked farther out into the room, noticing a tray set on the coffee table in front of the couch. There was a French press with coffee and a tray laden with pastries. Her stomach growled, a welcome sound after waking up too many mornings feeling vaguely nauseous.

And still, something continued to bother her.

But she figured she would work that out over some *pain au chocolat*.

"You're awake," Raphael said, striding into the room, a wide, flat velvet box clutched in his hand.

"Yes. I am. What's going on? Unless a morning order of flowers and pastries is business as usual for you. Which I kind of think might be a great tradition."

"All for you, *cara*." He moved nearer to her, holding the box up. "As is this."

Inside the box was the most incredible piece of jewelry she had ever seen. An ornate, glittering necklace composed of delicate strands of white gold braided together with gems sprinkled over it like dewdrops. And then, at the center, one large teardrop-shaped diamond that looked like it belonged at the center of a jewel heist.

And then she remembered. Last night, she had told him that she loved him. He had said nothing.

She looked around the room. This was…this was his response.

"That's…it's a lot," she said.

"Not too much for you," he said, his tone sincere, as though he were issuing her the greatest of compliments.

"Thank you," she said, waiting for…she didn't know what she was waiting for. He wasn't going to make a grand pronouncement, not today. But then, maybe it wasn't reasonable to expect one. Maybe she just needed to be patient.

"You don't sound very pleased."

He moved toward her, extending the jewelry box out to her. "I am," she said, taking it from him. "Who wouldn't want diamonds and butter?"

"Would you like to put the necklace on now?"

"No, thank you. I'm still in my pajamas. That would be a little bit ostentatious, don't you think?"

"You're free to be as ostentatious as you like," he said.

"That is a dangerous bit of permission. You have no idea what I'm going to do with it."

"I'm intrigued. I hope to see great acts of ostentatiousness in the near future."

"I will do what I can to oblige you."

"We are a headline this morning," he said casually. "As you suggested we might be."

"Oh," she replied, wincing a little bit. "How unflattering is it?"

"A couple of publications dared to be snide about how I was clearly forced to marry you. But others talked about how longingly you gazed at me during the party last night. And some of them even had photographs of us eating at the café, suggesting that the two of us clearly choose to spend time together in venues that are invisible because we enjoy each other's company, not just to court media attention."

That made her stomach sink. It made her wonder what his motivation had been for last night's impromptu walk through the city. She wondered if it had been a bit more calculated than it had appeared. She gritted her teeth, shutting that thought out. It didn't really matter. What had happened in the museum, in front of the clock, the entire city down below, that had been for the two of them.

So that had to count for something.

Sure, it meant that he wanted sex.

No, it was more than that. It was.

"I'm glad that we turned out a pretty good PR performance," she said, keeping her tone neutral. She was still deciding how she was going to handle all of this.

What it meant that she had told him she loved him and he had responded by buying her more things.

"If you have to be in the headlines, it is best if they're favorable."

"Oh, right. I forgot that all of this was a bit beneath you."

"It's a distraction," he said.

"From what?"

"From the actual job. There should not be so much glory in running a country. It should never be about you."

"Okay, that's interesting coming from the most arrogant man I have ever met."

He lifted a shoulder. "Perhaps you see me as arrogant. But from my point of view, it seems that it would do my country no good to see their ruler as a man who did not possess the utmost confidence in everything he did. Why should they trust me if I don't trust myself?"

"Well, sometimes there is strength in asking for help."

"No, that's a lie that helpless people tell themselves. People who don't want to feel weak, when they are in a desperate position. I don't blame them. If one finds themselves in a desperate position, one must handle it as they see fit. And I suppose there is strength within that. But I am not desperate. Not now, nor have I ever been. My father ruled in this fashion. And he created a nation that was strong, one that has weathered worldwide financial crises and war, without ever entering into either. Should I seek to change the way things are?"

"I suppose not," she said, taking those words and holding them close, turning them over. It was clear to her that he felt showing weakness of any kind was detrimental. Not just to himself but to an entire nation. It was difficult to argue with that. The most she'd ever been in charge of was a goldfish.

What did she know?

"The entire country trusts in me confidently." He lowered his voice then, looking at her, something in his dark eyes softening. "You can, too."

Those words warmed her, comforted her. After a morning of feeling off balance, they were exactly what she needed to hear. Well, if an *I love you* was unavailable, anyway.

"If you say so."

"I do. And my word is law."

"Oh, Raphael." She stood up, pressing her hand to his chest, emotion coursing through her. "I do love you."

She felt him stiffen beneath her touch. But she didn't really care. And suddenly, she was well aware of how she would proceed.

He might not love her yet. But he'd *chosen* her. He'd said. So she was just going to love him. There was no other alternative. Nothing more than keeping everything stuffed down inside, and she didn't want to do that. It would hurt her far more than honesty would.

"Do you have a list of things you wish to see today?" he asked.

Her heart twisted. But she kept her smile firmly in place. "Why don't you surprise me?"

He liked that. She could see it in the satisfied expression on his face. The gesture of trust, her simple admission that he could possibly do a good job with anticipating her needs.

"That," he said, "I can do."

The week in Paris went by too quickly, and when they returned to the palace, Raphael threw himself into dealing with affairs of state. Which, she supposed, was unavoidable seeing as he ran the entire country. He had left it in the capable hands of his staff for a while, but there were most certainly things that only the prince could see to.

She told herself she wasn't lonely. That she didn't miss having him around. That it was fine that she only saw him at night when he came to bed and took her with the kind of passion he withheld from her during the other hours of the day.

Most of all, she told herself that it was okay when he didn't say he loved her, too.

Oh, he had given her absolutely everything. More clothing than she could conceivably wear, especially considering it was maternity wear, and she would only need it for a few more months. Jewelry, books and then last week, an entire wing of the palace. All for her.

One day he had come in with a petite woman clutching a book at his side. "I know that back in Colorado we had discussed you finishing your degree," he said. "I have employed a teacher to assist you. She has compiled accredited curriculum and a university you can work with remotely. I want to make sure you have everything that you were promised and more."

The woman had smiled, looking down at Bailey's increasingly obvious bump. "Of course, we will work around your schedule," she said kindly. "I would not want you to feel overtaxed, Princess."

Nobody had ever cared if she was overtaxed when she was going to the University of Colorado. Nobody had cared that she was sick and tired of waiting tables when she had gotten pregnant before she had a title. Nobody at all.

It was strange to have people care so much about her condition.

And care they did. From the media to the staff at the palace, everyone was doting on her.

She had become a kind of icon for style when it came to pregnancy, but she really didn't feel like she could claim the glory for that. Raphael had appointed her a stylist who assisted her every time she went on an outing. If it were up to her, she would probably be in sweats. Though she had to concede that it wasn't really any more work to put on a dress and leggings.

She was very well taken care of. Possibly more than she had ever been in her entire life. But she still felt... empty. Because things weren't love. All of this wasn't love. It was deference, and it was...well, it was definitely care. But it wasn't what she felt for Raphael.

If there was no baby, she would have wanted him. If there was no title, and there was no expectation about marriage, she still would have wanted him. She had wanted him when she had thought he was just some kind of middle managing pharmaceutical rep.

But he hadn't wanted her. And even though he was doing a wonderful job of taking care of her now, even though he clearly still wanted her, she had doubts. And those doubts were insidious.

The doctor visit today had yielded results she knew would make him happy. The fact that she was having a boy. The kind of heir men like him were best off with. Or so she'd heard.

For some reason she was having a hard time finding the right moment to tell him.

"How are your studies going?" he asked, coming into the room that night.

"They're going very well. Professor Johnson has been extremely patient and helpful. I feel like I haven't even really fallen behind, because getting the one-on-one help has been so valuable."

"Perfect. What exactly are you going to do with a business degree?"

"Well, back when I was in Colorado I imagined that I might open my own business someday. And I thought it might just help me get more comfortable jobs until then. Maybe with slightly better pay."

"And now?"

"I feel like it's still valuable to understand the way things work. To understand a bit about the structure of these things, and where it all fits in with the economy. Surely there's value in that for a princess."

"If you find it valuable, then it is. And I'm sure that you can use it in any way you see fit. There are plenty of different charities you can get involved with. Organizations that would benefit from your insight, I'm sure. But I think a degree is one of the least things you have to offer something like that."

She sensed she was on the cusp of receiving a compliment, and so she pressed further. "Is that right?"

"You are fiercely determined. And a wonderful advocate. I can imagine you will get a great deal done. An iron will combined with the title is a wonderful thing."

"I'm glad you can appreciate my iron will."

"I appreciate it much more now that it isn't being turned on me with as much frequency."

She laughed. "Well, I make no guarantees."

Silence stretched between them, strange and slightly uncomfortable. She was so rarely uncomfortable with him anymore. She imagined it was because this silence was full of so many unsaid things. She wanted to tell him that she loved him again. Just to see what he would say. She told him every day. Had since that day in Paris. There had been no response. No response beyond giving her more and more.

"I have a very busy schedule tomorrow," he said, for no reason that she could discern.

"So, I won't see you?"

"Probably not."

"I haven't seen you enough lately," she said.

"I am very busy," he said, his tone getting hard. "It is something you will have to get accustomed to. I was around a little more than I would normally be when I first brought you back here out of courtesy to you. And because we were planning a wedding. And then, of course, we went to Paris, so we saw a great deal of each other. But it cannot continue. You will find a great many things to keep yourself busy."

"Is that why you're keeping me in school? Is that why you're talking to me about what I might do with my degree and all my spare time?"

"Yes, in part. You need to have something to keep you occupied. Something that will enable you to serve the country."

"I will also be parenting our child."

"Yes," he said, speaking slowly. "But mostly that responsibility will fall to nannies."

"No," she said, "it most certainly will not."

"You have a duty to the country, Bailey."

"I have a duty to our baby. Above and before anything else. I was ready to be a single mother, Raphael, because I had no idea if I would ever see you again. In my mind, I reshaped my entire life to accommodate this child. And while it seemed daunting, while I still don't know if I'm even half qualified to be a mother, I know that I want to devote my time to that."

"But it is not how it's done. Both because we will be busy ruling the nation, and because our child must be set on the right path from the first day, as I was."

"Being…bowed to by servants and held only by members of staff? Both worshipped and ignored all at the same time?"

"I was never ignored," he said, his tone hard. "I was essential. The heir to the throne. It will be the same for our child, and every portion of their childhood will be spent building to the moment they shall stand as I do, the prince or princess of Santa Firenze. It is how it has always been, and how it must continue to be."

"I don't care how it's been done for the past hundred years. I'm also the first nobody anyone in your storied royal lineage has married. Expect that I will do things differently. That I will have different expectations."

"So, your childhood was idyllic?"

"No," she said, "my childhood was awful. And you know that. My mother was eternally stressed and filled with resentment for me. She worked a job she hated and barely managed to keep us fed and clothed. We had no relationship. We have no relationship now. She resents me far too much for that. She made the decision to have me, and she regretted it ever since."

"So why," he said, his tone full of exasperation, "do you think the key to our child's happiness is you being around?"

"I don't think you understand. When I found out I was pregnant, I knew that I was in the exact same situation my mother was in. I knew that it would be so easy for me to spend my child's entire life resenting them. For interrupting my plans. For making things difficult. But they were my choices that led to that, Raphael, and I refused to punish my child for them. I thought long and hard about how I was going to avoid repeating the pattern that I had seen myself falling into. It was so important to me. But I realized, a few days after I found out I was pregnant, as I was lying in bed crying, ready to rend my garments in my distress, that it wouldn't be that way as long as I loved my child. As long as I loved my child more than I loved the dreams that I had built for myself. As long as I love my child more than my own comfort."

"Your child will be comfortable."

"But I want to be with them. I'm not going to fill up my days with busywork when I could be spending time with him or her. I like the idea of volunteering. I like the idea of having something of a vocation other than princess. But I'm not turning over the entire responsibility of my child to someone else."

"But it is how things are done." She could tell he was reaching the end of his temper. That he didn't understand—even after all this time with her—dealing with someone who wouldn't simply accept his word as law.

"Don't *you* want to spend time with our child?"

He waved a hand. "It has nothing to do with want, and everything to do with responsibility. It was thus for my parents, and it will be thus for me. You talk of love as if it is some kind of magic. As if it will move mountains, create time and keep a kingdom standing, but it is not. It is a potential distraction. Something that might prevent a ruler from acting in the best interest of his country. I cannot allow that. My father did not, and so I must not."

Her heart was pounding faster now, her stomach turning over. "You really think that love is the enemy?"

"I think it is an unnecessary distraction. I think a man in my position can afford to love nothing more than his country."

Those words hit hard, and she was reminded of that moment in the hotel room the night he'd first ended things with her. That grim finality. The evidence that he would not be moved. Not by tears or flying shoes.

"So, you'll never love me." It wasn't a question but a statement. Even as she spoke the words, they felt sharp in her throat, cutting into her, making it hard to breathe. "You're only ever going to love this country. You're not even going to love your own child?"

She had been willing to live in a situation where he didn't love her. Had been willing to try to figure that out. But the realization that he expected to have nothing to do with his own son or daughter was something she couldn't easily sweep under the rug.

"I told you this child mattered to me. There is a reason I had to marry you and not simply find someone else—"

"Will you love him?"

"I have never said those words to anyone," he said. "It has never been important to my existence."

"It is important now, Raphael. It's important to me."

"Have I not demonstrated how deeply I care for you?" he roared. "Have I not given everything to you that you could possibly want? And still, you behave as though it isn't enough."

"Raphael—"

"No. You are a waitress," he said, his tone harsh. "And I brought you here, to my palace, into my home, and I gave you all that it was in my possession to give. Still, you act as though somehow I am beneath you. You accuse me of being arrogant, and yet I think you best me on that score. Have I not given you an entire wing of this palace that has been in my family for generations? Did I not make you a DeSantis princess? You lived in a hovel, and I have elevated you in ways you never could have aspired to, and this is how you respond?"

"You're angry because I fail to be honored by the scraps that you've given me?" Rage was vibrating through her now, and she wasn't thinking entirely clearly. She didn't really care. She wanted to strike out at him. Wanted to hurt him the way that he had hurt her, all those countless times from that moment when he'd left her lying in the snow in Colorado. "That's what they are, and you have no idea. You think you can appease me with gold dust. Shiny things I never even wanted. That I should be grateful. But these are easy things, Raphael. So easy. For a man in your position, giving me a wing of your palace is nothing. You couldn't walk the length of it in an afternoon, so how will you ever miss a quadrant of rooms? You send me gifts, gifts that you have ensured I know are not extravagant enough to put a dent in your royal treasury. And you act as though you are somehow doing me a great favor. But how many necklaces can a woman wear? How many beautiful gowns?"

"That isn't the point," he said, sounding frustrated.

"Yes," she said, "it is the point. These things…they are easily replaceable. They are easily acquired for a man like you. But love? That is…it is so rare. And it is so beautiful. And so very, very costly. Don't you think that it has cost me every time I have told you that I love you and you've said nothing in return? That is a gift beyond price, and you don't even see it. You don't see everything that *I* have given to you. My body, my soul, my heart. I left my dreams, modest though they were, my dreams that you felt were somehow nothing, to come here and be with you."

Her angry words did nothing to cool his rage. "Look at all you have been given in return. Don't ask me to feel sorry for you. Don't pretend that you didn't love what we had in Paris. You didn't enjoy the extravagance."

"Of course I did. I'm only human. But all it will take is a financial crisis, a natural disaster, a war to wipe these things out. They are temporary. They are nothing. If the world catches fire, they'll burn away. And then what will be left? All that will be left standing is you and me, and without all of these shows of wealth and magnificence you don't know how to connect with me. You don't know who you are."

"But that will not happen," he said, his voice hard.

"Hopefully not. But you're still missing the point. These things are temporary. And they're not real. Not really. What I've given for you, that's real. What I feel for you? It *hurts*. It hurts whenever I breathe. It strips me of my pride by inches, day after day, every time I tell you I love you and you say nothing back. And what cost have I been to you? Truly."

"You are obsessed with that," he spat. "The cost. You wish to be an inconvenience? You wish to seem so high maintenance?"

"No. I wish to know that I'm not the only one sacrificing to have this. I wish to be something more than one of your possessions that you take out and put away at your will. That is what I want."

He exploded then. "You wish for the impossible. You wish to control how I feel. You have decided that my actions are not good enough. What good would it be if I felt things, and yet did nothing for you? If I told you that I loved you, and yet left you in that heap of an apartment in Colorado. Then you would not find these gestures so empty. If there was a lack of them, I imagine you would be saying that I clearly didn't love you because of what I failed to do."

"It's true," she said, her voice small. "I feel like those things kind of have to come together for them to matter."

"Is this how you were as a child?" he asked, the question hitting her like a slap. "Never able to be pleased? If your mother took care of you, but failed to demonstrate to you that her love was real, did you resent her?" His words dug beneath her skin, hit at her insecurity. But that wasn't fair. She refused to feel guilty for wanting someone to love her.

"That was low," she said, her voice vibrating. "Even for you, that was so damn low."

"It isn't throwing a shoe, I grant. But it's something to consider." He turned, his broad back filling her vision as he began to walk away.

"You're leaving now?" she asked.

"I can't talk to you at the moment. And so I refuse to."

"And your word is law," she said.

He turned again. "Yes," he said. "Yes, it is. And you would do well to remember that."

"Or what? You'll send me back to where I came

from? What does it matter if we are still together if you aren't even going to have me raise our child? If I don't mean anything to you?"

"I want you with me," he said.

"But why? To hear you tell it, I am nothing more than a waitress, and I am beneath you. You don't love me, and you never will. You don't need me to be there for our child. You think everything I came from is insignificant, that everything I want is something that doesn't matter. Why do you want me with you?"

He crossed the space between them, his expression lean and feral. "Because I want *you*," he growled, wrapping his arm around her and pulling her up against his body. It was hard and hot, everything she loved about him. Everything that always saw her weakening in his presence. She had to resist him now. She had to.

"It isn't enough. It's just another thing that will burn away."

"Never," he said, pressing his lips to her neck.

"Yes," she said, "it will. My body will change after I have this baby, and the years will soften it even more. I won't look like I did when you met me, when you first decided you wanted me. I'll be like every other old, unneeded thing littering this palace. And I will not submit myself to that."

"Have I not told you that your strength is valuable to me?"

"You have. But it isn't enough."

"And nothing less than what you want is enough?" He released his hold on her, taking a step back.

"Exactly. I've given you all that I am. All that I ever will be. I have submitted my future to you. And in return I want to know you. I want to have you. Every part of you. I want your love, I want your anger, I want everything messy and imperfect inside of you. I don't just want this distant arrogance, this blind insistence that you are law and above everything. I don't want it. I want all of that broken down and destroyed."

"Then you will never have it," he said.

She moved to him then, gripping his face, closing the distance between them and kissing him with all the pent-up rage that was inside her. Every twisted, ugly thing. All her selfishness, all her need. Her insecurity and her fear. And always, even now, every last bit of her love.

"Don't hide from me," she said, her voice vibrating.

"There is nothing to hide," he responded, his dark eyes blank.

"Liar," she said, claiming his mouth again.

He had told her more than once that she made him burn. That she had control over him no one else ever had.

Well, if ever he needed to go up in flames, it was now. And she was going to make sure it happened.

CHAPTER THIRTEEN

RAPHAEL KNEW THAT he should push her away. That he could not allow her to try to gain control in this way. He was Prince Raphael DeSantis, and no woman could manipulate him.

Except he could not bring himself to pull her lush mouth away from his. Could not deny the fire that burned between them.

He was being ripped apart from the inside out, piece by piece, and still, he could not bring himself to push her away. Still, he could not deny the desire that burned between Bailey and himself.

He would show her. He would prove to her, with this, that the need between them was enough. That it transcended use, that it went somewhere beyond beauty. There had been many beautiful women in his life. He'd always had his pick.

When he'd seen her, something had streaked through him, white hot and clean. It had been different than anything else ever had been. More. Deeper. It had been real. Real in a way nothing else before it had ever been. He would make her see. He would make her understand.

Raphael grabbed hold of her hair, twisting his fingers through the silken strands, tugging hard as he continued to kiss her, deep and long. As he took her seduction and flipped it against her.

Love.

They didn't need love. He didn't need it. It didn't matter. It wasn't important. And for a man in his position, it wasn't even possible. He had never wanted for it. Never once. He had always been given everything he needed.

But never love. Therefore, he could only assume that love was not among the necessary. Not for a man like him. If it were, his parents would have given him that, but they hadn't. Instead, he had been given education. He had been given staff. He had been given a room filled with the kinds of toys that would ignite any child's delight.

As a teenager, he had been given new cars. Well-fitted suits and private tutors who instructed him on how to best conduct himself in all situations.

Unlike Bailey, he had never been cold. He had never gone without. He'd had everything, always.

How dare this little witch come in and tell him that he lacked? How dare she make it seem as though he lived with a deficit? How dare she reduce everything that had always mattered to him to insignificant rubble? How dare she brush aside his gestures so casually?

He would not allow it. Not again. Not ever again. His blood was liquid fire in his veins as he ran his hands over her curves, reveling in her softness, in her heat. In her obvious need for him.

Yes, that was what he needed. He needed to feel how much she wanted him. And he needed it now.

He pushed his hands up beneath her skirt, his fingertips sliding easily beneath the edge of her panties. He felt that she was wet for him. Even angry, she still wanted him.

"You want me ugly?" he asked, his voice rough. "You want me out of control?"

He would give her all that and more. Here. Now. With his body. He would make her pay for this. For making him feel like his insides were made entirely of broken glass. For taking his well-ordered life and turning it completely upside down. For taking his perfect existence and proving to him that it was something less.

Yes. He would make her pay for that.

He pushed a finger deep inside her, watched as her mouth fell open, her eyes glazing over with pleasure. Yes, he wanted her like this. Mindless for him as he was for her, every damn day. Every moment, every breath. He wanted her to feel this desperation. To feel like it was all slipping away and there was nothing she could do about it. To feel hungry, aching, empty. As though nothing could ever fill the void. That was his entire existence with her. He wanted her to know that. To understand.

He had never felt like this. Everything he'd wanted, he'd had. And she insisted on keeping herself just out of reach. On making his best efforts not good enough.

She was ruining them. She was ruining him.

He would return the favor.

"Is this what you want," he rasped, adding a second finger to the first, rubbing the sensitive bundle of nerves at the apex of her thighs with his thumb. "You want me out of control?"

"I've *had* you out of control," she said. "From the beginning. But you won't admit what that means."

"It's sex. That's what it means. That we have very, very good sex."

He withdrew his fingers from her, rubbing her hips, sliding his hands down her thighs and lifting her, wrapping her legs around his waist, carrying her to the bed. He kissed her then, deep and long, with every ounce of his passion, every bit of his rage.

"No," she said, and he paused in his movements. "No, it's not sex. You chose me. You chose me, and that matters."

He said nothing, ignoring the pain those words inflicted on his heart as he pushed her skirt up her hips, dragging her panties down. Then he freed himself from his slacks. He didn't bother with more foreplay. Didn't bother with gentility. Instead, he thrust deep inside her, both of them gasping as he went deep. She was so tight, so wet and so undeniably his.

She could love him all she wanted. She did love him. Why couldn't that be enough for her? He didn't understand.

Don't you?

The howling beast inside him supplied the question, and he rejected it. Rejected all thought in favor of feeling. The feeling of her, the heat of her body, tight around him, the feeling of her fingernails digging into his skin. The sound of her needy cries as he pushed them both harder, higher. The feel of her hot breath against his neck as she panted, signs that she was getting closer to her peak.

That was his truth. It was all he cared about. He would exist in it now. Live in this moment, for as long as he could. He wanted nothing else. Nothing else, ever.

She was wrong. Wrong about him. Because if every-

thing else was stripped away. If he ended up a prince
with no palace, no kingdom, they would still have this.

*She will love you. She will pour everything out for
you. And what will you give in return?*

He gritted his teeth, thrusting harder, losing himself in the fractured rhythm that only the two of them
could ever dance to. The flames rose higher inside him,
and he didn't fight it. He let it consume him, his release
a shock of thunder inside him, shaking him, rattling
him to his core. And as he spilled himself inside her,
she found her own bliss. Her internal muscles clenched
tightly around him, wringing more pleasure out of him,
prolonging his orgasm.

It was always so with her. All of these things that he
had never thought possible. That he had never thought
to want.

And the truth of it all hung somewhere between
them, hovered over him like a cloud, and he was desperate to hide from it. To push it away. Because those three
words were the undoing of his entire life. Those three
words undermined everything he was, everything he
believed. They would shatter him. Utterly, completely.

He could not allow it.

He pushed himself away from her, forking his fingers through his hair, pacing the length of the room.

"I love you," she said.

He turned, that thing inside him savaging him now,
tearing him to shreds from the inside out. "No!" He
roared the words at her, satisfied when her face con-
torted with fear. With anguish. Because he had to make
her see. He had to make her see that this would not happen. That it could not.

"But I do." The simplicity of it…that was the worst

part. As though it simply had been and now always would be. As though he had no control at all.

"You shouldn't," he said. "No one ever has. Why should you? Why should you find it so easy to love me?"

"An entire nation loves you."

"Because of what I was born to be. Not because of who I am." Those words were far too heavy. They landed against the top of the well he kept covered. That bottomless, needy well that contained the dark truth about himself. About who he was and what that meant.

He never wanted it to open. He never wanted that truth to come out.

"I love you," she said again, defying his orders at every turn, as she always did.

Bailey, so strong and defiant, always. How had she become his? How had she decided that she loved him? How had she decided that she could love at all? With a life as bleak and difficult as hers sounded, how had she arrived at the conclusion that love meant anything?

He could ask her. But his mouth wouldn't form the words.

There was no point to them anyway. There was no point to any of this. It had all been a fiction from the very beginning. A dream.

Bailey talked a lot about dreams. About how she'd been afraid to have them. He had spent his life living an existence carefully constructed to appear like a dream, the kind of life that prevented him from having any aspiration that fell outside duty.

He had no idea what it was to dream. To want. To hope for anything that extended beyond what was expected. He had no idea at all.

She was his first dream. She had been from the mo-

ment he had walked into that diner. His first foray into
something that went beyond necessity and into desire.

He closed that off, ruthlessly, with great finality. He
could not allow himself to think such things. It was
nonnegotiable.

She was exactly what his father had always told him
something like this would be. A distraction. She was
a fatal weakness, something that could get right under
his skin, changing everything he was, everything he
was supposed to believe in.

She would become larger than Santa Firenze in his
heart, in his mind, and he could not allow it.

"I don't love you," he said, his voice rough. "I never
will."

Then he turned and walked out of the room, leaving behind a piece of himself he had never known existed. Leaving behind the most essential, vital part of
his heart. But it was for the best. It was all he could do.

The only other option would make his world fall
apart. And he couldn't allow that. Not when so much
depended on him standing firm.

He felt in that moment that if there were a snowbank
for him to throw himself into, he would do it.

The door to Bailey's room opened behind him, and
he turned. She was there, her blue eyes glittering.

"I don't know what you think my response will be,"
she said. "If I will accept it and tell you that's okay. If
I will continue on in this farce of a relationship simply
because you will it, and your word is law. But I don't
care about your pride, Raphael. Your pride needs to
burn. If it's the thing that separates us, then it is the
thing that has to go. I'm not staying."

"You have to."

"I will call the American embassy and tell them you're holding me captive."

"After we appeared in Paris together? After our wedding? The entire world knows you're carrying my child, Bailey. Do you honestly think you can pull something like that off?"

"I will, because I have to. Because you have finally killed the hope that I've been holding on to for all of these months. You built my trust back up, and now you've destroyed it again. And I'm not going to give you another chance. If you want to be involved in our child's life, you can. But you're going to have to come and visit us in Colorado. Because that's where I live. That's my world. And even if you never understand why it matters to me, that's the life I built for myself. It is not small. And neither am I."

She sucked in a sharp breath before continuing. "I was never just a waitress. I was never just anything. I have always, always been Bailey Harper. And that has always mattered. I pulled myself up with all of my own strength, and I will be damned if you reduce all of that effort to nothing. It will be good enough for my child, because it is what I built. And there will be love in my house. If your duty, or whatever you feel, is compelling enough to bring you across the world to visit, then I'll be happy with that. But I sincerely doubt anything less than love would compel a person to make that kind of effort. So I'll expect that you simply won't be involved."

"You can't do that," he said. "My child is my heir. The heir to this throne. He must be raised here. He must know of his heritage."

"A heritage of ice. A heritage so cold it will destroy him as soon as he touches it? No. That isn't the life that

I want for our child. And someday I think you'll see that I'm right. When your son grows up to be a more compassionate, more loving, more caring ruler than you will ever be. When he becomes the husband that you have been afraid to be."

"My son?"

"Yes. I had a doctor appointment today. And I was going to tell you. But then we fought."

"You tell me that you're having my son and are going to take him away from me?"

"You're taking him away from yourself, Raphael. That's the truth of it. But you don't want him. Not really."

"I do." He did. With everything. He didn't understand what was happening to him. Why he felt so torn, so bloody. So close to being destroyed.

"You like the idea of a wife. You like the idea of a son that you can raise and mold in your image. But you will always keep us at a distance. And I won't let that happen. You can break down that wall inside of you, that thing that keeps you from lowering yourself to accept my love."

"It has nothing to do with lowering myself."

"Maybe not. But you still won't do it. You're too proud."

"What are your demands?"

"Ready a jet to fly me back home. Arrange for me to gain entry into the US, and I will not make a scandal out of this. But I swear to you, I will strike your pride in any way that I can if you don't comply. Because I know that's the only thing you truly value."

Raphael could only stand there, stunned, wounded. And then he knew there was only one answer he could give her. That there was only one right thing to do. And it had nothing to do with pride and everything to do with the fact that he finally saw what she had been telling him from the beginning. What he had done to her was an insult. He had taken her, manipulated her and had never bothered to look deeper into his actions because he knew that doing so would require him to face deep, uncomfortable truths about his life and about himself that he had never wanted to face.

And so he did the only thing he could do. The only thing he could do and still survive.

"I will ready the jet. Be ready to leave early tomorrow."

Then he turned and walked away. Because he would be damned if he watched her leave.

CHAPTER FOURTEEN

HE WONDERED HOW a palace with so many people in it could feel empty. But it did. With Bailey gone it was empty.

And so was he.

He wandered the halls of the place he'd been so absurdly proud to bring her to. As if she would see it and crumble in humility and gratefulness because it was a palace, and there was no way she could have ever aspired to such a thing on her own.

She had worked for her life. For her education. For that apartment he'd insulted. He'd worked for none of this and yet held it up as some form of achievement.

Dio.

He was every bit as arrogant and unrelenting as she'd accused him of being.

But it was the only thing he had. The only thing that stood between him and the yawning void he tried so desperately to keep covered up.

It had cracked open now, and he was so terribly conscious of just how vacant and empty his entire existence was.

It made him question what he'd been taught. For the first time, he questioned his father. He'd never wanted to.

He'd so desperately wanted to preserve that image. Of a man who ruled a country with unfailing strength, who was the leader that Raphael had always aspired to be.

But he had been a terrible father and an even worse husband.

Raphael gritted his teeth, lowering his head and bracing himself against the wall. His staff continued to walk by, not speaking, not pausing. Why should they? That was the environment he'd continued to foster.

No connections. Nothing to interrupt business as usual.

Deference as a replacement for connection.

Prizing efficiency in a grand spectrum of days that all blurred together, instead of lingering in human connection.

He was breaking apart inside, and there was no one here to talk to. No one who would ever pause to ask why.

Oh, his Secret Service would take a bullet for him. But they would never talk to him.

Because that was what his father had taught him. What had been ingrained in him from childhood. He had never questioned it.

Never questioned when his father had yelled at his mother late one night for skipping an event because Raphael had been sick.

He knew he hadn't meant for Raphael to hear the argument, but he had.

"I needed you there tonight, and you were not. It split my focus!"

"Your son was sick," she hissed. *"I needed to be with him."*

"We have staff for that. An excellent staff. The boy wants for nothing. I, however, looked weak in front of

the ambassadors. Everyone's wife was in attendance except for you. You knew what this marriage was to be. You are to support Santa Firenze first. Above all else. Anything else is a distraction."

The next day he'd had a new toy. A gift from his father. The only contact the older man made during his illness. And after that his mother had been even more distant than before. An edict given by his father, because his son and heir could not be made dependent.

He'd done his best not to be a distraction. There and then he'd purposed to be the sort of man his father was. He never wanted his mother to be on the receiving end of his father's wrath for something concerning him, either.

The fault was his. It couldn't possibly be the old prince's. Not when the man was such a brilliant leader, not when he had done so much for the country.

He was also forced to remember the day his mother died. When his father had stood, stoic beside the grave of his late wife, and Raphael, only fifteen, had kept his face as hard as the old man's.

"Grief is a distraction, Raphael," he said later. "A weakness only other men can afford. You must never love anything more than you love your country."

"You don't?" he asked.

"No. And a good thing, because the nation won't pause for the loss of your mother. And neither can I."

Neither can you.

That had been the unspoken subtext of the conversation. That loss could never touch men like them. Because living life dictated by emotions was to walk on unsteady ground. He'd understood it.

And yet now he felt that even if it made sense, even if his father was right in his way, he was also wrong.

This kind of cold emptiness would break a man in the end. At least, it would break him. He was broken now, that was certain. Without Bailey, who had been the world's biggest distraction from the first moment he'd met her. The first spark of the unexpected in a lifetime of grim certainty.

Duty without love was empty. Life without love was empty. He could see that clearly now.

There was no cost to it. Bailey was right. If it cost nothing, it meant nothing. If you hid behind walls of control, and kept your wife and children at a distance, appeasing them with gifts...there was no love at all.

It didn't protect your country. It only protected you.

Building a wall like that, keeping out the elements... it could protect. But a life without sunlight could only leave you cold.

He had allowed it to make him a statue long before he'd been memorialized in death.

His father hadn't loved the country most. He'd loved himself and his protection most, and he'd taught Raphael to do the same.

He thought back to his mother's funeral. How much he would have given to get a hug from his father then. But the old man couldn't bend that way. Not for Santa Firenze, for his pride.

It had seemed like strength to Raphael then. But he could see now that the greatest strength would have been in showing weakness. For a son grieving his mother. A nation mourning a princess.

Instead, Raphael had been given a new car the next day.

A single moment sharing their loss would have been

so much more costly to his father. So much more valuable to Raphael.

The gifts had always been empty, but Raphael had wanted them to matter. So he'd believed his father. Believed him so that he could pretend he'd been loved.

You have been loved. You've been loved from the start by Bailey Harper, and just like your father, you pushed it away.

He pressed his hand to his chest, trying to staunch the flow of pain bleeding endlessly from his heart.

He had pushed away the best gift he'd ever received, because the cost of it had been too great.

What good was endless wealth if he couldn't afford love?

That was the damned rub. He couldn't buy love. He had to pay for it with the same. With humility and sacrifice. With discomfort. With his very soul.

As he looked around the palace and saw nothing but empty vanity, he knew that he had no other choice.

Her dream was over.

That was her predominant thought as the plane touched down in Colorado. It was what played in her mind over and over again as the car that Raphael had organized for her picked her up from the airport and drove her to a neighborhood that was unfamiliar.

"This isn't my house," she said when the driver pulled her up to a place with a well-manicured lawn that she had never seen in her life.

"These are the keys," he said. "My instructions were to bring you here and to give you these. Raphael said there would be an explanation inside."

Heart hammering, she took the keys from the driver's

hand and made her way up the front walk. She put the key in the lock, and it turned. She took a deep breath before walking inside. And then she did. It was beautiful. Modest, and certainly not a palace. But exactly the kind of place she had dreamed she might find herself in one day.

There was an envelope on the counter with her name written on it. She opened it, pulling out a simple note that was inside.

I know that you won't want to take this from me. I know that it will offend your pride. However, please consider this part of my child support. I am a prince after all, so you know that I can well afford it. This is the dream that you spoke about more than once when we were together. A house in a nice neighborhood. I wanted to make sure that you had this. That our child had this.

It wasn't signed. It didn't need to be. It could only be from one person. He was arrogant even when giving houses as parting gifts.

Her heart crumpled, and she looked around the room, feeling so adrift. This had been her dream. This little house, this kind of security. But it didn't feel like enough now. And that had nothing to do with the fact that she had just spent the last month being a princess. The last month living in a palace. No, all the feelings of inadequacy had to do with the fact that she had spent the last month sharing a bed with Raphael. And there was no room for him in this little house. In this little life.

Not for the first time, she wondered if she simply should have accepted what he'd given. Wondered if it

would have been enough. If she shouldn't have pressed
for more.

She shook that thought off quickly.

There was nothing else she could do, not really. It
had been the right thing. The right thing for herself,
and for her baby.

Anyway, it was too late to question it now. But this
gesture, this one last gesture, which wasn't a whole
giant mansion or anything crazy like Raphael would
normally do, was the first sign she'd really seen that
he had actually listened to her at all. That he saw value
in her dream. Beauty in it the same way that she had.

It was a little bit late now, but she would accept it.
Maybe, just maybe, he was starting to understand a
little bit. Maybe there was still hope.

*Or that's just what you want to think because you
spent the entire plane ride back here crying and feeling
like you'd been stabbed through the heart.*

Yes, there was that. That couldn't be ignored.

She did feel a little bit stabbed.

The days began to bleed together. She went to class
and came back home. She wasn't working, because she
was allowing Raphael to pay for a few things. Maybe
that was wrong. But he was the father of her baby and
currently still her husband. They weren't going to divorce officially until after the baby was born. All contact she'd had with him had been made through his
aides. She saw no reason to go against him on that.
Mostly, she just didn't have the energy. She was close
to six months pregnant, undeniably so, and unable to
muster up much energy to do anything. Though she
had a feeling the heartbreak was to blame, more than
the pregnancy.

She sighed heavily, throwing her purse down onto the couch, her body following quickly after. This place was starting to feel like home. Maybe that was a betrayal, seeing as it had come from Raphael. But it was one of the few bright spots in her life. This gift from him that was still extravagant by the standards of most people, but actually showed his willingness to listen.

She heard footsteps and sat up, her heart hammering hard. She was pretty sure she was hallucinating. Except then she looked toward her bedroom and saw a glorious figure standing there. He was wearing the same sort of well-cut suit that he always wore, his expression as lovely and arrogant as ever.

She felt like she was having déjà vu. Flashing back to the moment he had been in her apartment that first time he'd come to find her after their breakup. She felt like maybe she was dreaming, just as she had imagined she might be back then. She pinched herself.

"What are you doing?"

"Making sure that I'm not asleep."

"You are not," he said, taking a step toward her. It was then that she saw he did look different than he usually did. She noticed that he had dark circles under his eyes, and that the lines by his mouth were more pronounced than they usually were. It was then she noticed how exhausted he was. That his hair was disheveled as though he had been constantly running his fingers through it. It was then she realized just how affected he was by all of this. The same as she was.

"What are you doing here? I didn't realize that part of the deal with you buying me a house meant that you got to come and go in and out of it as you please."

"That was never my intent," he said, his voice rough.

"It was my intent to leave you alone. To honor what you said to me. It was my intent to let you go. But I have spent the past couple of weeks in agony, and I... I needed to see you."

"So we can have the same fight? So we can yell at each other some more? You can say more hurtful things, and I can counter with meaner things."

"No," he said, sounding ragged. "That isn't what I want. It's as far removed from what I want as anything ever could be."

"Why are you here?"

Suddenly, Raphael dropped down, landing on his knees, looking up at her with dark, tortured eyes. "I came to bow."

"You came to...what?" Her heart hammered wildly, her hands shaking. She couldn't reconcile what she was seeing in front of her. This proud, arrogant man, on his knees before her. As though he were the servant, and she were royalty.

"I was bowed to from birth," he said. "Not because anyone cared especially much, not because they were awed by their....deep emotion for me. But because of my blood. I was given everything from the moment I entered this world simply because I am a DeSantis. I have never, not once, debased myself for another human being. I will crawl across broken glass if it means having you, Bailey. I would spend the rest of my life on my knees before you if that was what it took."

She put her hands on her temples, hardly able to believe what was happening. "Raphael...you never had to do this. This was never what I wanted."

"But it is what must happen. I have been the most unbending, inflexible person, and I realize that. But I have been afraid that if I were to ever bend, I would break completely. And when you left, I did. I shattered. And I have spent the last two weeks trying to figure out what to do with the pieces of myself that you left behind. I have spent the last weeks trying to figure out what all of this means. Why your declarations of love offended me so much. Why I couldn't give them back. Why I had never...why I had never heard them before. Why I had never spoken them."

"Oh, Raphael." It hit her then, just then, that he had never felt chosen, either. That he had been born, and his fate had been set. But no one had ever chosen him.

She was from nothing and nowhere, and he was from a family as old as time, and they shared the same pain. Hers covered with pride and determination, his with arrogance and the insulation provided by his position.

But it was all pain.

"My father told me," he said, his voice breaking, "he told me that a ruler must never love anything more than he loved his country. Day after day he told me this. He told me this every time he had not a moment to spare to say a few words to me. He told me this every time he and my mother were traveling for my birthday. Every time I had dinner by myself. Except for the household staff. And in the place of my parents' presence would always be gifts. Everything a young boy could ever want."

"Gifts meant a lot to you," she said, her voice muted. Suddenly she felt...she felt foolish for not seeing that. For not realizing that for him those things had meant something. "Raphael, I am so sorry I didn't know."

"Of course not. But you see—they had to mean something to me. They were all I had. That and the... edict to always stand strong. My father told me that I couldn't allow love or grief to distract me. Even at my mother's funeral."

She put her hand over her mouth and shook her head. "No. I...how old were you?"

"Fifteen."

"He didn't comfort you or...or anything?"

"He bought me a car."

"To replace your mother?"

He shook his head slowly. "I think he bought me a car because it was...all he could really give. That was what I learned to place importance in. That and the title. The directive that was placed before me. And after he died... I told myself the only thing that mattered was ruling over my country in a way that would make my father proud. Making myself invulnerable so that I could be the best leader that I could be. To me, that's what it meant. And you have to understand that everything you said undermined that. If gifts are truly empty gestures, if things do not compensate for human connection, if arrogance and confidence are not the same as emotion, then I am a hollow, empty person with no connection at all. My father never said that he loved me. But I was able to take those things and create words from them. To fashion sentiments out of them that didn't exist. And you challenged that. From the moment that you first walked into my life."

She swallowed hard. "I'm sure that your father loved you." She wasn't sure. Because she wasn't sure her own mother had loved her. She could hardly speak for his father.

Raphael shook his head, pushing himself to his feet. "I don't think he did. But it doesn't matter to me, not now. That was part of my rock-bottom experience, you understand. I had to lay there on the floor for a while and fully come to terms with that. To accept what you had done to my worldview. To me. I got so angry at you because if what you said was true, then it meant my entire life was so much hollower than I had ever realized. If what you said was true, then I was never truly loved."

"You have an entire country of people who love you."

"Who revere me because of my bloodline. And maybe even love the idea of me. But no person who has ever known me has ever loved me. And, as I said, no one had ever spoken the words to me before you did. I wasn't conscious of the absence of them until you brought them into my life. I wasn't aware that I had never spoken them until you spoke them to me. And it was confronting. Because it demanded something of me that I didn't want to give."

"What's that?" she asked, her voice faint, splintered.

"Humility. To get on my knees and confess to you that I needed those words. That I had been missing them my entire life. Everything in me cried out for a kind of connection that I was always denied. That I needed love. That I needed someone to be close to me. That I was desperately aching for someone to get past all of that arrogance, to love me through it, to want me no matter what. Admitting that—"

"Raphael," she said, closing the space between them and wrapping her arms around him. "I love you. But more than that, I choose you."

His big body heaved, a broken sob escaping his lips. "I love you," he said, the words untested, unfamiliar and beautiful on his lips.

She clung to him. So tight she never wanted to let go. Not because she was afraid he'd disappear, but because they'd spent far too much time not holding each other at all. "I am so honored to be the first person to hear those words from you," she whispered.

"And you won't be the last. I will say them to our son. I will say them every day. I will withhold no good thing from my child. Not now that I've allowed myself to see what really matters. What really lasts. You're right. Everything I've ever put stock in my entire life has been vanity. So easily burned away by the things of the world. But this, this is real. It's deep. It's something that can never be taken away from me. Never be taken away from you. And I... I am so grateful. Because you have given me the one thing on earth that I could never buy. That I could never force someone to give to me simply because of my title. And I think that's why it terrified me so. I knew it was something I had no power within myself to acquire. I knew it was something you would have to choose to give me. Something I could never manipulate out of you. It's why I got so angry every time you asked for me to feel something authentic. To do something other than to simply wave my hand and commit an empty gesture. You asked for real things. For deep things. I knew that in order to achieve that, I would have to allow myself to feel something real."

"I know it hurts," she said, the words choked. "I know it does. I know what it's like to let your hopes shrink smaller and smaller, so that you aim for something you can manage at least, something that you might be able to have. Something that doesn't seem too spectacular."

"I never knew to dream," he said, his voice rough. "I was given all of this and told I had the world. How could I begin to disagree?"

Her chest tightened, and she looked up into his eyes. Haunted. Wounded. That arrogance was gone for now. She felt like she should look away so that she didn't... embarrass him. So that she didn't see him like this. So raw and exposed in a way he never had been before.

She saw it all for what it was now.

His protection. Not just from the world but from the truth that lurked inside him. The fear that he, of all people, may forever want something that he wouldn't be able to have. That his birthright didn't ensure for him.

"I thought..." he began. "I thought that I didn't know need. I thought that I had never needed anything in all my life. But it turns out I am a creature made entirely from need. Who has spent all of his life covering deficiency with a host of things. With possessions and powers, as I told myself that needing was the same as devotion. That deference and worship would somehow fill a hole in my heart." He brushed his thumb over her cheek. "I didn't need. And I didn't dream. Until I met you, Bailey."

He closed his eyes for a moment, and when he opened them again they were bright. "I was furious. Furious that you could show me something about myself I had never before seen."

"A lowly waitress," she said, her tone dry.

"Do not ever say that." He shook his head, his tone fierce. "You made a prince bow down to you—how could you ever be lowly?"

"I like that your standard of greatness relates back to you."

"Naturally."

She smiled then. "I'm pleased to see your arrogance hasn't been destroyed. Only reduced."

"I am still me."

"Yes," she said. "And a good thing, too, because you're the one that I love."

And then he did the impossible one more time and got to his knees in front of her. "I want you to be my wife," he said.

"I already am." Her throat was tight, emotion building in her chest until it was impossible to breathe.

"But this time I am not demanding. This time I'm asking. This time, it is with the understanding that I am not a great gift. Not with my title and my palace. You are the gift, Bailey. You. You have changed me, changed my world."

"After I broke it," she said, a little sob breaking the words.

"It was always going to break. You uncovered the void in me—you didn't create it. And you were the only one who could ever fill it. You're my only dream."

A tear slipped down Bailey's cheek, and she knelt down with Raphael, bringing herself to the ground with him. She bracketed his cheeks with her hands, her heart so full she thought it would burst.

"I never thought a girl like me would dream of a fairy tale. But here you are, my very own Prince Charming. And do you know what the very best thing is?"

"What?" he asked, his voice rough.

She pressed her lips to his as tears slipped down her cheeks. "We're going to live happily ever after."

EPILOGUE

SANTA FIRENZE REJOICED the day their prince and his princess gave birth to their first son. Raphael felt that he got much more credit for it than he deserved, and he was the first to tell everyone so.

If anyone was surprised by the prince's sudden show of humility, they didn't say. Especially as it ran only so deep.

He was still Prince Raphael DeSantis, after all.

When he and Bailey brought their son home, he didn't allow the residents of the palace to bow to him. Instead, they had a party in the newest DeSantis's honor. They had cake of every variety, cake that Bailey heartily approved of since, as she told him, she was completely secure in her husband's heart now.

There was laughter and music, happiness that was perhaps not fitting of a man who would one day join the statues out in the courtyard, but he didn't care. Love was more important than tradition.

The oldest members of staff held the little prince, kissed his forehead. Showed him affection in a way that Raphael had never been allowed to receive.

The sight made him feel like just maybe he would do

right for this child. That just maybe he would be able to care for him in the right ways.

Much later, when he was in the bedroom with Bailey, and she was holding their son close, feeding him at her breast, he was struck with a sudden swift surge of emotion so deep, so intense that he had to go down to the floor so he didn't fall forward.

And that was how the prince, who had been bowed down to from the moment of his birth, and all throughout his life, came to kneel before a waitress. Brought down to his knees by love.

* * * * *

Don't miss the first part of Maisey Yates's
HEIRS BEFORE VOWS *trilogy*
THE SPANIARD'S PREGNANT BRIDE
Available now!

And the trilogy concludes with
THE ITALIAN'S PREGNANT VIRGIN
Available January 2017

'What if we don't convince them?'

'That we are lovers?'

'Yes.' The word came out slightly strangled.

Leo straightened from the table. 'You assured me you could handle it. Are you getting cold feet already, Helena?'

She almost laughed at his choice of expression. Cold? Oh, no. No part of her felt cold right now. Not even close. Not when the prospect of playing lovers with Leo for an entire week had her blood racing so hot and crazy she feared her veins might explode.

He stepped towards her. 'There is one way to ensure we're convincing.'

'Oh?' She tamped down the urge to scurry to the other side of the room. 'How?'

'Drop the pretence.'

Her brain took several seconds to register his meaning. She blinked, a bubble of incredulous laughter climbing her throat. 'You're kidding, right?'

'You find the prospect of sex with me abhorrent?'

The question—so explicit, yet so casually delivered—triggered a fresh wave of heat that burned all the way from her hairline down to the valley between her breasts. Abhorrent? No. Dangerous? Yes. Terrifying? *Utterly*. Though not for any reason she was fool enough to admit.

Irresistible Mediterranean Tycoons

Impossibly arrogant, overwhelmingly sexy…
meet the men you can't say no to!

Gorgeous, powerful and darkly brooding,
Leo Vincenti and Nicolas César have dominated
their fields—not only in their home countries of Italy
and France, but across the globe.

Now it's time for them to turn their unwavering focus
on a different challenge: conquering two defiantly
delectable heroines of their own!

But have these billionaires bitten off
more than they can chew?

Find out in:

Surrendering to the Vengeful Italian
December 2016

Defying Her Billionaire Protector
January 2017

Don't miss this fabulous debut duet by Angela Bissell!

SURRENDERING TO THE VENGEFUL ITALIAN

BY
ANGELA BISSELL

First Published in Great Britain 2016
By Mills & Boon, an imprint of HarperCollins*Publishers*
1 London Bridge Street, London, SE1 9GF

© 2016 Angela Bissell

ISBN: 978-0-263-92142-7

Angela Bissell lives with her husband and one crazy Ragdoll cat in the vibrant harbourside city of Wellington, New Zealand. In her twenties, with a wad of savings and a few meagre possessions, she took off for Europe, backpacking through Egypt, Israel, Turkey and the Greek Islands before finding her way to London, where she settled and worked in a glamorous hotel for several years. Clearly the perfect grounding for her love of Mills & Boon Modern Romance! Visit her at angelabissell.com.

This is Angela's stunning debut for
Mills & Boon Modern Romance—we hope you enjoy it!

Look out for the next part of her
Irresistible Mediterranean Tycoons duet!

Defying Her Billionaire Protector

Available January 2017

For Tony. Because you never stopped believing.
And you never let me quit.
Love you to infinity, Mr B.

And for Mum.
The memories have left you but our love never will.
You are, and always will be, our real-life heroine.

CHAPTER ONE

HELENA SHAW HAD been sitting in the elegant marble foyer for the best part of two hours when the man she had trekked halfway across London to see finally strode into the exclusive Mayfair hotel.

She had almost given up. After all the effort she had devoted to tracking him down, she had almost lost her nerve. Had almost let cowardice—and the voice in her head crying *insanity*—drive her out of the plush upholstered chair and back into the blessed obscurity of the crowded rush-hour streets.

But she had not fled. She had sat and waited—and waited some more.

And now he was here.

Her stomach dropped, weightless for a moment as though she had stepped from a great height into nothingness, and then the fluttering started—a violent sensation that made her belly feel like a cage full of canaries into which a half-starved tomcat had been loosed.

Breathe, she instructed herself, and watched him stride across the foyer, tall and dark and striking in a charcoal-grey two-piece that screamed *power suit* even without the requisite tie around his bronzed throat.

Women stared.

Men stepped out of his way.

And he ignored them all, his big body moving with an air of intent until, for one heart-stopping moment, his footsteps slowed on the polished marble and he half turned in her direction, eyes narrowed under a sharp frown as he surveyed the hotel's expansive interior.

Helena froze. Shrouded in shadows cast by soft lighting and half hidden behind a giant spray of exotic honey-scented blooms, she was certain he couldn't see her, yet for one crazy moment she had the unnerving impression he could somehow sense her scrutiny. Her very presence. As if, after all these years, they were still tethered by an invisible thread of awareness.

A crack of thunder, courtesy of the storm the weathermen had been promising Londoners since yesterday, made Helena jump. She blinked, pulled in a sharp breath and let the air out with a derisive hiss. She had no connection with this man. Whatever bond had existed between them was long gone, destroyed by her father and buried for ever in the ashes of bitterness and hurt.

A hurt Leonardo Vincenti would soon revisit on her family if she failed to stop him seizing her father's company.

She grabbed her handbag and stood, her pulse picking up speed as she wondered if he would see her. But he had already resumed his long strides towards the bank of elevators. She hurried after him, craning her neck to keep his dark head and broad shoulders in her line of sight. Not that she'd easily lose him in a crowd. He stood out from the pack—that much hadn't changed—though he seemed even taller than she remembered, darker somehow, the aura he projected now one of command and power.

Her stomach muscles wound a little tighter.

Europe's business commentators had dubbed him the success of the decade: an entrepreneurial genius who'd turned a software start-up into a multi-million-dollar enterprise in less than ten years and earned a coveted spot on the rich list. The more reputable media sources called him single-minded and driven. Others dished up less flattering labels like hard-nosed and cut-throat.

Words that reminded Helena too much of her father. Yet even *hard-nosed* and *cut-throat* seemed too mild, too charitable, for a man like Douglas Shaw.

She shouldered her bag, clutched the strap over her chest.

Her father was a formidable man, but if the word *regret* existed in his vocabulary he must surely rue the day he'd aimed his crosshairs at Leonardo Vincenti. Now the young Italian he'd once decreed unsuitable for his daughter was back, seven years older, considerably wealthier and, by all accounts, still mad as hell at the man who'd run him out of town.

He stopped, pushed the button for an elevator and shoved his hands in his trouser pockets. Behind him, Helena hovered so close she could see the fine weave in the fabric of his jacket, the individual strands of black hair curling above his collar.

She sucked in a deep breath. 'Leo.'

He turned, his dark brows rising into an arch of enquiry that froze along with the rest of his face the instant their gazes collided. His hands jerked out of his pockets. His brows plunged back down.

'What the hell…?'

Those three words, issued in a low, guttural growl, raised the tiny hairs on her forearms and across her nape. *He'd recognised her, then.*

She tilted her head back. In her modest two-inch heels she stood almost five foot ten, but still she had to hike her chin to lock her gaze with his.

And oh, sweet mercy, what a gaze it was.

Dark. Hard. Glittering. Like polished obsidian and just as impenetrable. How had she forgotten the mind-numbing effect those midnight eyes could have on her?

Concentrate.

'I'd like to talk,' she said.

A muscle moved in his jaw, flexing twice before he spoke. 'You do not own a phone?'

'Would you have taken my call?

He met her challenge with a smile—if the tight, humourless twist of his lips could be called a smile. 'Probably not. But then you and I have nothing to discuss. On the phone *or* in person.'

An elevator pinged and opened behind him. He inclined his head in a gesture she might have construed as polite if not for the arctic chill in his eyes.

'I am sorry you have wasted your time.' And with that he swung away and stepped into the elevator.

Helena hesitated, then quickly rallied and dashed in after him. 'You've turned up after seven years of silence and come after my father's company. I hardly think that qualifies as *nothing*.'

'Get out of the elevator, Helena.'

The soft warning made the skin across her scalp prickle. Or maybe it was hearing her name spoken in that deep, accented baritone that drove a wave of discomforting heat through her?

The elevator doors whispered closed, cocooning them in a space that felt too small and intimate despite the effect of mirrors on three walls.

She planted her feet. 'No.'

Colour slashed his cheekbones and his dark eyes locked with hers in a staring match that quickly tested the limits of her bravado. Just as she feared that lethal gaze would reduce her to a pile of cinders, he reached into the breast pocket of his jacket and pulled out an access card.

'As you wish,' he said, his tone mild—*too mild*, a voice warned. He flashed the card across a sensor and jabbed the button labelled 'Penthouse Suite'. With a soft whir, the elevator began its stomach-dropping ascent.

Helena groped for the steel handrail behind her, the rapid rising motion—or maybe the butterflies in her belly she couldn't quell—making her head swim.

It seemed her ex-lover could not only afford the finest digs in London…he could afford to stay in the hotel's most exclusive suite.

The knowledge made her heart beat faster.

The Leo she'd known had been a man of understated tastes, stylish in that effortless way of most Italian men but never flashy or overt. She'd liked that about him. Liked his grit and drive and passion. Liked that he was different from the lazy, spoilt rich set her parents wanted her to run with.

And now…?

Her hand tightened on the railing. Now it didn't matter what she felt about him. All that mattered was the havoc he'd soon unleash on her family. If he and her father went head to head in a corporate war and Douglas Shaw lost control of his precious empire the fallout for his wife and son would be dire. Her father didn't take kindly to losing; when he did, those closest to him suffered.

'Has your father sent you?' The way he ground out the word *father* conveyed a wealth of hatred—a sentiment Helena, too, wrestled with when it came to Daddy Dearest.

She studied Leo's face, leaner now, his features sharper, more angular than she remembered, but still incredibly handsome. Her fingers twitched with the memory of tracing those features while he slept, of familiarising herself with that long, proud nose and strong jaw, those sculpted male lips. Lips that once could have stopped her heart with a simple smile—or a kiss.

Emotion rose and swirled, unexpected, a poignant mix of regret and longing that made her chest ache and her breath hitch.

Did Leo smile much these days? Or did those lines either side of his mouth stem from harsher emotions like anger and hatred?

Instinctively Helena's hand went to her stomach. The void inside where life had once flourished was a stark reminder that she, too, had suffered. Leo, at least, had been spared that pain, and no good would come now of sharing hers.

Some burdens, she had decided, were better borne alone. She let her hand fall back to her side.

'I'm not my father's puppet, Leo. Whatever your misguided opinion of me.'

A harsh sound shot from his throat. 'The only one misguided is you, Helena. What part of "I never wish to see you again" did you not understand?'

She smothered the flash of hurt his words evoked. 'That was a long time ago. And I only want an opportunity to talk. Is that asking too much?'

A soft ping signalled the elevator's arrival. Before he could answer with a resounding *yes*, she stepped through the parting doors into a spacious vestibule. She stopped, the sensible heels of her court shoes sinking into thick carpet the colour of rich chocolate. Before her loomed an enormous set of double doors. It was private up here, she realised. Secluded. *Isolated.*

Her mouth went dry. 'Perhaps we should talk in the bar downstairs?'

He brushed past her and pushed open the heavy doors, his lips twisting into a tight smile that only made her heart pound harder.

'Afraid to be alone with me?'

Helena paused on the threshold. *Should* she be afraid of him? In spite of her jitters she balked at the idea. Leonardo Vincenti wasn't thrilled to see her—that was painfully clear—but she knew this man. Had spent time with him. Been intimate with him in ways that marked her soul like no other man ever had.

Yes, she could sense the anger vibrating beneath his cloak of civility, but he would never lose control and lash out at her. He would never hurt her the way her father hurt her mother.

She smoothed her palm down the leg of her black trouser suit and assumed a lofty air. 'Don't be ridiculous,' she said, and strode into the room.

Leo closed the penthouse doors, strode to the wet bar and splashed a large measure of whisky into a crystal tumbler. He knocked back the potent liquid, snapped the empty glass onto the bar and looked at the woman whose presence was like a blowtorch to his veneer of calm.

'Drink?'

'No.' She reinforced her refusal with a shake of her head that made her auburn curls bounce and sway. 'But… thank you.'

Shorter, he noted. Her hair was shorter, the dark silky ribbons that had once tumbled to her waist now cropped into a sophisticated cut above her shoulders. Her face, too, had changed—thinner like her body and more striking somehow, her cheekbones strong and elegant, her jaw line firm. Bluish crescents underscored her eyes, but the rest of her skin was toned and smooth and free of imperfections. It was a face no man, unless blind, would pass by without stopping for a second appreciative look.

Helena Shaw, he reluctantly acknowledged, was no longer a pretty girl. Helena Shaw was a stunningly attractive woman.

Scowling, he reminded himself he had no interest in this woman's attributes, physical or otherwise. He'd been blindsided by her beauty and guise of innocence once before—a grave error that had cost him infinitely more than his injured pride—and he'd vowed his mistake would not be repeated.

Not with any woman.

And especially not this one.

'So, you want to talk.' The *last* thing he wanted to do with this woman. *Dio.* He should have bodily removed her from the elevator downstairs and to hell with causing a scene. He banked the flare of anger in his gut and gestured towards a duo of deep leather sofas. 'Sit,' he instructed, then glanced at his watch. 'You have ten minutes.'

She frowned—a delicate pinch of that smooth brow—then put her bag on the glass coffee table and perched on the edge of a sofa. She drew an audible breath.

'The papers say you've launched a hostile takeover bid for my father's company.'

He dropped onto the opposite sofa. 'An accurate summary.' He paused. 'And…?'

She puffed out a sigh. 'You're not going to make this easy for me, are you?'

Easy? That simple four-letter word made him grind his molars. This girl's entire life had been easy. Her family's excessive wealth, her father's connections, had ensured she wanted for nothing. Unlike Leo and his sister who, after their mother's death, had survived childhood in a murky world of poverty and neglect. For them, nothing came easy.

'You want me to make this easy for you?'

Like hell he would.

She shook her head. 'I want to understand why you're doing this.'

So she could talk him out of it? Not a chance. He'd waited too many years to settle this score with her father. He returned her gaze for an extended beat. 'It's business.'

She laughed then: a short brittle sound, not the soft, sexy laughter that resided in his memory. 'Please—this isn't business. It's…payback.'

Her voice conveniently wobbled on that last word, but her ploy for sympathy, if that was her angle, failed to move him.

'And if I said this *is* payback, what would you say?'

'I'd say two wrongs don't make a right.'

He barked out a laugh. 'A quaint sentiment. Personally, I think "an eye for an eye" has a more appealing ring.'

She dropped her gaze to where her fingers fidgeted in her lap. Her voice was husky when she spoke again. 'People aren't perfect, Leo. Sometimes they make mistakes.'

His gut twisted. Was she talking about her father? Or herself? 'So you're here to apologise for your mistakes?'

She glanced up. 'I tried that once. You didn't want to listen. Would it make any difference now?'

'No.'

'I was trying to protect you.'

He bit back another laugh. By driving a blade through his heart? Leaving him no choice but to watch her walk away? A bitter lump rose in his throat and he swallowed back the acrid taste.

Seven years ago he'd come to London to collaborate with a young software whiz on a project that, if successful, would have guaranteed his business unprecedented success.

As always, he was focused, dedicated, disciplined.

And then he met a girl.

A girl so beautiful, so captivating, she might have been one of the sculptures on display at the art gallery opening they were both attending in the West End.

He tried to resist, of course. She was too young for him, too inexperienced. Too distracting when he should be focused on work.

But he was weak and temptation won out. And he fell—faster than he'd ever thought possible—for a girl who, five weeks later, tossed him aside as if he were a tiresome toy she no longer wanted or needed.

He curled his lip. 'Remind me not to come looking for you if I ever need protection.'

She had the good grace to squirm. 'I had no choice. You don't understand—'

'Then explain it to me.' Anger snapped in his gut, making him fight to stay calm. 'Explain why you walked away from our relationship instead of telling me the truth. Explain why you never bothered to mention that your father disapproved of us. Explain why, if ditching me was your idea of *protection*, I spent the next forty-eight hours watching every investor I'd painstakingly courted pull their backing from my project.'

He curled his fingers into his palms, tension arcing through his muscles. Douglas Shaw had dealt Leo's business a significant blow, yet his own losses had barely registered in comparison to the impact on his younger sister. Marietta's life, his hopes and dreams for her future, had suffered a setback the likes of which Helena could never appreciate.

Sorry didn't cut it.

'Perhaps you wanted an easy out all along—'

'No.'

'And Daddy simply gave you the perfect excuse.'

'No!'

There was more vehemence behind that second denial than he'd expected. She threw him a wounded look and he shifted slightly, an unexpected stab of remorse lancing through him. *Hell.* This was precisely why he'd had no desire to see her. Business demanded a cool head, a razor-sharp mind at all times. Distractions like the beautiful long-legged one sitting opposite him he could do without.

A lightning flash snapped his gaze towards the private terrace overlooking Hyde Park and the exclusive properties of Knightsbridge beyond. His right leg twitched with an urge to rise and test the French doors, check they were secure. He didn't fear nature's storms—on occasion could appreciate their power—but he didn't like them either.

Didn't like the ghosts they stirred from his childhood.

A burst of heavy rain lashed the glass, drowning out the city sounds far below. Distorting his view of the night. He waited for the rumble of thunder to pass, then turned his attention from the storm. 'How much has your father told you about the takeover?'

'Nothing. I only know what I've read in the papers.'

Another lie, probably. He let it slide. 'Then you are missing one important detail.'

Her fidgeting stilled. 'Which is…?'

'The word "successful". In fact…' He hooked back his shirt-cuff and consulted his watch. 'As of two hours and forty-five minutes ago my company is the official registered owner of seventy-five percent of ShawCorp.' He offered her a bland smile. 'Which means I am now the controlling shareholder of your father's company.'

He watched dispassionately as the colour receded from her cheeks, leaving her flawless skin as white as the thick-pile rug at her feet. She pressed her palm to her forehead, her upper body swaying slightly, and closed her eyes.

A little theatrical, he thought, the muscles around his mouth twitching. He shifted forward, planted his elbows on his knees. 'You look a touch pale, Helena. Would you like that drink now? A glass of water, perhaps. Some aspirin?'

Her lids snapped up and a spark of something—anger?—leapt in her eyes, causing them to shimmer at him like a pair of brilliant sapphires.

Leo sucked in his breath. The years might have wrought subtle differences in her face and figure, but those eyes... those eyes had not changed. They were still beautiful. Still captivating.

Still dangerous.

Eyes, he reminded himself, that could strip a man of his senses.

They glittered at him as she raised her chin.

'Water, please.' She gave him a tight smile. 'You can hold the aspirin.'

Helena reached for the glass Leo had placed on the table in front of her and sipped, focusing on the cold tickle of the carbonated water on her tongue and throat and nothing else. She would not faint. Not in front of this man. Shock on top of an empty stomach had left her woozy, that was all. She simply needed a moment to compose herself.

After a third careful sip she put the glass down and folded her hands in her lap. She mustn't reveal her turmoil. Mustn't show any hint of anxiety as her mind darted from one nauseating scenario to the next. Had her father hit the bottle in the wake of this news? Was her mother playing the devoted wife, trying to console him? And how long before the lethal combination of rage and drink turned him from man to monster? To a vile bully who could lavish his wife with expensive trinkets and luxuries one minute and victimise her the next?

Helena's insides trembled, but it wasn't only worry for her mother making her belly quiver. Making her pulse-rate kick up a notch. It was an acute awareness of the man sitting opposite. An unsettling realisation that, no matter how many days, weeks or years came between them, she would never be immune to this tall, breathtaking Italian. She would never look at him and not feel her blood surge. Her lungs seize. Her belly tighten.

No. Time had *not* rendered her immune to his particular potent brand of masculinity. But she would not let her body betray her awareness of him. If her father's endless criticisms and lack of compassion had taught her anything as a child it was never to appear weak.

She laced her fingers to keep them from fidgeting. 'What are your plans for my father's company?'

A muscle in his jaw bunched and released. Bunched again. He lounged back, stretched out his long legs, draped one arm across the top of the sofa. 'I haven't yet decided.'

She fought the urge to scowl. 'But you must have some idea.'

'Of course. Many, in fact. All of which I'll discuss with your father, once he overcomes his aversion to meeting with me.' He paused. 'Perhaps he's hoping his daughter will offer his new shareholder some...incentive to play nice?'

Heat rushed her cheeks, much to her annoyance. 'I don't know what you mean.'

'Oh, come now. There's no need to play the innocent for me.'

Leo's hand moved absently over the back of the sofa, his fingers stroking the soft black leather in slow, rhythmic patterns. Helena stared, transfixed, then hastily averted her eyes. Those long, tanned fingers had once stroked her flesh in a strikingly similar fashion, unleashing in her a passion no man had unleashed before or since.

She pulled in a breath, tried to focus on his voice.

'You needn't look so worried, Helena. You won't have to dirty your hands with the likes of me again.' His fingers stilled. 'I have no interest in anything you could offer.'

As though emphasising his point, his gaze travelled her length, from the summit of her blushing hairline to the tips of her inexpensive shoes. 'As for the company,' he went on, before she could muster an indignant response, 'if your father continues to decline my invitations to meet, my board will vote to sell off the company's subsidiaries and amalgamate the core business with my own. A merger will mean layoffs, of course, but your father's people will find I'm not an unreasonable man. Those without jobs can expect a fair severance settlement.'

Her jaw slackened. 'Dismantle the company?' The one thing guaranteed to bring her father to his knees. 'You would tear down everything my father has worked his entire life to build?'

He shrugged. 'As a minority shareholder he'll benefit financially from any asset sales. He'll lose his position at the head of the company, of course, but then your father's no longer a man in his prime. Perhaps he'll welcome the opportunity to retire?'

She shook her head. For Douglas Shaw it wasn't about the money. Or retirement. It was about pride and respect and status. About winning. *Control.*

'You don't understand.' Her voice trembled. 'This won't hurt only my father. It will hurt others, too—my family. Is that what you want, Leo? To see innocent people suffer?'

His eyes narrowed, his gaze hardening under his dark slanted brows. 'Do not talk to *me* about suffering. You and your family don't know the first meaning of the word.'

Not true! she wanted to shout, but she held her tongue. Another habit deeply ingrained from childhood, when she'd been taught to avoid such indiscretions—to lie, if necessary, about her less than perfect home life.

She stifled a frustrated sigh.

Why did people think growing up with money meant a life filled with sunshine and roses? That might have been the case for some of her friends, but for Helena it had been nothing more than a grand, sugar-coated illusion. An illusion her mother, the ever-dutiful society wife, still chose to hide behind.

Leo lunged his powerful shoulders forward, planted both feet firmly on the floor. 'This is business. Your father knows that. Better than most.'

He rose to his full impressive height: six feet four inches of lean, muscled Italian.

'I could have made things much worse for him. You might remind him of that fact.'

For a moment Helena considered telling him the truth—that she'd not seen or spoken with her father in years. That she worked as a secretary and lived in a rundown flat in North London and visited her family only when her father was absent on business. That Douglas Shaw was a domineering bully and she didn't care a jot for the man, but she did care for those who would suffer most from his downfall. That she held no sway with her father and could offer Leo nothing in return for leniency except her eternal gratitude.

But caution stopped her. The man who stood before her now was not the Leo she'd once known. He was a tough, shrewd businessman, bent on revenge, and he would use every weapon in his arsenal to achieve it. Knowledge was power, and he had plenty of that without her gifting him extra ammunition.

Besides, he'd already accused her of lying—why should he believe the truth?

She unlaced her hands and stood.

'There must be other options,' she blurted. 'Other possibilities that would satisfy your board and keep the company intact?'

'My board will make their decisions based on the best

interests of my business. Not your father's interests and not his family's.' He looked at his watch. 'Now, if you have nothing else to discuss, there are more important matters requiring my attention.'

She stared at him.

More important matters?

A bitter laugh rose and died in her throat.

Really, what had she expected? Understanding? Forgiveness? A friendly chat over a cup of tea?

Humiliation raged through her. She was a fool, wasting her time on a fool's errand. She snatched up her handbag. 'Next time you look in the mirror, Leo, remind yourself why you despise my father so much.' She returned his stony stare. 'Then take a hard look at your reflection. Because you might just find you have more in common with him than you think.'

His head snapped back, an indication that she'd hit her mark, but the knowledge did nothing to ease the pain knifing through her chest. Head high, she strode to the door.

The handle was only inches from her grasp when a large hand closed on her upper arm, swinging her around. She let out a yelp of surprise.

'I am *nothing* like your father,' he said, his jaw thrusting belligerently.

'Then prove it,' she fired back, conscious all at once of his vice-like grip, the arrows of heat penetrating her thin jacket-sleeve, the faint, woodsy tang of an expensive cologne that made her nostrils flare involuntarily. 'Give my father time to come to the table. Before your board makes any decisions.'

Leo released her, stepped back, and the tiny spark of hope in her chest fizzed like a dampened wick. God. She needed to get out. *Now.* Before she did something pathetic and weak—like cry. She pivoted and seized the door handle. At the same instant his palm landed on the door above her head, barring her escape.

'On one condition.'

His voice at her back was low, laced with something she couldn't decipher. She turned, pressed her back to the door and looked up. 'Yes?'

'Have dinner with me.'

She blinked, twice. Three times.

'Dinner?' she echoed stupidly.

'*Si.*' His hand dropped from the door. 'Tomorrow night.'

Her stomach did a funny little somersault. Was he fooling with her now? She narrowed her eyes at him. 'Is that an invitation or a demand?'

The shrug he gave was at once casual and arrogant. 'Call it what you like. That is my condition.'

'Tomorrow's Friday,' she said, as if that fact bore some vital significance. In truth, it was all she could think to say while her brain grappled with his proposition.

His nostrils flared. 'You have other plans?'

'Uh...no.' *Brilliant.* Now he'd think she had no social life. She levelled her shoulders. 'A minute ago you couldn't wait to get rid of me. Now you want us to have dinner?'

His lips pressed into a thin line. Impatience? Or, like most men, did he simply dislike having his motives questioned?

He jammed his hands in his trouser pockets. 'You wanted an opportunity to talk, Helena. Take it or leave it. It is my final offer. I return to Rome on Saturday.'

Helena hesitated, her mind spinning. This could be her one and only chance for a calm, rational conversation with him. An opportunity to appeal to his sense of reason and compassion—if either still existed. The takeover was beyond her control and, if he spoke the truth, a *fait accompli*, but if she had even a slim chance of dissuading him from stripping the company's assets, convincing him to settle on a strategy more palatable to her father, she had to take it. Had to try, no matter how daunting the prospect.

She nodded. 'All right. Dinner. Tomorrow night. Where shall I meet you?'

'I will send a car.'

Her stomach nose-dived. The thought of Leo or anyone in his employ seeing where she lived mortified her. Her neighbourhood was the best she could afford right now, but the area was far from salubrious.

She fished in her handbag for pen and paper, jotted down her work address and her mobile number. 'You can pick me up from here.' She handed him the slip of paper. 'And my number's there if you need to contact me.'

'Very well.' With scarcely a glance at it, he slipped the note into his trouser pocket and pulled open the door. 'Be ready for six-thirty.'

With a nod, she stepped into the vestibule and pressed the elevator call button, having briefly considered then dismissed the stairs.

She would *not* bolt like an intimidated child.

The man who'd stolen her heart and left behind a precious gift she'd treasured and lost might be gone, the stranger in his place more formidable than she'd imagined, but she would *not* be cowed.

Ignoring the compulsion to glance over her shoulder, she willed the elevator to hurry up and arrive. When it did, her knees almost buckled with relief. She started forward.

'Helena.'

Leo's voice snapped her to an involuntary halt. Without turning, she braced her arm against the elevator's door jamb and tilted her head fractionally. 'Yes?'

Silence yawned behind her, turning the air so thick it felt like treacle in her lungs.

'Wear something dressy,' he said at last.

And then he shut the door.

CHAPTER TWO

LEO PICKED UP the half-empty water glass and studied the smudge of pink on its rim. *Had Douglas Shaw sent his daughter as a honey trap?* The idea was abhorrent, yet he wouldn't put it past the man. What Shaw lacked in scruples he more than made up for with sheer, bloody-minded gall.

He crossed to the bar, tossed out the water and shoved the glass out of sight along with the whisky bottle. Then he smashed his palms down on the counter and let out a curse.

He should have let her go. Should have let her walk out of here and slammed the door—physically and figuratively—on their brief, discomfiting reunion.

But standing there watching her strut away, after she'd stared him down with those cool sapphire eyes and likened him to her father; seeing the haughty defiance in every provocative line of her body...

Something inside him had snapped and he was twenty-five again, standing in a different room in a different hotel. Watching the girl who'd carved out a piece of his heart turn her back and walk out of his life.

Bitterness coated his mouth. He opened the bar fridge, reached past a black-labelled bottle of Dom Perignon and a selection of fine wines and beers and grabbed a can of soda.

At twenty-five he'd considered himself a good judge of character—a skill honed during his teens, when looking out for his sister, taking on the role of parent during their father's drink-fuelled absences, meant learning who he could trust and who he couldn't. Over the years he developed strong instincts, avoided his father's mistakes and weaknesses, but Helena remained his one glaring failure. For the first and last time in his life he'd let his feelings for a woman cloud his judgement.

He would not make the same mistake twice.

Just as he would not be swayed from his purpose.

Douglas Shaw was a bully who thought nothing of destroying people's lives and he deserved a lesson in humility. Leo didn't trust the man and he didn't trust his daughter.

He drained the soda and crumpled the can in his fist.

Shaw wanted to play games? Leo was ready. He'd been ready for seven years. And if the man chose to use his daughter as a pawn, so be it. Two could play at that game.

He threw the can in the wastebin, a slow smile curving his lips.

Si. This might be fun.

'Go home, Helena.'

Helena looked up from the papers on her desk. Her boss stood holding his briefcase, his suit jacket folded over one arm, a look of mock severity on his face. It was after six on Friday and their floor of the corporate bank was largely deserted.

'I'm leaving soon,' she assured him. 'I'm meeting someone at six-thirty.'

David gave an approving nod. 'Good. Enjoy your weekend.'

He started off, but paused after a step and turned back. 'Have you thought any more about taking some leave?' he said. 'HR is on the use-it-or-lose-it warpath again. And if you don't mind me saying…' he paused, his grey eyes intent '…you look like you could do with a break.'

She smiled, deflecting his concern. David might be one of the bank's longest-serving executives and knocking sixty, but the man rarely missed a beat. He was sharp, observant, and he cared about his staff.

She made a mental note to apply more concealer beneath

her eyes. 'I'm fine. It's been a long week. And the rain kept me awake last night.'

Partly true.

'Well, think about it. See you Monday.'

'Goodnight, David.'

She watched him go, then glanced at her watch.

She had to move.

The car Leo was sending was due in less than twenty minutes, and earning a black mark for running late was not the way she wanted to start the evening.

Shutting herself in David's office, she whipped off her trouser suit and slipped on the little black dress she'd pulled from the bowels of her wardrobe that morning, then turned to the full-length mirror on the back of the door and scanned her appearance.

She frowned at her cleavage.

Good grief.

Had the dress always been so revealing?

She couldn't remember—but then neither could she recall the last time she'd worn it. She seldom dressed up these days, even on the rare occasions she dated. She tugged the bodice up, yanked the sides of the V-neck together and grimaced at the marginal improvement.

It would have to do.

There was no time for a wardrobe-change—and besides, this was the dressiest thing she owned. She'd sold the last of her designer gowns years ago, when she'd had to stump up a deposit and a month's advance rent on her flat. Keeping the black dress had been a practical decision, though she could count on one hand the number of times it had ventured from her wardrobe.

She turned side-on to the mirror.

The dress hugged her from shoulder to mid-thigh, accentuating every dip and curve—including the gentle swell of her tummy. Holding her breath, she pulled in her stomach and smoothed her hand over the bump that no number of sit-ups and crunches could flatten.

Not that she resented the changes pregnancy had wrought on her body. They were a bittersweet reminder of joy and loss. Of lessons learnt and mistakes she would never make again.

She snatched her hand down and released her breath. Tonight she needed to focus on the present, not the past, and for that she would need every ounce of wit she could muster.

Outside the bank a sleek silver Mercedes waited in a 'No Parking' zone, its uniformed driver standing on the pavement. 'Ms Shaw?' he enquired, then opened a rear door so she could climb in.

Minutes later the car was slicing through London's chaotic evening traffic, the endless layers of city noise muted by tinted windows that transformed the plush, leather-lined interior into a private mini-oasis. Like the luxury suite at the hotel, the car's sumptuous interior epitomised the kind of lifestyle Helena had grown unused to in recent years—unlike her mother, who still enjoyed the baubles of wealth and couldn't understand her daughter's wish to live a modest life, independent of her family's money and influence.

She dropped her head back against the soft leather.

She loved her mother. Miriam Shaw was a classic blonde beauty who had moulded herself into the perfect society wife, but she was neither stupid nor selfish. She loved her children. Had raised them with all the luxuries her own upbringing in an overcrowded foster home had denied her. And when they'd been packed off to boarding school, at her husband's insistence, she'd filled her days by giving time and support to a long list of charities and fundraisers.

Yet where her husband was concerned Miriam was inexplicably weak. Too quick to forgive and too ready to offer excuses.

Like today, when she'd called to cancel their prearranged

lunch date. A migraine, she'd claimed, but Helena knew better. Knew her mother's excuse was nothing more than a flimsy veil for the truth, as ineffectual and see-through as the make-up she would use to try to hide the bruises.

Denial.

Her mother's greatest skill. Her greatest weakness. The impregnable wall Helena slammed into any time she dared to suggest that Miriam consider leaving her husband.

A burning sensation crawled from Helena's stomach into her throat—the same anger and despair she always felt when confronted by the grim reality of her parents' marriage.

She massaged the bridge of her nose. Over the years she'd read everything she could on domestic abuse, trying to understand why her mother stayed. Why she put up with the drinking, the vitriol, the occasional black eye. Invariably, when the latter occurred, a peace offering would ensue—usually some priceless piece of jewellery—and then Miriam would pretend everything was fine.

Until the next time.

Helena had seen it more times than she cared to count, but now the stakes were higher. Now her father stood to lose everything he held dear: his company, his reputation, his pride.

If Leo got his way the ShawCorp empire would be carved up like twigs beneath a chainsaw, and Helena had no doubt that if—*when*—her father went down, he would take her mother with him.

'Miss Shaw?'

She jolted out of her thoughts. The car had stopped in front of Leo's hotel and a young man in a porter's uniform had opened her door. Lanky and fresh-faced, he reminded Helena of her brother, prompting a silent prayer of gratitude that James was in boarding school, well away from all this ugly drama.

She slid out and the porter escorted her through the hotel

to a grand reception room with a high vaulted ceiling and decorative walls. The room was crowded, filled with tray-laden waiters and dozens of patrons in tailored tuxedos and long, elegant evening gowns.

'Have a good evening, miss.'

The young man turned to leave.

'Wait!' She clasped his arm, confusion descending. 'I think there's been some mistake.'

He shook his head, his smile polite. 'No mistake, miss. Mr Vincenti asked that you be brought here.'

Leo stood at the edge of the milling crowd, his gaze bouncing off one brunette after another until he spied the one he wanted, standing next to a wide marble pillar just inside the entrance. Weaving waiters, clusters of glittering guests and some twenty feet of floor space separated them, but still he saw the flicker of uncertainty in her eyes. The twin furrows of consternation marring her brow.

Satisfaction stirred. Last night the element of surprise had been hers. How would the minx cope when the tables were turned?

He lifted two champagne flutes from a passing silver tray and carved a path to her side.

'*Buona sera*, Helena.'

She spun, her startled gaze landing on the flutes in his hands, then the bow tie at his throat, before narrowed eyes snapped to his.

'*This* is dinner?'

Score.

He smiled. 'You look very…elegant.'

The look she gave him might have sliced a lesser man in half. 'I look underdressed.'

She smoothed an invisible wrinkle from the front of her short and exquisitely low-cut black dress.

'The other women are wearing ball gowns.'

'Your dress is fine,' he said—an understatement if ever

he'd uttered one. The dress wasn't fine. It was stunning. No eye-catching bling or fancy designer frills, but its simple lines showcased her lithe curves and long, toned legs better than any overblown creation could.

She stole his breath. As easily as she'd stolen his breath the first night he'd laid eyes on her. Her dress that night, however, aside from being a daring purple instead of black, had been less revealing, more…demure. By comparison, tonight's figure-hugging sheath was sultry, seductive, the tantalising flash of ivory breasts inside that V of black fabric enough to tempt any man into secret, lustful imaginings.

'It's a plain cocktail dress,' she said, fretting over her appearance as only a woman could. 'Not a gown for an event like this.' She pressed a hand to the neat chignon at her nape. 'And you're sidestepping the question.'

He extended a champagne flute, which she ignored. 'This—' he gestured with the glass at their lavish surroundings '—is not to your liking?'

'A charity dinner with five hundred other guests? No.'

He feigned surprise. 'You don't like charity?'

She glanced at a wall banner promoting the largest spinal injury association in Europe and its twentieth annual fundraiser. 'Of course I do.' Her eyebrows knitted. 'But I thought we'd be dining in a restaurant. Or at least somewhere…I don't know…a little more…'

'Intimate?'

Her eyes flashed. 'Private.'

'There's a difference?'

She glared at the flute in his hand, then took it from him. 'Do you make a habit of attending charity dinners at the hotels where you stay?'

'*Si.* When I'm invited to support a worthy cause.' He watched her eyebrows arch. 'There are better ways to spend an evening, admittedly, but this event has been a longstanding commitment in my diary. And it coincides with my need to do business in London.'

'Ah, well...' She paused and sipped her champagne. 'That's convenient for you. You get to mark off your social calendar *and* wreak revenge on my family—all in a week's work.' Her mouth curled into a little smile. 'There's nothing more satisfying than killing two birds with one stone. How eminently sensible for a busy man such as yourself.'

Leo tasted his bubbles, took his time considering his next words. Exert enough pressure, he mused, and a person's true colours would eventually surface. 'Revenge is a very strong word,' he said mildly.

Her eyes widened. 'Oh, I'm sorry. Do you have a different name for what you're doing?' She raised her palm. 'No, wait. I remember—"an eye for an eye", wasn't it?'

He studied the churlish set of her mouth, the dainty jut of her chin. 'I had not remembered your tongue being so sharp, Helena.'

Twin spots of colour bloomed on her cheekbones, but the glint of battle stayed in her eyes. 'This is retaliation for last night, isn't it? I turned up unannounced at the hotel and you didn't like it. Now you get to spring the surprise.' She raised her glass in a mock toast. 'Well-played, Leo. So... what now? You parade me on your arm at some high-profile fundraiser and hope it gets back to my father?'

He smiled—which only irritated her further if the flattening of her mouth was any indication. Her gaze darted towards the exit and the idea that she might bolt swiftly curbed his amusement.

Helena would *not* run from him.

Not this time.

Not until he was good and ready to let her go.

'Thinking of reneging on our deal?'

Her gaze narrowed. 'How do I know you'll keep your side of the bargain?'

'I've already spoken with your father's solicitor.'

'And?

'He has until Tuesday to get your father to the table.'

Her mouth fell open. 'My God...that's four days from now. Can you not give him longer?'

'Time is a commodity in business, not a luxury.' He didn't add that the solicitor's chance of success was slim, no matter the time allowed. Both men knew the invitation would be rejected. A great pity, in Leo's mind. He'd hoped to see for himself the look on Douglas Shaw's face when the man learnt the fate of his company. But Shaw's repeated refusals to turn up had denied Leo the final spoils of victory.

'He won't show.'

Her voice was so small he wasn't sure he'd heard correctly. '*Scusi*?'

'My father. He won't show. He won't meet with you, will he?'

He schooled his expression. Had she divined his thoughts? *Absurd*. He shook off the notion. 'You tell me. He's *your* father.'

'Leo, I haven't—'

'Leonardo!'

Leo heard his name boomed at the same time as Helena stopped talking and darted a startled look over his shoulder. He turned and saw a lanky, sandy-haired man striding forward with a petite blonde by his side.

Leo grinned. 'Hans.' He gripped the man's outstretched hand. 'I didn't know you'd be here. How are you? And Sabine.' He raised the woman's slender hand, planted a kiss on her knuckles. 'Beautiful, as always.'

She issued a throaty laugh. 'And you, my dear, are still the charmer.' Rising on tiptoes, she kissed him on both cheeks, then turned her sparkling eyes on Helena. 'Please, introduce us to your lovely companion.'

Leo shifted his weight, fielded a sidelong glance from Helena and sliced her a warning look. *Do not embarrass me.*

'Helena, this is Dr Hans Hetterich and his wife, Sabine. Hans, when he is not winning golf tournaments or sailing a yacht on the high seas, is one of the most prominent spinal surgeons in the world.'

'Nice to meet you, Helena.' Hans took her hand. 'And please pay my friend no attention. I am not nearly as impressive as he makes me sound.'

An unladylike snort came from beside him. 'I think my husband is not himself tonight.' Sabine commandeered Helena's hand. 'Normally he is not so modest.'

Hans guffawed and clutched his chest, earning him an eye-roll and a poke in the ribs from his wife. He winked at her, then turned a more sober face to Leo. 'Our new research unit in Berlin is exceptional, thanks to your support. Our stem cell procedures are attracting interest from some of the best surgeons in the world. You must come soon and see for yourself. And you are most welcome too, Helena. Have you visited Germany?'

Her hesitation was fleeting. 'Once, a long time ago. On a school trip.'

'Perhaps in a few months,' Leo intervened. 'When I get a break in my schedule.'

'How is Marietta?' Sabine said. 'We haven't seen her since her last surgery.'

His fingers tightened on his glass. 'She's fine,' he said, keeping his answer intentionally brief. He had no wish to discuss his sister in front of Helena. Proffering a smile, he gestured at the dwindling number of people around them. 'It appears the waiting staff would like us to be seated. Shall we…?'

With a promise to catch them later in the evening, Hans and Sabine joined the trail of diners drifting through to the ballroom. Leo turned to follow, but Helena hung back.

He stopped, raised an eyebrow. 'Are you coming?'

After a pause, she jammed her evening purse beneath her arm and shot him a baleful look. 'Do I have a choice?'

He gave her a silky smile—one designed to leave her in

no doubt as to his answer. But just to ensure she couldn't mistake his meaning he leaned in and said softly, 'You don't.'

Gorgeous. Devastating. *Lethal*.

Those were three of a dozen words Helena could think of to describe Leonardo Vincenti in a tuxedo. And, judging by the lascivious looks he was pulling from every corner of the ballroom, she wasn't the only female whose hormones had clocked into overdrive at the mere sight of all that dark, brooding masculinity.

He spoke from beside her. 'The fish is not to your taste?'

She cast him a look from under her lashes. 'It's fine. I'm not very hungry.'

The treacle-cured smoked salmon served as a starter was, in fact, superb, but the knots twisting her stomach made the food impossible to enjoy. Which really was a shame, some part of her brain registered, because she rarely had the opportunity these days to sample such exquisite cuisine.

She laid her fork alongside her abandoned knife and leaned back in her chair. So much for a quiet dinner *à deux* and the chance for a serious talk. She almost rubbed her forehead to see if the word *gullible* was carved there.

Surreptitiously she watched Leo speak with an older woman seated on his left. His tux jacket, removed prior to appetisers being served, hung from his chair, leaving his wide shoulders and lean torso sheathed in a white wing tip shirt that contrasted with his olive skin and black hair. He bowed his head, murmuring something that elicited a bright tinkle of laughter from the woman, and the sound scraped across Helena's nerves.

Age, evidently, was no barrier to his charms.

She averted her gaze, smothered the impulse to get up and flee. Like it or not, she'd agreed to be here and she would not scarper like a coward. If she was smart, bided her time, she might still persuade Leo to hold his plans for her father's company. A few weeks...that was all she needed. Time to make her mother see sense before—

'Bored?'

Leo's deep voice sliced across her thoughts.

She drummed up a smile. 'Of course not.'

'Good.' His long fingers toyed with the stem of his wine-glass. 'I would hate to bore you for a second time in your life.'

Helena's smile faltered. His casually delivered words carried a meaning she couldn't fail to comprehend. Not when her own words—words she'd bet every hard-earned penny in her bank account had hurt her more than they'd hurt him—were embedded like thorns in her memory. *I'm bored, Leo. Really. This relationship just isn't working for me.*

She shifted in her seat, her face heating. 'That's unfair.' She glanced around the table, pitching her voice for his ears alone. 'I tried once to explain why I said those things.'

After he'd left that awful message on her phone—telling her what her father had done, accusing her of betrayal and complicity—she'd gone to his hotel room and banged on his door until her hand throbbed and a man from a neighbouring room stepped out and shot her a filthy look.

'You didn't want to listen.'

He shrugged. 'I was angry,' he stated, as if he need offer no further excuse.

'You still are.'

'Perhaps. But now I'm listening.'

'I doubt that.'

'Try me.'

She arched an eyebrow. He wanted to do this *now*? *Here?* She cast another furtive glance around the table. *Fine.*

'I needed you to let me go without a fight,' she said, her voice a decibel above a whisper. 'And we both know you wouldn't have. Not without questions. Not unless I—' She stopped, a hot lump of regret lodging in her throat.

'Stamped on my pride?' he finished for her.

Her face flamed hotter. *Must* he make her sound so cruel? So heartless? She'd been nineteen, for pity's sake, staring down the barrel of her father's ultimatum. *Get rid of the damned foreigner, girl—or I will.* Naive. That was what she'd been. And unforgivably stupid, thinking she could live beyond the reach of her father's iron control.

She smoothed her napkin over her knees. 'I did what I thought was best at the time.'

'For you or for me?'

'For us both.'

'Ah. So you were being…how do you English like to say it…cruel to be kind?'

His eyes drilled into hers, but she refused to flinch from his cutting glare. She didn't need his bitter accusations. She, too, had paid a price, and however much she longed to turn back the clock, undo the damage, she could not relieve the pain of her past. Not when she'd worked so hard, sacrificed so much, to leave it behind.

She mustered another smile, this one urbane and slightly aloof—the kind her mother often wore in public. 'Hans and Sabine seem like a nice couple. Have you known them long?'

The change of subject earned her a piercing stare. She held her breath. Would he roll with it?

Then, 'Nine years.'

He spoke curtly, but still she breathed again, relaxed a little. Perhaps a normal conversation wasn't impossible? 'You never talked much about your sister,' she ventured. 'Sabine mentioned surgery. Is Marietta unwell?'

Long, silent seconds passed and Helena's stomach plunged as the dots she should have connected earlier—Leo's choice of fundraiser, Hans's reputation as a leading spinal surgeon, talk of the Berlin research unit followed by the mention of Marietta and surgery—belatedly joined in her head to create a complete picture.

A muscle jumped in Leo's cheek. 'My sister is a paraplegic.'

The blood that had heated Helena's cheeks minutes earlier rapidly fled. 'Oh, Leo. I'm... I'm so sorry.' She reached out—an impulsive gesture of comfort—but he shifted his arm before her hand could make contact. She withdrew, pretending his rebuff hadn't stung. 'I had no idea. How... how long?'

'Eleven years.'

Her throat constricted with sympathy and, though she knew it was silly, a tiny stab of hurt. Seven years ago they'd spent five intense, heady weeks together, and though he'd mentioned a sister, talked briefly about their difficult childhood, he'd omitted that significant piece of information.

Still, was that cause to feel miffed? She, too, had been selective in what she'd shared about *her* family.

'Did she have an...an accident?'

'Yes.' His tone was clipped.

'I'm sorry,' she said. 'I didn't mean to pry. I can see you don't want to talk about this.'

She lifted a pitcher of iced water in an effort to do something—anything—to dispel the growing tension. She'd half filled her glass when he spoke again.

'It was a car accident.'

Startled, she put the pitcher down and looked at him, but his head was angled down, his gaze fastened on the wineglass in his hand.

'She was seventeen and angry because we'd argued about her going to a party.' His black brows tugged into a deep frown. 'I didn't like the neighbourhood or the crowd, but she was stubborn. Headstrong. So she went anyway. Later, instead of calling me for a ride home, she climbed into a car with a drunk driver.' He drained his wine, dropped the glass on the table. 'The doctors said she was lucky to survive—if you can call a broken back "lucky". The driver and two other passengers weren't so fortunate.'

Helena tried to imagine the horror. Teenagers made bad decisions all the time, but few suffered such devastating, life-altering consequences. Few paid such an unimaginable price.

She struggled to keep her expression neutral, devoid of the wrenching pity it was impossible not to feel. 'Sabine mentioned surgery. Is there a chance...?'

Leo's gaze connected with hers, something harsh, almost hostile, flashing at the centre of those near-black irises. 'Let's drop it.'

Slightly taken aback, Helena opened her mouth to point out she *had* tried to drop the subject, but his dark expression killed that pert response. 'Fine,' she said, and for the next hour ignored him—which wasn't difficult because over the rest of their dinner another guest drew him into a lengthy debate on European politics, while the American couple to Helena's right quizzed her about the best places to visit during their six-month sabbatical in England.

When desserts began to arrive at the tables the compère tapped his microphone, waited for eyes to focus and chatter to cease, then invited one of the organisation's patrons, Leonardo Vincenti, to present the grand auction prize. After a brief hesitation Helena joined in the applause. In light of his sister's condition Leo's patronage came as no real surprise.

His mouth brushed her ear as he rose. 'Don't run away.'

And then he was striding to the podium, a tall, compelling figure that drew the attention of every person—male and female—in the room. On stage, he delivered a short but pertinent speech before presenting a gold envelope to the evening's highest bidder. People clapped again, finished their desserts, then got up to mingle while coffee was served.

Twenty minutes later Helena still sat alone.

Irritation sent a wave of prickly heat down her spine. *Don't run away.*

Ha! The man had a nerve.

She dumped sugar into her tea. Gave it a vigorous stir. Was he playing some kind of cat-and-mouse game? Or had he cut his losses and gone in search of a more agreeable companion for the evening?

Another ten minutes and finally he deigned to show. He dropped into his chair but she refused to look at him, concentrating instead on topping up her tea.

'You have no boyfriend to spend your Friday nights with, Helena?'

Her pulse skipped a beat. No apology, then. No excuse for his absence. Had his desertion been some kind of test? An experiment to see if she'd slink away the minute his back was turned? The idea did nothing to lessen her pique.

She piled more sugar in her tea. 'He's busy tonight.'

'Really?' His tone said he knew damn well she was lying. He lifted his hand and trailed a fingertip over the exposed curve of her shoulder. 'If you were mine I would not let you spend an evening with another man.' He paused a beat. 'Especially not in that dress.'

Carefully, she stirred her tea and laid the spoon in the saucer. He was trying to unsettle her, nothing more. She steeled herself not to flinch from his touch or, worse, tremble beneath it.

His hand dropped and she forced herself to meet his eye. 'You said my dress was fine.'

His gaze raked her. 'Oh, it's fine. Very fine, indeed. And I am sure not a man here tonight would disagree.'

Did she detect a note of censure in his voice? She stopped herself glancing down. She'd been conscious of her plunging neckline all evening, but there were dozens of cleavages here more exposed than her own. And, though the dress was more suited to a cocktail party or a private dinner than a glittering gala affair—cause at first for discomfort—there was nothing cheap or trashy about it.

She crossed her legs, allowing her hem to ride up, until

another inch of pale thigh defiantly showed. 'And you?' She watched his gaze flicker down. 'I wouldn't have thought a man like you would need a last-minute dinner date. Where's your regular plus-one tonight?'

His lips, far too sensual for a man's, twitched into a smile. 'A man like me?'

'Successful,' she said, inwardly cursing her choice of words. 'Money attracts, does it not? The world is full of women who find wealth and status powerful aphrodisiacs.'

One eyebrow quirked. 'When did you become a cynic?'

'Oh, I don't know.' She pursed her lips. 'Maybe around the time you were getting rich.'

He lounged back in his chair, the glint in his eye unmissable. 'In answer to your question, I'm between mistresses.'

'Oh...' She fiddled with the handle on her teacup.

Not girlfriends or partners. *Mistresses*. Why did that word make her heart shrink? So he enjoyed casual relationships. So what? His sex life was no business of hers.

She sat back, forced herself to focus. She couldn't afford to waste time. The evening was slipping away. If she didn't speak soon her chance would be lost. 'Leo, my father and I are estranged.'

In a flash, the teasing light was gone from his eyes. Her stomach pitched. Should she have blurted the words so abruptly? *Too bad*. They were out there now.

A vein pulsed in his right temple. 'Define "estranged".'

She hitched a shoulder, let it drop. 'We don't talk. We don't see each other. We're estranged in every sense of the word, if that's what you're asking.'

'Why?'

She hesitated. How much to tell? The bitter memory of that final violent confrontation with her father was too disturbing to recount even now.

'We fell out,' she said, her tongue dry despite the gallon of tea she'd consumed. 'Over you and what he did after

we—after *I* broke things off. I walked out seven years
ago and we haven't spoken since.' She paused and glanced
down. Her hands were shaking. She lifted her gaze back
to his. 'I dropped out of university and went to live in a
rented flat. Father cut off my allowance, froze my trust,
so I work at a full-time job. As a...a secretary. In a bank.'

Leo stared at her, his face so blank she wondered if he'd
heard a single word she said. Her insides churned as if the
tea had suddenly curdled in her belly. She wished she could
read him better. Wished she could interpret the emotion in
those dark, fathomless eyes.

And still the silence stretched.

God, why didn't he say something?

'You gave up your design studies?'

She blinked. *That* was his first question? 'Yes,' she said,
frowning. 'I couldn't study full-time and support myself.
The materials I needed were too expensive.'

Other students on her textile design course had jug-
gled part-time jobs along with their studies, but they'd had
only themselves to think about. They hadn't been facing
the same dilemmas, the same fears. They hadn't been in
Helena's position. Alone and pregnant.

Careful.

She shrugged. 'I might go back one day. But that's not
important. Leo, what I'm trying to tell you is that I'm not
here for my father.'

'Then why *are* you here?'

She leaned forward. 'Because what you're doing will
hurt the people I *do* love. And before you remind me that
my father—and thus his family—stands to gain financially from having his company torn apart, it's not about
the money.'

Helena hesitated. She had to choose her words with care.
Miriam Shaw might be too proud to admit to herself, let
alone the world, that she was a victim, but she was none
the less entitled to her privacy. Her dignity. She wouldn't

want the painful truth about her marriage shared with a stranger. Who knew what Leo might do with such sensitive information?

'My father can be...difficult to live with,' she said. 'At the best of times.'

Leo sat so still he barely blinked. Seemed barely to breathe. 'So what exactly do you want?'

'I want you to reconsider your plans for ShawCorp.' The words tumbled out so fast her tongue almost tripped on them. 'At the very least give my father more time to come to the table. Offer him a chance to have a say in the company's future. Maybe keep his position on the board.'

He gave her a long, hard look. 'That's a lot of want, Helena. You do realise my company is overseen by a board of directors? I am not the sole decision-maker.'

'But you have influence, surely?'

'Of course. But I need good reason. Your concern for your family is admirable, but this is business. I cannot let a little family dysfunction dictate corporate strategy.'

'Can't you at least delay Tuesday's deadline by a few weeks?'

His eyebrows slammed down and he muttered something under his breath. Something not especially nice.

He rose. 'We will finish this talk later.'

Warmth leached from her face. Her hands. Had she pushed too hard? Said too much? 'Why can't we finish it now?'

He moved behind her chair, lowered his head to hers. The subtle scent of spice twined around her senses. 'Because we're about to have company.' His hot breath fanned her cheek. 'Important company. And if you want me to consider your request you will be very, *very* well behaved.'

CHAPTER THREE

LEO STRAIGHTENED AND quelled the urge to mutter another
oath.

Of all the damnable luck. This night was going from bad
to worse. First a call on his mobile from a board member
whose angst over a minor matter had required twenty minutes of placation, followed by his relief at finding Helena
hadn't done a runner in his absence turning into stunned
disbelief over her staggering revelations—revelations his
reeling brain had yet to fully process.

And now Carlos Santino. Here in London. At this hotel.
At *this* function.

Tension coiled in his gut as the older Italian approached.
Santino stood a full head shorter than Leo, but the man's
stocky build and confident gait more than made up for his
lack of stature. Add to that hard, intelligent eyes above a
beaked nose and a straight mouth, and you had the impression of a man who tolerated weakness in neither himself
nor others.

Leo liked him. Respected him. Santino Shipping dominated the world's waterways, and in the last three years
its cyber security needs had generated sizable revenue for
Leo's company. The two men shared a business relationship based on mutual trust and respect.

But Leo had not seen Carlos Santino for several months.
Not since he'd rejected the man's daughter.

'Carlos.' He gripped Santino's hand. 'This is unexpected. What brings you to London? I thought few things
could prise you away from Rome.'

His client grunted. 'Shopping. Shows. Anything my
wife and daughter can spend my money on.' A chunky gold

watch and a heavy signet ring flashed in the air. 'Nothing they cannot get in Rome, or Milan, but you know women—' he shrugged expressively '—they are easily bored.'

Leo fired a loaded glance at Helena, but she was already rising, gifting the newcomer a million-dollar smile that drove a spike of irrational jealousy through his chest because *he* wasn't the recipient.

'Helena, this is Carlos Santino, head of Santino Shipping.' A deliberate pause gave his next words emphasis. 'One of my company's largest clients.'

She extended a slim hand. 'A pleasure to meet you, Mr. Santino.'

'The pleasure is mine.' Santino's hand engulfed hers. 'And, please, call me Carlos.' For a long moment he studied her face in a frank appraisal that nearly but not quite overstepped the bounds of propriety. By the time he released her hand, her cheeks glowed a delicate pink. He turned to Leo. 'Business is not your only good reason for visiting London, *si*?'

Leo forced a smile that almost made his eyes water. 'This is a coincidence, running into you here.' He pulled out a vacated chair for his client. 'Maria and Anna are with you?'

Carlos waited for Helena to resume her seat before taking the proffered chair. 'This was Anna's idea. She remembered you were patron of this organisation and...well—' another very Italian shrug '—when my wife planned the weekend Anna called your office and asked if you would be in London.' His smile offered only the vaguest apology. 'You know my daughter. She is resourceful and persistent. And furious with her *papà* right now. She woke with a bad cold this morning and I forbade her to come out. The tickets were already purchased and Maria insisted she and I still come.' He waved his hand. 'My wife is here somewhere—no doubt talking with someone more interesting than her husband.'

Some of Leo's tension eased. The young, voluptuous Anna Santino was an irritation he'd spent several months trying hard to avoid. Running into her this evening, or rather running *from* her, would have turned the night into a complete disaster.

Carlos switched his attention to Helena. 'It is fortunate, I think, that my daughter could not be here tonight. I fear she would be jealous of such a beauty at Leo's side.'

The provocative compliment heightened her colour but her hesitation was brief. 'I'm so sorry to hear your daughter is too ill to come out, Mr San— Carlos. That really is most unfortunate.' Her voice sang with sympathy. 'I do hope she'll be back on her feet again soon. You must tell her she has missed a wonderful, wonderful evening.'

Leo fought back a smirk. She might blush like a novice in a convent, but there was backbone beneath that pseudo-innocent charm. He noted a quirk at the corner of Santino's mouth. A flash of approval in his eyes.

Carlos inclined his head. 'I will, my dear.' To Leo, he said, 'I owe you an apology, my friend. When you told my daughter you had someone special in your life I assumed you were letting her down gently with a lie. I see now I was mistaken. You do have a special lady, indeed. And I am pleased to make her acquaintance at last.'

Leo felt the flesh at his nape tighten. He'd known that small white lie would come back one day and bite him. But flat-out rejecting the daughter of a client as powerful as Santino had seemed as sensible as cementing his feet and jumping into the Tiber. Claiming he was committed to another woman had seemed a kinder, more effective solution.

Carlos's focus returned to Helena. 'How often are you in Rome, Helena?'

Her lips parted and Leo shot her a hard, silencing look. She closed her mouth and frowned at him.

'Not often,' he interceded. 'Business brings me to London on a regular basis.'

'Ah, shame. In that case you need a reason to bring her to our great city.' Carlos's sudden smile drove a shaft of alarm straight to the centre of Leo's gut. 'My wife and I are celebrating our twenty-fifth wedding anniversary next weekend. Maria has organised a party—something large and extravagant, knowing my wife. Please join us. We'd be delighted to welcome you both.'

In the fleeting moment of silence that followed Leo caught a movement from the corner of his eye, but not until he felt the press of her palm on his thigh did he get his first inkling of what Helena intended.

Too late, his brain flashed a warning.

'Thank you, Carlos,' she said, her voice as smooth and sweet as liquid honey. 'That's very kind of you. We'd love to come.' She turned her head and flashed him a dazzling smile. 'Wouldn't we, darling?'

She squeezed his leg and heat exploded in the muscle under her hand. He tensed, biting back an exclamation, the fire shooting straight from his thigh to his groin. *Madre di Dio*. If the vixen inched her fingers any higher he would not be responsible for his body's reaction. He gritted his teeth until pain arced through his jaw—a welcome distraction from the killer sensations stirring south of his waist.

'I will need to check my schedule.' He forced the words past the hot, viscous anger building in his throat. *What the hell was she doing?* 'I may have another commitment.'

'Of course.'

Carlos stood and Leo rose with him, unseating the hand that was dangerously close to setting his pants alight.

'My assistant will contact your office on Monday with the details.' Carlos inclined his head. 'I look forward to seeing you again, Helena. And now I must find my wife before my absence is noted. Leo—good to see you. It has been too long.'

Leo nodded and watched his client's retreating back, the

tension in his chest climbing into his throat until it threatened to choke off his air supply.

He turned, glared at her. 'Get your bag.'

'What?' She stared up at him, wide-eyed. 'Why?'

'Just do it.'

When she hesitated, he grabbed her bag and wrapped a hand around her upper arm, hauled her to her feet.

She snatched her bag from him. 'Where are we going?'

'Somewhere private. To talk. Is that not what you wanted?'

She didn't utter a single word as he marched her out of the ballroom.

The instant the elevator doors closed Helena jerked her arm out of Leo's grasp. 'There's no need to manhandle me.'

He punched the button for the top floor of the hotel and threw her a look so thunderous a sliver of fear lodged in her spine. She edged away, reminded herself with a hard swallow that not all men were physically abusive. But if he was planning to shout she wished to God he'd get on with it. Anything had to be better than this…this tense, oppressive silence.

Moments later he slammed the door of his suite closed and rounded on her. 'What the *hell* was that?' His roar rose to the ceiling, echoed off the walls and reverberated through her chest like a boom of thunder.

She stood calm even as her insides quaked. 'I don't know why you're so angry. I thought you'd be grateful.'

'Grateful?' The word barely escaped his clenched teeth.

'Yes.' She pulled her brows into a delicate frown. Ignored the jelly-like quiver in her knees. 'You were in a sticky situation and I was being helpful.' Not to mention reckless and impulsive and out of her mind crazy. *Lord help her.* Whatever she'd done, it was either very clever or very, *very* stupid. 'Or would you have preferred I set Carlos straight about us?'

'*Dio.*' He threw his tuxedo jacket over a lounge chair, ripped his bow tie from around his neck. 'I should have known you'd have another stunt up your sleeve.'

Oh, now, *that* was rich. 'You brought me here tonight,' she reminded him. 'Not the other way around. I couldn't have foreseen your client turning up.'

'But you didn't waste a second in twisting it to your advantage, did you?'

She let out a clipped laugh. 'And *you* made no effort to correct his notion that we're a couple. I'm not a mind-reader, Leo. How was I to know I shouldn't play along?'

'It was simple, Helena.' He enunciated each syllable as if she were missing a few critical brain cells. 'All you had to do was keep your mouth shut. Oh, but wait—' he flung his arms wide '—you're a woman. That would have been impossible!'

He tossed down the tie, tore loose the buttons at his throat, raked lean fingers through his thick black hair. Gone was the cool, suave businessman from the charity dinner. In his place stood a man who looked hard. Fierce. *Dangerous.*

Helena drew a calming breath. She couldn't bottle now. Not when she could see the future looming with such frightening clarity. The takeover was only the beginning. If her mother thought things were bad now, they were only going to get worse. Leo didn't want to own ShawCorp; he wanted to destroy it. And when he succeeded her father's rage would need an outlet. A victim. Helena could not sit on the sidelines. She couldn't stand idle while her mother became that victim.

'Look, I…I'm sorry if I made things worse.' She tried for a softer, more apologetic tone. 'But maybe we could turn this to our advantage? Come to some…arrangement that would benefit us both?'

He stalked towards her and stopped inches short of their bodies touching—so close she could feel the heat emanating from him. In sharp contrast, his dark eyes carried a chill that needled into her flesh like icy midwinter sleet.

'Newsflash, Helena. Mutual benefit works best when each party has something the other needs. And, like I told you last night, you don't have anything I want—or need.' He spun on his heel and strode to the bar, pulled a large bottle from a black lacquered cabinet.

For her own benefit, not his, she straightened her spine. 'You need a girlfriend for your client's party next weekend.'

'Wrong.' He fired the word over his shoulder as he uncapped the bottle. 'On Monday my assistant will advise Santino's office that I am, regrettably, unable to attend.'

'Carlos will be disappointed.'

Amber liquid sloshed into a crystal tumbler. 'He'll get over it.'

'And next time you see him? What if he asks about me? Will you pretend there's still *someone special* in your life?'

'That is not your concern.'

'It is if you pretend that someone is me.'

He turned, the whisky untouched on the counter beside him. 'I will tell him our relationship ended.'

She dropped her purse on the arm of a sofa and sauntered over. 'I'm sure his daughter—Anna, was it?—will be delighted by that news.'

Was that a growl in his throat? She lifted the tumbler of whisky, inhaled the eye-watering fumes and, before she could think twice, helped herself to a generous swallow. The fiery liquid shot down her throat and extinguished the air in her lungs, but the molten heat spreading through her innards fired her courage.

Frowning, he snatched the glass back. 'What exactly are you proposing?'

Hope flared. 'That I attend the party with you in Rome—at your expense, of course—and help you prove to Carlos and his daughter that you're a happily attached man.'

His brows sank lower. 'And in return?'

'In return you defer your divestment of ShawCorp's assets and keep any announcements under wraps until my father agrees to meet you. In the meantime the company operates as normal and my father retains his position on the board.' It would give her father a sense of security. A belief, albeit false, that he still wielded some control.

Leo fell silent for long seconds and she imagined his brain ticking through the options.

'What makes you think your father will come around?'

She hesitated. Chances were he wouldn't. He was too arrogant, too proud, and that was what she was counting on. Because she didn't want to *prevent* her father's downfall. She only wanted to delay it—long enough for Miriam Shaw to accept some hard truths, come to her senses.

'We can agree a time limit. Say...four weeks.'

In two smooth motions he downed the remaining whisky and set the glass on the counter. 'Let me get this straight. You want to play-act at being my mistress—'

'Girlfriend.'

He flicked a hand in the air. 'Same thing—in return for granting your father a grace period?'

'Of sorts. Yes.'

He closed his eyes. Ran a wide palm over his jaw. 'That's insane.'

Totally.

She hiked her chin, swatted away the inclination to agree with him. 'Why? We'd each be doing the other a favour. What's so insane about that?'

'Because I don't need—'

'I know. I know.' Her turn to flick a hand. 'You don't need or want anything from me.' She let that hang a moment. 'But Carlos has met me now, and you said yourself he's an important client. Why decline his invitation if you don't need to? And, assuming you do want Anna to get the message loud and clear that you're unavailable, why not make use of the opportunity?'

He folded his arms, his shirt stretching over biceps that bunched and flexed with what she guessed was a surge of testosterone-fuelled pride. 'I can handle Santino's daughter without your help.'

She let a knowing smile curve her mouth. 'I'm sure you can. And, let's face it, you've done a stellar job so far. So stellar, in fact, that she went to all the trouble of tracking your whereabouts and arranging to be at the same event as you—in a different city. A different *country*.' She shook her head, turned her smile into a pitying grimace. 'I hate to say this, Leo, but that's not a girl who's accepted no for an answer. That's a woman still hot for the chase.'

His muscles deflated slightly, though the arrogant set of his jaw remained. 'That's quite some proposition, Helena. You and I pretending to be lovers. How do you think your father would feel about that?'

Helena swallowed, or tried to, but her mouth had gone suddenly dry. *Lovers.* The word had skimmed off his tongue with such ease and yet it drove home the reality of what she'd suggested. Of precisely the kind of role-playing required to convince a crowd of partygoers that she and Leo were a committed couple. Her belly quivered with something much more unsettling than nerves, but she couldn't back down now.

She moistened her lips. 'I don't mix in my father's circles. Not any more. Few people of note would recognise me, and certainly not in Rome. And if they did, well...why would you care? Isn't that the reason I'm here tonight? Because you like the idea of getting under his skin?'

He frowned at that, eyes narrowed, his fingers yanking loose another button at his throat. He tugged at the collar and the shirt gaped, exposing the base of his strong neck and a triangle of chest deeply bronzed and dusted with fine whorls of dark hair.

Helena jerked her gaze north of his chin. *Focus.*

'There's no reason this can't work. If people in Rome

question why they haven't seen us together before we'll say we wanted to keep our relationship private until we'd figured out the long-distance thing. If we're convincing, Anna will back off and lose interest, and once she's moved on you can tell Carlos we broke up. That way he won't ever have to know you lied to his daughter—' she paused for a significant beat '—or to him.'

His jaw ground from side to side. 'You really think you could pull that off? Convince the Santinos and their hundreds of guests—and there *will* be hundreds—that we're a couple?'

'Sure.' She shrugged, strove for nonchalance. 'Why not? We were lovers once.'

Briefly, admittedly, and then only after she'd convinced him that at nineteen, besides being a legally consenting adult, she was a level-headed young woman who knew her own mind. He had been older, yes, but six years was hardly cradle-snatcher territory. She'd wanted it, wanted *him*, as she'd never wanted anything before. And not once had she regretted what they'd shared—even in the days and months of heartache that followed. Sex with Leo had been the most intense, most beautiful and physically liberating experience of her life.

Nothing, and no one, had come close since.

Drawing courage from the alcohol warming her blood, she stepped forward and cupped a hand around his jaw. 'It wouldn't be so difficult, would it? Pretending we're lovers? Pretending we're enamoured of each other?'

She swayed her hips—a gentle, seductive grind that bumped their bodies and sparked a slow blossoming of heat low in her pelvis.

Bone and muscle shifted under her palm. He ground out an oath, seized her wrist. 'What are you doing?'

'Proving I can play the part. I *can*, Leo, if that's what you're worried about.'

There was no mistaking the growl in his throat this time.

Or the sudden flash of heat in his eyes. His grip tightened and she thought for one heart-stopping moment he was going to kiss her—haul her against him, crash that harsh, beautiful mouth down on hers and kiss her. Her breath stalled. Her heartbeat hitched. A tiny, forbidden thrill of anticipation skimmed her spine.

Then his head was snapping back, his hand thrusting hers away as if he found her touch, her very proximity, repugnant. 'How do I know your father didn't put you up to this? That everything you've told me tonight isn't more lies? Tell me why I should trust you.'

Heat seared Helena's face even as the flare of desire in her belly iced over.

Because I loved you once! she almost shouted. *Broke my heart in two for you. And, by God, doesn't that make me the world's biggest fool?*

She bit the lining of her cheek. Distrust was written all over his face. In the hard, narrowed eyes, the implacable jaw. The contemptuous twist of his mouth.

She looked him in the eye and spoke with a quiet dignity that camouflaged the turmoil inside her. 'I lied to you once, Leo. I don't deny it and I'm not proud of it. I made up a weak, hurtful excuse to end our relationship because that was what my father wanted. *Demanded.*'

She passed a hand over her eyes, the strain of recent days coupled with sleepless nights taking its toll.

'My greatest mistake was believing that if I obeyed him, did what he wanted, that would be the end of it. Why he went after you I'll never know. Maybe he was punishing me. Maybe he did it simply because he *could.* Whatever his reasons, I can assure you this—I did *not* tell him anything about you or your project. Wherever he got his information, it wasn't from me.' She exhaled on a heavy sigh, the last of her energy rapidly waning. 'Is it really so hard for you to believe me now?'

His gaze held hers, no softening visible in those midnight depths. 'After the stunt you just pulled, what do you think?'

She backed up a step, the ice in her belly trickling into her veins. Astonishing that a man could nurse his anger, his resentment, his need for retribution for so many years. Pride, rage, distrust—whatever the emotions that drove him, they were too strong, too ingrained for her to fight against and win.

She collected her purse, turned to face him one last time. 'You really want to know what I think? I think you're right. This is insane, and I'm sorry I suggested it. Manipulation might be my father's forte, maybe even yours, but it's not mine.' She walked to the door and glanced back, her smile brittle. 'Good luck with taking my father down a peg or two.' She inclined her head. 'I believe he might have met his match.'

She opened the door and paused a moment, half expecting a presence to loom at her back, a hand to fall on her shoulder. But she heard no footfalls, no rustle of movement behind her. She stepped out, closed the door and rode the elevator down to the foyer.

Minutes later, striding through the brisk evening air to the nearest tube station, she angrily dashed the tears from her eyes.

She would *not* let them fall.

Leo didn't deserve her anguish.

Not seven years ago, and not now.

Leo stopped pacing just long enough to glare at the whisky bottle and dismiss the notion of refilling his glass.

Getting tanked so he could obliterate this evening from his memory held a certain appeal, but he'd cleaned up his father's drunken messes too often as a kid to condone such mindless excess. Not to mention he'd have one hell of a hangover. Besides, his pilot had scheduled an early-morning return to Rome, and a flight-change was out of the question. If he turned up to Marietta's first ever art exhibition a dishevelled, ill-tempered wreck he'd spend days, if not weeks, earning his little sister's forgiveness.

He flung his restless frame into a chair, his muscles stiff after the effort of holding his body in check. Of stopping himself from charging after Helena like some raging Neanderthal and forcing her to press those sultry curves against him one more time.

Scowling at the flash of heat in his groin, he got up to pace again. He was too wired to sit, his head too full of questions clamouring for answers. Answers he needed if he were to make any sense of Helena's actions. The idea that she'd come to him without her father's knowledge, that she and Shaw were estranged and had been for years, that she'd abandoned her studies, now lived alone in the city, worked nine-to-five as a secretary in a bank...

He shook his head as if he could clear the overload from his brain.

Truths, half-truths, or carefully constructed lies?

Whatever the answer, there were more layers to this situation than met the eye. And if his years of dealing with wily competitors and cut-throat corporates had hammered home any lessons, they were never to accept anything at face value, never to underestimate your opponent, and never to assume he'd go down without a fight.

Turning on his heel, he retrieved his tux jacket and pulled out his mobile. He placed a call and his friend Nicolas answered within two rings. Leo skipped the pleasantries—Nico didn't do small talk—and launched into his request.

'I need this ASAP,' he finished.

A short silence came down the line, then Nico's deep voice. 'No problem, *mon ami*. I will have something for you in forty-eight hours.'

Gratitude surged, even though Leo had known his friend would do him this favour, no questions asked. Nicolas

César ran a global security firm with an investigative arm reputed for its reach and discretion. He was a man with the resources to uncover the secrets of the world's most powerful and influential people. Confirming a few basic facts about an Englishwoman would amount to little more than child's play.

Leo tossed aside his phone, stripped off his clothes and headed for the en suite bathroom. He turned on the shower and let the steaming jets of water ease the tension from his muscles.

If Nico delivered with his trademark efficiency Leo would soon know if there was any truth to Helena's claims. And whatever his friend's probing unearthed, whatever truths—or lies—were revealed, she would soon discover this was far from over.

Whether she had planned to or not she'd started something tonight, and Leo intended to finish it.

The next time Helena Shaw walked out of his life it would be on *his* terms.

On Monday morning Helena stepped out of the elevator on the forty-second floor of the bank and knew at once something wasn't right. For a start the receptionist grinned at her, and prim, efficient, fifty-something Jill didn't grin. She smiled. Professionally. No grinning allowed.

'You're late,' Jill announced.

'I know,' Helena said, flustered enough without Jill stating the obvious. 'The Underground was a nightmare this morning.' And the last thing she'd needed on the heels of a long, sleepless weekend. All she wanted was to get to her desk and bury herself in work. 'Any mail for David?'

'He collected it ten minutes ago—along with your visitor.'

Helena stopped. 'My visitor?'

'A man.'

And there it was again. Not a smile. A *grin*. Helena

couldn't recall ever before seeing so many of her col-
league's teeth.

'He said he was a friend, so once Security cleared him
I had them send him up. When David arrived and I mentioned you had a visitor he took him through to your office. His name was...' She picked up a piece of notepaper.
'Yes, that's right. Mr Vincenz—no, Vincenti.'

Helena blinked. She wasn't at the office at all. She was
still tucked up in bed. Dreaming about the infernal man
who had single-handedly ruined her weekend.

Jill frowned. 'Helena? Are you okay?'

No. 'Yes,' she said, forcing herself to rally. To *think*. She
managed a smile. 'Thanks.'

Before Jill could probe further, she pushed through the
glass security doors and followed the executive corridor
down to her workspace. With every step the tremor in her
knees threatened to escalate into a full-blown quake.

At her desk, she dumped her bag, removed her blazer—
the temperature in the office had soared suddenly—and
glanced around. No tall, dark, brooding Italian in sight. She
could, however, hear voices in David's office, and when a
burst of laughter carried through the half-open door any
lingering doubts were swiftly dispelled.

She clutched the edge of her desk, her stomach clenching in response to that rich, full-bodied sound and the con-
firmation that Leo was not only here, at her office, *in her
boss's office,* he was having a nice little one-on-one with
David while he waited for her to arrive.

Confusion followed by a spurt of alarm jolted her into
action. Without knocking, she pushed open David's door
and two heads swung in her direction. In a matter of seconds her brain registered two things.

First, David was not behind his desk but seated out front,
beside his guest—a relaxed approach he only ever adopted
with her or with people he especially liked. And second,
though by no means less noteworthy, was the simple fact

that Leonardo Vincenti looked just as mind-blowingly sexy in a silver suit, pale blue shirt and striped tie than he did in any formal tuxedo.

Helena's mouth went dry. No wonder Jill had been grinning like a schoolgirl.

'Ah, here she is,' said David, and then both men were on their feet, greeting her with smiles, the megawatt force of Leo's almost knocking her back on her heels.

He walked over, slipped his arm around her waist and dropped a featherlight kiss on her temple. Her knees nearly gave out.

'Morning, *cara*.' The firm press of his hand in her side sent a message—or was it a warning? 'My meeting was cancelled at the last minute and, since I was nearby, I thought I'd take the opportunity to see your offices.' He drew her into the room. 'And to meet David, of course.'

Her gaze darted to the older man, who now wore a grin to rival Jill's. She opened her mouth, but the dryness had crawled down her throat and no sound came out aside from a slight wheeze.

She gave herself a mental kick. 'Sorry I'm late, David. Problems on the tube…'

He waved off the apology. 'It's a nice change to beat you into the office for once. And I must say it's been an unexpected pleasure to chat with your man, here.'

Her man. The floor lurched and it was only Leo's grip that kept her steady, despite the unsettling effect his touch had on her insides. She wanted to swat his hand away, sink into a nearby chair. She forced herself to concentrate on David's voice.

'I was just telling Leo how seldom you take any leave, and he mentioned how keen he is to get you to Italy.'

He paused, rocked on his heels, looking immensely chuffed with himself all of a sudden. Helena felt faint.

'He also tells me you're off to Rome at the weekend and it would be the perfect chance for you to stay longer.' The men exchanged a glance. 'I think it's an excellent idea. Why don't you take a week?'

Helena couldn't help herself; she gaped at her boss. 'A...a *week*?'

Leo's fingers dug into her side but she refused to look at him. If he flashed her another of those devastating smiles she'd lose her ability to think, let alone remain upright.

She stared at David. 'I...I couldn't. Things are much too busy.'

'Nonsense. The office won't grind to a halt in your absence and neither will I. Hire me a temp who's half as efficient as you and I'll survive the week just fine.'

'Perhaps you should listen to your boss, *cara*,' came a silky voice in her ear, and she stifled the adolescent urge to stamp her heel onto his foot.

'I'll think about it,' she said to David. 'I promise. But right now we should get back to work. I'm sure Leo's taken enough of your time.'

A slight shift in her stance dislodged his hand from her hip. She turned, forced a smile onto her stiff lips.

'Shall we grab a quick coffee before you go?'

CHAPTER FOUR

HELENA OPENED THE door to a vacant meeting room, stood to one side and waited for Leo to enter. He paused, gave the room a cursory once-over, then crossed to a large bank of windows overlooking the River Thames and the City of London's eclectic skyline of spires and towers.

'Not bad, Helena.' He turned his back to the view. 'You were a little stiff, but we can work on that.'

She closed the door, sucked in a deep breath and counted to twelve before the urge to shout had safely passed.

She expelled the air from her lungs. 'Why?'

'Why do we need to work on it?'

She made a ticking sound in her throat. 'Please don't play games with me.'

One eyebrow hooked up, as did one corner of his mouth—a subtle shift of facial muscles that barely qualified as a smile, yet Helena had the distinct impression he was enjoying himself.

'The only game I'm playing is the one you wanted to play, *cara.*'

'Stop calling me that.' She crossed her arms over her chest. 'And stop avoiding the question. I assume you've changed your mind about things since Friday? Why?'

Moving with more grace than a man of his height and size should possess, he propped his hip on the long conference table dominating the room. 'You're assuming my mind was made up.'

'Wasn't it?'

'No.'

'Then why did you let me leave?'

He shrugged. 'I wanted time to consider your proposal.'

She huffed out a breath. The possibility that in the interim *she* might change *her* mind clearly hadn't occurred to him. She changed tack. 'Why are you here?'

His brow furrowed. 'Did we not just establish that?'

'No, I mean why are you *here*? At my office. Talking to my boss.' She narrowed her eyes at him. 'How did you know where I work?'

'You gave me the address yourself.'

She thought about that, then bit her lip. He was right. She'd jotted down the address so he could send a car to collect her on Friday. A simple enquiry at the downstairs security desk would have filled in the rest. Still, it didn't excuse his turning up here with no warning. He had her mobile number. He could have phoned.

Like you could have phoned him before turning up at the hotel?

She slammed a lid on that voice. 'And your little *tête-à-tête* with David? What was that all about?'

His mouth quirked again. 'He invited me into his office. Refusing would have been rude, no?' The quirk lingered a few seconds more. 'Your boss seems a pleasant man—he speaks very highly of you, by the way. But tell me...' He paused, all trace of levity leaving his face. 'Why are you wasting your time in a job like this?'

His question stung. It shouldn't have, but it did. It reminded her of her father and all the hurtful criticisms she'd endured as a child. The small, painful barbs that pierced the protective wall her mother tried to erect between father and daughter. Her list of faults was exhaustive. And while being born a girl surely drove the first of many nails into her coffin, opting for design school over a law degree and dating a man not of her father's choosing certainly hammered in the last.

She lifted her chin. 'You're belittling my job now?'

'Not at all. I appreciate the value of a skilled assistant. I have an excellent one myself, and she is an asset to my office. But this—' he lifted a hand to indicate their surroundings '—is not the career you were planning seven years ago.'

Not the answer she'd expected. Still, she didn't need to justify her choices. Her job was *not* the dream career in design she'd once envisaged, but hopes and dreams, just like people—just like tiny, innocent, unborn babies—could unexpectedly die.

She dismissed his censure with a shrug. She worked hard, made an honest independent living, and no one—not her father and certainly not this man—had any right to judge her. 'Plans change. People change. And how I make a living is no business of yours.'

His black-lashed eyes treated her to a long, intense regard that made her tummy muscles tighten. 'You are right—it's not my business,' he said at last, though his tone wasn't in the least contrite. 'What you do in the coming weeks, however, *is*. Assuming you want to proceed with this little plan of yours?'

She stared at him, a prickle of unease tiptoeing down her spine. *Weeks?* Her arms fell to her sides. 'You're not serious about me spending a whole week in Italy?' Her stunned gaze met his cool, unwavering stare. She shook her head. 'Oh, no. That…that wasn't the agreement.'

His brows snapped together. 'We had no agreement, as I recall. You chose instead to put me in a difficult position with my client and then used it as a means of blackmail.'

Blackmail? 'I did no such thing!' Her face flamed. With indignation, she told herself. Not with guilt. Definitely not guilt. '*You* chose not to correct Carlos's assumption about us. I simply played along and then suggested we might come to some…some mutually beneficial arrangement.'

'Ah. Yes. The "mutually beneficial arrangement" in which I grant your father a grace period of four weeks, and in return you give me the pleasure of your company for—' his eyebrows rose '—one night?'

She smoothed her palms down the front of her black knee-length skirt. 'One *evening*,' she corrected, keeping her chin elevated. 'And, yes, that would be the arrangement to which I'm referring.'

He laughed—a deep, mellifluous sound that seemed to reach out and brush her skin like the rub of raw silk.

Her anger spiked. 'Is something amusing?'

'Only your ability to play naive when it suits you.'

'What is that supposed to mean?'

'It means you are well aware those terms are weighted in your favour and not mine.' He took his time adjusting a silver cufflink on his left sleeve. When he looked up, his expression had hardened. 'Did you think I would simply roll over for you, Helena?'

The undercurrent of menace in his voice made her knees quiver again. 'But why?' she blurted. 'What could you possibly want with me for a week?'

One side of his mouth kicked up. 'What, indeed?' he murmured, his gaze sweeping her length in an unhurried appraisal that set her teeth on edge—more so because she knew her clumsy question had invited it. 'Let's call it a balancing of the odds.' His eyes flicked back to hers. 'It would be a crime, would it not, if one of us were to feel…cheated?'

An enigmatic response at best. A deflection of her question as skilful as it was irritating.

She crossed to a window, leaned her hip against the metal sill and attempted nonchalance. 'So our pretence of being a couple—you're suggesting we keep that up for the entire week?'

'*Si.*'

'Why?'

'People will want to see us.'

'What people?'

'The people who have heard about you.' He tilted his head and smiled. 'Do not look so puzzled, Helena. You know how it is among the rich and privileged—the gossip mill is a voracious beast. And Rome is no different from London. Worse, in fact. We Italians love our drama.'

Her temples started to throb. 'But I met Carlos only three nights ago.'

He gave another of his maddening shrugs. 'Carlos tells his wife. His wife tells their daughter. Anna tells a friend… or twenty. News travels. You know how it works.'

Yes. She knew how it worked—that brittle, superficial world of the social elite. It had been her world once and she rarely missed it. Scratch the surface of gloss and glamour and every time you'd find a bitter core of hypocrisy and backstabbing.

She massaged the growing pressure in her temples. What madness had she started? 'What if we don't convince them?'

'That we are lovers?'

'Yes.' The word came out slightly strangled.

He straightened from the table. 'You assured me you could handle it. Are you getting cold feet already, Helena?'

She almost laughed at his choice of expression. Cold? Oh, no. No part of her felt cold right now. Not even close. Not when the prospect of their playing lovers for an entire week had her blood racing so hot and crazy she feared her veins might explode.

He stepped towards her. 'There *is* one way to ensure we're convincing.'

'Oh?' She tamped down the urge to scurry to the other side of the room. 'How?'

'Drop the pretence.'

Her brain took several seconds to register his meaning. She blinked, a bubble of incredulous laughter climbing her throat. 'You're kidding, right?'

'You find the prospect of sex with me abhorrent?'

The question—so explicit and yet so casually delivered—triggered a fresh wave of heat that burned from her hairline all the way down to the valley between her breasts. Abhorrent? No. Dangerous? Yes. Terrifying? *Utterly.* Though not for any reason she was fool enough to admit.

Her brain scrambled for a foothold. 'I don't understand.' That sounded lame. 'You said you didn't—that you weren't—that you no longer...' *Wanted me.* Were those the words he'd used? She squeezed her eyes shut. No. His exact words had been, *I'm not interested in anything you could offer.*

A shard of pain in the vicinity of her heart made her wince.

'What is there to understand?'

She opened her eyes to find him standing in front of her. Startled, she stepped back, the windowsill's sharp edge biting into her thighs.

'We know we're compatible in bed,' he said, his voice so calm, so matter-of-fact she wanted to scream. 'Why not make the most of our arrangement—throw some pleasure into the mix?'

Lightheaded suddenly, she gripped the ledge behind her, its hard metal surface cool and reassuringly solid beneath her palms. She breathed in. Out again. Summoned calm. He was toying with her...having fun at her expense. Needling for a reaction he wasn't going to get.

She tightened her fingers on the sill. 'I still don't believe you're serious.'

'And you still haven't answered my question.'

'What question?'

'Do you find the prospect of sleeping with me abhorrent?'

She looked him in the eye. She wouldn't lie.

'Of course not.'

But neither would she pander to his ego.

'But that doesn't mean I have any great desire to jump into your bed.'

He shifted closer and she shrank back—away from the

wall of masculine heat threatening to envelop her. A tell-tale pulse galloped at the base of her throat and she cursed her body's irrepressible responses. Why, oh, why could she not control her reactions to him?

'Is that so?' He lifted a finger and traced a fiery line from her jaw down to that delicate pulse-point in her neck. 'Then why do I make you nervous? Or is there another reason your heart is beating so wildly right now?'

She smacked his hand away and tried to straighten, barely daring to breathe. If she swayed the tiniest fraction their bodies would connect. Just the thought made her nipples peak hard and sensitive under the cotton layers of her bra and blouse.

'Don't flatter yourself,' she snapped, but his gaze was already dipping, taking in the evidence of her body's swift, mortifying arousal.

When his eyes reclaimed hers, the naked hunger in those inky depths nearly took her knees from under her.

'Your body betrays you, Helena.'

Before she could utter a denial his hands spanned her waist, his palms searing like hot iron through thin cotton as they slid upwards, coming to rest beneath the swell of her breasts. He dragged his thumbs up and outward, gliding them over taut, sensitive peaks. Her breath locked in her throat, a combination of panic and unbidden craving making her blood pulse at a dizzying speed.

'I think you are not as immune to me as you would like to believe,' he crooned in her ear.

And then he was setting her away from him. Stepping back. Giving her room to breathe.

Leaving her hot and flustered and confused.

He straightened his silver tiepin. 'Those are my terms.'

His tone had turned crisp, businesslike, his face impassive, and she wondered with a touch of hysteria if the lust she'd seen in his eyes had been imagined or real.

'Take it or leave it, Helena. But I need your answer—*now*.'

She hesitated, her thoughts splintering, scattering in too many directions. *Too unexpected...too overwhelming... too crazy...*

She drew a shaky breath and expelled it. 'I...I don't know...'

'In that case we have no deal.'

And just like that he turned to go.

Stunned, she stared after him, motionless at first, then with teeth clenched, hands fisting by her sides. She closed her eyes, the throb in her temples building to a painful crescendo. *What was she doing?* Was she really going to stand here and watch him leave? After he had, in essence, offered her what she wanted? He'd asked for one week in return—one week out of her life. Was that sacrifice so unthinkable?

For her mother?

She snapped open her eyes. 'Wait!'

He stopped, glanced back, one hand raised to the door. *'Si?'*

'Five days,' she croaked.

His arm lowered. *'Scusi?'*

She cleared her throat. 'Five days,' she repeated, certain he'd heard her well enough the first time. 'And my own room.'

'Seven.' He turned, his dark eyes glinting. 'And I can guarantee you'll find more satisfaction in my room.'

Cocky bastard. She smiled thinly. 'My own room.'

He shrugged, unconcerned. As if, for all his baiting, where she slept mattered to him not one way or the other.

'And my father gets six weeks.'

A mirthless laugh rumbled in his chest. 'Nice try.'

'Five, then.'

'Four.'

They stared at one another, eyes locked in challenge, each waiting for the other to concede. He wouldn't, she knew, but she needed this final moment of defiance.

Needed to savour these last precious seconds of sanity before she plunged off the edge into madness.

The prospect alone had fear clawing her insides, but it wasn't the promise of night-time pleasures with the man who had once owned her heart that frightened her beyond measure. It was the hot, delicious, burgeoning spark of desire in her belly she could neither extinguish nor control.

She squared her shoulders. Hiked up her chin. *Please don't let me regret this.*

'We have a deal.'

On Thursday, close to noon, Helena's mobile phone rang. She answered on the run, dashing out to collect a sandwich for David and a salad for herself prior to a lunch meeting.

'You're panting.'

Leo.

'I'm running.'

Well, almost. Walking briskly. She dodged a flying cycle courier, who in turn dodged a double-decker bus.

'Contrary to popular belief, secretaries don't spend all day sitting on their backsides.'

An unexpected chortle came down the line. A deep, sexy, gravel and velvet laugh that reminded her, fleetingly, of the old Leo. Her stomach flip-flopped.

'A car will pick you up tomorrow, at six p.m., to take you to the airport. Where do you wish to be collected?'

She jostled her way into a popular sandwich bar, wondered if he was still in London or back in Rome, then wondered why she cared.

She mimicked his cool, no-nonsense tone. 'From the office.'

'Fine. Six o'clock. Don't be late.' He ended the call as abruptly as he'd commenced it.

Helena frowned at her phone, then shoved it back in her blazer pocket and smothered a flash of annoyance. Letting his lack of geniality irritate her was silly—a waste of mental energy when she had none to spare. They weren't a couple, and nor were they friends. Out of the public eye there was no need for pleasantries or false sentiment. And as for his taunts about her sleeping in his room, sharing his bed—turning their ruse into reality—they had been nothing more than that.

Taunts.

Unfortunately that thought didn't placate her nerves later that evening as she stared at the neatly packed contents of her suitcase. Stomach churning, she ran through the list in her head one last time, confident she hadn't overlooked any essential items. Tomorrow the compact roller case would wheel easily on and off the train to work and her canvas carry-on, holding her passport, purse, and the jeans and tee she would change into for travelling, was light enough to hitch over one shoulder should she need a hand free.

Satisfied, she made some peppermint tea to pacify her tummy and settled on her sofa. It was late now—well after eleven—and her flat was silent, the tenants upstairs and the neighbourhood streets finally, blissfully quiet. She sipped her tea, let the fragrant brew circulate and soothe, then put down her cup and picked up the envelope she'd pulled from her nightstand drawer earlier in the evening.

She lifted the flap and pulled out a photograph—a picture of a tiny baby swaddled in the soft folds of a hospital-issue blanket. For long moments she studied the image, noting every detail even though she could close her eyes and still know every individual feature by heart. From the adorable tufts of jet-black hair to the miniature half-moons of delicate lashes and the sweetest little Cupid's bow mouth she'd ever seen on a child.

She'd named her son Lucas, and he would have been six now had he lived. She had other mementos of him, too. Small treasures. Keepsakes. Stored in the beautiful wooden memory box her mother had bought. But this image of her son—so tiny and precious, cradled in her arms as if he simply slept—was by far her favourite.

She swallowed and breathed through the dull, familiar ache that settled in her chest whenever she thought of her stillborn son.

Carefully, she slipped the photo back into the envelope.

Leo had been long gone by the time she had learnt she was pregnant, and though she'd known in her heart she had to tell him she hadn't found the courage to do so. He'd been so angry the last time they'd spoken, his declaration that he never wanted to see her again so adamant and final. Far easier, she had discovered, to let fear and hurt rule her head than to step back into the firing line.

And yet the day she gave birth to their son—the moment she cradled his tiny, silent, still warm body in her arms—all that fear and hurt became trivial. Irrelevant. Because she knew. Knew that if Lucas had been gifted life she could never have kept him from his father. Could never have denied Leo the chance to know he had created such a beautiful, perfect little boy.

She rose, went to her bedroom and slid the envelope back into her nightstand drawer.

Months of counselling had helped her to move on with her life, overcome her feelings of anger and guilt, but those dark, endless days of soul-destroying grief—she wouldn't wish those on anyone. Not her worst enemy and not Leo. What could be gained now by dredging up all that heartache and sorrow? Nothing. It was history. Water under the bridge. Whatever cliché one wanted to assign it.

Some burdens, she reminded herself, were better borne alone.

Leo stood at the head of the steps that scaled the private jet and checked his watch for the fifth time in as many minutes.

Damn it: Why did his shoulders feel as if they were

roped into knots the size of fists? And why couldn't he shake this weird, jittery feeling from the pit of his stomach?

Granted, he'd expected the car he'd sent for Helena to have arrived by now, but it was Friday rush hour and this was London. Traffic would be hitting its peak and a fifteen-minute delay was negligible. If the driver had encountered any serious hold-ups, or if Helena had failed to show, he'd have heard by now.

All of which meant he needed to kill this obsession with his watch and *relax*.

This arrangement of theirs might top the scale of hare-brained ideas, but his impromptu return to London on Monday had at least gained him an edge. In less than an hour he'd blindsided Helena at her office—fair payback for ambushing him at the hotel—tossed her firmly on to the back foot and enjoyed their verbal sparring to boot.

Though not nearly as much as he'd enjoyed putting his hands on her.

His fingers curled at the memory of her skin's heat penetrating his palms through her thin blouse and the way her nipples had pebbled in response to his touch. At some point the vibrant girl with her bold colours and creative ambitions had given way to a woman too content with mediocrity, yet he'd seen a spark of fire in her blue eyes that convinced him some remnant of that passionate, captivating girl still existed.

A flash of reflected sunlight at the edge of the Tarmac caught his eye and he squinted into the lowering sun. A silver SUV with tinted windows approached, cruising to a stop in the traffic safety zone alongside the aircraft hangar. The driver sprang from the vehicle and made for the other side, but his passenger had already climbed out. Smiling at the man, her loose curls tossed by the evening breeze, she spoke a few words Leo strained to hear but couldn't catch from where he stood.

He sucked in his breath, the edgy, irritable mood that

had plagued him all day dissipating beneath an entirely different kind of tension.

Dio.

Even casually attired, the woman was a breathtaking vision. A perfect combination of long, slender limbs and feminine curves in all the right places. An ache stirred deep in his groin as he watched her cross the Tarmac, her rounded breasts clearly outlined beneath her figure-hugging tee, the denim of her jeans stretched over shapely hips and slender thighs. In one hand she carried a jacket, in the other a small holdall.

He descended the steps. When she neared he took her bag, slipped an arm around her waist and pulled her flush against him. Her eyes widened, her mouth forming a perfect O of surprise.

'*Ciao*, Helena.' He lowered his head, intending to drop an experimental kiss on those sweet, inviting lips, but she averted her face and his mouth collided instead with her cheek.

Her body stiffened. 'People are watching,' she hissed.

He glanced at the men in overalls working around them, some engrossed in their tasks, others paused and openly staring.

'So they are.' He dragged her closer, some deep, primal instinct urging him to send a clear message to the onlookers. *Mine.* He turned his attention back to her mouth. 'Perhaps we should not disappoint them?'

Her eyes narrowed to pinpricks of sapphire and she pulled in a breath, but whatever retort hovered on that pretty pink tongue she chose not to share it. Instead she twisted from his grasp and started up the steps, the mesmerising roll and sway of her hips holding his gaze captive. He tightened his grip on her bag, his amusement tempered by a sting of annoyance.

Was this how she planned to fulfil her role as his mistress? By tolerating his touch only when it suited her?

Think again, cara.

'Drink?' he offered after he'd stashed her bag in an over-head locker and snapped the cover closed. For a woman she travelled exceptionally light. The carry-on he'd just stowed was small and compact, the single piece of luggage the driver had removed from the SUV not much larger.

The observation gave him pause. A week ago he'd have shrugged it off, assumed she planned to hit the shops in Rome and buy an extra case to carry home her purchases. Now, after Nico's report, he knew that scenario was un-likely. Despite her family's enviable wealth, Helena's life-style appeared modest, even frugal. A revelation he found oddly disturbing.

She tossed her jacket over a seat. 'Yes, please.'

He moved to a built-in bar where a bottle of champagne sat chilling on ice. He filled two long-stemmed flutes, handed one to Helena and raised the other in a toast. 'To our arrangement.'

She hesitated before touching her glass to his. The crys-tal sang sweetly as the rims clinked. 'To our arrangement.'

Her head arched back on her graceful neck as she took a surprisingly long swig of the effervescent liquid. She lowered the glass, gestured a hand at the cabin's interior.

'You travel in style.'

He considered the gleaming mahogany fixtures, fine Italian leather and thick cut pile carpet. The expansion of his business into Asia and North America over the last few years had demanded extensive travel, and his board had deemed the corporate jet a justifiable expense.

'You sound surprised.'

She shrugged. 'It's more luxurious than I'd expected.'

'And you disapprove?'

For a second the question seemed to throw her, then her features morphed back into an aloof, dignified mask. 'No. Of course not. It's just…not what I'm used to these days.'

'And what *are* you used to?'

Her eyebrows tugged together. 'I don't know. Things more…ordinary, I suppose.'

'In that case—' he took her glass, placed both flutes on the bar '—you will need to reacquaint yourself with things less…ordinary.'

He moved closer, enjoying the way her eyes flared wide, the titillating glimpse of her tongue as it darted across her lower lip. She was nervous, despite her cool, controlled demeanour. The skittering pulse at the base of her throat gave her away.

'And there is one more thing you must become accustomed to.'

She notched her chin. Quietly defiant. Utterly beautiful. 'And that is…?'

He captured her jaw between thumb and forefinger. 'Me.'

CHAPTER FIVE

HELENA SWALLOWED. THE generous mouthful of bubbles she'd foolishly imbibed on an empty stomach was meant to give her sass and courage. Instead she felt lightheaded and shaky on her feet. She wanted to turn her head, tear her gaze from those mesmerising eyes, but his fingers held her captive.

'I don't know what you mean.'

'Then I will demonstrate.'

The instant his head lowered, panic seized her. 'Wait!' Her hands flew to his chest. 'What are you doing?'

He halted, his lips mere inches from hers, his black-fringed eyes glittering like a star-studded night. *With what? Amusement? Desire?*

'Demonstrating my point.'

She pushed harder, her fingers tingling, his warmth—his vitality—seeping through the fabric of his shirt and into her nerve-endings. 'What point?'

'That you seem to have developed an untimely aversion to me.'

He grasped her wrists, the latent strength in his long fingers making her bones feel small. Fragile.

'No one will believe we are lovers if you balk at my touch.'

She tried to free herself but he held fast, keeping her hands anchored to his chest. Under her palms his heart beat strong and steady, unlike hers, which had launched into the cardiac equivalent of a Fred and Ginger tap routine.

'We agreed to play lovers in public.' *Why did her voice sound so high and breathless?* 'Not in private. And I've proved to you I can do this.'

'Yet you stiffen in my arms like an innocent.'

He pulled her hands upward, linking them behind his neck. Dragging her body into agonising contact with his.

'It will not do, Helena. Carlos Santino is an astute man, his daughter no fool. If we are to convince them you must learn to relax with me.' His big hands circled her waist. 'And now is the perfect time for a lesson.'

Heat spiralled through her, but she fought the shiver of desire gathering momentum in her muscles. He was testing her boundaries, pushing her limits, and she would not give him the satisfaction of seeing her quiver. She dropped her arms and willed her body to go lax. Unresponsive. She could struggle, make it difficult for him, but he was strong. He'd kiss her anyway. Better to play it cool and aloof and retain at least some scrap of dignity.

She closed her eyes, pressed her lips together and waited, but the expected pressure of his mouth didn't come.

His hot breath skimmed her lips as he spoke. 'Your little martyr act doesn't wash with me, *cara*. Admit it. You want my kiss. My touch. Your body craves it—' his hand rose to the back of her head and closed around a fistful of curls '—just as mine does.'

She opened her eyes and shook her head—or tried to. Moving was difficult with his long fingers tangled in her hair. 'You're wrong.'

'Are you sure about that?' His teeth flashed, his quick smile too sharp. Too knowing. 'I remember the nights you begged for my touch…the nights you lay naked beneath me, panting and pleading—'

'Stop!' His brazen words evoked a hot rush of erotic memories. Fresh panic spurted in her chest. 'Maybe this was a…a mistake.'

His eyebrows hiked. 'This was your idea, remember? What are you afraid of?'

Myself.

'Nothing.'

Amusement rumbled deep in his chest. 'Liar.'

He tugged her head back, tilted her face to his, and she knew in the span of a single panicked heartbeat she was headed for trouble. Knew the instant his mouth covered hers this kiss would not be the hard, demanding, alpha-take-charge kiss she'd expected. No. This kiss was something altogether different. Something far more calculated and disturbing. A skilled, sensual assault that sent his mouth and tongue moving in long, lazy strokes over her tightly clamped lips.

Helena's nostrils flared, her sharp inhalation drawing in the heady spice of his cologne, and a whimper of protest caught in her throat. Or was it a moan? Either way, Leo showed no sign of relenting. His lips coaxed, his tongue teased, his teeth lightly grazed. And with every stroke, every nip and tug, her resolve to refuse him access suffered another crippling blow.

Ruthless, she thought, the floor tilting under her, the bones in her legs melting like heated wax. He was ruthless and she was drowning, oblivious to everything except the hard male body imprisoning hers and the sweet, blistering assault of his mouth.

Belatedly she registered a tugging at her waistband, a whisper of cool air on her midriff—and then the explosive charge of flesh against heated flesh. She jerked with surprise, but the hand behind her head held firm while the other rose to cup her breast. Deft fingers hooked aside cotton and lace and closed around one hard, almost painfully taut peak.

Helena arched her back and groaned. She couldn't help it. Her body was on fire and she couldn't douse the flames. Her lips parted, her lungs desperate for air, and she did nothing to resist when Leo's tongue swept in and tangled with her own. He growled—with satisfaction or triumph?—and then she was lost, unable to remember why she didn't want this. Didn't want *him*. With a moan of surrender, she wound her arms around his neck. Arched into his touch. Opened herself to his kiss.

'Ahem…'

Helena froze.

Oh, no, no, no.

That could *not* be the sound of a man clearing his throat inside the cabin. Heat of a different kind crawled up her neck as she realised that Leo, too, was motionless, his mouth locked on hers, one hand twined in her hair while the other cradled her breast beneath her tee.

Horrified, she wriggled to snap whatever spell held him frozen. Slowly his head lifted, his gaze blazing into hers with momentary intensity before shifting to the uniformed man standing near the entry to the cockpit. Her cheeks flamed. Why didn't Leo release her? Remove his hand from her breast? She squirmed, mortified.

'Five minutes to take-off, sir,' the attendant said, his voice neutral, his face devoid of expression.

Leo nodded. *'Grazie.'*

The man retreated behind a floor-length curtain and she dragged in a breath, waited for the curtain to fall, then shoved at Leo's chest. Her trembling arms possessed just enough strength to break his hold. Hastily she rearranged her bra and tee, conscious of her smarting cheeks. Her tingling lips.

One kiss.

And she'd lost herself completely. Been ready to give him whatever he wanted. Whatever he demanded. How could she be so weak? So pathetic?

Was this what her mother did every time she kissed and made up with her husband? Did she let herself get played? Sucked in by some practised seduction routine that made her forget all the hurt that had gone before? All the ugliness that would surely follow?

Anger flared, at herself. At him. 'Is this part of our

deal?' She yanked the hem of her tee into her jeans. 'That you get to maul me whenever you feel like it?'

He had the nerve to smile. A cool, sardonic smile that made her want to throw something—preferably at his head.

'You call that being mauled?'

'What would *you* call it when a man forces himself on a woman?'

His soft laugh jarred her nerves. 'Force?'

She would have spun away if his hand hadn't risen with startling speed to capture her jaw. Her pulse skittered.

'Don't fool yourself, *cara*.' He dragged his thumb over her mouth, parted her lips. Ran his tongue over his own as if recalling how she tasted. 'You enjoyed that as much as I did.'

A sharp denial danced on her tongue but she choked it back. His heated appraisal, the glitter in those dark eyes, told her he felt the pull of their physical attraction as surely and inexorably as she. Refusing to acknowledge what they both knew existed was futile. Dangerous. Instinct warned he'd take great pleasure in proving her wrong—again.

She jerked free of his grasp, moved to a window seat and strapped herself in. Outside, the ground crew completed their final safety checks and she stared out the window, feigned interest in their activity.

Leo made her feel vulnerable, exposed, and she hated it. Hated that her desire for him was so plain to see. Hated the ease with which he zeroed in on it, ruthlessly exploiting her weakness for him.

Her father did the same thing—found people's weaknesses, their soft spots and vulnerabilities. Was that why her mother stayed? Did he wield her fears and weaknesses against her? Use them as leverage so she didn't leave?

Helena blinked away the burn of tears. She'd never make her mother's mistake. She'd rather die a dried-up old spinster than tolerate a man who didn't treat her with respect.

If only Leo's kiss hadn't made her blood sing. Hadn't fired every dormant cell in her body to glorious life.

With a ragged sigh, she closed her eyes and let her head fall back against the seat.

So much for cool and aloof.

Leo closed his laptop as the pilot announced their descent into Rome's Fiumicino Airport. The flight had been uneventful and he'd passed the time with work, sifting through emails and reports while Helena had mostly slept. Or pretended to. He wasn't sure which. Either way, she'd avoided engaging with him, stirring only once in two hours to visit the restroom and accept refreshments.

He studied her in the seat opposite. Her eyes were closed, long lashes the same dark auburn as her hair fanned over ivory skin, and the slopes of her breasts rose and fell in time with the steady, hypnotic rhythm of her breathing. Her hair was shiny and tousled and the thick, lustrous curls he'd enjoyed twining his fingers through tumbled in soft waves to her shoulders.

His groin stirred, unbidden. She was a temptress. Beautiful as a mythical siren and twice as dangerous with those sweet, alluring lips that could test the restraint of any man with a libido and a heartbeat.

They had certainly tested his.

He let his gaze linger a few seconds longer, then dragged his focus to the window and the vast sprawl of lights in the blackness beyond.

This version of Helena was a mystery to him and he didn't like mysteries—or secrets. He liked staying one step ahead of the game. The takeover was a done deal, but writing off his opponent would be premature. Douglas Shaw would be seeking ways to retaliate, and the man had a reputation for playing dirty. The possibility that he'd reached out to his estranged daughter, manipulated her in an effort to undermine his adversary, was one Leo couldn't afford to ignore.

The jet's wheels hit the Tarmac and Helena stirred. She straightened, blinked, looked out the window, then peered at her watch.

'One hour,' he said.

She glanced up. 'Sorry?'

'Turn your watch forward one hour. It's just after ten.'

The plane taxied to a stop near a large hangar. Fifteen minutes later customs formalities had been completed and their luggage transferred to the trunk of a black Maserati convertible. He guided Helena into the front passenger seat, then slid behind the wheel, anticipating at once the dichotomous feelings of control and freedom he enjoyed whenever he took charge of the sleek, powerful machine.

'The Eternal City,' Helena murmured when, a short time later, he manoeuvred them into busier, more densely populated streets. She stared out her side window at the illuminated façades of elegant old buildings, towering columns and ancient timeworn structures.

'You've never visited Rome?'

She shook her head. 'I never got around to it.'

He glanced at her. Was that a wistful note in her voice? Seven years ago she had bubbled with excitement when he'd suggested bringing her to Rome. He didn't know why the fact she hadn't come with a boyfriend or lover in the years since should give him a small kick of satisfaction—but it did.

'I'd love to explore while I'm here.'

'You can sightsee during the days, while I'm working. I will arrange a driver and a guide.'

He sensed rather than saw her sharp look. 'I don't need a babysitter.'

'I am not suggesting you do.'

'But you'd be happier if someone kept an eye on me,

right?' Her sigh was loud. 'You really *do* have trust issues, don't you?'

A young couple on a red scooter swerved in front of the car, forcing him to brake. 'Meaning…?'

'Meaning I'm not going to run off the minute your back's turned. We made a deal and I don't plan to renege on it. I'm here, aren't I?'

The scooter sped off down an alley and he hit the accelerator again. 'Rome is a vast city, Helena. An experienced guide can ensure you see the best sights. Go to the right places. There are areas I would not like to see you, or any woman unfamiliar with the city, go to alone.'

'I can take care of myself.'

He smiled. Briefly. 'I have no doubt. But if you wish to sightsee you will have a guide. I will not debate with you on this,' he ended, injecting a note of finality into his voice.

Helena averted her face and he wondered if she would sulk. He didn't recall her being the petulant type, but then neither did he remember her being so argumentative. Perversely, he liked it.

'Are you always so over-protective?'

Her voice was soft, laced with curiosity rather than the irritation that had spiked her earlier words. He frowned, a ripple of discomfort sliding through him. The question felt intrusive, too personal, and for several awkward moments an answer eluded him.

'I do not consider the use of good sense to be over-protective,' he said at last.

Silence met his statement, and when he glanced over she was studying him intently. He tightened his grip on the steering wheel. Marietta, too, had accused him of being over-protective at times, but taking care of his sister was a responsibility he would never shirk—no matter how vociferously she objected. He knew the consequences of failing in that duty and he never wanted to feel the devastation of such failure again. Loving someone, being responsible for them, was no trifling task. Most days it scared the hell out of him.

Setting his jaw, he crunched the Maserati's gears and turned into the narrow lane that ran down the side of his apartment building. He pressed a key fob on his visor and a wrought-iron gate rattled open, granting access to the secure courtyard he shared with his tenants. He nosed the car past two others and stopped in a reserved space beneath the leafy branches of a mature orange tree.

Helena peered up at the building's ornate façade. 'You live right in the city?'

He shut off the engine. 'Apartments in central Rome with private parking are rare. When one of my clients put the building on the market last year I considered it a good investment.'

She gaped at him. 'You bought the entire building?'

He shrugged. 'It's convenient. My office is a few blocks from here.'

She shook her head and climbed out of the car, completely absorbed, it seemed, in her surroundings. Leo retrieved their luggage from the boot and hoped their previous discussion was over and forgotten. With any luck she'd realise the futility of defying him and accept his edict about the sightseeing.

If she didn't...?

Well, he could think of several ways to silence her arguments. And he wasn't above a few dirty tactics of his own.

Leo's penthouse apartment was spectacular.

Stylish modern furniture, richly textured rugs and great expanses of glass created a slick, contemporary oasis that floated in peaceful isolation above the heart of the ancient city.

Helena tried hard not to look impressed.

Tried harder still to calm the flutter in her belly as he took her to a bedroom with stunning views from a floor-to-ceiling window and an en suite bathroom so massive she could have swung a tiger. She slipped her holdall off her shoulder, her gaze landing on the gigantic bed with its big, plump pillows and soft ivory comforter.

A steady flush crept up her neck.

'Hungry?'

She darted him a look. 'A bit.' On the plane she'd snacked on biscuits and fruit between bouts of sleep. Now her stomach craved something more substantial. Not to mention her mouth. Dry as a sandpit. 'Thirsty more than anything.'

He laid her case on the upholstered ottoman at the end of the bed. 'Settle in, then come and find me in the kitchen when you're done. Back down the hall on the right.'

Left alone, and with a burst of energy born of nervous tension, Helena made short work of unpacking. Not that the task required much effort. Even with all her clothes arranged on individual hangers she'd utilised only a fraction of the gargantuan wardrobe. She straightened the skirt of the long black gown she'd bought on impulse from a store selling pre-loved designer fashion, stashed her case in the rear of the wardrobe, then checked her phone.

No messages, but she hadn't expected any. She'd told her mother she was going out of town, visiting a girlfriend in Devon and then attending a team-building course with colleagues during the week. Small, innocuous lies that had caused a pang of guilt, but there was no reason her mother should know about her arrangement with Leo.

She tucked her phone away. Recent conversations with her mother had been stilted, tense, but Miriam *had* agreed to meet and talk the following weekend, and that, if nothing else, was progress. In the meantime Douglas had run off to Scotland to shoot deer and no doubt seek solace in a bottle or two of single malt: typical behaviour for a man who thought himself untouchable. But on the upside her mother was safe. For now, at least. The coward couldn't lay hands on his wife while he wallowed in denial four hundred miles away.

Expelling her father from her thoughts, Helena ventured into the hall and followed the faint aroma of garlic and basil until she came to a big, stainless steel and black granite kitchen.

Leo stood behind a large central island, his hand wrapped around the handle of a sharp knife, a partially sliced tomato on the thick wooden board in front of him. An open can of soda sat on the granite. He appeared relaxed. At ease. And more achingly handsome than any man had a right to look, standing at a bench chopping vegetables.

She raised her eyebrows. 'You cook?'

He glanced up. 'Bruschetta is hardly cooking. But, yes, when I have the time. My housekeeper stocks the kitchen for me.'

A housekeeper. That explained the spotless floors and gleaming surfaces everywhere she looked.

'You said you were thirsty. Wine, juice or soda?'

Wine was tempting, but her lack of control after the bubbles on the plane made her shy away from that idea. 'Juice, thanks.' She raised a hand when he paused his work. 'I can help myself.' Better that than stand there gawking at him. She crossed to a stainless steel double-door refrigerator, surveyed its impressive contents, and selected a carton of apple juice. 'Glasses?'

'Cabinet on your left.'

After filling a tall glass and savouring her first thirst-quenching swallow, she hovered awkwardly. 'Anything I can do?'

He scooped the cut tomato onto a platter with thin strips of prosciutto, sliced mozzarella, fresh basil leaves and fat cloves of garlic. 'If you still like Cerignola olives, there's a jar in the fridge door. Small bowls are in the same cabinet as the glasses.'

Her mouth watered. Years ago he'd introduced her to the

large, sweet-flavoured Italian olives and she'd loved them. Still did. The fact he remembered that tiny detail made her heart clench in an unexpected way.

What else did he remember?

She found the jar and grabbed two ceramic bowls—one for the olives and one for discarded stones.

It didn't matter what he remembered. Or what he didn't. She wasn't here for a waltz down memory lane.

She hunted out a spoon and fished out the olives, putting them into a bowl, careful not to transfer too much of the oily brine.

She couldn't resist. The olives were plump and juicy and she was ravenous. She popped one straight from the jar into her mouth, paused a second to anticipate the burst of flavour on her tongue—then nearly inhaled the olive whole when two large hands circled her waist from behind. Her hand jerked and the spoon slipped, catapulting an olive over the benchtop like a miniature green missile. Helplessly she watched it shoot off the end and roll, leaving a wet, glistening trail over the limestone floor.

Leo pulled her against him. 'Relax,' he murmured in her ear, and she bit through the flesh of the olive.

The temptation to do exactly that—relax into him, let her shoulders and buttocks mould to his hard, muscular contours—was too strong. Too dangerous.

She gripped the edge of the bench.

Oh, God.

She wasn't ready for him to touch her like this, hold her like this, whisper in her ear like a sweet, familiar lover. No more than she'd been ready for the mind-blowing impact of his kiss. Yet in less than twenty-four hours she had to be ready. Tomorrow people would watch them closely. Especially the Santinos. And Italians were demonstrative people, unafraid to express themselves in front of others. She and Leo couldn't simply claim to be lovers. They must *behave* like lovers.

She forced her grip on the bench to loosen.

'I'm just getting in some practice.' His warm lips brushed the sensitive skin below her earlobe, inciting an involuntary shiver in her muscles. His arms tightened around her. 'You are cold?'

Damn him. She wasn't cold and he knew it. The evening was humid and sultry. She shook her head, not trusting herself to speak.

'So quiet, Helena…' His mouth trailed to the ultra-sensitive spot between her neck and shoulder. 'What are you thinking?'

That I want this. I want you. I want you to stop and I want you never to stop.

She removed the olive stone from her mouth and very carefully placed it in the empty bowl. 'I'm thinking I'd quite like that glass of wine now.'

He straightened. And chuckled? Yes, she could hear the gravelly purr in his throat. Feel the vibrations in his chest. His hands slid off her waist and she returned to her task. Focused on her breathing in an effort to slow her heartbeat.

He placed a glass of wine beside her.

'Thanks.' Somehow she managed to sound normal rather than breathless. Lifting the glass to her nose, she inhaled the spicy, berry-scented aroma. Did he also remember her preference for red wine?

Eager to avoid the onset of a tense, awkward silence, she sipped and said, 'Mmm…nice.'

'Vino Nobile di Montepulciano.'

She blinked. 'Pardon?'

'Noble Wine from Montepulciano. Not to be confused with the more commonly known wine derived from the Montepulciano grape in Abruzzo.' He extracted a tray of rustic-style bread slices from the oven's grill. 'Montepulciano is a hill town surrounded by vineyards in southern Tuscany. Vino Nobile di Montepulciano is one of Italy's oldest wines.'

'Tuscany?' Was he trying to put her at ease now with idle chitchat? Okay. Fine. It was safe ground—safer than where they were before. She'd go with it. She had to. She wouldn't survive the week if she couldn't handle a harmless conversation with him. 'I hear that part of Italy is beautiful.'

'*Si*. Very.' He transferred the platters to a slab of granite extending from the island and pulled out two high leather stools. 'I have a villa in the province of Siena, not far from Montepulciano.'

She sipped her wine, quietly digested that snippet of information. A villa in Tuscany. A penthouse in Rome. Exclusive hotel rooms in London. Not forgetting the house-keeper and, of course, his company jet. However severe his setback at the hands of her father, it hadn't stopped his meteoric rise to success.

She perched on a stool, decided that now was not the time to challenge him on that, and focused on the food. 'I'm hungry.' She studied the platters. 'Where do I start?'

'Here. Like this.' He rubbed a garlic clove on a piece of grilled bread, drizzled over olive oil, piled on tomato and mozzarella and topped it with basil leaves and a grind of salt and pepper. He handed it to her. 'Bruschetta—*tradizionale*.'

'Looks wonderful.'

And it tasted just as good.

They ate and drank and she asked him about Rome and Tuscany, quizzing him on the culture, history and climate of each region. He seemed content to keep their conversation light, the topics neutral, and gradually the pretence of normality eased her tension. Or was that thanks to the wine she'd consumed?

When Leo picked up the bottle again she covered her glass and shook her head. The wine had helped her relax, but too much would lull her into a false sense of comfort.

'We need a story about where and when we met,' he said,

his gaze fastening on her mouth as she fired in another olive. 'I suggest we use a version of the truth.'

Conscious of his scrutiny, she removed the olive stone as daintily as she could and washed the pulp down with a gulp of wine. 'The truth?'

'That we met at an art gallery in London some years ago and have recently become reacquainted.'

She nodded slowly. 'How recently?'

He sipped his wine, considered. 'Five months.'

Five months? Did that account for the time since he'd rejected Anna Santino and then some? Or had it been five months since his last mistress? Abruptly, she killed that line of thought. She didn't need to know. Didn't want to know.

'Okay. Five months.'

'Good.' He put his glass down, reached for an olive, the movement bringing his arm into contact with hers. The touch was fleeting, inadvertent, yet instant heat flared beneath her skin.

Without meaning to, she flinched.

His brows slammed down. '*Damn* it, Helena.'

'I'm sorry.'

'I don't bite.'

'I know.'

'Then why leap like a scalded cat every time I touch you?' Lines bracketed his mouth—deep grooves of displeasure that made her stomach lurch. 'Do you find my touch so repellent?'

Her eyes flared. 'No—'

'Perhaps you were right to have second thoughts.' He balled up his paper napkin and tossed it over the benchtop. 'We'll never pull this off. The whole thing is crazy. *Pazzo.*'

Panic surged up her throat. 'It's not. I *can* do this.'

'Can you?'

She pushed off her stool. 'Yes,' she said, her tone low and fierce, and before she could stifle the impulse she fisted her hands in his shirt, shoved him against the granite and slammed her mouth over his.

Reckless! a voice in her head screamed, but she silenced it. What better way to prove her ability to play his mistress than with a kiss? A kiss that had to knock him dead, she told herself, letting instinct and boldness take over as she flicked her tongue into his surprise-slackened mouth.

Heat combined with the taste of salt and red wine exploded on her tongue, and when he grunted she thrust deeper, a second time and a third, until his grunt became a low growl against her lips.

Leo moved, shifting his weight on the stool, and she felt the hot imprint of his big hands curving around her buttocks. Then he hauled her in close, his powerful thighs parting to accommodate her, and angled his head to give their mouths a better fit.

And, Lord, the man knew how to kiss. Knew how to use those sensual lips and that wicked tongue to devastating effect. He stroked into her mouth, his tongue hot, demanding, and she almost lost her grip on his shirt. Almost lost her grip on *herself.*

A warning shivered through her.

How easy it would be for her to let hunger overcome sense and give in to the hot need pulsing at her core. But this kiss wasn't about sating her needs, or his. It was about taking control. Proving a point. To herself as much as to him.

She wrenched her mouth away, stepped back and watched a range of expressions roll over his chiselled features. Her heart slammed against her ribs and she balled her hands, concentrated hard on calming her breathing.

Leo made no such effort. His breath fired from his chest in short, harsh bursts and a dark flush rode high on his cheekbones. She took in his bunched shirt, wet lips, stunned gaze. He looked like a man who had been thoroughly kissed.

Please, voice, don't tremble. 'I can handle this, Leo.'

She leaned in and rubbed her thumb over his mouth, wiping away the moisture from their kiss. His eyes darkened and his hands reached for her, but she backed off before he could touch her.

'Thanks for supper,' she said lightly. 'If you don't mind, I think I'll turn in. It's been a long day and I'm rather tired.' She paused in the doorway, forced a smile onto her lips. 'Goodnight.'

By the time Helena closed the door of the guest bedroom her heart was pounding so hard she felt short of breath and dizzy.

With swift, robotic movements that required blessedly little co-ordination, she brushed her teeth, shed her clothes and pulled on pyjama shorts and a matching cami. Then she crawled under the covers of the huge bed and groaned into a pillow.

These seven nights in Rome were going to be agony.

CHAPTER SIX

LEO PUNCHED HIS pillow three times, and when that failed to appease him he sat up and hurled it across the room. The pillow sailed through the air, hit the far wall with a dull, satisfying thud, and slumped to the bedroom floor.

Juvenile behaviour, but it felt good.

He swung his legs off the bed, glanced at the digital clock telling him it was five minutes past six a.m.—ten minutes since he'd last glared at it—and pulled on some sweats. He needed to expend some energy, and since bed-wrecking sex with his house guest wasn't an option—not a wise one, at any rate—he'd have to settle for exercise.

Hard, punishing, sweat-drenching exercise.

Damn the minx.

He slung a towel over his shoulder, padded down his hallway to the small, well-equipped gym at the far end and set himself a gruelling pace on the treadmill.

Forty minutes later every muscle from his groin to his Achilles tendons strained and burned. Without slowing he swigged from his water bottle, yanked his tee shirt over his head and threw the sweat-soaked garment to the floor.

Perhaps if he'd made time for a mistress in recent months he wouldn't be struggling now to harness his libido. But his work in the lead-up to the takeover had consumed him day and night, leaving scant time for distractions of the female variety no matter how tempting or willing. A blonde, career-driven attorney in New York had been his one indulgence—a brief bedroom-only affair that ended by mutual agreement after his last visit eight, maybe nine weeks ago.

Nine weeks.

He cranked up the speed on the treadmill. No wonder he

was fit to explode after Helena's little sexpot performance in the kitchen last night. His memories of their lovemaking had remained vivid over the years—more so than he cared to admit—but he couldn't recall her ever having kissed him so senseless. Even now he could feel the imprint of her mouth, her tongue driving him wild, firing his body into a state of near-painful arousal.

With a grunt he stopped the treadmill, grabbed his towel and tee shirt and headed back to his room for a cold shower.

Helena was a paradox…a hotbed of unpredictability. Cool and flighty one minute, scorching the next. Estranged from her father yet willing to do almost anything, it seemed, to delay his day of reckoning. What game was she playing? So far nothing about her actions made sense. Nothing sat quite straight in his mind. And wasn't that the reason he'd brought her here? To keep her close until her true motives were revealed?

He snapped off the water, towelled himself dry and dressed in jeans and a button-down shirt. Feeling rejuvenated, he glanced at the clock. Still early, but he had emails to sift through, a mountain of paperwork to sort. He'd allow her another hour of beauty sleep. Two at the most.

And then, cara mia, *it's game on.*

'Morning, *cara.*'

Helena opened her eyes. Scowled. Shut them. She was dreaming again. Except this time Leo wasn't hot and naked and tangled in her sheets. He was sitting on the bed, fully clothed.

She threw her arm over her eyes.

Get lost, Mr Sandman.

'Your coffee is going cold.'

She snatched her arm down, blinked three times, then bolted upright so fast a galaxy of tiny stars danced in front of her eyes. 'Oh, my God!' *Not dreaming.* 'Wh…what are you doing here?'

'Breakfast.' He inclined his head towards a tray on the nightstand. 'Orange juice, *cornetti* and coffee. Unless you prefer tea in the morning?'

'I prefer *privacy* in the morning,' she snapped, to which he simply responded with a bone-melting smile.

Her heart tripped and fell and she swallowed a groan. Why must he look so crisp and gorgeous? She yanked the sheet to her chin, pushed a hand through her jungle of curls. 'What time is it?'

'Nine o'clock.'

'Oh…' She frowned, dismayed. 'I don't normally sleep so late.'

The tantalising smells of strong coffee and warm pastry wafted from the nightstand. She eyed the *cornetti*, all fresh and fluffy and tempting. Had he gone out especially for them?

She tried for a conciliatory smile. 'If you give me a few minutes I'll get up and dressed.' *In other words, get out. I can't breathe with you here.*

'Take your time.' He stood, and her shoulders sloped with relief—only to inch up again when he sauntered to the wardrobe. He flung open the doors. 'What are you wearing tonight?'

She blinked. 'I beg your pardon?'

He started riffling through her clothes and she leapt forward, one foot hitting the floor before she remembered her skimpy pyjama shorts. She sank back, frowning when he pulled out the long black dress.

He held it up. 'This?'

Her hands fisted in the sheet gathered against her chest. 'Yes. Does that meet with your approval?'

'It is black.'

'You're very observant.'

'And boring.'

She gritted her teeth. Okay, the high neckline and long

sleeves *were* a little conservative. But it was elegant and practical. 'I think the term you're looking for is classic.'

He tossed the dress onto the bed, flicked an imperious hand at the rest of her clothing. 'Where is the colour?'

She shrugged, but the tension in her shoulders made the gesture jerky. Where was he taking this? 'I'm a working girl now. Neutrals are more practical.'

He studied her intently. 'You used to like colour.'

His observation was hardly profound, yet all the same her insides twisted. 'Well, now I don't.' She reached for the orange juice, her throat suddenly parched, but her hand trembled and she put the glass down again.

She'd rather die of thirst than admit it, but he was right. Colour had been her passion. Her talent. Her joy. And her textile design degree, had she graduated, would have turned that passion into a career. But the day she buried her son—*their* son—the colour vanished from her world, and though she looked for it, tried desperately to reconnect with her passion, all she saw for the longest time were lifeless shades of grey. Bright colours had felt wrong. Artificial. Like painting the outside of a house to make it pretty while the inside remained neglected and rotten.

'I want to see you in something eye-catching tonight,' he said. 'Something more befitting my mistress.'

She stiffened. 'I don't measure up to your standards now?' An old familiar ache sparked in her chest. How many childhood years had she wasted, trying to live up to her father's impossible standards, knowing that no matter what she did it would never be good enough?

Leo's eyes narrowed. 'I'm talking about the dress. Not you.'

'Well.' She hiked her chin, tamped down her old insecurities. 'It will just have to do. It's the only gown I've brought.'

'Then we will shop today and buy you another.'

She shook her head. 'I can't afford anything new.'

'We agreed I would take care of expenses, *si*?'

'Travel costs. Not clothes. I don't need your charity.' *Or to be told what to wear.*

His eyebrows plunged into a dark V. 'Do not mistake my intent for charity, Helena. Outside of these walls you are my mistress, and tonight many eyes will be upon us. I will not have you fade into the background like an insipid wallflower.' He walked to the door, paused and glanced back. 'Enjoy your breakfast. We will leave as soon as you are ready.'

Helena sucked in her breath to hurl a refusal, but he was gone before the words could form on her tongue.

Insipid?

She glared at the closed door, seething for long minutes until a loud, insistent grumble from her stomach dragged her attention back to the pastries. Huffing out a resigned sigh, she picked up a fat *cornetto* and studied its golden crust. If she couldn't avoid the excursion, she could at least take her time getting ready.

Slightly mollified by the thought, she slouched against the pillows, bit off a chunk of pastry and chewed very, very slowly.

'Not this one.'

Helena dug her heels into the cobbled stones outside yet another exclusive boutique. She eyed the name etched in discreet letters above the door. If the prices in the last three stores had been outrageous—and they had—here they would surely qualify as scandalous.

Leo's grip on her hand firmed. 'It is not to your liking, *cara*?'

For what seemed like the hundredth time that day she let his endearment slide over her, forced a blithe smile and suppressed the inevitable shiver that single, huskily spoken word evoked. Like everything else, it was all part of their ruse—a ruse he had evidently decided to embrace today with unrestrained relish. Indeed, from the time they'd left his apartment scarcely a moment had passed without him touching her in some way: a hand at her waist, his thigh brushing hers, a random kiss on her mouth or temple.

And when, sitting at a quaint sidewalk café for lunch, he'd wiped a dash of cream from the corner of her mouth and sucked it off his thumb, her body had damn near dissolved into a puddle of liquid heat.

Worse—he *knew*. Knew that every touch, every lazy, lingering look from his hooded eyes, was making her quiver and burn.

She kept her voice low. 'It looks too expensive.'

His lips curved into the same tolerant smile he'd worn for much of the day, fuelling her suspicion that this exercise was less about buying a gown and more about some underlying battle of wills.

'I will decide what is too expensive.' He tugged her forward. 'Come.'

Inside, the routine was much the same as it had been at the other boutiques, only here the saleswoman was twice as elegant, the gowns four times more exquisite, and the proffered beverage not espresso or latte or tea, but sparkling wine served in tall, silver-rimmed flutes.

Helena pasted on a smile, as determined now as when they'd started out to find nothing she liked.

'I'm sorry,' she said to the tireless saleswoman four gowns later. 'It's just not my style.'

'Ah, pity...' The woman smiled, too professional to exhibit more than a glimmer of disappointment. 'The blue is perfect with your eyes.'

Helena carefully peeled away the layers of beaded chiffon and offered up an apologetic smile. 'It's beautiful, really, but the detailing is too fussy for me. I'd prefer something...plainer.'

A male cough, loud and lacking any kind of subtlety, came from beyond the mirrored screen.

Helena ground her teeth, then raised her voice. 'But nothing in black, please.'

Undeterred, the saleswoman tapped a red fingernail to her lips, then set off with a look of renewed focus.

As soon as she'd gone Helena pulled a silk robe over her bra and knickers, yanked the sash into a knot and stepped out from behind the screen. 'This is ridiculous.'

Leo sat—or rather, lounged—in a blue and gold brocade chair in the private sitting room, a half-consumed glass of champagne at his elbow, his long legs stretched out over a plush velvet rug.

He didn't bother glancing up from his phone. '*Scusi*?'

She scored her palms with the tips of her nails. 'Don't *scusi* me. You heard me perfectly well. This is pointless.'

He pocketed the phone and raised his head, his gaze travelling with a discernible lack of haste from her feet to her face. She squirmed, heat trailing over her skin in the wake of his indolent scrutiny. Teeth gritted, she fought the urge to adjust the robe over her breasts.

'Pointless only because you are being stubborn.'

She snorted. 'I'm not stubborn. I'm just…selective. I haven't seen anything I like, that's all.'

'You have tried on fourteen dresses.'

He was counting? She crossed her arms. 'And I told you—I haven't seen anything I like.'

'Then I suggest you find something you do.'

'And if I don't?'

'I will choose for you.'

The desire to stamp her foot was overwhelming. But no doubt he would enjoy her loss of composure. She settled for raising her chin. 'I don't know what type of relationships you have with the women in your life, and frankly I don't care. But I, for one, do *not* like to be bullied.'

In a single fluid movement of his powerful frame Leo surged off his chair. He prowled towards her and her nerves skittered, but she held her ground. He stopped just short of their bodies touching and locked his gaze on hers.

'My mother gave me three pieces of advice before she died.'

It wasn't remotely what she'd expected him to say. She frowned, uncertain. 'Did she?'

'*Si*.' His right index finger appeared in front of her face. 'One, to take my schooling seriously.' His middle finger rose beside the first. 'Two, to learn English and learn it well.' His third finger snapped up to join the others. 'And three, always to choose my battles wisely.'

Her frown deepened—a convulsive tug of the tiny muscles between her brows. During their brief time together he'd not spoken of his mother except to say that she'd died when he was eleven. Her heart squeezed now at the thought of a young boy grieving for his mother and it stirred a ridiculous urge to comfort him—this proud, infuriating man who wouldn't accept her comfort if they were the last two people on Earth.

'Your mother was a sensible woman,' she ventured, unsure how else to respond.

'*Si*.' He hooked his fingers under her chin. 'And her advice has served me well. As it will you, if you have the sense to heed it.'

She gave him a blank look. 'I was a straight A student, thank you very much. And I think you'll find my English is perfect.'

His teeth bared in a sharp smile that mocked her attempt to miss the point. 'Then you will have no trouble understanding this.' He lowered his mouth to her ear, his breath feathering over her skin in a hot, too-intimate caress. 'Wisdom is not only in choosing your battles with care, *cara*. It is knowing when to concede defeat. We will stay here until you choose a dress or I will choose one for you. Those are your options. Accept and decide.'

'I—'

He planted a brief, hard kiss on her mouth, stealing her breath along with any further attempt at protest, then held her gaze in mute challenge until she gave a grunt of anger and whirled away.

'Bully,' she muttered, but he either didn't hear or chose to ignore the slur, and by the time the saleswoman reappeared he was seated again, dark head bowed, his attention back on his phone.

With mammoth effort she mustered a smile and cast a critical eye over the two latest gowns, both backless halternecks with ankle-length skirts, one a bright turquoise, the other a deep, stunning claret. She ran an appreciative hand over the latter.

The saleswoman removed the dress from its hanger. 'Beautiful, *si*?'

Helena had to agree. 'How much?' she asked quietly.

The Italian woman quoted a number in euros that dropped the bottom out of Helena's stomach. The equivalent in pounds would pay the rent on her flat not for weeks, but for months.

She slipped into the gown and it was even more beautiful on, its weightless silk gliding like cool air over her body, the shimmering claret a striking contrast against her pale ivory skin. She performed a little pirouette in front of the mirror, her stomach fluttering with a burst of unexpected pleasure.

The saleswoman smiled. 'This is the one?'

Helena hesitated. Could she *really* allow Leo to buy her this dress? She studied her reflection. A lot of skin was exposed, and the style called for going braless, but he *had* said he wanted her in something more eye-catching. Something more *befitting his mistress*.

She chewed her lip. She could go out there, parade for his approval, but pride and some residual anger over his high-handedness stopped her. Maybe she lacked the glamour of his usual mistresses, and maybe her wardrobe was a little staid, but she still had enough feminine savvy to know when she looked good.

Confidence swelled. *Yes*. She could do this. She could play her part and convince the world—or at least the Santinos and their guests—that she and Leo were lovers. She had to. If she wanted to honour her end of their bargain—if she wanted Leo to honour *his*—there could be no half-hearted performances. She either did this properly or not at all.

She gave the ever-patient saleswoman a beatific smile. 'This is the one.'

Leo eased the Maserati to a stop in the gravel courtyard outside the Santinos' palatial mountainside villa. Behind him a long queue of taxis, luxury cars and black-windowed limousines stretched into the distance. Valets swarmed like worker ants on a sugar trail, keeping the line moving as guests poured from the vehicles and watchful dark-suited security men oversaw the hustle of activity.

He glanced at Helena, sitting silent in the passenger seat, but her face was angled away and he couldn't gauge her reaction.

He liked the way she'd styled her hair tonight, her glossy curls piled high on her head, a few random ringlets left loose to float around her face. He *didn't* like that all he could think about was how it would feel to pull out the pins and watch those silky tresses spill over his hands... his sheets...*his thighs*...

He killed the engine. 'Are you ready for this?'

Her head swung around, her blue eyes inscrutable under their canopy of dark lashes. 'Yes. Are you?'

He smiled at the challenge in her voice. 'Always.' He fired off a wink that earned him a frown, then climbed out, grabbed his suit jacket from the back seat and shrugged it on.

On the other side a valet opened Helena's door and she stepped out, a swathe of rich burgundy silk cascading like wine-infused water down her body. She smiled, and the kid's face split into a goofy grin that lasted all of three seconds—until he met Leo's dark stare.

'One scratch,' he warned in Italian, handing over his key, 'and I will find you.'

The young man nodded, his Adam's apple bobbing as if jerked by an unseen string, and Leo eyeballed him until he disappeared into the driver's seat.

The vehicle purred to life and Helena froze, her eyes widening. 'The gift!' She whirled and tapped on the side window as the car started to move. When it stopped she pulled open the back door and reached into the footwell.

Behind her Leo dug his fingers into his palms. Did his damnedest not to notice how the sheer dress clung to her hips and buttocks below her naked back. An exercise in futility, no less. He'd have to be blind not to notice all that smooth ivory skin. Those beautiful curves.

Dio.

He should have let her wear the black dress. It might remind him of a nun's habit, but at least his thoughts wouldn't be steeped in sin.

She turned and stilled, the gift-wrapped antique silver Tiffany bowl clutched in her hands. 'You can stop looking at me like that.'

Like what? Like he wanted to slide her dress up her thighs and bend her over the hood of his Maserati? He unfurled his hands. Tried to blank his expression. Hell, was he that transparent?

'I'm not going to screw this up, so you can wipe that frown off your face,' she said, her voice tinged with exasperation. 'Here—' she thrust the gift at him '—you take this. It's your gift.'

And a detail he'd have overlooked if she hadn't asked him earlier in the day what he'd bought the Santinos. Normally his PA took care of such things, but Gina had had a family emergency on Tuesday and he'd told her to take the rest of the week off work. He'd cursed at the over-sight, but Helena had promptly set about finding some-thing suitable—and pricey, he'd noted when handing over his credit card. Funny... Once she'd overcome her reluc-tance to choosing a dress she'd warmed noticeably to the idea of spending his money.

Inside, a waiter took the gift, offered them wine and guided them through a long piano hall doubling as a ball-room and outside to the uppermost of three sprawling ter-races. A floodlit swimming pool dominated the middle tier and in the distance, beyond the landscaped grounds, the lights of Rome winked like fallen stars under a purpling sky, painting a view of the ancient city that might have been impressive—breathtaking, even—had the flash and dazzle of the party guests crowding the travertine terraces not eclipsed the panorama beyond.

'Oh, my.' Helena stood beside him, one hand resting in the crook of his arm, the other cradling a glass of ruby-red wine. 'It's very...um...'

Leo dragged his gaze from the landscape back to the glittering assemblage before them. 'Flamboyant?' He didn't bother hushing his voice. The music piped into every corner of the grounds, mixed with the babble of a hundred con-versations and the chiming of crystal and laughter, made discretion unnecessary.

'That's one description.'

'You can think of others?'

'Mmm... Nothing as polite. You should have told me I'd need my sunglasses.'

Her wry humour extracted a grin from him. 'We Ital-ians know how to do bling, *si*?'

After a short silence she squeezed his arm. 'Thank you.'

He looked down at her. 'For what?'

'For not letting me wear that "boring" black dress.'

He shrugged. 'It wasn't—'

'Charity.' She looked him in the eye. 'Yes. I know. But thank you all the same.'

Her gratitude caused a ripple of guilt to radiate through him. The truth was she could have worn a sack and still outclassed every woman here—a fact he'd been confident of long before they'd arrived—but he had wanted to see her in something other than the nondescript black that seemed to have become her standard default. Had wanted, for reasons he refused to examine too closely, to see a glimpse of the old Helena.

She turned, lifted her face and broke into a smile that struck him square in the chest. 'Whisper in my ear and kiss me,' she said, her voice urgent, breathy. 'Carlos is on his way over. And he has company.'

Well, hell... That was an invitation he didn't need to hear twice. Without a beat of hesitation he put his lips to her ear, murmured a few words in Italian, then angled his mouth over hers.

And tried not to groan at the feel of her soft lips parting under his.

Just for show, he reminded himself, as the temptation to run his tongue into those warm, honeyed depths proved a true test of his restraint. Even knowing that his host approached and others looked on, he wanted to prolong the kiss into something far less chaste and fit for public display.

Helena, by contrast, appeared in full control, and by the time Carlos—and his daughter—reached their side she was rubbing the gloss off his lips and giggling as if they'd just shared some private joke.

Anna Santino glowered at them.

'Good to see you again, my friend.' Grinning, Carlos took Leo's hand in a strong grip. 'And Helena.' He turned, clasped her hands and kissed her on both cheeks. 'You look radiant, my dear. I am delighted you could make it.'

'Thank you, Carlos.'

Her voice was husky, her cheeks tinged a delicate shade

of pink. From the compliment? Or their kiss? The latter, he hoped.

'And congratulations on your wedding anniversary. What a wonderful party your wife has thrown. Thank you again for inviting us both.'

Carlos inclined his head towards the dark-haired girl by his side. 'May I introduce my daughter, Anna?'

Helena extended her hand, smiled warmly. 'It's a pleasure to meet you, Anna.'

'Likewise,' the younger woman said, her pretty face barely cracking a smile.

Had Leo been a betting man he'd have wagered that Carlos had dragged her over, told her to be polite, but the young socialite's pout said she was in no mood to be gracious.

She dropped Helena's hand and nodded at Leo, her brown eyes dark. Petulant. 'Leo.'

'Anna,' he said, and felt Helena's slender hand slide into his.

She pressed close and he caught a drift of the light, summery scent she wore on her skin. He tightened his hand over hers and she squeezed back, the contact spreading a peculiar warmth up his arm.

Smiling, she addressed Carlos. 'Leo has persuaded me to stay in Rome for an entire week. I'm planning to sightsee while he's working, but it's hard to know where to start. There's so much of your fabulous city to see.'

Smart girl. A safe, neutral topic and an irresistible opening to a man passionate about his city. Asking questions, listening intently, she kept the conversation alive until finally Carlos excused himself, invited them to a Sunday luncheon for their out-of-town guests, and moved on with his hosting duties. His sullen-faced daughter, who'd uttered not a word since the introductions, trailed away with him into the crowd.

Helena stared after them. 'She looks so miserable I almost feel sorry for her.'

He snorted. 'Don't.'

'Why not?'

'She's a pampered party girl with three priorities in life. Money, attention, and getting what she wants.'

Helena's expression was contemplative. 'She didn't get *you*.'

Thank God. He almost shuddered with relief. 'And see how she sulks.'

'Yes.' Helena sighed. 'A tragedy in the making, no doubt.' She hooked her arm through his. 'I dare say the poor girl's heart is ruined. You do realise she may never get over you?'

He narrowed his eyes. 'Are you mocking me, Helena?'

Her lashes swept down, but not before he'd caught the bright glitter of amusement in her eyes. He felt a thump under his ribs. A stirring of recognition in his blood. *There. That's her. That's the girl you remember.*

She signalled a passing waiter, swapped her empty wine-glass for a full one and turned her mischievous eyes back to him. 'Darling…' she cooed, loud enough for those nearby to overhear. 'Make fun of *you*?' She pursed her lips in mock reproach. 'Never. You're too sensitive. It's one of the things I adore about you. Come on.' She grabbed his hand. 'The night is young. Let's mingle.'

Letting her lead him into the crowd, Leo filed a mental note to teach her later about the perils of overacting. He could think of any number of activities he'd enjoy performing with her right now. Mingling wasn't one of them.

Yet mingle they did. For two endless hours. Hours during which his eyes glazed over and he repeatedly fought the urge to glance at his watch. Small talk was an art he'd mastered over the years out of necessity, not preference. Business dinners and charity events—the select few he supported—at least had a deeper purpose. But the kind of meaningless prattle that typified gatherings like this invariably wore at his patience.

'Signor?'

Assuming it was a waiter who had spoken behind him, Leo turned to say that he didn't want a drink or another damned canapé. What he wanted, he thought moodily, was Helena back by his side. How long did a woman need to powder her nose?

He frowned. The waiter was not bearing the usual tray of decadent offerings.

'Signor Vincenti?'

His frown sharpened. '*Si.*'

'Signorina Shaw would like you to know she is resting in the salon off the piano hall.'

Resting? 'Is she all right?'

The man hesitated. '*Si.* But there has been a small incident—'

Leo didn't wait for the man to finish. He powered up the steps of the terrace and into the hall, skirting the edge of the surging, overcrowded dance floor until he found the salon. He paused in the doorway. In the far corner Helena sat on a red velvet divan, and a kneeling waiter held a compress to the top of her left foot. Off to the side, a middle-aged couple hovered. As if intuiting his arrival, Helena glanced up and smiled and his chest flooded with relief.

He strode over.

'I'm fine, darling,' she said, her game face firmly in place. 'I just had a minor mishap.'

The middle-aged woman stepped forward. '*Je suis vraiment désolée*—I am so sorry,' she added in heavily French-accented English. 'I was clumsy. We were dancing and I did not see her walk past behind me.'

Leo took in the woman's solid frame and six-inch stilettos, then glanced at Helena's foot with renewed concern. '*Scusami,*' he said to the waiter, indicating that he should lift the compress, and then knelt on one knee to examine the damage.

'It's not serious,' Helena said quickly. She looked up to the woman. 'Please don't feel bad. It's just a scratch.'

More like a gouge and the promise of a decent bruise, but, no, it wasn't serious. He stood, picked up her purse and the high-heeled sandal she had removed and put them in her hands. Then he bent and hooked one arm around her back, the other under her knees, and lifted her against his chest.

'Oh!' Her exclamation came out on a gush of air. She frowned at him even as her arms looped around his neck. 'Really, darling.' She gave a little laugh. 'This isn't necessary. I can walk.'

He ignored her protest. 'Thank you for your concern,' he said to the couple. 'Please enjoy the rest of your evening.' He nodded to the waiter. '*Grazie.*'

Then he strode from the room and made for the nearest exit.

'We're leaving?' She stared at him, wide-eyed, her cheeks flushed, Her lips soft and pink. She looked sexy. Adorable. *Beddable.*

'*Si.*'

'But it's only ten-thirty.'

'You want to stay?'

She shook her head so quickly, so adamantly, a long auburn curl slipped its binding and bounced against her cheek.

His answering smile was swift. Satisfied.

'Good. Neither do I.'

CHAPTER SEVEN

LEO CONTROLLED THE urge to floor the Maserati's accelerator until they'd cleared the mountain roads and had hit the expressway back to the city. Without traffic delays the journey time was forty minutes. He reckoned he could do it in thirty.

Helena leaned forward in the passenger seat, removed her other sandal and massaged her ankles. 'I swear high heels were invented by men as instruments of torture.'

She sighed—a soft, breathy sound that coiled through his insides like a ribbon of smoky heat.

'Could we have the air-con up a bit, please? It's awfully warm.'

Happy to oblige, he adjusted the controls and glanced over as she settled back in her seat. Her eyes were closed, her features smooth apart from a slight frown, and for a moment he was reminded of his sister. Of that intriguing combination of strength and vulnerability some women seemed naturally to possess.

A sudden tightness invaded his chest—the same suffocating sensation he always felt when he thought of Marietta and the battles she'd had to face. He gripped the steering wheel, his knuckles whitening. He had no business comparing Helena with his sister. They were poles apart. He loved Marietta. She was his blood, and he'd give his life for hers in a heartbeat. The feelings Helena stirred in him were rudimentary, nothing more than lust—a lust he intended to sate before this evening was out.

Thirty minutes later, in the courtyard of his apartment building, he pulled open the passenger door.

Helena glanced up. 'I can walk,' she said, gathering her shoes and purse before climbing out.

'We should see to that foot.'

She shook her head. 'It's fine. Really. It doesn't hurt all that much.'

Inside, he ushered her into the building's single elevator and watched her back into a corner, her belongings clutched in front of her like some sort of shield. Against what? Him? He thought of their too-fleeting kiss and all the little intimate touches and quips that had driven him slowly insane tonight. Anticipation spiralled in his blood.

'The skin's broken,' he said, looking at her foot. 'We should at least clean and dress the wound.'

They entered the apartment and he cupped her elbow, steered her towards the living room. Ignoring her mumbled protest, he sat her on the sofa and went to fetch the first aid kit from the kitchen. When he knelt in front of her she lifted her dress, obediently stuck out her foot and allowed him to clean the shallow gash. He finished by applying a neat dressing.

She offered up a smile. 'Thanks.'

He nodded, but didn't rise. Didn't speak. He held her gaze until her lashes fell and she shifted slightly.

'Leo...'

Liking the husky little catch in her voice, he sat back and hooked his hands behind her knees. Her teeth captured her lower lip and he held back a groan. The sight of her gently biting her own soft flesh was inordinately sexy. He pulled her to the edge of the sofa, spread her legs and moved between them.

Slim, toned muscles trembled under his hands. 'Leo, please... Don't do this.'

Undeterred by her soft plea, he cupped his hand under her left breast, cradling its fullness and weight in his palm. Only a sheer layer of silk separated his fingers from her flesh.

'This...?' He slid his thumb back and forth over the slippery fabric, teasing her nipple to a hard nub beneath the burgundy silk.

A tiny groan escaped her lips—a groan he might have mistaken for protest had she not arched into his touch.

'Yes.'

Her throat convulsed around that single word, drawing his gaze to the base of her neck where the skin looked so soft, so delicate, it begged to be kissed.

He leaned in and pressed his lips to the fluttering pulse there. *Oh, yes*. Soft. Warm. Sweet. He breathed in her summery scent, used the tip of his tongue to taste her skin.

'And this…?'

No words this time. No protest. Only a silent shudder that rode her body like the crest of a powerful fever. Satisfaction rippled through him. The message her body conveyed was unequivocal: she wanted him, hungered for him as fiercely as he hungered for her.

He shifted to cover her mouth with his, but she pulled back. Desire roughened his voice. 'Do not tell me you don't want this.'

'You know I do.'

Her candid, husky confession kicked his pulse up another notch.

'But that doesn't mean we should.'

'Tell me why not.'

'It will only complicate things.'

His laugh was short. '*Cara*, our physical attraction is the only thing between us that is *not* complicated. What could be more simple, more natural, than desire between a man and a woman?'

She shook her head. 'I didn't come here to sleep with you.'

'Yet you just admitted you want to.' More than anything else that frank admission fired his blood. Drowned out the rational part of his brain urging him to concede this was a bad idea.

She wedged her palms against his chest, shoved with surprising strength. Caught off guard, he rocked back on his heels.

'Is this how it works, Leo?' She shot to her feet and glared down at him, arms akimbo. 'You buy me a dress and expect me to demonstrate my gratitude with sex?'

For a second he stared at her. Then, as her words sank in, he launched himself up, his blood roaring in his ears like the bellow of a wounded bull. The idea that he would use material gifts as leverage for sex was galling. Distasteful. He balled his hands lest he do something foolish like grab her and shake her. Demand an apology.

She collected her purse and shoes. 'I'm tired,' she said, her gaze avoiding his. 'I'm going to bed.' *Alone*. She didn't need to say the word; it was implicit in her tone.

Hands fisted, heart thumping furiously, Leo stood silent and watched her stalk from the room. When he heard the closing snick of the guest room door he snatched up the first aid kit, strode into the kitchen and rammed it in a drawer.

He shoved his fingers through his hair.

Air. That was what he needed. And lots of it.

He shed his jacket, stepped onto the terrace and stared out over the endless tiled rooftops and church domes of Rome. He closed his eyes and breathed deeply, forcing his chest to expand and contract with each lungful of air. His anger slackened in a matter of minutes but his body stayed tense, trapped in a state of aching arousal he was powerless to quell.

Powerless.

He clenched his jaw. No. That wasn't right.

'Powerless' was holding on to his mother while the skies thundered and raged and the cancer stole the last of the light from her eyes. 'Powerless' was watching his father drown in the murky waters of addiction that had blinded him to his children and finally taken his life. 'Powerless' was walking into an ICU and seeing his sister's broken body, then turning around and walking out so she wouldn't see her big brother cry.

'Powerless' was *not*, by any stretch of its definition, some pathetic inability to bring his libido under control.

And yet this burning need Helena aroused in him, this inferno in his belly, would not be doused.

Turning on his heel, he marched inside and headed down the hall.

This night was not over.

Not by a long shot.

Helena stood barefoot in the en suite bathroom and stared at herself in the mirror. 'Congratulations,' her reflection sneered. 'You just earned the rank of first-class bitch.'

She laid her palms on the cold marble vanity unit and closed her eyes. Her body hummed with a current of sexual energy, her nipples felt exquisitely sensitive, and the wet heat of arousal lingered between her thighs.

Dammit. Why had he pushed? Why had she panicked? And why had she let that awful accusation fly from her mouth? His shocked face flashed into her mind and another burst of regret soured her tongue. She'd expected him to get angry with her; she hadn't expected him to look *hurt*.

She straightened and ran her hand over her stomach. If she and Leo *had* made love would he have noticed any changes in her body? Any subtle post-pregnancy differences?

She had no stretch marks, thanks to the diligent use of hydrating oils and the benefit of youth. And, while her mid-section was slightly more curvaceous than before, overall her body was thinner. No. She would not have needed to worry, she thought with an odd mix of certainty and regret. Her body would not have given up her secrets.

Heaving a sigh, she pulled the pins from her hair, undid the gown's halter neck and let the seamless fabric glide down her body. With a tiny pang of regret she went to the wardrobe and hung up the dress, well away from her own clothes. The stunning silk creation had made her feel sexy and confident, more feminine than she had in years, but she could not accept it as a gift.

Just as she could not fall into Leo's bed.

Oh, she would find a night in his arms explosive and unforgettable, of that she had no doubt. But they had a history of heartache and hurt, a past they couldn't erase, and there was no escaping the fact he still didn't trust her. Why would he? She was Douglas Shaw's daughter, guilty by association in Leo's eyes.

Perhaps seducing her and bedding her would have been no more than an opportune means of revenge?

Suppressing a shiver at the idea of such a callous motive, she closed the wardrobe door, pivoted on her heel—and screamed.

Leo.

Not inside the room, but standing in the doorway, his large frame silhouetted by the lighting from the hall. His hand rested on the handle of the door she knew she'd closed behind her. Had she been so lost in thought she hadn't heard the latch click? Or had he worked the handle with deliberate stealth?

He stared at her—silent, unsmiling—then stepped into the room and quietly closed the door.

Fright galvanised her. 'Get out!'

She hugged her arms over her breasts, glanced at the bed and considered diving for the safety of the covers. But he was already advancing.

'Leo, stop.' She was naked except for a thong! 'This isn't fair.' She backed up, felt the wardrobe door colliding with her bare buttocks and back. 'Get out,' she repeated, but this time her demand sounded weak. Unconvincing.

He stopped in front of her, leaned the underside of one forearm on the wood above her head. The suit jacket was gone, the black silk shirt unbuttoned to a point midway down his chest. She dropped her gaze and caught an eyeful of hard muscle under a dusting of fine hair. Before she could stop it, a groan rose in her throat. She wanted so very badly to slide her hands inside that shirt. To run her palms over his wide shoulders and thickly muscled chest.

'Tell me you are not a liar.'

She blinked up at him. 'Wh...what?'

'Tell me,' he barked, making her jump.

She scowled to let him know she didn't appreciate being shouted at—or being backed against a wardrobe naked, for that matter—but the set of his jaw told her he didn't give a damn what she did or didn't appreciate.

She found her voice. 'I'm not a liar.'

'Tell me I can trust you.'

She hesitated. *Test or trap?* Both, probably. She licked her dry lips. 'You can trust me.'

His gaze held hers. 'Now look me in the eye and tell me you do not want me, do not want *this*—' The fingers of his right hand skimmed down her stomach, slipped inside her thong and, before she could fully realise his intent, pushed into her slick folds. 'And then I will leave.'

Heat erupted between her thighs, flared like wild-fire through her pelvis. Gasping, modesty forgotten, she dropped her arms and wrapped her hands around his wrist. 'Don't!' she croaked.

He thrust one finger upward, straight into her hot, moist core, then withdrew and circled his wet fingertip around her sensitised nub. Her legs nearly collapsed.

'Tell me, Helena.'

His rough command sent a hot shiver racing over her skin.

'Tell me exactly what you *don't* want.'

Convulsively her hands tightened on his wrist, his strong tendons flexing in her grip as his fingers stroked and teased. She bit her lip to keep from crying out, tensed her muscles to stop her body trembling. God help her. How could she tell him *no* when every inch of her flesh screamed *yes*?

'So wet,' he murmured, his other hand cupping the back of her head, his fingers tangling in her hair. 'So ready for me.'

He kissed her until her bottom lip came free of her teeth,

then sucked the tender flesh into his mouth. His tongue explored, invaded, as bold and shameless as his fingers— a dual assault that spun her senses until she couldn't tell which way was up.

He eased back enough to speak. 'Soon I won't be able to stop, so if you want me to leave—if you do not want this—you need to tell me now.'

She squeezed her eyes closed and prayed for sanity even as a part of her scoffed. *Sanity?* She'd forfeited that the moment she'd agreed to spend seven days with him in Rome. And no matter how many reasons she gave herself for why they shouldn't do this, why she shouldn't give in—why everything about this was wrong—one incontrovertible truth remained. She wanted this man, burned for him, and it really was that simple. That natural. Just as he'd said.

She let go of his wrist. 'Please...' she whispered, not caring how breathless and needy she sounded. 'Don't stop.'

He did stop, and she groaned, opened her eyes and frowned her dismay.

He gave a throaty laugh. 'Do not fret, *cara*.' He cupped his hands under her bottom, lifted her off her feet and headed for the bed. 'We are going somewhere more comfortable.' He started to walk and pressed an open-mouthed kiss to the base of her throat, his tongue dipping into the delicate hollow there.

She shivered with delight. If she came to her senses, told him to stop, would he honour his word and leave? She wrapped her legs around his torso, hooked her ankles behind his back. She didn't want the answer to that question. Didn't want to contemplate anything, *feel* anything, beyond the hot rush of anticipation in her veins. Surging her hands into his hair, she pushed his head back and covered his mouth with hers. He shuddered, growled something against her lips, and she sensed his control, like hers, was starting to slip.

When they reached the bed, her reluctance to unwrap

her legs had him overbalancing. He crashed down on top of her, crushing her breasts, spreading her thighs wide beneath his hips. Their mouths jerked apart and the air left Helena's lungs with a *whoomph*.

'*Dio!*' He levered his weight from her with one elbow. 'Are you hurt?'

She shook her head, too breathless for words, too aroused to care about anything other than getting her hands inside his shirt. His skin next to hers. She reached for a button, her fingers fumbling, shaking, until he closed a fist over her hands and stilled them.

'Soon,' he murmured, dropping a long, wet kiss on her mouth that made her forget what she was doing. 'First, I have something to finish.'

He lowered his head, closed his lips over one erect nipple and sucked the aching peak deep into his mouth. Then, when a shudder racked her body and she moaned, he turned his attention to the other.

Helena arched her back and dug her nails into the bedding. She couldn't decide which was more exquisite. More erotic. The graze of his teeth or the flick of his tongue. She writhed. 'Leo...'

As if responding to her strangled plea, he surged up, knelt between her thighs and slid his palms behind her knees. Their gazes locked and her breath hitched in her throat. She could see the intent in his smouldering eyes, knew that what he had in mind would drive her over the edge in seconds.

He spread her legs and stared down at her. 'I want to know if you taste the same, *cara*. If you are still sweet and hot.'

She rolled her head, tried to grasp his wrists. 'No... Wait...' *Too soon.* She would come apart too soon. And she wanted this to last. Wanted to savour every spark, every touch, every spine-tingling sensation. Wanted him to ride the swells of pleasure with her. *Inside* her. 'Not yet...'

He wasn't listening. Hands braced on her thighs, he

dropped to his stomach, hooked aside her thong, and used his mouth and tongue to take her to the crest of a swift, shattering climax. She bucked against his hands, cried out something—his name?—and then she was arching up, her thighs clenched, her fingers plunging into his hair, holding tight as each powerful wave of her orgasm rocketed through her.

Her blood pulsed. Her breath came in ragged little bursts. And through a dizzying haze of sensation she felt his hands release her thighs. Felt wet, searing kisses trailing across her hips and tummy, over her breasts and up her neck.

'Like honey,' he rasped. 'Hot liquid honey.'

He slid his mouth over hers, his kiss scorching, possessive, then pushed to his feet, tore off his shirt and tossed it to the floor. Shoes and socks next, then belt, trousers—a short pause to extract something from a pocket—and lastly his briefs. All removed in seconds.

He leaned down, hooked a finger in her thong. 'As sexy as this is, it needs to come off.' And with one yank it too was gone.

Her mouth dried. He was magnificent. Like a modern-day centurion with his wide shoulders and deep chest, his hard, flat stomach. A line of dark hair tapered south, drawing her gaze down until her eyes stopped at the sight of his impressive arousal. For a second she thought about reaching out, wrapping her hand around him, but a surge of belated shyness kept her hands by her sides, made her contemplate sliding under the covers so she didn't feel so exposed.

Leo didn't suffer the same affliction. He stood proud, unashamed of his arousal, his eyes trailing over her body like a starved man surveying a banquet, unsure which delicacy to devour first. The fierce glow in his eyes, the strength of his physical desire, told her he hadn't begun to sate his appetite.

He ripped open a condom packet, sheathed himself, and stretched out beside her on the bed.

'Beautiful.' His teeth nipped her earlobe, grazed her jaw, tugged at her lower lip. 'You are more beautiful than I remember.'

And as he kissed and nibbled and murmured words in Italian she didn't understand, his hands roamed and explored, rediscovering all the secret places from the backs of her knees to the delicate tips of her ears that he knew would drive her wild.

'And responsive,' he added, drawing one of her moans into his mouth. 'Still so responsive.'

'Leo?'

He nuzzled her neck. *'Si?'*

'Please shut up and make love to me.'

A brief moment of stillness, then a smile against her skin, a low, husky laugh that made her heart skip a beat. He moved over her, pushed his knee between hers, the chafe of his hair-roughened thigh exquisite on her sensitive skin.

He cupped her jaw with one hand, forced her to look at him. 'No regrets.'

She frowned. 'What—?'

'Say it,' he insisted.

'Okay.' *Whatever.* Whatever he wanted to hear. She needed him inside her. Now. She held his gaze. 'No regrets.'

The words had barely left her lips and he was poised for entry, braced above her, his hot tip pressed against her opening. She knew she was slick, ready to take him, yet still that first powerful thrust had her gasping aloud. She reached up and curled her fingers into his rippling shoulders. When it seemed he'd filled every inch of her he pulled out, the movement slow, torturous, then slid back in, setting a rhythm that started to build once more into that hot, sweet pressure deep inside her pelvis.

She closed her eyes, tipped her head back, let the feel of him, the scent of him, overtake her senses. For so long she'd gone without luxuries, denied herself pleasures, but tonight she would not deprive herself. Tonight she would indulge. Tonight she would take everything Leo wanted to give her and more. And tomorrow—or the next day, or the next—she would deal with the consequences.

'No regrets...' she whispered, and she moved her hips, matched his rhythm, urged him on faster and harder, until she flew apart a second time and Leo threw his head back and roared.

Leo kicked the sheets off his body, stared at the ceiling and listened to the sound of running water through the closed bathroom door.

After a long night of incredible sex he should be lying here feeling sated and spent. Instead he wanted more. More of the woman he was right now picturing in the shower, her long limbs and lush curves all soft and slippery and wet. His body stirred and yet as much as he ached to join her under the water, hoist her against the marble tiles and lose himself once more in her velvety heat, he needed to employ some restraint. Needed to bank his lust and make sure his head—the one on his shoulders, at least—was still on straight.

Anyway, she'd be too sore to take him a fourth time, and he already felt caddish on that front. Not that he hadn't tried to be the gentleman when, in the faint light of dawn, she'd winced as he'd entered her and clung to him when he'd tried to withdraw. He hadn't wanted to hurt her— had told her as much—but she'd wrapped her endless legs around him, sunk her fingernails into his buttocks and pulled him in deep, driving all thoughts of chivalry straight out of his head.

He expelled a breath, aimed another kick at the sheets.

Did her soreness mean she hadn't been sexually active for a while? In London she'd alluded to a boyfriend but he'd seen through that lie and he couldn't believe she'd be here now if she were in a relationship.

He scrubbed a hand over his bristled jaw.

Seven years ago he had taken her virginity, and though he'd been furious with her afterwards for not warning him, secretly he'd been flattered, his ego pumped by the fact she'd chosen *him* to be her first lover. In a primitive and yet deeply satisfying way he'd stamped his mark on her, and for the first time in his life he'd known the powerful pull of possessiveness—the fierce, unsettling desire to know that a woman was exclusively his.

He craned his head off the pillow and glared at the bathroom door. How many lovers had she taken since? One or two? A handful? Too many to keep count? A dark curiosity snaked through him. He should have given Nico a broader remit. Should have told him to look beyond her finances and living arrangements and dig a little deeper into her personal life: her friendships, her relationships. *Her lovers.*

He dropped his head back down and scowled.

Dio. What was wrong with him? Her liaisons with other men were no concern of his. Last night they'd indulged their mutual desire for one another—nothing more. A few hours of mind-blowing sex didn't change their past, and it sure as hell wouldn't change their future.

He swung off the bed, scooped his clothes off the floor and fired another look at the bathroom door. Either she'd managed to drown herself in three millimetres of water or she was taking her sweet time, hoping he'd give up waiting and leave.

Did she already regret their lovemaking?

The possibility turned his stomach to lead. He'd seen regret and something too much like pity in her eyes once before, the night she'd ended their relationship. He'd vowed he'd never let a woman look at him like that again.

As if he was a mistake she wanted to undo.

Naked, his chest tight, his shoes and clothes bunched in his fists, Leo turned on his heel and strode from the room.

CHAPTER EIGHT

HELENA FLICKED A speck of lint off her black trousers and cast a sideways look at Leo. 'Lunch was nice,' she ventured, adjusting the car's seatbelt over her blouse. 'The hotel gardens were beautiful.'

His gaze remained on the road. '*Si.*'

Silence fell. She waited a moment. 'Anna was conspicuous by her absence, don't you think?'

He spared her a fleeting glance. '*Si.*'

'I didn't expect her mother to be so pleasant. We had a lovely chat over dessert. Do you know Maria well?'

'No.'

Helena sighed. *Excellent*. Three monosyllabic answers in a row. She sank down in her seat. This was not the man who'd sat by her side at the long luncheon table in the sun-drenched gardens of the Hotel de Russie. That man had been charming and attentive, playing the role of affectionate lover with such consummate ease she had, for a time, confused pretence with reality. Had actually indulged the notion their lovemaking might have meant something more to him than just a convenient lust-quenching tryst.

A wave of melancholy threatened but she fought it back. *No regrets.* Wasn't that what she'd promised Leo? Promised herself?

She touched her mouth, tender still from his kisses, and conceded she'd allow herself one regret—that Leo hadn't joined her in the shower this morning. Her fault, she supposed, for being a coward. For letting her fear of what the morning might unveil in his eyes send her scurrying for the bathroom. What she'd really wanted to do was run her tongue over his salty skin, straddle his hips and take brazen advantage of his desire for her in spite of her body's tenderness.

When she'd finally emerged from the bathroom, her skin waterlogged from too long in the shower, Leo had been gone, the tangled sheets and the lingering smell of hot bodies and sex the only signs he'd been there.

She shifted in her seat, a sudden shiver cooling the warmth in her veins. Their lovemaking had been exquisite, everything she had expected, but in the sobering light of day nothing about their situation had changed. He was still a man driven by vengeance and she was still the daughter of the enemy he loathed.

Nothing would alter those facts.

Nothing.

Ten long, silent minutes later, they walked into Leo's apartment. Helena didn't bother opening her mouth. She turned down the hall and headed straight for the guest room.

'Where are you going?'

The question brought her up short. She whirled around. 'To my room. Is that all right with you?' She couldn't keep the pithiness out of her voice. His taciturn behaviour had bugged her and, dammit, it hurt. 'I'm going to change and go for a walk. Or do I need your permission for that, too?'

'Don't push my buttons, Helena.'

His deeply growled warning only fuelled her pique. 'And what buttons would they be? Clearly not the ones that control your power of speech, or I might have got more than three words out of you in the car.'

A deep frown puckered his brow. 'Why are you angry?'

She gave him an incredulous look. 'Why am *I* angry? That's a joke question, right?'

'I am not laughing.'

No, he wasn't. And neither was she. She stepped back, took a deep breath and tried for calm. Maybe they both needed some space. Maybe, after last night, she wasn't the only one feeling awkward and confused.

She retreated another step. 'I think we both need some breathing space,' she said, and turned.

'Do not walk away from me, Helena.'

Ignoring his grated command, she strode down the hall. She needed the refuge of her room. Needed to break the spell his presence cast over her. He looked so big and dark and formidable, and yet her pulse quickened not with anxiety or fear but with the vivid memory of all the ways his hands and mouth had explored her body last night.

She reached the bedroom doorway but he was right behind her, his arm bracing against the door before she could close it. 'Please go away,' she said, her voice steady even as her insides trembled.

He followed her into the room. 'Why? So you can have your "breathing space"? Is that what you need after a night in bed with me, Helena?'

She frowned at him, perplexed. 'I think *you* need some space, given your present mood.' Heart pounding, she put her purse on the dresser and removed the earrings that were starting to pinch. 'What is *wrong* with you, anyway?'

'I don't like being dismissed.'

She paused to stare at him. He looked utterly gorgeous in a light blue open-necked shirt and navy trousers, even with his features drawn into hard, intractable lines.

She put the earrings down. 'I have no idea what you're talking about.'

'No regrets. That is what we agreed, *si*? And yet this morning you could not face me. You hid in the bathroom until I gave up waiting and left.' He stalked forward. 'Why, Helena? Was the idea of waking up beside me so unpalatable?'

'Of course not!'

Her heart climbed into her throat. *Oh, God.* Had her act of cowardice unwittingly hurt him? As swiftly as the idea entered her head she rejected it. Leo wasn't the vulnerable type. Men like him were thick-skinned. Impervious. More likely his pride had suffered a blow. He probably wasn't used to women deserting his bed. Anyway, it wasn't even *his* bed she'd deserted.

'What is this really about, Leo?' She shored up her courage with a flash of anger. 'Your ego?'

Before he could answer she spun away, but he caught her wrist and swung her back to face him. The action was firm, not rough, and his grip didn't hurt, but still an ugly memory snapped in her mind. Reflexively she ducked her head, instinct driving her forearm up to protect her face.

A sharp, indistinct sound came from Leo's throat. He released her and she glanced up, saw the colour drain from his face.

'*Mio Dio.* Did you think I would strike you?'

Her chest squeezed. 'No, I… Of course I…I mean, you would never…' She bit her tongue and mentally cursed. Her babbled response had only worsened his pallor. She pulled in a deep breath. 'No,' she repeated, firmly this time. 'Of course I didn't.'

She reached out to touch him, to show she wasn't afraid, but this time he was the one who spun away.

'Leo, wait…'

But he didn't. And before she could find the right words to stop him, to erase that bleak look from his face, he was gone.

Leo stood on the terrace in the sultry afternoon heat and raked his fingers through his hair. His insides churned. The idea of Helena believing he would physically hurt her—despite her claim to the contrary—turned his stomach.

'Leo?'

He gripped the railing, loath to turn. Loath to look at her lest he see that flicker of fear on her face again.

'Leo, I…I'm sorry.' She appeared at the railing beside him. 'It was just a stupid reflex, that's all.'

He stared across the rows of tiled rooftops baking under the brilliant Roman sun. 'I would never harm you. I would never harm *any* woman.'

Her hand covered his, squeezed lightly, then slid away. 'Of course. I know that.'

Did she? Or was she offering words she thought would mollify him? The need to test that theory overtook him and he turned, lifted his hand and brushed the backs of his fingers down her cheek. She didn't flinch, and his relief was a balm more powerful than he could have imagined.

He dropped his hand. 'I am sorry. I scared you and that was not my intent.'

'I wasn't scared. Like I said, it was just a reflex.'

Leo studied her for a long moment. 'You assumed I would hit you, Helena.' Just saying the words made his stomach roil again. 'For most people that is *not* a natural reflex.'

'So I'm not "most people".' She shrugged, a smile flickering briefly on her lips. 'Really, it's no big deal. Let's forget about it.'

He wasn't fooled. Not by her dismissive tone nor by that brave attempt at a smile. Her determination to downplay the matter only sharpened his interest. He moved, putting Helena between him and the view and gripping the railing either side of her, hemming her in. He wouldn't touch her or frighten her again—not intentionally—but he would have the truth.

'Was it a boyfriend?' His gut burned, outrage simmering like a vat of hot oil beneath his calm.

Her lashes lowered. 'No.'

His hands flexed on the railing. 'Your father?'

She hesitated and the burn in his gut grew hotter. Thicker.

'You said he was difficult to live with,' he prompted, when the silence stretched.

Finally she looked up, her face pale even as a hint of defiance shimmered in her blue eyes. 'Must we have this conversation now?'

'*Si*,' he said. 'We must.'

Her gaze tangled with his for a long, taut moment, then she pulled in a deep breath and puffed it out. 'In that case I think I need to sit.'

Leo set two glass tumblers on the coffee table in the living room and poured a finger of whisky into each. He recapped the decanter, sat on the brown leather sofa and faced Helena. Inside him acid churned, along with a hefty dose of impatience, but pushing her would have the reverse effect. So he waited.

'My father's a consummate Jekyll and Hyde,' she said finally. She picked up her glass and stared into the pale bronze liquid. 'Charming when he chooses to be, lethal when he doesn't.'

'And he has struck you?'

Helena swirled the whisky, then sipped, grimacing a little as she swallowed. 'Twice.' She put the glass down, slipped off her shoes and curled her legs beneath her, favouring her bruised foot. 'The first time I was thirteen. My mother was good at running interference between Father and me, but I provoked him one day when she wasn't around. He backhanded me across the face.'

The acid rose into Leo's throat. A man could inflict pain on a woman or a child with an open-handed slap, but a backhand was a whole different level of vicious. He clenched his jaw.

'It hurt,' she went on, her gaze focused inward now, presumably on the past and whatever unpleasant images her memory had conjured. 'But the pain didn't make me cry nearly as much as the argument my parents had afterwards.'

Her chin quivered. The tiny movement was barely visible, yet still a deep-rooted instinct urged him to fold her in his arms.

He resisted.

Not only because he had told himself he wouldn't touch her unless invited, but because the compulsion stirred a dark, remembered sense of futility and loss. Of how he'd felt as a child, wanting to protect his mother, then his father, only to face the bitter reality that loving them, believing he could save them, had not been enough.

Loving them had only made his sense of inadequacy, of life's unfairness, more unbearable when they were gone.

Leo swallowed, tightened his jaw. He wouldn't let emotion distort his thoughts. Not now, in front of Helena—the woman for whom he'd once lowered his guard, opened himself to the possibility of love, only to have life serve him yet another reminder that love only ever led to disappointment and loss.

He dragged his hand over his face. Pieces of past conversations were slotting together, crystallising into a picture he didn't much like. *This won't hurt only my father. It will hurt others, too—my family.*

He refocused. 'This grace period for your father and his company—who are you really buying time for?'

She blinked, but didn't prevaricate. 'My mother.'

'Why?' He knew the answer—it had already settled like a cold, hard mass in his belly—but he wanted to hear her say it.

'When my father is angry or drunk or upset about something he can't control—like losing his company...' She paused, and the brief silence practically crackled with accusation. 'He lashes out at her.'

Leo pushed to his feet, his blood pounding too hard now for him to sit. He stared down at her. 'So you're telling me the takeover has put your mother at a greater risk of abuse?'

'Yes.'

He scraped his fingers through his hair. Frustration,

along with another, more disturbing emotion he didn't want to identify, sharpened his tone. 'Why did you not tell me this a week and a half ago?'

Her chin snapped up. 'I told you I was worried for my family.'

'But you didn't give me the whole story.' He paced away and back again. '*Dio*, Helena!'

Her posture stiffened, cords of tension visible in her slender neck. 'This is my mother's private life we're talking about—an issue that's sensitive and painful. Not to mention perfect fodder for the gossipmongers. I couldn't trust what you might do with the information.'

He bit back a mirthless laugh. *She* didn't trust *him*? He let his disbelief at that feed his anger, because the other emotion—the one that was feeling a lot like guilt—was burning a crater in his gut he'd prefer to ignore.

'Besides...' Accusation blazed in her eyes. 'Would you have reconsidered your plans if I'd told you everything then? Are you reconsidering them now?'

Dammit. Did he have an answer for that? He dragged in a deep breath, reminded himself that Douglas Shaw was the villain in all this. Not himself. 'Violent men can have many triggers, Helena. The takeover has clearly upset him—' *as intended* '—but any number of things could set him off. Changing my plans will not change the fact that your mother is in a volatile relationship and constantly at risk of abuse.'

'I understand that. But when my father learns that you plan to dismantle the company it isn't going to "trigger" a bad mood. It's going to trigger a major meltdown. I need more time before that happens—time to convince my mother to get out.'

'And our arrangement gives you that time, does it not?' Time he could extend, if he so chose. But not by much. Convincing his board to back the takeover hadn't been easy.

The buyout of shares had been costly, and divesting the company's assets would be critical for balancing the books.

Helena's shoulders suddenly lost their starch. Her gaze slid from his. 'Yes. It does. And hopefully it'll be enough.'

The resignation in her voice, the slope of her shoulders as she stared down at her hands, undid him.

His anger drained and he sat down.

'Your mother's never considered leaving?' He strove for neutrality but still the censure crept into his voice. He knew domestic violence was a complicated issue. Understood that fear and circumstance could deprive victims of freedom and choice. But surely Helena's mother had resources? Options? Why would she tolerate abuse?

'It's easy to judge from the outside looking in, Leo.'

The reproach in her tone made the tips of his ears uncomfortably warm.

'There's a hundred reasons women stay trapped in abusive relationships. Fear of reprisal. Fear of isolation from loved ones. Fear of being alone. Believe me, I've tried talking to her, but she shuts me down every time.'

He heard the tremor in her voice, saw the quiver in her lip she tried to suppress, and cursed.

To hell with not touching.

He shifted over and lifted her into his lap. She stiffened, surprise flitting over her pale features. But as he wrapped his arms around her, her body softened, acquiesced, and she dropped her head on his shoulder.

'I am sorry, *cara*,' he murmured against her hair. 'I know how painful it is to watch someone you love suffer.'

Everyone *he'd* loved had suffered. His mother with cancer. His father from grief and addiction. Marietta, whose life had been irreversibly altered by that one fateful decision.

Helena turned her face into his neck and he buried his fingers in her hair, the soft, peachy scent reminding him of the organic fruit orchards surrounding his villa in Tuscany.

He closed his eyes.

Five weeks they'd had together in London.

Five short, intense weeks. Barely enough time to get to know one another, and yet he'd fallen like a teenager on his first romantic crush.

Hell.

Had he really thought he could bring Helena to Rome for seven nights, keep her in his home, his bed, and not risk a return of the insanity that had proved his downfall the first time around? It was a colossal mistake—one he would no doubt regret. But not today. Not yet. Not until he had all the answers he needed.

'You said your father hit you twice.'

Instantly her body tensed. He waited until she relaxed, her breath warm on his neck as she released a pent-up breath.

'After that first time I'd never seen my mother more furious—or more willing to stand up to my father. It was the most violent argument I'd ever heard them have—and I'd heard a few.' She paused. 'I was in my room and couldn't hear it all, so I don't know everything she said to him, but I do know he didn't lay a hand on me again for six years.'

Swiftly Leo calculated that she'd have been nineteen when Shaw had next assaulted her. His brows sank. *Nineteen.* Her age when he'd met her. Coincidence? A sick feeling in his gut told him it wasn't.

'The night you wouldn't see me…after you sent me away from your hotel,' she said, her words segueing from his thoughts with uncanny accuracy, 'I went to confront him. I knew Mum was out at some charity thing but I was too angry for caution. Too upset to notice he'd been drinking.' A faint quiver undermined her voice. 'One minute he was cool and condescending, the next…he lashed out so quickly I never saw it coming.'

Leo gritted his teeth.

'My lip split,' she said before he could speak, 'and I fell, hit my head on the fireplace. When he came at me a second time I picked up the first thing within reach—an iron poker—and swung it at him.'

'*Dio!*' She'd fought back? Gutsy, but unwise if she'd had the safer option of fleeing. He smoothed her hair back, pulled her chin up so he could look at her. 'That could have been dangerous, *cara*.' He ran his thumb over the soft skin of her cheek, made the mistake of imagining that cheek bruised, her mouth bloodied. Tension coiled in his muscles. 'What happened?'

'I struck him,' she whispered, emotion creeping in now, her shoulders hunching forward. 'And he…he went down. I was horrified. I felt sick. There was a gash on his head and…and a lot of blood. I ran to help him, but he was already staggering to his feet and he shoved me away—so hard I fell again.' She shook her head, as if trying to dispel the ugly images. 'I got out as fast as I could and… Well, you know the rest. I haven't seen or spoken to him since.'

'And he cut you off?'

'He cut off my allowance, stopped paying my college fees, but *I* chose to make it on my own. As long as he supported me financially I was bound by his rules. His dictates. I wanted freedom, for myself and—' She stopped suddenly.

'Helena?'

She pulled her chin from his grasp, looked down. 'I… I wanted to live free of his control.'

Her fingers plucked at a button on his shirtfront and he covered her hand, stilled her fidgeting. 'Your father never met me, yet he took exception to our relationship. To me.' Even now, years later, that rankled deep. 'Why?'

Her hand curled into a delicate fist under his. 'Father had rules for everything—including who I dated. Boys who were wealthy, British and well-connected were the only ones deemed acceptable.' She emitted a soft snort. 'He never tried to hide his disappointment that his first-born wasn't a son. He once said my greatest worth was as marriage material, so I should at least choose someone he could benefit from.'

Leo's stomach clenched. He'd thought his loathing for the man couldn't deepen. He'd been wrong.

Helena shifted and he tensed. The glide of her soft, rounded buttocks over his groin was doing nothing to quell the desire he'd been struggling to subdue from the moment her backside had landed in his lap.

Her eyes rounded with comprehension. 'Sorry—'

'Sorry,' he said at the same time.

They both stopped, and half-laughed, half-groaned.

Before lust could incinerate his restraint, he gently moved her off him. Then rose and pulled her to her feet.

'Thank you.' He tipped up her chin. 'I know those weren't easy things to talk about.' He tucked a curl behind her ear, something tender, perplexing, moving inside him. 'Do you still want that walk?'

She stared up at him 'No,' she said.

And then she leaned in and pressed her lips to his—a move so entirely unexpected that for a moment he simply stood there, inert, caught by the sweetness of her breath and the subtle sizzle of promise in that tentative kiss.

Then her tongue darted out, stroked over his lips, and in one red-hot second her kiss had escalated from sweet to incendiary.

Leo groaned, hauled her against him and thrust into her mouth, needing to feel her, taste her, unable to get enough even when her fingers stabbed into his hair and pulled his head down for a deeper kiss. His clothes felt too tight, chafing his skin.

Too many layers.

Too much fabric between them.

He wanted the barriers gone.

Wanted her naked, laid bare—just for him.

His pulse firing with a flammable mix of impatience

and lust, he scooped her up, enjoying the warm nuzzle of her lips on his neck as he carried her to his bedroom. He lowered her feet to the rug beside his four-poster bed, satisfaction roaring when she tore at his shirt with an urgency that matched his own frantic need to get naked.

In seconds their clothes were shed and Helena was spreadeagled on his bed, her slender limbs pale against the dark cotton coverlet. He kissed her jaw, her collarbone, then sucked the hard, rosy peak of one breast into his mouth.

A low moan vibrated in her throat. When he slid his finger along her hot, wet seam her legs widened in a brazen invitation. Her fingers scraped over his scalp, her hips writhing as he circled her clitoris with his thumb and slid one finger, then two, deep inside her.

'Oh, yes…' Her moan fractured into soft little cries that stoked his desire. 'Please…I want you… Don't make me wait.'

I want you.

The words snapped his restraint. Shredded his intent to touch and taste and savour before burying himself inside her.

Hands unsteady, he pulled a condom from his nightstand and tore into the packet. Helena rose on her elbows and watched him roll on the sheath, her eyes glazed, her lips moist and slightly parted.

Leo moved between her thighs, positioned himself at her entry and began to nudge in. But she raised her knees, wedged her heels into his buttocks and tilted her hips so he slammed full-length into her searing heat.

'Dio!'

Stars exploded in front of his eyes and he squeezed them shut, opening them again when her hands framed his face and he heard his name whispered over her lips. He held himself rigid above her.

'You don't need to be gentle with me,' she said, and rocked her pelvis.

The sensual rhythm created an exquisite friction that forced another rough exclamation up his throat. He searched her face for any hint of the fear he'd seen earlier but saw only the flush of desire. The stark look of hunger in her eyes that mirrored his own.

He surrendered control and started to move, stroking his hard length in and out, building to a frenzied rhythm that she matched thrust for thrust until, a second before he climaxed, she sank her teeth into his shoulder and arched in violent orgasm beneath him.

A feral, utterly alien sound was torn from his throat, the intense pleasure of release amplified by the erotic pain of her bite and the feel of her internal muscles convulsing around him.

Moments later his strength gave out and he rolled onto his back, dragging Helena with him. Sensations came and went. Rapture. Languor. Satisfaction. But they were all fleeting. And as his heartbeat slowed and his breathing returned to normal Leo had the disquieting sense that *he*, not Helena, was the one laid bare by their lovemaking.

CHAPTER NINE

THE TINY *TRATTORIA* tucked down a cobbled lane a few blocks from Leo's building was not what Helena had expected when, after a steamy afternoon in bed, he had declared they would go out to eat. From the moment the owner had greeted them with a broad smile and a back-slap for Leo, then ushered them into a cosy booth, however, everything about the place had charmed her.

She chased down her last bite of crispy Roman pizza with a large sip of Chianti. 'You were right.' She wiped the corners of her mouth with a red-and-white-checked napkin. 'That is quite possibly the best pizza in the world.'

He smiled, and her heart missed a beat even though she tried to be unaffected. Tried to wedge a solid wall between her head and her heart. Sitting here sharing a casual meal felt too...*ordinary*—and nothing about their contrived relationship or the things she had told him this afternoon was ordinary. Letting a few hours of phenomenal sex, a little easy talk over pizza and a disarming grin convince her otherwise was naive...and yet there was no harm in relaxing for a bit, surely?

She sipped her wine, savoured the intense flavour of ripe cherries on her tongue. She was pleasantly full, but the warm, contented feeling inside her wasn't only thanks to good food and wine. It was a carryover from earlier, when Leo had held her in his arms. When he'd listened to her talk about things she'd never talked about with anyone and made her feel safer, more secure, than she ever had in her life.

'You seem to know the owner well,' she remarked. 'Are you a regular?'

He leaned back, extended his long jean-clad legs under

the table. 'I worked here as a delivery boy during my first few semesters at university—one of three jobs that supported us while I studied.'

She couldn't hide her surprise. The man who ran a multi-million-dollar global business had delivered pizzas?

'Us?' she said.

'Marietta and me. My father was still alive then, but he was drunk most days and the people he mixed with were undesirable. My sister needed a better environment, so as soon as I could afford the rent I took her with me to a bedsit in a safer neighbourhood. It was cramped, but clean—and secure.'

Helena frowned. 'Your father was an alcoholic?'

'He turned to drink after my mother's death. He never got over her loss.'

Sympathy bloomed. Leo and his sister had had such a traumatic childhood and then, as if they hadn't dealt with enough, Marietta's paralysing accident had happened. By contrast Helena's childhood, though far from perfect, had at least afforded material comforts, her father's wealth ensuring she'd wanted for nothing except the one thing money couldn't buy. The one thing she'd constantly craved as a child. His love.

'I'm so sorry,' she said, meaning it. 'I can't imagine the hardships you and your sister endured.'

He shrugged. 'We survived.'

She twirled the stem of her wineglass. They'd survived because Leo had made sacrifices, worked hard to keep his sister safe and create a better life for them both. Leo didn't trust or forgive easily, but he looked after his own. It was a quality in a man impossible not to admire.

'Does Marietta live in Rome?'

'*Si.* She has her own apartment and she's largely independent—both at home and at work.'

'What does she do?'

'She's curator at a contemporary art gallery—and an

artist in her own right. She recently had her first exhibition.' His voice resonated with pride. 'The landscape in my entry hall is her work.'

Helena's eyebrows shot up. 'Wow! I was admiring that just this morning. It's fabulous.'

'The accident quashed her ambition for a time, but with encouragement from her physical therapist she resumed painting a few years ago.'

'It would have been a shame if she hadn't. Talent like that shouldn't be wasted.'

'No,' he agreed, watching her intently. 'It shouldn't.'

Something in his tone made Helena's hand still on her glass. He wasn't talking about his sister now and they both knew it. She dropped her gaze, a flicker of unease chasing the warmth from her insides. She couldn't let the conversation go down this road. Couldn't explain the real reason she'd abandoned her textile design degree.

Desperately she cast around for a diversion, but only one sure-fire tactic sprang to mind.

Stifling a twinge of guilt, she reached under the table and slipped her palm over one muscle-packed thigh. 'So, are we staying for dessert…?' She glided her hand higher until, under cover of the table, she found the impressive bulge in his snug-fitting jeans. 'Or should we indulge at home?'

She ran the tip of her tongue over her lips and watched his pupils dilate, his throat muscles work around a deep, convulsive swallow.

He clamped his hand over her wandering fingers and leaned close, eyes glittering darkly. His voice, when he spoke, was a low, sexy rumble. 'You, *tesoro mio*, are insatiable.'

A breathless little laugh escaped her. The flash of raw hunger in his gaze—the knowledge that he wanted her even now, after hours of lovemaking—was a potent aphrodisiac in her blood.

Keeping pace with him on the walk back proved a challenge. By the time they tumbled through the front door of his apartment—hot, gasping for breath—his roving hands had already driven her mindless with need. He toed the door shut, backed her up against the hallway wall. For a long moment they stood panting, gazes locked, the heat of desire a living, pulsing thing in the air around them. Then his head came down, and his possession of her mouth was swift, almost brutal.

Helena's body responded with a powerful throb and she wrapped her arms around his neck, hungry for the crush of his mouth, the hot slide of his tongue against hers.

Lord.

He was right.

Her need for him was insatiable. Beyond her control.

Somehow they reached his bedroom, a haphazard trail of shoes, clothes and undergarments strewn in their wake. And then he was sheathed and inside her, filling her to the hilt with the hard, powerful thrusts of his possession.

Taking her to a place where there was only him.

Only her.

Only pleasure.

And then, too quickly, she was climaxing, her body arching wildly under him, multiple waves of pleasure radiating from her core as her internal muscles milked his simultaneous release. Her orgasm was so swift, the sensations flooding her so intense, she had to bury her face in his neck and hold back a sob of some inexplicable emotion as he rolled onto his side and cradled her into his chest.

When, a short while later, he carried her into his massive marble shower and started soaping the sweat from their bodies, she didn't have the energy to talk or move. She simply closed her eyes, clung to his wide shoulders and let the hot soapy water and his gentle touch prolong her bliss.

Back in bed, dry and cosy, snuggled into his side, she

drifted towards sleep. She was teetering on the edge of that sweet abyss when his fingers tilted up her chin. She kept her eyes closed, muttered a protest.

'Promise me something, *cara*.'

She frowned. They were doing *this* again? 'No regrets...' she mumbled, and tried to drop her head back onto his chest.

His grip firmed. 'A different promise.'

Sighing, she fluttered open her eyelids. 'Hmm...?'

'Promise me you'll never let your father—never let *any-one*—tell you you're worthless.'

She hesitated, her throat growing painfully tight. 'I promise,' she whispered, and *damn* if that warm glow from earlier hadn't flared back to life.

Leo emerged from the tendrils of a deep, dreamless sleep and sensed he was being watched. He opened his eyes and blinked, adjusting to the pale morning light slanting through the gaps in the blinds. Helena lay half atop him, her naked body warm and soft, her chin propped on the slim hand splayed over his chest.

His groin stirred.

'Morning, *cara*.'

Her smile held a hint of mischief, as if she knew how easily she aroused him and revelled in the knowledge.

'Morning.' She ran the tip of one finger down his jaw, her nail scraping through a thick layer of bristly stubble. 'Are you properly awake?'

He moved slightly, his erection nudging her hip. 'One hundred per cent.'

A pretty blush stole over her cheeks.

'Can I ask you a question?'

He crooked an eyebrow. An early morning Q&A session was not quite what he'd had in mind. *'Si,'* he said, gliding his hand over her satiny shoulder, down the back of her ribs to the dip of her waist and lower.

'Leo.' She smacked the fingers that had grabbed a handful of soft, delectable buttock. 'I'm serious.'

Reluctantly, he moved his hand to her waist. Helena
chewed her lip, her expression growing pensive, and a sudden stab of instinct warned that he wouldn't like her question.

'Why do you need to do it?' Her voice was soft, curious rather than accusatory. 'Why do you need to ruin my
father after all these years?'

The heat of arousal in his veins instantly cooled. It was
a candid question, one he had failed completely to anticipate, and had she asked it twenty-four hours earlier he'd
have refused to be drawn.

But that had been yesterday. Before she had opened up
to him. Before she'd answered a few equally tough questions with the kind of honesty his conscience was telling
him he owed her in return.

Hell.

He expelled the air from his lungs. Gently he shifted her
from him and climbed out of bed. 'Wait here.'

He scooped his briefs off the floor and pulled them on.
Then he pushed a button on the wall to raise the blinds,
padded down the hall to his study and riffled through a
drawer till he found what he wanted.

When he returned Helena was sitting cross-legged on
the bed, the top sheet tucked around her middle. The morning sun fell across her bare shoulders and created a halo of
rich amber in her tousled hair.

Her gaze went to the items in his hand. 'Photos?'

She took the two six-by-four snapshots he held out and
studied the top one, an old shot of a tall, leggy girl messing around on rollerblades.

'Your sister?' She glanced up for affirmation, then down
again. 'Taken before her accident, obviously. She's absolutely stunning.' She studied the other photo, this one more

recent. Her brow furrowed. When she looked up, her eyes were solemn. 'Still beautiful.'

'*Si*. Still beautiful.'

A familiar weight dragged at his insides. Even seated in a wheelchair, the lower half of her body visibly frail, Marietta Vincenti was a striking young woman. Nevertheless, the contrast between the photos was sobering.

Leo sat on the bed. 'Do you remember the Hetterichs from that charity dinner in London?'

'Of course.'

'Sabine mentioned Marietta and you asked me about her afterwards.' And he'd shut her down—hadn't wanted to discuss it.

'I remember.'

'For the last decade Hans has led the field in experimental stem cell surgery for spinal cord injuries and patients with varying degrees of paralysis.'

'Oh…I've read about that.' She sat forward, eyes bright with interest. 'It's a bit controversial, isn't it?'

'It's *very* controversial.' For a time he'd waged his own internal war over the ethics of it, but watching a loved one suffer did wonders for liberalising one's attitudes. 'After Marietta's accident I took an interest in Hans's work. I followed the early trials and eventually I contacted him. After reviewing Marietta's case he believed she'd be a good candidate for surgery.'

Helena frowned again. 'It wasn't successful?'

He took the photos and placed them on the nightstand. 'There is a window of time following the initial trauma during which the procedure has a greater chance of success. Marietta was already on the outer cusp of that time period.'

'So…it was too late?'

'*Si*. In the end.'

'In the end?'

'The surgery was delayed—by a year.'

Confusion clouded Helena's face. 'But…why?'

The old tightness invaded Leo's chest. Talking about this wasn't easy. The anger, the guilt, the gut-wrenching disappointment and the dark emotions he'd wrestled with had nearly destroyed him, and he had no desire to bring them to the fore again. Yet for some reason he couldn't define he felt it was important to make Helena understand.

'The surgery was only available privately, and it was expensive—beyond the means of most ordinary people. I had taken some aggressive risks to grow my business, tying up most of my assets and capital, but I had investors in the wings who were interested in a project with enormous potential. I knew if I could secure those investors I would be able to free up some of my own funds for the surgery.'

A stillness crept over Helena. 'How long ago was that?'

'Seven years.'

Her comprehension was instantaneous, the paling of her features swift. She placed her hand over her mouth and closed her eyes. When she opened them her lashes glistened with something he hadn't expected—tears.

'It was the project my father derailed?'

He nodded, his chest growing tighter. One by one his potential investors had backed off, suddenly claiming his project was too high-risk, too pie-in-the-sky for a young entrepreneur whose start-up was a tiny David in an industry full of Goliaths. When cornered and pressed, two of those men had let slip the name of Douglas Shaw. Somehow the man had used his power, his influence and connections, to identify Leo's investors and scatter them to the winds.

'Eventually I resurrected that project, but my business had taken a serious hit, and it was many months before I could reverse the damage—over a year before it was stable enough financially for me to reconsider the surgery.'

For that he'd wanted to hunt Shaw down and rip his head clean off. Instead he'd bided his time. Nursed his anger. Planned every detail of his retribution.

'Hans warned us that the chance of success was severely diminished, but I encouraged Marietta to have the procedure anyway.'

'And it was a failure?'

'She has some increased sensation and movement in her leg muscles, but nothing more significant. Barring a miracle, she will never walk again.'

Helena swiped a hand across damp cheeks. 'I...I had no idea,' she croaked. 'I'm so very sorry.'

He swore under his breath. 'Don't,' he said gruffly.

'Don't what?'

'Apologise for something that's not your fault.'

Her mouth twisted. 'But it *is* my fault, isn't it? I knew my father wouldn't approve of our relationship and I took the risk anyway. And in the end you paid the price for my stupidity. You...and Marietta.' She grimaced. 'No wonder you hate me.'

Leo rubbed a hand over his jaw. Of all the disturbing emotions that had churned through him these last forty-eight hours, hate had not been among them. 'I do not hate you, Helena.'

She gave him a look. 'You don't have to humour me. I know you think I walked away from you fully aware of what my father intended.'

An accusation he couldn't refute. Not with any degree of honesty. Seven years ago he had judged and condemned her, too blinded by ego to consider that her role in Shaw's machinations might have been as victim, not conspirator.

He tipped her chin up. 'Where you are concerned, *tesoro*, I am fast learning that what I think I know is more often than not incorrect.'

He leaned in and pressed a soft, lingering kiss to her lips. When he pulled back he noted the pulse beating at the base of her throat, the flush of colour down her neck and chest—sure signs he wasn't the only one so easily aroused. His body stirred again, his blood heating. Pool-

ing. He trailed a fingertip over her collarbone down to the
sheet covering her breasts.

Enough talking.

'We have one hour before I leave for work and your
guide is due.'

She jerked back, frowning. 'My guide?'

'Si.' He curled his fingers into the sheet and yanked it
down, exposing her lush breasts to his unabashed scrutiny.
'The guide who is taking you sightseeing today.'

Her mouth opened, no doubt to voice a protest, but Leo
was already moving. With easy strength he tumbled her
beneath him, pinned her to the mattress and smothered her
squeal of outrage with a hard, ravenous kiss.

Six hours later, sitting on the Spanish Steps awaiting the
return of the five-foot-two bundle of feminine energy that
was her tour guide, Helena admitted that she'd have to eat
every ungracious word of protest she had mumbled that
morning.

She'd had fun—an absolute blast, in fact—and her
guide, Pia, had been a delight: smart, funny, full of knowledge and, thanks to her local connections, able to leap even
the longest tourist queue in a single bound.

In just a few hours Helena had counted the great marble
columns of the Pantheon, shivered in the dungeons of the
Colosseum, stood next to the towering four-thousand-year-
old Egyptian obelisk in St Peter's Square, gazed in awe at
Michelangelo's famous frescoes on the Sistine Chapel's
ceiling, and performed the traditional right-handed coin-
toss over her left shoulder into the beautiful Trevi Fountain.

Phew!

Now she basked in the sunshine of yet another glorious
Roman afternoon, watching crowds of people mill about the
Piazza di Spagna while she waited for Pia, who'd vanished
on a one-woman mission for fresh lemon *gelato*.

She pushed her sunglasses up on her nose and smiled

at the antics of two young boys playing at the foot of the centuries-old steps. Both had dark hair and olive skin and didn't look dissimilar to how she imagined her son would have looked as an energetic boy of five or six.

Just like that her meandering thoughts caught her like a sucker punch, and she hugged her knees into her chest.

It had been impossible to sleep with Leo these last two nights and not think at least once about the life they'd inadvertently conceived. About the child she'd carried in her womb with such deep maternal love and the tiny grave where every year, on a frigid February morning, she would kneel on the cold, damp ground and mourn the loss of their son.

But she wasn't ready to tell Leo about Lucas. To inflict pain where so much hurt had gone before. Not when this truce between them was so new. So fragile.

Their revelations—hers yesterday and Leo's this morning—had caused a subtle shift in their understanding of each other. A sense of growing mutual respect. She couldn't bear it if they slipped backwards. Not now. Not when she had a tiny bubble of hope inside her. A blossoming belief that maybe—just maybe—once the dust had settled from the takeover, they could have something more. Something *real*.

'Helena!'

Pia called out from the foot of the steps and Helena rose, shelving her thoughts. This was not the time to sit and ruminate. Leo had no doubt paid good money for Pia's services. The best way Helena could show her gratitude was to enjoy the day.

Aware that eating on the steps was forbidden, she descended to the bottom. A minute later, around a mouthful of cold, creamy *gelato*, she said, 'Oh, Pia, this is divine!' And then muttered, 'Darn it...' when a muffled ringtone came from her bag.

'Here—let me.' Her ebullient, ever-present smile in

place, Pia relieved Helena of her cone so she could rummage for her mobile.

She checked the display and frowned. 'Mum?'

But it wasn't her mother on the line; it was her mother's housekeeper. And as the woman started to speak, her words rushed, the line scratchy in places, a chill that bore no relation to the cold *gelato* she'd eaten slid down Helena's spine.

She gripped the phone and stared at Pia, thinking dimly that the look on her face must be quite a sight. Because suddenly Pia's smile was gone.

Leo slouched in his office chair, threw his pen across his desk and scowled at the strategy paper he'd been attempting to red-pen for the last ninety minutes.

Buono dio! Had he ever had a day at the office this unproductive? And since when had a weekend of sex so completely annihilated his ability to focus?

He rolled his shoulders, twisted his head and felt a small pop of release in his neck.

Better. *Marginally.*

He blew out a heavy breath. Blaming his lack of concentration on the sex—no matter how spectacular—was a cop-out. It was the hot tangle of emotion in his gut that he couldn't unravel that had him distracted and on edge. He glared again at the papers on his desk and conceded he'd have to open his laptop and start from scratch.

He rubbed his eyelids, not thrilled by the prospect. His board of directors was expecting a detailed plan for divesting ShawCorp's assets. Instead he was drafting a recommendation for keeping the company intact—at least in the short term.

No doubt they'd all think he'd lost his mind.

Chances were they'd be right.

Aware of a dull ache taking root in his temples, he hit the button labelled 'Gina' on his phone and waited impatiently for his PA to pick up.

When she burst into his office moments later, a stricken-faced Helena hot on her heels, a jolt of surprise drove him to his feet. He strode around his desk, the pain in his head forgotten.

'*Cara*?'

She walked into his arms, her body trembling, her eyes enormous saucers of blue in a face as pale as porcelain.

'I need to go home,' she said, her grip on his arms verging on painful. 'My mother's had a fall. She's in Intensive Care—in an induced coma.'

CHAPTER TEN

MIRIAM SHAW REMAINED in a medically induced coma for two days.

Though her recollection of the incident was hazy, it was apparent she'd suffered a severe knock to the head that caused a swelling on her brain. Her sprained wrist, the bruising along her left hip and thigh, the presence of alcohol in her blood and the location in which the housekeeper had found her all pointed to an unfortunate and—though Helena balked at the idea—drunken tumble down the stairs.

'Helena?'

She jerked awake, lurched forward in her chair and reached on autopilot for the guardrail of the hospital bed. A second later her overtired mind registered the deep, rich timbre of the voice that had spoken.

She twisted round as Leo placed a plastic cup filled with black watery coffee on the small table beside her.

He grimaced. 'The best I could find, I'm afraid.'

She settled back in her chair—one of several in her mother's private room on the ward. 'It's fine. I'm used to it after four days.' She managed a smile. 'Thanks.'

He dropped into the seat beside her and reached for her hand, lacing his fingers through hers, his other hand loosening the tie at his throat. He'd swapped his jeans for a designer suit today, having gone to a business meeting in London, but the look of unease he wore every time he came to the hospital remained.

She met his gaze and her breath caught, her belly tugging with a deep awareness of him that was inappropriate for the time and place. *Incredible.* Even dulled by worry and fatigue, her senses reeled from his impact.

'Don't say it,' he said, his brows descending, his jaw, clean-shaven for the first time in three days, clenched in sudden warning.

'I wasn't going to say anything,' she lied, unnerved by his ability to read her. Somehow he'd known she was on the brink of telling him—for the hundredth time since they'd left Rome—that he didn't need to be here. That he shouldn't have come to London. That her mother's welfare wasn't his concern.

He felt responsible in some way. He hadn't said so—not in so many words—but every time Helena looked at him she sensed a storm of dark emotions swirling beneath his veneer of control.

'Has she been lucid today?'

She shifted her attention to her mother, restful in sleep and less fragile-looking now, without all the tubes and wires that had been attached to her in the ICU. She'd been brought out of her induced coma two nights ago. So far the doctors were pleased with her recovery.

'We've had a few brief chats. And she talked with James before he returned to boarding school this afternoon.'

The chance to spend a few hours with her brother had been bittersweet, in the circumstances. By contrast, coming face to face with her father in a packed ICU waiting room had just been...*bitter*. She was surprised he'd bothered returning from Scotland. Thank God he'd turned up when Leo wasn't there.

'Have you seen your father again?'

Helena shook her head. She didn't want to discuss her father with Leo. Not when she had the sneaking suspicion he was secretly hankering for an outright confrontation with the other man.

His hand squeezed hers. 'He cannot hurt you, *cara*. I won't let him.'

A lump rose in her throat. When he said things like that, looked at her the way he was looking at her now, she was filled with confusion. Torn between the cynical voice that said he was using the situation—using *her*—to get to her father, and the whisper of hope urging her to believe he truly cared.

'Helena?'

She started. The voice uttering her name this time was not deep and manly but soft and feminine. Her mother's. Pulling her hand free, she jumped to her feet.

Leo rose beside her. 'I'll take a walk,' he murmured, turning to go. 'Call me when you're ready to leave.'

'Or you could stay.' She touched his arm. 'You barely said more than hello to her yesterday.'

He rubbed the back of his neck. 'Another time. I have some calls to make.'

Helena didn't push. She understood his unease. Her mother was the wife of the man whose company he'd set out to destroy.

She dropped her hand and waited for the door to close behind him before moving to the bed. She pulled up a chair, took her mother's hand. 'How do you feel, Mum?'

'Fine, apart from this awful headache.' A weak smile formed on her pale lips. 'He's very handsome, isn't he?'

Helena looked down, frowned at the mottled purpling on the back of her mother's hand where an IV catheter—now gone—had ruptured a vein. Yesterday she had stretched the truth. Told her mother she and Leo were seeing each other, trying to work some things out. In reality she didn't have a clue *what* they were doing—and she didn't think he did either.

'I'm sorry he didn't stay.'

Miriam's smile vanished. 'You mustn't apologise, darling. For anything.' She closed her eyes, frowning, as if the pain in her head was suddenly too much to bear.

Alarmed, Helena sat forward. 'Mum?'

Miriam's eyes opened again. 'I've made choices,' she said, her blue eyes latching on to her daughter's. 'Choices

I know you don't understand. But I only wanted the best for you, darling. And for James. Douglas is a difficult man, a proud man, but he gave us the best of everything. You can't argue with that.'

Damned if she couldn't. But she swallowed the bitter retort. Now was not the time to catalogue Douglas Shaw's many failings as a husband and father.

Miriam gripped Helena's hand. 'It wasn't all bad, was it? We had some good times. After James came along things were better, weren't they? Douglas was happy for a while.'

'Yes,' Helena agreed, reluctantly. 'I suppose he was.'

In fact the years following her brother's birth had been the most harmonious she could remember, her father seemingly content for once—because, she supposed, he'd finally got what he wanted. A son.

'But, Mum, that was a long time ago. And things…well, they aren't fine now, are they?'

The proud, resolute look she knew so well came into her mother's eyes. 'I can *make* them fine.'

Helena donned a dogged look of her own. 'For how long? Until the next time he's angry and drunk?'

She reached out, gently touched the faint discoloration under Miriam's left eye. Last week's bruise had faded, but in time there'd be another. And another.

'Things are only going to get worse. *He's* only going to get worse. You do see that, don't you?'

Miriam's mouth quivered, just for a second, before firming. 'I have to think of James.'

'Who's nearly sixteen,' Helena pointed out. 'Old enough to understand that marriages can fail. Parents can separate. I love him, too, but you can't wrap him in cotton wool for ever.'

Most of the year her brother was at boarding school, limiting his exposure to the tensions at home. But he was a smart boy, perceptive, and Helena suspected he already knew more than he let on. To her knowledge their father had never laid a hand on his precious son, but that could change. Violent men were unpredictable—especially when fuelled by rage and drink. She would sit James down and talk with him, make sure he understood his options. Ensure he was safe.

'It's a few weeks yet till the summer break,' she said. 'When he comes home he can decide who he stays with. Who he sees.'

A tiny tremor ran through her mother's hand. 'No. Your father won't let go that easily. He'll force James to choose between us.'

That was a possibility. One Helena couldn't deny. 'You're his mother,' she said gently. 'That will never change. He loves you.'

Miriam's throat worked for long seconds, then she whispered, 'I'm proud of you, darling. Do you know that? You had the courage to walk away when I didn't.' Her grip tightened on Helena's hand. 'I don't think I can be as brave.'

'Oh, Mum.' Helena hugged her, hiding the rush of moisture in her eyes.

Brave? The word seemed to hover in the air and mock her. Brave was not how she'd felt these last few nights, lying in Leo's arms as she searched in vain for the courage to talk about their son.

Cowardly was a more fitting word.

Maybe even *selfish*.

She pulled back and gave her mother a steady look. 'You can,' she said, the conviction in her voice as much for herself as for her mother.

She mightn't have a clue where she and Leo were headed but one thing she did know—she loved him now just as she had seven years ago. If they were to have any shot at a second chance she had to overcome her fear. Do the right thing and tell him about his son.

She squeezed her mother's hand. 'You *can*,' she repeated.

Miriam's eyes filled with tears. 'Your father will never agree to a divorce. And if he does where will I go? What will I do? I grew up with nothing, Helena. I can't go back to that. And I'm too old to start over on my own.'

'Mum, you're not even fifty! And you'll be entitled to a divorce settlement. We can find you a good lawyer.'

Somewhere in the distance a man raised his voice, the strident sound out of place in the quiet of the ward.

Helena tuned out the disturbance, her mind already too full of noise. 'Please, Mum,' she said. 'Let me help you.'

Miriam's tears spilled down her cheeks. She nodded and pulled her daughter into a tight hug.

'Miss Shaw?'

Helena straightened and turned. A nurse stood in the doorway.

'I'm sorry to interrupt,' the woman said, her tone brisk, her face serious. 'But could you come with me, please?'

Leo stood in the empty visitors' room at the end of the ward and stared out of the rain-spattered window. Outside, London was gearing up for another five o'clock rush hour and the frenzy of people and traffic on the wet streets below matched his edgy, restive mood. He swayed forward, letting his forehead bump the cool glass.

Why was he still here?

It was Thursday and he should be back in Rome, presenting his report on the ShawCorp takeover to his board—a task he had, until recently, anticipated with relish.

Now, not so much.

And wasn't that one hell of a kicker?

Seven years he'd planned this victory—*seven years*—and in a matter of days the taste of triumph had turned to ash in his mouth.

Footfalls echoed in the room and he straightened, pulled his hands from his pockets. Time to get some air, stretch his legs. Then he'd wait in the limo and clear his emails.

The hospital's sterile surroundings were closing in on him and, as mean-spirited as it sounded, he was in no mood for polite chitchat with the relative of a sick person.

The roar that rent the air before Leo had fully turned from the window gave him a split second to react. Even so, the fist flying towards him caught the left side of his jaw and sent a shard of pain ricocheting through his skull.

'Bastard!'

Douglas Shaw spat the word before lunging again, but Leo was ready this time. He dodged the blow and with a swift, well-timed manoeuvre seized Shaw's wrist and twisted his arm up his back.

'Calm down, you old fool,' he grated into the man's ear.

'Don't give me orders, Vincenti.'

Shaw struggled and Leo firmed his grip, inching the man's wrist higher up his back.

In a second, Shaw's voice went from gruff to reedy. 'You're breaking my arm.'

Making a noise of disgust, Leo let go with a shove, giving himself room to counter another attack if Shaw was stupid enough to try.

The older man wisely calmed down. He rubbed his arm. 'What the hell are *you* doing here?'

Leo returned his hands to his pockets, adopting a casual stance that belied the tension in his muscles, his readiness to act. He studied Shaw's hostile face—a face he had, until now, seen only in media clippings and corporate profiles. Hollows in the man's cheeks and a grey tinge to his skin made him look older in the flesh. Strong cologne and the waft of alcohol tainted the air.

Leo suppressed a grimace. 'I'm surprised you recognise me, Shaw. After all those declined invitations to meet I was beginning to think you had no interest in your new majority shareholder.'

'Is that why you're here?' Shaw snarled the question. 'Looking for a chance to gloat?'

Leo threw his head back and laughed. 'Don't flatter yourself, old man. I have better ways to spend my time.'

Shaw stepped forward, his sore arm and Leo's superiority in the strength department clearly forgotten. 'Maybe I should teach you another lesson—like the one I taught you seven years ago.'

Leo freed his fists, leaned his face close to Shaw's. 'You can try, but we both know your threats are empty. The truth is you're a coward and a bully. I know it. Your wife knows it. And your daughter knows it.'

A deep purple suffused Shaw's face. 'By God, I should—'

'Stop it! Both of you!'

A female voice sliced across the room, silencing whatever puerile threat Shaw had been about to deliver.

'This is not the time or place.'

Helena glared at each man before turning to murmur something to the nurse hovering in the doorway behind her. The woman muttered a reply, levelled a stern look at the men, then disappeared. Helena came into the room, her movements short, stiff, and stood shoulder to shoulder with Leo.

This time Shaw threw his head back and laughed. 'Of course!' he exclaimed to the ceiling. 'I should have guessed.' He snapped his chin down, pinned his daughter with a contemptuous stare. 'Some things never change— you're still a disloyal slut.'

Rage exploded in Leo's chest. Before his brain could intervene his muscles jolted into action. Within seconds his hands were twisted in the front of Shaw's shirt and he had the man pinned to a wall.

'Leo—stop!'

Helena's voice barely registered over the roar in his ears, but her firm touch on his arm dragged him back to his senses. Sucking in a deep breath, he dropped his hands, appalled by how swiftly the urge to do violence had overtaken him. That was Shaw's MO, he reminded himself with a flare of disgust, not his.

He stepped back and Shaw eyed him with a supercilious sneer that made Leo, for one tenth of a second, want to wipe the look off his face and to hell with being the better man.

Shaw straightened his attire and brushed himself off as if Leo's touch had left him soiled.

Pompous ass.

Helena turned to her father, her pale features set in the cool, dignified mask Leo had learnt to recognise as her protective armour. A week ago that very mask had bugged the hell out of him. Now her poise under pressure drew his unbridled respect.

'Leo's right,' she said, her voice as cold and sharp as a blade of ice. 'You're nothing but a coward and a bully.'

Shaw's face darkened, but Helena showed no fear. She stepped closer, and Leo braced himself to intervene if Shaw made any sudden moves.

'You tried so often to make me feel like a failure as a child. To make me feel worthless. But the truth is there's only one failure in this family and it's not me or Mum.' Her chin jutted up. 'It's *you*. It's *always* been you.' She pulled the strap of her handbag higher up her shoulder. 'Go home, Douglas,' she said, her voice quieter, weary now. 'My mother doesn't want to see you.'

And then she stepped back, looked at Leo.

'I'm ready to go whenever you are.'

Stiff and proud, she strode out of the room and Leo bolted after her, ignoring the man whose bluster had withered to a hard, brittle silence. A few days ago Leo would have sold his soul for a chance to face off with the man. Now there Shaw stood and Leo couldn't care less. The only face he wanted to see was Helena's.

He caught her in the corridor, pulled her gently to a stop. The tears on her cheeks caused a sharp burning sensation in his chest.

She swiped at her face with the heel of her hand. 'Please, just take me home.'

He frowned, picturing the cramped flat he'd cast an appalled eye over four days ago. He had announced with unequivocal authority that she would stay with him at the hotel.

'Home?' he echoed, his stomach pitching at the idea of taking her back there.

'I mean the hotel. Just anywhere that's not here.'

His innards levelled out. '*Si.* Of course.' He cradled her damp face in his hands, pressed a kiss to her forehead. 'Will you wait here one minute for me?'

She nodded and he kissed her again—on the mouth this time—then released her and headed back to the visitors' room.

Shaw hadn't gone far. He stood by the window, much as Leo had earlier, staring down at the rain-soaked streets.

He glanced over his shoulder, his top lip curling. 'What do you want now, Vincenti?'

'To give you some advice.'

Shaw snorted. 'This should be good.'

Leo stood a few paces shy of the older man. 'Next time you feel the need to lash out,' he said, undaunted by the sudden fierce glower on Shaw's face, 'stay away from your wife. If you do not, and I hear that you have harmed her, know that I will come after you and do everything in my power to see you prosecuted in a court of law.'

He eyeballed Shaw just long enough to assure the man his threat was genuine, then started to leave, his thoughts already shifting back to Helena.

'Let me give *you* a piece of advice, son.'

Leo stopped, certain that whatever gem Shaw intended to impart wouldn't be worth a dime. He turned. 'What?'

'There are two kinds of women in this world. Those who understand their place and those who don't. Miriam always knew how to toe the line, but she coddled that girl far too much. If you want obedience in a woman you won't find it in Helena. She'll bring you nothing but trouble.'

Dio. The man was a raving misogynist. 'You don't know Helena.'

Shaw sneered. 'And you *do*?'

'Better than you.'

The sneer stretched into a bloodless smile that raised the hairs on Leo's forearms.

'In that case, since the two of you are so close, I assume you know about the baby?'

At that moment a grey-haired woman entered the room and headed for the kitchenette in the far corner.

Shaw stepped forward and Leo tensed, but the other man's hands remained by his sides.

He leaned in to deliver his parting shot. 'The one she buried nine months after you scarpered back to Italy.'

For a suspended moment Shaw's words hung in the air, devoid of meaning, and then, like guided missiles striking their target, they slammed into Leo's brain one after the other. His lungs locked. The skin at his nape tightened. And when Shaw walked away, his expression smug, Leo couldn't do a damn thing to stop him. Because his muscles—the ones that had been so swift to react earlier—had completely frozen.

Through a dark, suffocating mist, he registered a touch on his arm. He looked down.

'Are you all right, my dear?' The elderly woman peered up at him through round, wire-rimmed spectacles. 'You're as white as a ghost.'

'Tell me about the child.'

Helena stared at Leo's implacable face. 'Stop standing over me.'

She wished she hadn't sat down as soon as they'd entered the suite. She fought back a shiver. She'd thought his silence during the limo ride from the hospital had been unbearable. Having him tower over her now, like some big, surly interrogator, while she cowered on the sofa was ten times worse.

He gritted his teeth—she could tell by the way his jaw flexed—then visibly flinched.

'You should ice that,' she blurted, eyeing the livid bruise beneath his five o'clock shadow. She still couldn't believe her father had punched him.

'So help me, Helena, if you do not—'

'I wanted to tell you.' She jumped to her feet, unable to sit there a moment longer while he glowered down at her. She circled around the sofa, gripped the back for support. 'I was just...waiting for the right time.'

Oh, God. How weak that sounded—how very convenient and trite. He'd never believe it. Not now. Not in a million years.

She searched his face, desperate for a glimpse of the warmth and tenderness she'd grown accustomed to in recent days. But all she saw was anger. Disbelief. Hurt. She thought of her father and his smug expression as he'd passed her in the hospital corridor. A flash of hatred burned in her chest. He'd ruined everything. *Again.*

'You were waiting for *the right time*?' Leo plunged his fingers into his hair. 'Did you not think seven years ago that it was "the right time"?'

Her legs shook and she dug her nails into the sofa. 'You left,' she reminded him. 'You went back to Italy.'

'Because I had nothing to stay for. Your father had seen to that.'

'You said you never wanted to see me again.'

'I had no idea you were carrying my child.'

'Neither did I.'

Only once had they burst a condom, and she'd sensibly taken a morning-after pill. And since her cycle had always been erratic her overdue period hadn't, at first, been cause for concern.

'And when you *did* find out? Did it not occur to you *then* to find me and tell me I was going to be a father?'

'No—I mean...' She shook her head. '*Yes*. But I was confused. Frightened.'

'So you were thinking about yourself? Not me? Or what was best for our child?'

His words cut like the vicious lash of a whip. Smarting, she prised her hands from the back of the sofa then walked around it, her insides trembling.

'Be angry with me, Leo,' she said, stalking into his space. 'But don't judge me. Don't pretend you have *any* idea what it's like to be pregnant and scared and alone. I made some foolish decisions—some *bad* decisions—but don't think for a moment I didn't realise that. Don't think I didn't hold our son in my arms and regret, to the very bottom of my soul, that I had denied you that privilege.'

Leo's face suddenly paled and the flash of anguish in his eyes sliced through her heart.

'A son?' He dropped onto the sofa and bowed his head for a long moment. 'How...?'

He didn't finish the question. He didn't need to.

She sat beside him, close but not touching, and pulled in a deep breath. She spoke quietly. 'He was stillborn. He died in my womb two days before he was due.'

She stared at her hands, pale against the dark denim of her jeans. She didn't need to look at Leo to know his reaction. His shock was palpable.

'I knew something was wrong because I could no longer feel him kicking. I went straight to the hospital and they confirmed that he didn't have a heartbeat. The doctors couldn't tell me why it had happened. Apparently it just does sometimes.'

She curled her nails into her palms. Her memory of that day was still vivid: the horror, the pain. It was a dark stain on her soul she would never be able to erase.

'They offered an autopsy but I...I turned it down. I

didn't want our little boy cut open,' she said hurriedly, feeling she had to justify that decision. 'The results weren't guaranteed to be conclusive. And it wasn't going to bring him back.'

She looked up and Leo's expression was so stark she wanted to reach out and touch him. But there was no comfort she could offer him. No words of solace. Pain, she knew, eased with time. Nothing else.

'I'm so sorry,' she whispered.

Abruptly he stood, grabbed his jacket off the chair where he'd tossed it earlier and shrugged it on.

She swallowed, her heart plummeting. 'Where are you going?'

He looked at her, the emotion in those dark eyes impossible to fathom.

'Out. I need a drink.'

'You have a bar here.'

Ignoring that, he strode to the door.

Disbelief drove Helena to her feet. 'So you're just going to walk out? You don't even want to talk about it?' She blinked back tears.

Damn him. He was hurting. In shock. She got that. But he wasn't the only one who'd been through an emotional grinder today.

He stopped and turned. Several beats of silence pulsed between them, each one long and unbearably tense. For a moment she thought he would say something. He didn't. He spun on his heel and walked out through the door.

CHAPTER ELEVEN

DARKNESS SHROUDED THE suite when Leo returned.

Had she gone? he wondered. Back to that grim flat of hers? Back to whatever bland, colourless life she'd consigned herself to since the death of their son?

He flicked on a light and blinked. He wasn't drunk. In fact he'd nursed a single Scotch in the hotel bar for over an hour before the need to move had overtaken him. And then he'd walked. From the streets of Mayfair to the teeming pavements of Soho and Piccadilly Circus and back to the tree-lined greens of Hyde Park. He'd walked until his feet burned and fatigue stripped away his anger, leaving in its wake the galling knowledge that he'd behaved appallingly.

He dumped his jacket and looked at his watch. Nine-thirty p.m. Three hours since he'd left—plenty of time for her to pack up and flee. But had she? He moved through the suite, a hard knot forming in his chest at the prospect that she really had gone.

But, no. Her clothes were still in the bedroom, her toiletries sitting in a neat row on the bathroom vanity.

So where the hell was she?

He went back to the lounge and found his phone. He'd switched it off earlier. Maybe she'd left a message? He powered it on and had his code half entered when he heard a noise at the door. A few seconds later it swung open and Helena walked in, carrying a bag and wearing a grey hooded jacket with damp patches on the shoulders.

He frowned, disguising his relief. 'You're wet,' he said. Inanely. Because it was better than shouting, *Where the hell have you been?*

'It's just started raining again.' She glanced at him, put

down the bag and took off her jacket. Her face was flushed, her breathing a little uneven. 'I only caught a few drops.'

'Where have you been?' He surprised himself with how reasonable he sounded. How *not* angry.

'I went home.'

He raised his eyebrows. 'How?'

'On the tube. You know…that thing called public transport—for common folk who can't afford limos.' Her sarcasm lacked any genuine bite.

He put his phone down. 'Why?'

'I needed to get something.'

She knelt by the bag and lifted out a wooden box, roughly the size of a document-carrier. It looked hand-crafted, its golden wood polished to a beautiful sheen, the lock and key and silver side-handles dainty and ornate. She placed it on the coffee table by the sofa and straightened, holding out her hand to him.

'I named our little boy Lucas,' she said, a smile trembling on her lips. 'And he was the most beautiful thing I had ever seen.'

Helena watched Leo's expression crumple in a way she'd never have imagined it could. He closed his eyes and turned away, his shoulders hunched, his head bowed.

'No. I can't.'

She walked over and touched his shoulder. 'You can,' she said, as firmly as she'd spoken those very same words to her mother. 'Our son was *real*, Leo. He didn't cry or open his eyes or take a breath, but he had ten fingers and ten toes and everything else a perfect baby should have.' She squeezed his shoulder, felt a tremor run through the hard muscle under her hand. 'Please,' she said, willing him to look at her. Willing him to trust her. 'Let me show you our little boy. I promise it will help.'

Endless seconds ticked by. Taut, silent seconds that stretched her nerves and amplified each painful beat of her heart. At the very moment her shoulders started to slump, weighted by defeat, he turned.

'*Si*.' He dragged a hand over his face. 'Show me, then.'

Relief—and a glimmer of hope—trickled through Helena's veins. She took his hand and led him to the sofa. He sat and she kicked off her shoes, knelt on the floor and opened the box. The first item made her heart give a painful squeeze.

Hands shaking, she passed it to him. 'I knitted it myself.'

Leo's big, masculine hands dwarfed the tiny purple beanie. He turned it over several times, his eyebrows inching up as he fingered the multi-coloured pompom. 'It is very…bright.'

She waggled a pair of fire-engine-red booties. 'I liked colour, remember? Pastels didn't get a look-in, I'm afraid.'

His soft grunt might or might not have been approval. Sitting forward, he peered into the box. 'Is this…?' He lifted out a small white plaster mould. '*Mio Dio*.' He ran his thumb over the tiny indentations created by his son's hand. His voice deepened. Thickened. 'So small…and perfect…'

'There are moulds of his feet, too,' she said, blinking away the sudden prickle of tears. 'And a lock of hair. Some outfits.' She delved into the box, removed more items, including an envelope. 'And I…I have photos.'

Leo shifted suddenly, sinking to the floor beside her, so close his warm, muscled thigh pressed against hers. He reached for the miniature mould of Lucas's foot, handling the tiny object with infinite care.

Helena watched, her throat growing hot, tight. Perhaps this hadn't been a crazy idea after all? If everything fell apart from here—if *they* fell apart—at least they would have shared this.

He put down the mould and turned his attention to the other items she'd laid out, taking his time to handle and examine each one in turn. When he eventually came to the photos he studied them for a long time in silence.

'He looks like he's sleeping,' he said at last.

'Yes.' The ache in her throat became a powerful throb. 'He does.'

She sat back on her heels. She could weep right now. For the son she had lost. For the strong, proud man sitting beside her. For the future for which she had dared to hope.

Instead she climbed to her feet and looked down on Leo's bowed head. 'I'm tired, and cold. I think I'll grab a shower before bed.' She hovered a moment, but his focus remained on the photo in his hand. 'Will you...be coming to bed?'

As she waited for his answer, her muscles tense, her body shivery from tiredness, she realised how much she wanted him to say yes. How badly she needed his arms around her tonight. How desperately she ached for his warmth, his touch, *his love*.

'Soon,' he said, and his eyes, when he glanced up, revealed nothing.

But when Leo finally came to bed, over two hours later, he didn't put his arms around her. He didn't touch her. He didn't even turn in her direction. And though it was only a matter of inches that separated their bodies, the gap might as well have been a chasm. A chasm Helena feared was too wide, too dark and too deep for either of them to bridge.

Leo stood at the French doors and watched lightning fork across the night sky, the jagged streaks of white light searing his retinas.

Or was it the tears making his eyes burn?

Dammit.

He hadn't cried since the night of Marietta's accident, but that box had been his undoing. Unravelling him in ways he hadn't thought possible. Flaying his emotions until his insides felt raw. And yet his pain must be nothing compared to what Helena had suffered. Helena had borne her loss alone, grieved for their son without him because she had been too afraid to tell him she was carrying their child. Too afraid because the last words he'd spoken to her—shouted through a closed hotel door, no less—had been hard, unforgiving words, fired without a care for how deeply they'd wound.

Thunder boomed, closer now, and he stepped back from the glass. *Idiota*, standing here watching the storm. Inviting memories of the night his mother had died.

As a child he'd thought thunder was a sign of God's anger. Had thought losing his mother was his punishment for boyhood sins: avoiding homework, skipping chores, cornering the big bully who'd pulled Marietta's hair and punching him in the nose—twice.

Since then he'd hated thunderstorms. Hated the idea of something so powerful and beyond his control.

Maybe God was punishing him now?

For his pride. His anger. His failure to forgive.

He had targeted one man with single-minded purpose and spared not a thought for collateral damage. Now a woman lay in hospital. Another in his bed.

And what of her? his conscience demanded. Would Helena, too, become collateral damage when all this was over? Or would the only damage where she was concerned be to his heart?

'Leo?'

He started, the soft voice behind him catching him by surprise. When he had thrown off the sheets and padded, naked, through to the lounge he had thought Helena asleep—undisturbed, it seemed, by the storm.

'What are you doing?' she said, drowsy. 'It's three a.m.'

He didn't turn. Didn't know what to say to her. What *could* he say? *I'm sorry?* No. Useless. Mere words couldn't express his regret for his behaviour today. His behaviour seven years ago.

He'd stormed back to Italy like an angry bear, licking

his wounds when he should have been here looking after her, sharing the burden of responsibility.

Of loss.

He glanced over his shoulder. Her form was a willowy outline in the glow of the single lamp he'd switched on in the corner of the room.

'I couldn't sleep,' he said.

'The storm?'

'I don't like them.' The words just spilled out. He didn't know why. He didn't make a habit of highlighting his weaknesses to people. But then, Helena wasn't *people*. She was... Hell, she was so many things—none of which he was in any mood to contemplate.

'Why?' She was right behind him now.

He shrugged. 'Bad memories.'

He could feel her breath on his shoulder, and the tantalising scent of warm, sleepy woman enveloped him. He scrunched his eyes closed, the rush of blood to his groin turning him hard against his will.

He wanted her.

Even with his gut in turmoil, tears drying on his cheeks, he wanted her.

He heard a rustling behind him and then her arms were slipping around his middle, her slender fingers splaying over his abs. Her heavy breasts pushed into his back, her hips against his buttocks, and his desire surged with the realisation that she'd shed her pyjamas and was now, like him, completely naked.

He groaned. 'Helena...'

'Shh.' She ducked under his arm and took his face in her hands.

When he drew breath to speak again she tugged his head down and silenced him with a long, drugging kiss.

Her taste exploded in his mouth, hot and sweet and undeniably erotic. He shuddered, closed his arms around her and surrendered to the burning need only she could assuage. The solace only she could offer. He hoisted her up and her legs hooked around his waist, their mouths continuing to meld and devour—until he started for the bedroom.

She wrenched her mouth away. 'No,' she whispered, lowering her legs, pulling him back to the French doors. She sank to her knees at his feet. 'Here. Take me here.'

He stared down at her, his blood pounding, his heart pumping so hard he feared it might punch from his chest.

This woman stripped him bare. Of his pride. His anger. His guilt. Everything but this deep, compelling need for her.

'Why?' he said, his throat raw.

She reached for his hands and dragged him down to the carpet, pushed him onto his back. 'To replace your bad memories with new ones,' she said, and mounted him so quickly he almost came the moment her slippery heat encased him.

He dug his heels into the carpet, seized her hips in an urgent bid to slow her. He wasn't wearing protection and she was hot and slick, her internal muscles a tight velvet sheath pulsing around him.

The sensation was exquisite.

'Condom...' he rasped.

'I'm on the pill.' She grabbed his wrists, guided his hands to her breasts and arched her back, taking him deeper. Her dark curls tumbled around her shoulders and her features were illuminated as another bright bolt of lightning tore the sky.

Leo stared up, captivated by the sight of her riding him, by the bold, sensual grind of her pelvis driving him to the brink faster than he'd have liked. Thunder rolled down from the heavens, loud and near, a boom so powerful it slammed into his body with an almighty thud.

'Come with me,' he ground out, grasping her waist, forcing her to still so he could satisfy his need to drive up into her.

'I…I'm close.' Her body flexed, her thighs squeezing his sides, a taut O of ecstasy shaping her mouth. 'Oh, yes… Now, Leo… *Now*…'

He plunged upward, penetrating deep, and she screamed at the same instant another flash lit up the sky. Her cry of release was all he needed and he let himself go, his orgasm thundering through him in a climax so intense it bordered the line between pleasure and pain and racked his entire body with a series of long, powerful shudders.

With a whimper Helena slumped onto his chest. She buried her face in his shoulder, made a soft mewling sound against his skin, and he stroked his hands up and down the graceful lines of her back.

He didn't deserve her compassion—didn't deserve *her*—but she felt so good nestled in his arms he didn't want to let her go.

He cradled her close.

He *would* let her go. It was the right thing to do. The only thing to do. And the sooner he did, the better.

Helena navigated the bedroom on autopilot as she packed up her things. The painkillers she'd forced down earlier hadn't worked and her temples throbbed, her eyes gritty from the crying jag she'd indulged in. Silly to have allowed emotion to overwhelm her simply because she'd woken to find Leo's side of the bed empty and cold. He'd left a note, at least. A bold, handwritten scrawl advising her that he'd gone to a meeting and would be back by noon.

She looked around for her pyjamas, frowned when she couldn't see them, then remembered and went through to the lounge.

Yes—there. On the floor by the sofa, where she had discarded them so brazenly in the night.

She reached for them and a sudden powerful sob of emotion rushed up her throat. On shaky legs she sank to the sofa, hating it that she felt so off-balance, so raw and exposed.

But how could she not?

She wasn't the same woman who had left London a week ago. She felt different—more aware of herself. As if someone—no, not 'someone', *Leo*—had shone a great floodlight inside her and illuminated all the parts of herself she'd ignored for too long.

He made her feel desired. Wanted.

Worth something.

Made her want to rip down the safe, boring black and white walls she'd erected like a concrete tower around herself.

She rubbed her chest as if she could banish the ache within.

She loved Leo, but what future could they hope for? One in which he spent his days trying to forgive her and she spent hers trying to earn back his trust?

A shudder rippled through her. Her mother had endured a miserable marriage and she didn't want that for herself. She wanted a partnership based on honesty and respect. On *love*. That last especially. Because if two people loved each other they could overcome anything, surely?

She forced herself to her feet, returned to the bedroom to finish her packing.

She didn't know if Leo loved her—didn't know if what he felt for her ran any deeper than lust—but she would not play the desperate, needy lover. She would not pout and demand that he declare his feelings for her. *No.* She would do this with dignity and strength. With self-respect. The kind she had often wished over the years her mother possessed.

And if Leo chose to let her walk away…if he was content to see the back of her…she would have her answer.

Relief. That was what Leo told himself he was feeling. When he walked into the suite and saw Helena sitting on

the sofa, her bags packed beside her, he felt relief. She had
come to her senses. Realised in the cold light of day that
she could do better. Better than a man who had let her down
when she'd needed him most.

'You're leaving.' He kept his voice flat. Neutral. As if
those words *hadn't* stripped the lining from his stomach.

She rose, her expression serious and her eyes, he realised
on closer inspection, bloodshot and puffy. Self-loathing
roiled in his stomach. No doubt *he* was the cause of her
misery. He thrust his hands into his trouser pockets before
he did something selfish, like haul her into his arms and
beg her not to leave.

'I think that's wise,' he said.

'Do you?' She looked at him, her gaze wide, unblinking.

'*Si.* Of course.'

He strode to the wet bar, pulled a soda from the fridge.
Later he'd need something stronger. For now he just needed
something to do—an excuse not to look at her. Not to
drown in those enormous pools of blue.

'Our seven days are up, are they not?'

Silence behind him. He popped the tab on the can,
quashed the temptation to crush the aluminium in his fist.
Instead he took a casual swig and turned.

She took a step towards him, her clasped hands twisting in front of her. 'Yes,' she said. 'And I know you can't
stay here for ever. Neither can I—which is why I'm going
back to my flat…' Her voice trailed off, an awkward silence descending.

'I video-conferenced with my board this morning, regarding my acquisition of ShawCorp.' He kept his delivery brisk. Businesslike. 'They've agreed to a delay on the
asset divestment.'

'Oh?' Her eyebrows lifted. 'How long?'

'Nine months, initially—provided costs can be restricted
and profits improved.' He put the soda down. 'Time to

see how the company performs and consider options for its future.'

She blinked. 'I...thank you.'

'Don't thank me, Helena.' A bitter edge crept into his voice. 'We both know you don't owe me any gratitude.'

Something flashed in her eyes. An emotion he couldn't decipher. Her hands continued to fidget and he fought not to reach out and still them.

'When will you return to Rome?'

'Tonight.' A decision he had just now made. Why stay? He couldn't sleep here. Not knowing she was in the same city, close and yet untouchable. He needed land, water, miles between them.

'I see. Will you—?'

His mobile chimed and he pulled it from his pocket, saw it was his PA calling and answered with a clipped greeting. He listened to Gina relay an urgent message from his second-in-command, then asked her to hold.

He glanced at Helena. 'I need to take this,' he said, and without waiting for an acknowledgement he moved through the French doors onto the balcony.

Ten minutes later Leo ended his call and turned away from the view. Instinctively, before he even stepped into the room, he knew Helena was gone.

Inside, the fragrance of her perfume lingered in the air—a bittersweet echo of her presence.

Relief, he reminded himself, but the cold, heavy weight pressing on his chest didn't feel like relief. Nor did the sudden insane urge to run after her.

He flung himself into a recliner and closed his eyes. When he opened them long minutes later his gaze landed on a small unsealed envelope on the coffee table. Frowning, he reached for it, lifted the flap and removed the single item from within.

A photo of their son.

The one he had studied so intently the night before.

He turned it over, and as he read the neat lines of hand-writing on the back his eyes started to burn.

He was special because we made him.
Carry him in your heart, as I do in mine.
I love you—and I'm sorry.
H.

CHAPTER TWELVE

'LEONARDO VINCENTI, ARE you listening to me?'

Marietta's voice, sharp with exasperation, jerked Leo from his thoughts. He looked up from the dregs of his espresso, guilt pricking him. 'Sorry, *carina*.'

His sister's expression softened. 'You were miles away.'

He pushed his empty cup aside and cursed himself. This was Marietta's night. He'd brought her to her favourite restaurant in the upmarket Parioli district of Rome to celebrate the lucrative sale of two of her paintings, and yet all he'd managed to do was put a dampener on the occasion.

'What's wrong?' she said.

'Nothing is wrong.' If he didn't count the fact that he hadn't slept in weeks. Or eaten properly. Or achieved anything more productive than pushing paperwork from one side of his desk to the other.

'*Something* is going on with you.' She leaned in, elbows propped on the table, eyes searching his. 'Talk to me.'

Marietta's sweet-natured concern only amplified his guilt. He forced a smile. 'Tell me about this loft you found.'

She frowned at him, but she didn't push. Instead she said, 'It's perfect. Lots of natural light and open space.' A spark of excitement lit her eyes. 'And there's a car park and a lift, so access isn't a problem.'

His sister had searched for months for a space she could purchase and convert into a dedicated art studio. The need for wheelchair access had made the search more difficult, but she'd tackled the challenge with the same determination she applied to everything in her life.

Pride swelled. 'How much do you need for it?'

Her frown reappeared. She sat back. 'I have money saved for a deposit. I don't need a loan, Leo.'

'Of course not.' As if he'd ever *loan* his sister money and expect her to repay him. He could afford to buy her ten studios—one was hardly an imposition. 'You'll need a notary for the purchase contract. I'll call Alex in the morning.'

She threw her hands in the air. 'You're doing it *again*.'

'Doing what?'

'Taking over. Going all Big Brother on me. I can do this on my own—without your help.'

Leo stared at her, his jaw clenching, a stab of intense emotion—the kind he'd been feeling too much of lately—lancing his chest. He tried to smooth his expression, but Marietta knew him too well.

She reached for his hand. 'You know I love you?'

A fist-sized lump formed in his throat. '*Si*. I love you, too.'

'I know.' Her fingers squeezed his. 'And that's all I need.'

Leo swallowed. That damned lump was making it difficult to speak. 'It doesn't feel like enough,' he admitted, and realised he had never said those words out loud before.

Marietta's eyes grew misty. 'Enough for what? For this?' She tapped the arm of her wheelchair. When her question met with silence, she shook her head. 'Oh, Leo. This isn't your fault and you know it.'

'The surgery—'

'Wasn't successful,' she cut in. 'Maybe we waited too long, or maybe the delay made no difference—we'll never know for sure. But I've made peace with it and you must, too. My life is good. I have my job, my art, *you*.' She sat forward, her dark eyes glistening. 'I'm happy, Leo. Yes, my life has challenges, but I'm strong and I don't need you to prop me up or catch me every time I fall. All I need is for you to be the one person in the world I can rely on to love me—no matter what.'

Her fingers wrapped more tightly around his.

'There's one other thing I need, and that's to know my brother is happy, too.' She gave him a watery smile. 'Maybe you could start by sorting out whatever has turned you into such a grouch these last few weeks?'

Leo scowled, but underneath his mock affront his sister's words were looping on a fast-moving cycle through his head, their impact more profound than he cared to admit. He felt something loosen inside his chest. Felt the heavy shroud of darkness that had weighted his every thought and action for almost a month start to lift.

He reached across and tweaked her chin. 'I do love you, *piccola*. Even when you are giving me lip.'

She grinned. 'I know. Now, stop scowling. You're scaring off the waiter and I want my dessert.'

An hour later, after seeing Marietta safely home, Leo ignored the lift in his building and bounded up the seven flights of stairs, a burst of energy he hadn't experienced in weeks powering his legs.

He loved Helena. He had reached that conclusion within days of returning to Rome. Within minutes of walking into his apartment and realising how empty it felt—how empty *he* felt—with her gone.

For more than three weeks he'd clung to the belief that she deserved better than him.

But how could she do better than a man who would love her with everything he had for the rest of his life?

Paris, eight days later...

Helena pulled off her strappy sandals and took the stairs two at a time inside the old building near the bustling promenades of Les Grands Boulevards.

The apartment she and her mother had rented for the week was small but charming, with shiny wooden floors, decorative finishes, and a sunny balcony where each morning they soaked up the beauty of Paris over coffee and croissants.

It was a girls' holiday. A chance for mother and daughter to reconnect and a celebration of sorts. For Helena because she'd worked out her notice at the bank, and for Miriam because, following her discharge from hospital, she had walked out of the home she'd shared with her husband of twenty-nine years and retained one of London's most successful divorce lawyers.

The weeks since had been challenging—tongues had wagged and Douglas had refused to 'play nice'—but Miriam was holding strong and Helena was proud of her.

Warm from her stroll and the three-storey climb, she reached the landing, glad she'd worn her new dress today instead of shorts or jeans. With its camisole bodice and little flared skirt the yellow sundress was cute and bright, and she'd worn it to buoy her spirits as much as anything. She was doing her best to move on, to live the life she should have lived these last seven years, but still she had plenty of dark, desolate moments when all she wanted to do was curl into a ball and cry. When it seemed she would never excise Leo from her thoughts or her heart no matter how hard she tried.

It didn't help that he'd called her mobile several times this past week. She hadn't answered and he hadn't left any messages—which was good, because she wouldn't cope with hearing his voice. And, really, what could he say that she wanted to hear? Or vice versa? That last day at the hotel his lack of interest couldn't have been any clearer. The man who'd held her with such heartbreaking tenderness in the aftermath of their lovemaking had, in those final stilted moments, barely forced himself to look at her.

Sighing, she fished her key from her tote and ousted Leo from her thoughts. She was in Paris and the sun was shining—good reasons to smile. And she couldn't wait to tell her mother, who'd opted for an afternoon of lounging in the sun with a book, about the incredible street art she'd found nearby.

Helena pushed open the door. 'Mum!' she called. 'I found the most amazing—' She stopped short. Her mother had been outside on the balcony when she'd left but now Miriam sat in the cosy sun-filled lounge. And with her, looking utterly incongruous in an easy chair covered in pink floral upholstery, sat the man Helena decided some wistful part of her imagination must have conjured.

Her key and tote dangled from her fingers, forgotten. 'Leo?'

He rose and he looked…magnificent. Big and dark and sexy in faded jeans and a snug-fitting black tee shirt.

'*Ciao*, Helena.'

The deep baritone fired a zing of awareness through her she didn't welcome. Questions crowded her mind until one emerged from the jumble. 'How did you find me?'

His gaze roamed her face, her bare shoulders. For a second she thought she saw a flicker of heat in his eyes.

'When I couldn't reach you I contacted David. He told me you'd resigned.' His voice carried a note of surprise. 'He also said you'd planned a trip to Paris. The rest—' He shrugged. 'Let's just say I know someone who's good at tracking people down.'

She wanted to be annoyed. She wanted to be so very, *very* annoyed. But all she could focus on was fighting the desire to reach out and touch him.

She pulled in a breath and realised her mother was by her side, bag in hand.

'I want to check out that little bookstore and café we spotted yesterday.' Miriam touched Helena's cheek, her smile tender, then gave her daughter a quick hug. 'Hear him out,' she whispered, and then she was gone.

On rubbery legs, Helena went and perched her tote on the end of the small breakfast bar.

'I like this,' Leo said behind her, and she turned, ready to agree that the apartment was indeed likable.

But he wasn't looking at the chic decor, or the quintessentially Parisian views. He was staring at *her*—or, more specifically, at her dress.

He stepped closer and slid his finger under a thin daffodil-yellow strap. 'It's pretty.'

'And it's not black,' she quipped, nerves—and something else—jumping in her belly.

One corner of his mouth kicked up. 'It's certainly not that.' He fingered one of her curls, bleached amber by the sun, and let it spring free. 'So...no more black?'

'Well...*less* black.' She couldn't afford to ditch half her wardrobe. She'd made no definite decisions about her future, but whether she chose art school or simply a job that offered scope for creativity she'd need to stretch her savings. She shrugged. 'I guess I'm rediscovering my love of colour.'

'And what brought that about?'

'You did.' Her candour made her blush but she couldn't regret the words. She wanted to be truthful with him, even though it wouldn't change anything. 'You challenged me. Made me think twice about what I'd chosen to give up.'

He had reawakened her passion for art and life. For that, among other things, she would always love him.

She moved away, sat in a comfy chair, needing to escape the heat his close proximity generated.

'What do you want, Leo?' The question came out sharper than she intended, but that was all right. She needed to keep her barriers up. Already the sight of him was spreading unwanted warmth. Making her forget how cold and remote he'd been during their last encounter.

He reached for a jacket she hadn't noticed over the arm of a chair. He pulled an envelope from a pocket, tossed the jacket back down and dropped to his haunches in front of her. When he slid the photo out and handed it to her, back side up, a thick wad of emotion clogged her throat.

'Read it to me,' he said.

She glanced up, opened her mouth to refuse, but the firm set of his jaw made her reconsider. She looked down again, studying the words even though she didn't need to. They were carved for eternity on her heart.

She prayed her voice wouldn't wobble. '"He was special because we made him. Carry him in your heart...as I do in mine."'

The next line blurred in front of her eyes.

'Read the rest.'

Her throat thickened. 'Why?'

'Because I need to hear you say it.'

'Why?' she repeated, fighting back stupid tears. 'So you can watch me humiliate myself?'

He placed his hands on the arms of her chair. 'Why would those words humiliate you?'

'Because!'

She glared at him, discomfort turning to anger. Anger to resentment. He would do *this* to her? Make her pour out her wretched feelings? Confess her love in person to satisfy his ego? She should never have never written those words. *Never.*

'Because it *hurts*!' she cried, thumping the heel of her hand against his chest. 'It hurts to love someone and know they don't love you back.' She thumped again, her palm bouncing off a wall of immovable muscle. 'It hurts to know you've lost any chance with that person. It hurts, Leo—' She hiccuped on a stifled sob and whacked his chest a third time. 'Because I do, damn it. I love you!'

The silence that fell in the wake of her outburst threatened to suffocate her. As did her surge of outrage when she glimpsed the satisfaction on Leo's face. With a shriek of fury she shoved at his chest and tried to rise, but he seized her wrists, his grip strong. Unyielding. Instead of standing she fell on his lap, straddling his thighs, trapped against the chair with her dress hiked around her hips.

Her chest heaved, another mortifying sob rattling through her. She couldn't fight him any more than she could fight the hot stab of need in her belly. Being this close to his big, powerful body was agony. She writhed, helpless, conscious of her sprawled legs, her exposed panties.

'*Tesoro mio...*'

She stilled, but she had no time to wonder at the rawness in Leo's voice. He released her wrists, folded his arms around her and buried his face in her neck. His scent engulfed her. His body, so warm and strong, sent her pulse into overdrive. She couldn't move, could barely breathe he held her so tight.

'Leo...?'

Finally he pulled back. His hands cupped her face. 'I love you, *cara*,' he said, and Helena didn't know if it was the intensity in his dark eyes or his words that stole her breath. 'I loved you seven years ago and I love you now. And, like a fool, I let you get away from me—not once, or even twice, but three times. Believe me when I tell you—' his voice roughened '—it will not happen again.'

Shock. Disbelief. Hope. Too many emotions to process at once rushed through her. Her body shook. Her brain, too—or at least that was how it felt. As if her mind couldn't contain the enormity of what he'd just said.

She studied his face, unwilling to let hope take hold too soon. 'What makes you so sure you love me?'

Leo stared at the strong, stubborn, beautiful woman who had ignored every one of his calls these last eight days and driven him to the brink of despair. The smile he gave was tortured.

'Aside from spending every waking hour wanting to know where you are, who you're with, what you're doing... and whether or not you are thinking of me?' He brushed away the lone tear that rolled down her cheek. 'I've been a fool and a coward, *cara*. Paralysed by fear.'

'Fear?'

He touched his forehead to hers. 'Fear that I couldn't be the man you deserve. The kind of man you can depend on.' He lifted his head. 'I failed you, *cara*.'

Her brow pleated. 'How?'

'Seven years ago I sent you away because I was angry and hurt, my pride wounded. I refused to give you a second chance, and because of that I wasn't there when you needed me.'

'Oh, Leo…' She laid her palm along his jaw. 'That's not on you. I should have found you and told you I was pregnant but I wasn't brave enough—and that was *my* bad, not yours. You deserved to know and I denied you that.' Her mouth trembled, her eyes searching his. 'Can you ever forgive me?'

He shook his head. 'There is nothing to forgive. We have both made mistakes.' He offered up another smile, this one crooked. Rueful. 'I believe it is called being human.'

Two more tears slipped down her cheeks. He brushed each one away.

'We can't change our history,' she said. 'Undo our mistakes. What if you can't trust—?'

He laid his finger over her lips, then took her hand and pressed her palm to his chest. '*Il mio cuore è solo tuo.*' When she blinked, he translated. 'My heart is yours.' He punctuated the statement with a gentle kiss. 'There is nothing more valuable I can entrust to you. And I promise you this, *tesoro*. You will never have to fight for my love.'

The way she'd had to fight for her father's.

'It is yours. Unconditionally. Tell me it is enough,' he demanded. 'Tell me—'

His command went unfinished. Because Helena cut him off with a kiss. A sudden, fierce, full-on-the-mouth kiss that smashed the breath from his lungs and caused an explosion of heat in his blood. He groaned. She tasted of heaven. Warm, sweet—a taste he wouldn't tire of for as long as he lived.

When she finally pulled back they were both panting for breath. Her eyes were moist, her smile shaky but wide. 'It's enough, my darling,' she said. 'It's enough.'

She pressed her face into his throat and they stayed like that for long, contented minutes. Then he eased her back and let his gaze rove her face, her body. *Hell.* He loved the yellow dress. Bright. Bold. A little bit cheeky. It was the girl he remembered. The one he hoped was back for good. The one whose blue eyes sparkled now with a hint of mischief.

Her smile was coy. Sexy. 'I think my mother will be gone for at least an hour.'

Leo responded with a wolfish grin, sealed their future with a scorching kiss, and then set about demonstrating one of the many ways in which he planned to love his woman.

EPILOGUE

One year later...

HELENA PRISED THE lids off the two test pots of paint and
smiled at the colours. The first, Sugar and Spice, was a
gorgeous lilac with a pretty shimmer. The second, Surf's
Up, was a deep purple-blue.

Neither colour was the one she'd originally planned for
this sunny room on the second floor of the Tuscan villa, but
when she'd started her flurry of redecorating she'd imagined the room as a studio. A dedicated space where she
could work on her projects for the interior design course
she'd undertaken and, in her downtime, dabble in creative
pursuits.

She'd even thought she might try her hand at painting
some landscapes under Marietta's expert tutelage. The Tuscan countryside, with its sun-drenched hills, fragrant orchards and acres of lush vegetation, offered no shortage
of inspiration.

She and Leo spent most of their weekends here, escaping the bustle of London or Rome. It was calming, reju-
venating, and she wondered how he would feel about the
villa becoming their more permanent home.

Her mobile whistled, indicating a text message, and she
rose from the canvas sheet on the floor. Leo was en route
from Rome, and he'd already texted to say he wanted her
naked when he arrived. They'd been apart only two nights,
but according to her husband of six months that was two
nights too long.

She rarely came to the villa by herself, but she'd needed
to organise some tradesmen and their short separation had

given her some time alone. Time to absorb the news that made her tummy flutter with a mix of excitement and nerves every time she anticipated the moment she would tell Leo.

She swiped the screen of her phone. His message said he was thirty minutes out and— Heat flooded her as she read the rest.

She grinned, shaking her head. Her husband was wicked. And sexy. And she loved him with every atom of her being.

Half an hour later the crunch of gravel and the low purr of the Maserati's engine heralded his arrival.

Pulse leaping, Helena put down her brush and leaned out of the open window. Leo climbed from the car and she waved to him.

'Up here!'

He looked up, late-afternoon sunlight bathing his bronzed features, and she knew she'd never get used to him smiling at her like that. As if she was his favourite person in the entire world.

He disappeared into the house and she heard his footsteps thunder up the curved staircase.

She barely had time to run her fingers through her dishevelled hair before she was in his arms, her legs wrapped around his waist, her breath stolen by his ferocious kiss.

'*Dio*,' he growled when he broke for air. 'You are beautiful.'

She laughed. 'Hardly.' Her curls were a wild mess, not a trace of make-up adorned her face, and she wore the old short denim dungarees she kept for painting and decorating.

'Do not argue, *tesoro.*' Still holding her high, he started out of the room. 'And—speaking of disobedience—did I not request my wife be naked when I arrived?'

She giggled and squirmed. 'Leo, wait. Put me down. I have something to show you first.'

He stopped and gave a pained sigh, but did as she'd bade him. Heart thudding, she led him by the hand to the section of wall where she'd painted a large square of Sugar and Spice and another of Surf's Up.

'What do you think of these colours?'

He shrugged. 'You know I trust your choices...' He glanced around the room and frowned. 'But this is to be your studio, *si*? Had you not decided on orange?'

'I thought we might use this room for something else,' she said, and moved closer to the wall. She pointed to the shimmery lilac. 'I was thinking this might be nice for a...a girl. And this one...' She pointed to the other square, her hand trembling, her throat tightening on the words. 'This would be good for...for a boy.'

Her breath stopped as she watched the rapidly changing expressions on Leo's face. From bemusement to confusion and finally a dawning comprehension.

He stared at her, his jaw gone slack. 'Are you telling me...? Do you mean...? Are you...?'

'I'm pregnant,' she blurted, taking pity on her gorgeous tongue-tied husband. She blinked, her eyes growing hot and prickly. 'Seven weeks—'

She didn't get to finish her sentence. Leo pulled her into a hug so tight, so engulfing, she couldn't draw breath to speak. He broke into a string of Italian she partly followed, thanks to months of lessons. Mentally, she translated the words she understood.

Incredible...so happy... I love you.

At last he pulled back, his hands curling gently over her shoulders—as if she might suddenly break.

'How do you feel? Do you need to rest instead of...?' His voice trailed off, a deep furrow creasing his brow.

'I'm good,' she assured him.

'Are you sure—?'

'Leo.' She took his strong, familiar jaw between her hands and gave him a reassuring smile. 'I promise you I'm one hundred per cent healthy.'

But she understood his sudden caution, the dark glimmer of anxiety in his eyes. Beneath her own excitement lay a shadow of apprehension. A fear that she would lose this child as she had lost Lucas.

But even that flicker of fear could not eclipse her joy or hope for the future.

Because this time she was not alone. This time she had Leo by her side. This time, whatever ups and downs life had in store, they would face them as one.

He was perfect. Ten fingers, ten toes, a fine thatch of black hair and the loudest, gustiest cry the nurses said they'd ever heard from a newborn.

Not for the first time since his son's miraculous arrival into the world two hours ago, Leo thought his chest might explode from the torrent of emotions coursing through him. Pride. Elation. Relief. And, of course, love. So much love it threatened to overwhelm him.

It had certainly stolen his ability to find words for such a momentous occasion. To tell his beautiful, incredible wife in the wake of her ten-hour labour how proud he was of her. Of their son.

He looked up from the tiny bundle in his arms. Despite the rings of exhaustion around her eyes Helena was radiant, her glow of happiness reflecting his own. He shifted on the edge of the hospital bed and gently laid their son in her arms.

For a long moment he stared at the woman and child he would spend the rest of his days loving, supporting, protecting. 'I love you.' He dropped a kiss on her mouth, another on his son's downy head. 'I love you both.'

'I love you, too.' She smiled at him through her tears. 'No regrets?'

He looked at his sleeping son—the most amazing sight in the world—then back to his beautiful wife.

He smiled. 'None.'

* * * * *

*If you enjoyed Angela Bissell's debut
don't miss the final part of the*
IRRESISTIBLE MEDITERRANEAN
TYCOONS *duet:*
*DEFYING HER BILLIONAIRE PROTECTOR
Available January 2017!*

MILLS & BOON®

MODERN™

POWER, PASSION AND IRRESISTIBLE TEMPTATION

A sneak peek at next month's titles...

In stores from 15th December 2016:

- **A Deal for the Di Sione Ring** – Jennifer Hayward *and*
  Married for the Greek's Convenience – Michelle Smar
- **A Dangerous Taste of Passion** – Anne Mather
  and **Bought to Carry His Heir** – Jane Porter
- **The Italian's Pregnant Virgin** – Maisey Yates
  and **A Child Claimed by Gold** – Rachael Thomas
- **Bound by His Desert Diamond** – Andie Brock
  and **Defying Her Billionaire Protector** – Angela Bissel

Just can't wait?
Buy our books online a month before they hit the shops!
www.millsandboon.co.uk

Also available as eBooks.

MILLS & BOON®

EXCLUSIVE EXTRACT

Hotel magnate Nate Brunswick's faith in marriage
has been destroyed by his father – but searching
for his beloved grandfather's lost ring leads the
illegitimate Di Sione to an inconvenient engagement!
Mina Mastrantino can only pass the ring on once
she's married. A divorce should be easy…
but their exquisite wedding night gives them
both far more than they planned!

Read on for a sneak preview of
A DEAL FOR THE DI SIONE RING
by Jennifer Hayward

"You're an honorable man, Nate Brunswick. *Grazie.*"

"Not so honorable, Mina." A dark glitter entered his
eyes. "You called me improper not so long ago. I can
be that and more. I am a hard, ruthless businessman who
does what it takes to make money. I will turn a hotel
over in the flash of an eye if I don't see the flesh on the
bones I envisioned when I bought it. I will enjoy a
woman one night and send her packing the next when
I get bored of her company. Know what you're getting
into with me if you accept this. You will learn the
dog-eat-dog approach to life, *not* the civilized one."

Why did something that was intended to be a warning
send a curious shudder through her? Mina drew the wrap
closer around her shoulders, her gaze tangling with
Nate's. The glitter in his eyes stoked to a hot, velvet

shimmer as he took a step forward and ran a finger along the line of her jaw. "Rule number one of this new arrangement, should you so choose to accept it, is to not look at me like that, *wife*. If we do this, we keep things strictly business so both of us walk away after the year with exactly what we want."

Her gaze fell away from his, her blood hot and thick in her veins. "You're misinterpreting me."

"No, I'm not." He brought his mouth to her ear, his warm breath caressing her cheek. "I have a hell of a lot more experience than you do, Mina. I can recognize the signs. They were loud and clear in my hotel room that day and they're loud and clear now."

She took a deep, shuddering breath. To protest further would be futile when her skin felt like it was on fire, her knees like jelly. He watched her like a cat played with a mouse, all powerful and utterly sure of himself. "The only thing that would be more of a disaster than this day's already been," he drawled finally, apparently ready to have mercy on her, "would be for us to end up in bed together. So a partnership it is, Mina." He lifted his glass. "What do you say?"

Don't miss
A DEAL FOR THE DI SIONE RING
by Jennifer Hayward

Available January 2017
www.millsandboon.co.uk

MILLS & BOON®

Why shop at millsandboon.co.uk?

Each year, thousands of romance readers find their perfect read at millsandboon.co.uk. That's because we're passionate about bringing you the very best romantic fiction. Here are some of the advantages of shopping at www.millsandboon.co.uk:

* **Get new books first**—you'll be able to buy your favourite books one month before they hit the shops

* **Get exclusive discounts**—you'll also be able to buy our specially created monthly collections, with up to 50% off the RRP

* **Find your favourite authors**—latest news, interviews and new releases for all your favourite authors and series on our website, plus ideas for what to try next

* **Join in**—once you've bought your favourite books, don't forget to register with us to rate, review and join in the discussions

Visit **www.millsandboon.co.uk** for all this and more today!

MILLS_WEB